# PNV

A Cocoon of Earth's Metamorphosis

E.F. GELLER

# Copyright

PNV

Copyright © 2015 by E.F. Geller

Editing by Kelly Lynne Schaub

Cover art by YellowAnt

Publishing History
First edition Ebook and print March 30, 2015

ISBN  978-0-692-39894-4

# Dedication:

I especially dedicate this book, PNV—to my editor Kelly Lynne for her positive attitude, encouragement, and remarkable skills and experience in editing and her extra efforts and time put into this book to make it possible; to web designer YellowAnt, who designed the book cover and book trailer video for me free-of-charge; to my old dad, who imparted to me my first astronomical knowledge; and to my mom, who told me bedtime Bible stories.

# 1

# Sighting of a Mysterious Giant Flying Creature

South Texas, mid-21st century

Down the valleys of South Texas, footprints of bigwigs and trespassers tracked on the same hunting ground one after another. The former were remarkable foreign dignitaries but the latter were desperate, poverty-stricken illegal foreign vagabonds, and the faithful bald eagles soaring idly over the distant sky were the only witnesses of such a drastic exchange.

The rough and thorny vast Texan landscape created a natural camouflage, perfect for a group of illegal game-poachers to dwell undetected within its hinterlands. By dusk, they were preparing a big feast and campfire by a stream; as usual, some of them were already drunk even before the feast began. A few young couples were kissing behind mesquites and soon their tossed attire twined over different scrubby branches.

An overworked, tired, lonely young mother dejectedly looked her husband's direction. He was drinking and playing poker with his friends, all of them displaying typical selfish and insensitive chauvinistic attitudes. One glance at them showed they would never share their overworked wives' daily chaos.

She gave a forlorn sigh and decided to put her baby under a nearby mesquite unattended before proceeding to her chores. Right before she placed her baby down next to the mesquite, she heard noises coming out from behind the tree. Curiously, she took a peek and saw a couple in a compromising position, moaning and rocking ecstatically. Embarrassed, but without a second thought, she walked off and began searching for a more suitable and quieter spot away from these rackety merrymakers.

* * * * * *

Over the cloudless summer night sky, the moon shone bright on the land. When it lurked behind lush green foliage, there was no premonition of any impending phenomena abnormal to human eyes; only its looming luminosity could selectively render human beings' imperfection and reflect through their madness.

When primordial rays released from the earth's central core rectified an incoming spectrum of refracted moonlight and cosmic rays, a serendipitously powerful trajectory converted to penetrate one of the most enduring mystical enclaves on Earth.

For a moment, the atmosphere turned silent when the mystical enclave camouflaged at its mundane earthly border modulated and converted into neutral ground. Under the darkness, the earth's most primitive navigation and migration signals soon linked up with each other one after another. Undetectable by human vision, soon one of the frequencies began to mislead a hungry primitive giant creature from its mystical, confining, primitive habitat into an obsolete ancient hunting track that linked to our known earthly habitat.

Subsequently, the atmosphere received a sudden gush of cool refreshing air that quickly induced earthly diurnal living things, including human beings, into their deepest sleeping state.

* * * * * *

In the valley, a half drunken old Mexican man with a Tequila bottle in his left hand, was on and off singing mariachi songs and playing dominoes, alone on the back porch of his little house.

2

While he sang, "Oh—*la Luna—la Luna*—" instinctively he began to search for a moon over the horizon, but his opened mouth froze instantly in the middle of his song as an immense flying creature zoomed toward him. Awestruck, he thought it was going to attack him, but it swooped over the roof in the direction of the nearby ranch. Then he saw a pair of agitated birds pursuing the flying creature but soon they all vanished over the horizon.

In semi consciousness, he caressed his big fat fallen buttock; he managed to return to the rocking chair and soon dozed off.

\* \* \* \* \* \*

The tired, yawning mother with a now sleeping baby cuddled in her arms had finally spotted an ideal tree quite a distance away from the rowdy people. This tall giant was remote; however, it was the only desirable tree available among other shorter trees with thorny scrub underneath them.

When she reached the tree, she placed the sleeping baby inside a straw basket and left it in a gap between aerial roots. The mother was unaware that in the darkness, a sinister prying creature was now perched right above her baby and staring interestedly at the proffered prey. The woman soon left to clean the dishes over the stream.

Thirty minutes later, she returned to collect her baby, ready for a good evening's rest. But when she looked at the empty straw basket, chills ran down her spine. Nervously, she began to turn her head around, searching for a possible place that her baby could be. "Where's my baby?" she whispered to herself.

Straining her ears for the least noise, she ran as quickly as possible toward the mesquite tree with the young couple she encountered before, but she stopped abruptly in front of the mesquite and listened attentively to make sure she didn't embarrass herself again.

"Oh baby—Oh babe...eee!"

3

*Could he be talking about my baby?* She hesitated, but in the desperate situation, she still crept forward, extending her neck to probe.

"Oh babe!—oh—don't sssss—uck—too hard!"

Instead she saw a man moaning in ecstasy. She turned away at once with a red face and as greatly disturbed as she was, she went further on, losing her mind. She searched frantically everywhere, with no sign of her baby, and in dismay she cried out hysterically for help.

This attracted everyone's attention but while everyone searched, it was all in vain, for neither the baby, nor any single clue that could explain how the baby disappeared could be found.

The tragic occurrence was over in a flash, too mysterious and odd with no witness of what had happened. The missing baby incident was not reported officially and thus it merely became a rumor over those old country cafes in the valleys; it simmered painfully forever in the hearts of the beholders but was easily forgotten by gossipers.

* * * * * *

Rodriguez Ranch, Corpus Christi, Texas

The Rodriguez Ranch looked like any successful commercial ranch in Texas, especially famous for cutting. To the naked eye, people saw Dorper breed sheep, imported Merino sheep, mavericks, and thoroughbred and Arabian horses grazing across vast grassland, and these herds often attracted visiting rich Arabs and Chinese upstarts seeking acquisition of some of those rare breeds.

Deeper into the ranch, under a canopy of giant pines and bushy tall grass, stood simple farm houses and huts, and yet concealed deeper underneath them was a vast underground cellar, where its owner operated and plotted his underground illegal activities. He often had to closely tango with the CIA, who would usually play the good friendly cops, while he also received information that he was under close surveillance by the FBI, who would play the bad cops.

4

He enjoyed his life with pretty, voluptuous women, flashy sports cars and good Cuban cigars. Above all his addictive interests, his favorite hobby was cock fighting. What made him different from other fugitives was that he seemed to obviously enjoy his life while earning his money, as his indulgence in items and hobbies provided him a mix of pleasure with business.

He liked to smoke Cuban cigars, so he smuggled them into the country and now he was enjoying the aroma. He also liked exotic women; he smuggled them too from all over the world to work as prostitutes, and now a rare beauty from the East was giving him an intimate service.

Smuggling and illegal gambling activities had grossed him an easily fifty-million dollar annual income, and he would travel as far as casinos in undeveloped third world countries of the Far East for money laundering.

During the last season, some of his rival's cocks were on par with his famous fearless cocks and thus threatened his position as "The King of Cocks," which really bothered and embarrassed him. He came across a newspaper report about a Texas A&M-Kingsville professor's special breed that was believed to be one of the highest IQ and fiercest warrior fowls endemic to a remote volcanic island called Kikicoo, somewhere in the southern hemisphere. Immediately he sent one of his subordinates to the island to smuggle in a few indigenous fowls with the aim to breed or crossbreed in order to produce superior fowls to become champion roosters.

When someone knocked on the door to request his audience, Mr. Rodriguez's mood abruptly changed. His annoyed glance emitted a killing spark when he heard the voice. He pushed away the prostitute, unexpectedly stood up and pounced forward to seize the newcomer's neck and growled, "I asked you to bring me back TWO PAIRZZZ of roosters and hens from the island down south near Antarctica, now you must go fuck those four hens to produce the chicks!" He slightly released his grasp; the man immediately struggled and broke free.

5

The lackey coughed to catch some breath before replying, "The natives told me that they were two roosters."

"Oh yes! You trusted those damn *mezquinos* who probably can't tell their own sex and species. If you can make these hens crow, I will go fuck them now!"

"Daddy Rod...I have a better idea. Why don't we go 'borrow' Professor Rochester's rooster? We also can test its abilities to fight and to use it for mating with our four hens at the same time."

"Now get the fuck out of here, don't come back here without Rochester's rooster!" He threw the man a menacing look, right before the door closed behind him. The prostitute already started to cling all over him, annoying him further. He ordered the man again, "Call in three more 'hens' for me RIGHT NOW!"

"Sure, Daddy Rod," *Three hens?—no—should be three puta!* Actually, it took some time for the man to figure out what his boss wanted.

* * * * * *

Alice, Texas

A famous gospel singer had just finished her rehearsal for a Sunday service special solo. She pulled out in her newly-purchased Ford convertible and headed home, but halfway, she closed the top due to the chilly, late evening autumn winds.

Just as she was about to turn into the driveway of her parents' ranch, suddenly under the dusty sunset light, she saw a gigantic owl-shaped creature swoop down toward her convertible. Its wingspread exceeded the width of the driveway as it flew against the side of the vehicle.

The singer panicked; instinctively she applied the brake to slow down her car, then the giant bird swiped the front windshield and began to attack the car. Under her panicking eyes in semi-darkness, she determined the beast was an unusually large owl. Its thrashing wings, pecking beak and scratching talons were so enormous she was afraid it might push the car into the ditch, so she accelerated. The giant owl pursued her for a distance then suddenly changed its course, pouncing on a nearby lamb, crushing its head mercilessly within its vise-like talons.

The gospel singer felt an instant relief and felt lucky that she had closed the convertible top earlier on; she thought otherwise she might not be still sitting inside her car. The incident happened as though it were a nightmare, but the scratched-off paint and dents left on the front of her new car assured her that this was not a dream.

* * * * * *

A few days later, just five miles away from the singer's destination, six brothers were playing out in an open field with their new gifts—the colorful bird and butterfly kites their uncle brought back for them from Malaysia, where he worked as an oil company exploration engineer.

They were not aware a mammoth hungry creature was foraging in the area and it soon perched on a sturdy limb of a tall tree a distance away, prying curiously at those boys while its body gradually tensed for the pounce.

At dusk, just before the last twilight faded, the boys started to rewind their kite-strings. They watched the gradually descending kites—one of them happened to be an owl kite—unaware as a gigantic flying creature dove toward one of them with lighting speed and absolute silence. Talons sank into cloth and hair as massive wings pushed down against the air, carrying the smallest boy away from the ground.

Stunned for a moment, the brothers stared. "Oh gosh, it's a giant owl!" one of them warned, but they saw the giant owl had already picked up their brother by his windbreaker hood, lifted him up three feet from the ground and carried him a few yards away from the ambush spot. The sturdy boy was too heavy for the owl to lift any higher, and the bird struggled to gain distance. Quickly, the boys chased after the giant owl to rescue their brother.

7

Beneath the violent and unearthly screech of the giant owl, the group of brave and fearless boys picked up the larger pebbles and stones from the ground to aim at its wide, red eyes. It simply closed its clear, nictitating membranes and then gave a few blinks with upper eyelids like that of a man's, and this really scared the kids.

Under the sharp talons, the victim's windbreaker hood was tightly clutched; however, the brave little captive attempted to break free by slipping his body through the windbreaker. One of his tallest brothers finally managed to grab one of his legs from underneath after several attempted hops. "Hurry up! Pull your arms out the sleeves before it goes higher...don't worry, we'll catch you when you drop," the brothers assured the boy.

At the moment when the little boy released his arms from the bottom of windbreaker to free himself, his father was returning from work. From a distance away, he saw a gigantic bird grasping something large and struggling in the air. To his awe, he realized this was no jackrabbit but his son who dropped to the ground, and soon all his sons also fell to the ground.

Without any hesitation, he accelerated his truck to the spot. "Come on! Run and hide in the truck," he shouted to his sons, pulling out his shotgun.

The giant creature was not afraid of the truck or man at all. It flipped its wings a few times and then approached its new target—the two barking dogs in the truck bed—but they quickly jumped down to the ground, gave a few frightened yelps and cringed, with tails tucked between their hind legs, under the truck. The boys shouted too with the car door half-open, "Daddy, hurry up! Hide in the truck, too!"

The father ignored his children's pleading. "Now, close that door and lock yourself in there—don't come out until I say so!"

The hungry owl didn't give up attacking the two hiding and yelping dogs under the truck. It pushed its immense feathered mass against the truck until it almost toppled, groping toward the dogs with its deadly talons. Soon a gunshot rang out; the man couldn't fire at the bird without endangering his children, but the concussive noise had the desired effect. The owl dodged away from the truck with loud and angry screeching sounds then flew off, to everyone's relief.

These sightings and attacks from giant owls were not reported due to the victims' belief that they would not be taken seriously by the local wildlife authorities. Whoever heard of an owl as tall as a man? An owl that hunted human children?

\* \* \* \* \* \*

The headline of one of the only remaining newspapers in Texas, The Texas State Daily, announced: KINGSVILLE INTERNATIONAL PIANO COMPETITION WINNER TO BE AN INSTANT MILLIONAIRE. The big red font on the front page had attracted an old couple showing up in the early morning at the Kingsville SEG Filling Station.

After the woman read the Daily's headline on her husband's arm, she remarked, "Huh, this is the pianists' version of lotto."

"Yeah, I heard some of them hop from one competition to another, hoping to win a big one like this." His eyes were already staring on the news:

An envelope containing a check of three million dollars was presented to the Kingsville International Piano Competition by an unnamed Texas A&M University-Kingsville alumnus.

The unnamed benefactor said he always felt indebted to TAMUK for awarding him a scholarship when he was a poor international student, and he had always wanted to do something in return.

For past decades, this KIPC has had good opportunities to promote TAMUK, its little county, Kingsville, and one of the world's largest ranches.

As it was announced that this year's competition winner would become an instant millionaire, the KIPC has attracted thousands of entries from all over the world and even from some very young, budding, prodigious pianists.

Only twenty-four semi-finalists were selected to compete for the finals from the thousands of entries based on a performer's profile, performance experience, and audition records.

\* \* \* \* \* \*

Texas A&M University-Kingsville

A seven-year-old New Zealand music prodigy was the youngest competitor among the twenty-four selected Kingsville International Piano Competition's semi-finalists. His mother was even more thrilled to revisit her old Texas campus after returning to New Zealand twenty years ago.

During the competition's eve, upon entering the music department's main entrance, they could feel the resonance of the thundering cacophony vibrating the whole building as well as vibrating their bodies, too. The selected contestants were competing with the remaining time to practice diligently on their respective repertoires.

When the woman and her two children walked past the music library, they even saw a few aggressive contestants fighting for an old piano they discovered. The mother felt privileged being offered the use of a kind piano professor's studio for practicing, through ff-mail contact. She unfolded her ff, a dainty, malleable modern smart tablet designed like a folding-fan, and accessed her ff-mail to review the room number. Closing the ff again allowed the multipurpose penetrating and positioning system, MPPS, to point her in the right direction.

She looked around; finally she located the professor's piano studio. She waited until nobody was looking, then she ushered her children into it. "We better keep quiet that we have this kind of privilege. Can you believe this—actually this room used to be my Polish piano professor's studio," she told her son.

"Wow, Mum, look at these two 12-foot-long Steinways with extended keys. How many keys?" the boy said to his little sister. "Let me count...wow...96 keys!"

Giggling in delight and awed at her brother's counting prowess, the three-year-old girl tapped her tiny patent-leather Mary Jane shoes on the hard floor and pressed on the extra keys to hear the new notes.

"Darling, it's amazing right?" The mother guided the eager girl's hands away from the expensive instrument. Then she told her son, "Now you can start to practice your concerto; just sing out the orchestral part by yourself. I'll go greet some of my old friends and old professors. I shall return soon to accompany your concerto, and after that we'll take a stroll around the old campus sites."

Two hours later, pedestrians who passed by the music department could hear Beethoven's Moonlight Sonata through an open window of a studio, synchronizing with the full moon that shone brightly upon the campus. Countering and superimposing this soothing music were also several layers of reverberation of some of the most difficult classical piano tunes; *Islamay, Toccata, Appasionata, Estampe, Memphis Waltz* and the *Grand Polonaise*. The practiced ear might also pick out Britten's, Khachaturian's, and Ravel's left hand concerti and forefront Chinese composer Mimi Mao's hit *Pentatonic Concerto*, nicknamed *Yellow Mountain Seas of Cloud*, that required a 96-key super grand piano.

The homecoming TAMUK alumna took a deep breath of the Texan autumn air before leisurely walking past the liberal arts building with her children, headed back to their rental car and from there to the hotel. Subconsciously she traced her steps into her familiar old routes while her mind wandered off, reminiscing about the past. Soon she stopped and pointed to a corner. "Look, that's the spot where I played piano with the university jazz band." A large garbage bin was placed there now. Nostalgia dissipated in her dismay at the current use of the space. Her children lost interest and started playing "catch me if you can" in the open common area.

Suddenly, a massive dark flying object appeared right above her and was silently plunging toward her children. Instinctively she hastened her pace, running after her children. "Hide—under the tree!" she cried vainly to warn them.

The snatching happened so fast she only made it in time to pick up her poor son, who screamed hysterically, and her daughter was already ten feet high above the ground struggling to get out of her pink jacket, gripped tightly under the razor sharp talons of a giant owl.

Regardless of those helpless crying and screaming from the ground, the giant owl remained fearless; it ascended calmly with the struggling captive underneath and quickly disappeared from the scene.

# 2

# It's a Giant Owl!

Not far away from Texas A&M-Kingsville's campus, Senator Spencer was having a garden party with a Hawaiian theme. The arriving guests, with colorful floral printed Hawaiian outfits, were welcomed with fresh flower *leis* and kisses by passionate pretty girls, a band played at a corner next to the pool. Guests were smoking Cuban cigars, drinking champagne and trying a range of appetizers.

A twelve-candle candelabrum centerpiece decorated the lavish buffet table, along with a big bouquet of assorted Hawaiian hibiscus nestled among spicy exotic foods and tropical punch.

The evening went as planned under a lovely poolside ambience with fine people, fine foods and fine music. But just before the guests could go for a third round, suddenly Senator Spencer's pet calico Persian cat growled fiercely. First it jumped over the long dining table and dropped into a big bowl of Malaysian beef curry; after it got out, soon it fell into another Thai green curry. When it finally got out, with additional colors staining its long wet fur, it zoomed into the kitchen and dripped the curries all over the Persian runner.

"Oh...gosh! How did our neighbor's Rottweiler get into our yard?" Senator Spencer turned around angrily, ready to go after the dog. Then he heard a loud splash followed by his wife's hysterical screaming. Immediately, he rushed to the poolside in time to see his wife running after something. "My baby!" When she saw her husband, she cried desperately to him, "Help! A giant owl took Ruby!"

"A giant owl...?" He wondered what his wife was carrying on about. Bewildered, he looked at his broken-down wife but at the same time he also noticed a little girl he didn't know splashing and struggling inside the swimming pool; without any hesitation he dived in the pool.

* * * * * *

In the living room of a secluded, brown, modern-designed villa with solar panels mounted all over its roof situated in the outskirts of Kingsville, Associate Professor of Biology Maximilian "Roc" Rochester was now engaged in a repetitive ff-call with his mother.

"Why you didn't attend Senator Spencer's party?" his mother asked. A week ago, when his mother heard that Senator Spencer was having a party, she asked her local friend if she could arrange her son attending such a party, in hope that he would be able to meet some nice girls there.

Roc rolled his eyes. "Your good friend called me this morning, angrily informing me that her request was turned down by Senator Spencer. The reason was because I am just an unknown TAMUK professor without tenure—a nobody," he replied amusedly. Not going to a frou-frou event didn't bother him at all.

"Ha, sweetie pie, that's why I told you to return here at once." His mom had never given up on begging her only son to quit teaching and return to New York to help his aging father in his financial business. Roc had left that field for ornithology; teaching was just a means to an end to remain in the research environment, far away from finance, neckties, cubicles, and the City.

"Come on, Mom, I'm not the girl you kept wishing for forty years ago that I need to get matched up at a party like a spinster."

"Honey, I really think it's time you stop chasing around chicks in Texas."

*What's the difference between "sweetie pie" and "honey"? They're both sweet; she just wishes she had a daughter.* "Come on! Dad's still young. Working in Texas is not my 'jail sentence' yet. There's another eight months to go in the school year," he again made excuses.

"No, I checked your TAMUK contract. The end date is at the end of fall semester! Now, you have exactly three more months left to go chasing after those dream chicks and then your future will be at my disposal. I really don't understand you, there's plenty of pretty chicks right here in the city, too."

"Come on, Mom, I chase birds, not chicks...Leave me alone, please! Five years ago, I promised you that one day I would bring along a daughter-in-law for you from your home state. If I don't stay put here, how can I find a nice Texan girl?"

"It doesn't matter anymore, just pick one!"

"Mom, I am here to fulfill your dream," he coaxed her.

Finally, the call ended. Having rid himself of his cheeky, manipulating mother with his smooth talk, he yawned while scratching his scalp and mellowed to murmurs. "I doubt if I would be able to find a perfect 'chick' here or there." He liked the smart ones but they were mostly fat or ugly or flat-chested; Roc liked six-times-six double-D chicks...but the ones he'd met had no brains. Those pretty, smart and rich chicks were fussy with no taste, and the elegant, eloquent and talented ones were born materialistic, usually with a mouthful of lies, and loved to show off. The wild and fun chicks were unfaithful; tame and wise chicks were too clingy and boring...

He muttered aloud, "Texas chicks? Or...small dainty New York City chicks? All the girls I've met are only good for a roll in the—"

"A what?" He had been unaware that his latest girlfriend had been standing right behind him listening; she roared angrily about what she had just overheard. "I didn't realize that's all I was good for! Ugh—you're such a crude little boy!" She flung a house keycard out of her purse and it hit him right in the nose. "I'm so out of here." She stormed out, big Texas hair flouncing.

Roc simply responded to her fuming exit with a cold-hearted chuckle. "Finally I've gotten rid of that used baggage and saved myself from extreme physical exercise tonight." He was glad to be able to retreat for an earlier night's sleep after a day of chasing an unknown species of bird that suddenly appeared in South Texas. He turned out the lights and retreated to bed.

Suddenly, a rooster crowed. He called out fondly to his pet rooster, "Hey, you out there! This is Texas! Are you dreaming you're still in Kikicoo? That's the moon shining out there in the sky, not the morning sun. Stupid bird." While mentally calculating the time of day in Kikicoo, he slowly dozed off.

* * * * * *

Around midnight, Roc lay half-awake on the bed, wondering if he was having a series of nightmares, as frantic emergency calls from the KIPC competition chairman and the county sheriff subsequently rang one after another, attempting to inform him that a giant owl had "kidnapped" one of the competitors' three-year-old sister.

He took a look at the clock; it was exactly twelve minutes after twelve. *This is the police's duty. Shit...Why are they so persistent on calling me this time of night?* Although ignoring those ff-calls with a sense of uneasiness, he still managed to doze off again.

Fifteen minutes later, the sheriff further annoyed him with another ff-call to inform him that the girl had been "released" by the giant owl in exchange for Senator Spencer's baby. *That's none of my business, right? I'm just an inconspicuous professor, and the giant owl was not a specimen from my lab. Why is the sheriff reporting to me everything that happened? When did I turn into the director of the FBI?* Soon he dozed off again.

At 1:30 a.m., an imperative personal call from Senator Spencer heightened the sense of urgency that awakened Roc fully.

"I'm sorry to bother you at this late hour, Professor. It took a while for several people to convince me you were the only suitable candidate to lead this search and rescue expedition."

Roc gritted his teeth and glared at the clock. "Why don't you ask that famous Dr. Dick to help you? Wasn't he invited to your house last night? Now at this insane hour you ask me to go out there catch a bird? Sorry, but I'm losing sleep."

Roc provoked the snobbish senator deliberately. The reason he'd been declined for the party was because the senator thought Dr. Dick Fisher's dad was a famous anchorman. Roc refused to call him "Dr. Fisher." The guy was a dick.

"No! No! You are the best biologist in this region and you are also one of the finest specialists in birds. Our SAR team really needs your expertise and experience to search for that bizarre giant owl that stole my baby."

"Ornithologist."

"Sorry for my ignorance. Please, will you come lead the search?"

The amenable tone in the man's voice mollified Roc. "Hmmm—all right, I'm on my way now."

After Senator Spencer put down his ff-phone he remembered just two days ago he had refused a request from a former Miss Texas to invite a TAMUK professor he never heard of to attend his party. *Oh shit...that's him!*

\* \* \* \* \* \*

A group of hidden thieves from Rodriguez Ranch couldn't believe their luck. Just as they were preparing to steal Professor Rochester's rooster, their prying eyes noticed the professor's house suddenly brightening up and they saw him bustling around.

Soon they saw him leaving the house in a great hurry—hopping into his vintage Land Rover and zooming off with a blast of trailing thick black smoke that dissipated under the streetlights and soon into the darkness.

The thieves who had been crouching and waiting behind the shrubs nervously breathed easier; they now had the freedom to take a few puffs before proceeding to steal the rooster as planned.

They approached the coop with an imitative cock's crowing in their thick soothing voices, "Cock-a-doodle-doo...cock—oh FUCK!"

These thieves weren't aware that this particular species of primitive fowl could recognize its master and even its master's voice, thus it would act very aggressive toward any stranger.

Painful screams were muffled but replaced by clear, undertoned curses. "Shit! Oh, damn fowl! I'll castrate you—let's see if you're able to cluck or rock with your hens anymore!"

"Hey, this bastard can't understand you. Let's get out of here quick."

Soon all the noises dwindled, followed by five or six creeping black shadows camouflaged under the darkness. They skedaddled and soon disappeared from Professor Rochester's house with one of them carrying a rooster-filled cage.

* * * * * *

For the past five years, Roc had enjoyed his anonymous, quiet life in Texas. His students and colleagues only knew that he drove a thirty-year-old Land Rover and wore a fifty-dollar Seiko watch that he purchased ten years ago in Jakarta. He put on a free pair of all-terrain army boots donated by his American Ranger buddy while on a research fellowship to conduct studies on different Texas bird species' behaviors, specifically their nature and nurture.

He usually wore a pair of old, faded, torn jeans and an equally torn out TAMUK T-shirt. Once the weather got colder, he would pull on an equally tatty leather jacket, which was further torn by the thorny brush out in the Texas wilderness during his bird watching expeditions.

Several decades ago, an ex-dean of TAMUK's College of Arts and Science also reported seeing a six-foot-tall owl perching on a giant tree right outside his study during a late night. Could this menacing owl at the senator's party be the same species?

Fifteen minutes after leaving his home, Roc pulled into Senator Spencer's driveway. He saw a joint-force SAR expedition team in full gear on standby, anticipating his arrival.

He hopped down from his Land Rover and was immediately surrounded by Senator Spencer's entourage. Surprisingly, nobody greeted him. "I'm Professor Roc. The senator needs me to help you track the owl." Everyone was looking at him oddly. He swept a hand through his hair, which was likely still bed-messy. "Sorry about the exhaust...This antique uses diesel and was one of the most efficient diesel model vehicle produced by Land Rover in the 20s. I keep saying I'm going to get rid of it and go solar..."

They entered the living room full of frantic chaos, crying and angry words. Their arrival immediately received Senator Spencer's personal attention and soon the SAR team was led into a big conference room.

A dozen people were anticipating Roc's arrival. Roc was dismayed to find among them two young kids who looked barely out of high school and a few adults who didn't look up to a rugged hike. This was to be his search crew? No wonder they'd desperately called in an expert on owls in the middle of the night.

Sheriff Eddie Shih showed Roc his earlier request to track the senator's baby based on its MPPS ankle chain. Data points showed the MPPS was in motion.

After Roc read the given information, he unfolded his ff to touch its projector button. An enlarged map was projected on the wall. "Look at this dotted line that I just added; we can't miss this Pythagorean course, right? Due to an unknown reason, the MPPS tracking was intermittent on the screen, but we still can tell these broken lines make an obvious straight line, and very clearly the data points also indicate that the target, after the sharp 30-degree turn shown here just a minute ago, has been now flying on the hypotenuse. I have a hunch where it's heading. We should be able to meet the baby face to face somewhere if we move from the opposite end of this hypotenuse line. But we need to move quickly." Aloofly, he folded up his ff, turned and left the room.

"Professor Rochester," a lady called him from behind.

He pretended he didn't hear her soft voice.

"Professor Rochester!"

When he felt the lady touching his back, he finally stopped walking and turned around to face her. A tiny, attractive Asian woman with shoulder-length black hair and red-rimmed, almond-shaped eyes plucked at his sleeve anxiously with one hand.

"Sorry to bother you. I am Mrs. Spencer. Actually I have something to confide in you—Ruby's MPPS ankle chain was broken last night. I just pinned the unbroken rings with a safety pin outside the basket. It has me worried sick that it may drop any time. Please don't tell this to my husband or he would be very mad at me." She showed him a photograph on her ff screen of a Japanese designer baby basket, with a zippered cover that would hold the baby inside and a hood to protect its face from the sun. He'd seen plenty of these on his many research visits in the Far East; they were as ubiquitous as car seat baskets were in the United States.

"So far, from the tracking, we can tell it's still pinned on the baby basket," he assured her. Likely, the owl had been drawn to the basket in the first place by the baby's prey-like cries. With luck, the contraption would be too big for the owl to swallow and it would not bother to tear it apart.

"Thank you so much for agreeing to help us." Promptly she gave him a proper forty-five-degree bow. He had long heard that Mrs. Spencer was a Japanese-American beauty. This bow had showed she still held strongly to her Japanese roots. He returned her bow, which seemed to surprise her. Before she could say more, he had already walked a distance off. Mrs. Spencer reminded Roc of his Japanese ex-girlfriend when they studied together in Cambridge about fifteen years ago; his heart gave a brief squeeze at her memory.

On the driveway's assembly point, Roc gave a briefing to the SAR expedition members; he surmised to them that the thinning ozone layer and environment abuse could have disrupted the giant owl's natural food chain, thus it could be looking for other sources of food away from its usual territory. Within city limits that meant pets and small children were at risk.

"Last piece of information for you before departing for our search: King Ranch is one of the world's largest ranches and its area is bigger than Rhode Island. I have long suspected that a particular remote area in or next to the range could be the habitat for several owls. We'll begin our search there and fan out if necessary.

"And one last thing—we are not to harm the bird if at all possible. An owl is protected under federal law. We don't get to make the kill decision. We bring that bird in alive."

# Commencement of SAR

The search and rescue expedition finally managed to leave Senator Spencer's residence right before astronomical dawn. Under Roc's lead, they passed through a quiet neighborhood to get out of the county. They entered a winding country road with very few solar energy streetlights, which segued to dark country highway, then eventually they turned off on a remote dirt road with total darkness. The uneven surface evaded the Land Rover's headlights; the vehicle seemed to go around corners before the light could illuminate the road ahead. Still, Roc sped along at thirty miles per hour.

"Professor Roc, this is crazy! How could you manage to drive so fast when the road ahead is so dark?"

After a few sharp turns at high speed that chilled his on-board passengers to the bone, he replied, "Now you know why I insisted on driving this ancient four-wheel-drive vehicle?" But everyone kept quiet. "It runs best and most stable on this kind of bumpy country road, but of course I could drive blindfolded on this route as well, and I also know every existing pothole here," he informed them confidently.

"They won't be able to keep up with you," someone said, reminding him that he was not traveling alone and indirectly asking him not to speed. He had heard of this "dog"; they called him Bloodhound. *Indeed a smart, two-legged Bloodhound. I like his retro, blood-red, spiked Trojan style hair but it doesn't fit his face. He looks like that guy who founded Microsoft...Bill Gates.*

Curiously, he took a look at the rearview mirror; when he didn't see any car lights, he relented and slowed down his Land Rover to let the Tesla electric and hybrid solar-electric

SUVs that should be trailing right behind him to catch up with him.

Fifteen minutes later, according to MPPS, they had successfully approached the shortest surmised route and brought themselves closer to their target, but they also found that they had just reached a fringe of unpenetrated woods of thick lush foliage, tall-grass prairie, thorny trees and shrubs. Roc made a quick decision to leave behind their vehicles to proceed on foot instead.

After chopping off some overgrown weeds, they managed to clear a small passable path, but soon they began to encounter a sudden heavy fog and a stiff breeze, and this further limited their speed and visibility for the ongoing journey. The party was reliant upon their ff instruments to find the target.

Many of them were merely following Roc and Bloodhound, chattering and stomping through the brush. Roc doubted the wisdom of bringing such a large party to search out a bird of prey. Owls had exceptional hearing and the ability to fly; their quarry couldn't help but hear them coming and retreat.

After some time of tracking with the guide from MPPS, they were puzzled to find some previously marked or colored strings hung by Bloodhound—their SAR communications person in charge, and they also started to notice unmistakably familiar landmarks.

Only then did Roc wonder if they had been repeatedly returning to the same spot. They had to have been roaming in the same small circle. Bloodhound surmised a local phenomenon must be interfering with the ff-signal.

He called a halt to figure out how to get back their orientation senses. Luckily, this strange phenomenon only went on for around five minutes, according to Roc's watch, before the signal resumed as normal, pointing in a single direction.

Soon after they crossed through another canopy of thorny creepers, brush and giant trees, a piece of vast ranch appeared in front of them.

"Gosh...I'm bushed! Why are we wasting our time? We should have asked for permission to use King Ranch road," the most talkative team member, the twenty-ish boy, was complaining again to his girlfriend.

His just as bubbly girlfriend snubbed him sarcastically, "Yeah, I'm tired too. Sometimes a bumpy winding ranch road is not necessarily the shortest route, but it is constructed for those asses who can't take a hike." She looked Roc in the eye and put on a saucy smile, jutting her breasts forward and pushing one hip to the side. The desperation in the move turned him off.

Being annoyed all this while by their loud giggling, talking, music and games, Roc had been waiting for this right moment to get rid of the two kids. "Since both of you are getting tired already, and this search expedition requires physical endurance, it's best you both not join us further, as we might have to walk for another week before we find the owl. Why don't you both accompany each other, perhaps another fifteen minutes, trailing back on our cleared path?"

The two could be free-of-charge security guards and valets to park their vehicles for an unknown period of time. He was also a shrewd businessman at heart; he wouldn't let anyone take advantage of him literally. "You can wait with the vehicles, and if we aren't back by morning, why don't both of you get someone to move our vehicles to park in Senator Spencer's compound?"

After they left, he immediately imposed some rules for the team members. "This is a SAR expedition, not a high school camping trip. We're tracking a predatory bird with the hope of catching up to it before it swallows this baby whole. I don't want to hear any more shouting, swearing, loud music or games from now on."

"Professor Roc, don't worry! Actually, we got annoyed by them too," one of the adult team members revealed.

He felt relief instantly.

"Professor Roc, I think that girl had a crush on you."

*Hmm—so I was not oversensitive.* He had long noticed that the girl was trying hard to impress and seduce him. She was so young the result was more embarrassing than titillating.

Soon the rescue team resumed their tracking but stopped when they heard a group of sheep nearby bleating sadly. "Aha...something may have just eaten one of their lambs." Roc hoped the owl might have released the baby as it did before, but this time obviously in exchange for more toothsome prey—a lamb. Owls in Texas primarily ate rodents and rabbits, maybe the occasional possum, but an owl the size of a man would naturally seek larger prey. He hoped to God a baby in a basket would prove too difficult to swallow, but ranchers wouldn't take kindly to losing livestock to this predator either.

From the unfolded ff screen, Roc received a signal. "The target is on the ground, hurry up!" but soon, to their disappointment and worry, they only found baby Ruby's dropped MPPS ankle chain.

Roc ordered immediately, "Okay, hurry up folks! Please split into four groups to conduct a fan-search now. Turn on your MPPS's SAR devices."

Roc decided to choose the area with thick foliage to continue his search. From his avian experience, knowledge, and also his gut instinct, he felt there was a high chance the baby could be there.

Ten minutes later, with an extra help from the MPPS thermo-imaging camera, he located little Baby Ruby high in the foliage. The silent basket was just about a hundred yards away from their starting point. Nervously he unzipped the basket's cover. A baby stared up at him, actively kicking her legs and moving her arms, although the basket's handle had been badly torn by the owl's talons, and he also found an empty milk bottle discarded next to the tree.

He looked once more at Baby Ruby, and she returned to him a sweet smile and began to burble. "Gosh, pretty girl, you sure were lucky being buckled-up, zipped-up and concealed inside the basket securely like this by your mommy." Then he took a look at the sky. "You sure were also lucky enough to land in a thick pile of dead brown foliage and not upside down. Did you enjoy your flight?"

Ruby cooed.

Roc signaled the others, then attempted to examine the baby for any possible cuts or puncture wounds, which could be dangerous. But before he could do more thorough checking, the baby began to cry, facing a group of curious strangers.

"Bloodhound, please tell them to dispatch a SAR serescopter now." Baby Ruby seemed all right to him; he decided to leave her alone for the paramedics to examine instead. "Now y'all stay away from her; obviously she only likes me," he joked to them.

Just as Roc expected, the SAR Serescopter CN999 Mini Dragonfly had been anticipating their call and thus it could arrive the scene at its fastest speed. Within fifteen minutes, Baby Ruby was examined by county SAR's best paramedic team and on her way to the hospital.

* * * * * *

The SAR members on the ground split up. Most of the team, interested only in finding the baby, headed back to their vehicles; Roc kept Bloodhound, his buddy Melvin, and the two other capable men to continue the much more relaxing search for the owl. A predator snatching children needed to be wrangled. Roc was sure the bird was menacing loose pets as well as livestock.

Most of them were still feeling excited after their successful rescue operation and some of the guys began to crack dirty jokes. Amidst the guffaws, they overlooked the surrounding atmosphere that had gradually turning gustier, mistier, and soon the group was enveloped by a chiffon of sinister fog.

Soon Roc noticed jet-like stream of fumes ascending from the ground. He quickly figured out that whenever the others spoke, obvious jets of foggy fumes discharged from the ground.

"Hey guys, I think there is a lady spirit staying right beneath our feet, and obviously she doesn't like your indelicate jokes," he advised. The others cajoled him for being prudish, but soon noticed the strange phenomenon of jets of fumes released from the ground whenever they started to talk.

Some of his team members began to communicate with each other using sign language; when their facial expressions and signals started to get abusive and crude, he signing to them to take a rest and have their breakfast.

After the breakfast, the strange phenomenon also subsided. They resumed the search deeper into the area for the giant owl, unaware that the deeper they tracked, the trace of animals and the sound of birds chirping grew lesser. Not until they had reached a sinister area with complete silence did they realize something was wrong, but it was too late for them to retreat. A thick cooling mist had enshrouded them, trapping, engulfing and rendering them to minimum visibility.

Through the mist, Bloodhound called out, "Professor Roc, our ff and its MPPS have both gone haywire again. I'll try to find a spot where it might work..."

Bloodhound's voice and visible figure gradually diminished when he trailed further away, until he completely disappeared. After a moment, the team members realized Bloodhound had disappeared. Roc quickly figured out Bloodhound's likely direction, and he ordered, "Now, everyone lock your elbow with someone else's. We'll go the direction we last saw Bloodhound go. Keep calling out his name and if anything weird happens, don't get panicked and don't let go."

* * * * * *

When Bloodhound detected a deadly silence, he turned his head back, wondering why his team did not respond after he called out for them several times. He still hadn't heard anyone's reply and neither could he see anybody. He was confused why everyone had disappeared all a sudden. Had they walked off and left him?

He didn't want to be left alone as a straggler, so according to his sixth sense of where his friends were, calmly he reversed direction, soon confirming his position when he saw some of his discarded colored strings.

Then he began calling out repeatedly, "I'm here, can y'all see me? Can y'all hear me?—" But his voice got sucked up into an acoustic cloak close around him.

Bloodhound could neither see nor hear his team members calling for him. Suddenly a chill ran down his spine and he felt his goose pimples rise; involuntary, he tucked his hands into the side pockets of his jacket and inadvertently one of his hands touched something cold and metallic. At once, he took the whistle out and began blowing it non-stop as he walked.

The fog began to disperse from his surrounding when he started to blow the whistle. Suddenly he tripped into something and fell to the ground. He scrambled on hands and knees to escape, adrenaline prompting him to flee. A familiar voice cursed loudly.

"Damn you, Bloodhound! Now stop blowing that damn shrill whistle of yours."

He stopped and turned his head to confirm that was his friend Melvin before got up. He stared at the group, all with elbows locked, circled around him.

"Ouch...Didn't you notice you bumped right into my butt?" His teammate was groaning and massaging his back and his buttock.

"Why were you trying to run away from us?" another teammate mocked him.

"Sorry, I got goose bumps all of a sudden and I wondered how could I trip and fall over something invisible."

"You thought we were a group of invisible ghosts?"

"Yes, you were!"

"No, we're your disciples! You were just like the resurrected Jesus suddenly appearing in the midst of his disciples," someone else suggested, laughing.

"All right, guys, attention please! I think this vicinity is too weird for us to continue the owl search. Now we'll figure a way out and go home," Roc decided. The responsibility to ensure a large group's safety was too risky after this bizarre experience. He would send them back first and return later with an even smaller group of people; maybe he'd bring his grad students from the university who had bird experience.

"Anyway, why did it take you guys so long to find me?" Bloodhound snapped, temper covering fear and embarrassment.

"No, actually we found you fairly quick," Roc informed him.

While Bloodhound stared back at them, perplexed, his voice became muted in between syllables and delayed partially and inconsistently, like a bad ff-signal. "Lo—ok a— us! All of us now h—be...com—a mutated ghooooost, mov...ing in...air!"

The delayed broken voices affected the rest of the team too as Roc looked around. Their delayed, looming, fragmented body movements constantly shifted like waves in the ocean. He thought of an X-ray that saw through a body; perhaps they were experiencing a kind of wavelength that would make a physical being appear invisible and delay their movements and sounds.

A ray of bright sunlight penetrated the foliage, temporarily blinding him. The team's whole physical outlook resumed once again but it didn't last long.

Once again, the strange phenomenon repetitively went on and off, and this reminded him of the sunrise light that shone in their eyes where they had found baby Ruby.

"Hur...ry up, let's hold...each o...ther's h...ands... ...again! We have to get out this ghostly land immediately.

Keep moving on toward the sunlight and......s...ee what will happen, we need to r...*et*......urn to our pre...vious ea...st...ward ro...u...te..."

Bloodhound hesitated in doubt. "Professor, should we turn to the opposite direction where I got lost? Once the MPPS indicated I was facing the east, only when I turned my back run...ning to...ward you in the opp...osite direction, it st...o...pped fun...c...tion......ing."

"A...re y...o...u......s...ure?" Roc hesitated too but he decided to trust the sunrise light instead.

"Hi, stray......ing hound," one of his team mates jeered at him, "you bet......ter fo......llow the......l...ea...der! I wonder if your MPPS was working reliably dur......ing th...e w...ei...rd mo......ment!"

What Roc didn't know was that his badly delayed watch couldn't function correctly anymore according to earthly time, and what he assumed to be sunrise twilight actually was the refracted sunset twilight that penetrated from the earthly dimension.

Eventually they followed Roc's wrongly perceived heading, marking earthly sunset rays from three days later as their reliable eastward direction that deceived and misled them deeper into an unknown realm.

After tracking the wrong earthly time by following the assumed refracted "sunrise rays" that penetrated to the primordial zone from time to time, time and motion seemed to return to normal; however, a thick layer of sinister fog had just begun to slowly envelop them from every direction again.

"Hooray! We're no longer ghosts!" one of them cheered loudly.

"Are you sure? Now we might be walking in a true ghost's land," Bloodhound replied ironically.

Melvin also started to doubt, goose pimples running across all over his body. He whispered to Bloodhound, "I also strongly feel that this is the wrong way."

The SAR team had carried a few dozen flares for emergency use. Roc called out, "All right, guys, since our haywire ff has an unreliable signal, we better pick an open ground to launch some flares to see if we're lucky enough to get someone's attention."

When the flares detonated in midair, they wondered if that would work out or not, but soon they heard the intermittent noise of a distant serescopter.

Due to the time warp surrounding their present enclosed enclave, they did not know it took the serescopter more than thirty minutes to reach their vicinity. They were still unaware of the extreme time differences between two existing space-time atmospheric vaults, both hovering on the same Earth.

The CN999 rescue-serescopter had been circling above them for quite some time before one of the members asked, "Why can we only hear the serescopter but not see it? Is it possible we're invisible now like what happened before between Bloodhound and us?"

The question reminded Roc of what had happened earlier to Bloodhound, and how they had managed to get him back to the team. "Well, it could be possible. These flares were not invisible. Let's hurry up! Launch another batch of flares."

\* \* \* \* \* \*

After circling at search altitude for at least thirty minutes without seeing any trace of human existence, the pilot was in a dilemma, wondering if he should or shouldn't persist in the search. While hesitating whether he should leave the vicinity soon, more flares appeared; these signals gave him confirmation to descend the serescopter right on the location detected earlier via MPPS.

Soon, the descending serescopter became increasingly visible to the people on the ground. When it reached one hundred yards above the ground, everyone could finally see the whole serescopter and soon after, all the communication networks began to function again.

"Where were you guys? I have been hovering here for quite some time already. I could see the flares, I could see the trees, but why couldn't I see any of you until now?" the pilot complained. "When you're being searched for, stay out of the trees."

"How could you say you didn't see us, yet you could see the flares and the trees? We were standing in open ground, not too far from the flares." Roc shouted into his ff over the rotor noise.

"No, we didn't see anyone until around two hundred yards up. We would have returned to the base if we hadn't confirmed earlier your position on MPPS right before it went haywire."

"Hey something weird happened to us just a while ago on the ground. One team member couldn't see or hear us calling him and neither could we see him or hear him, but after he blew his whistle, suddenly he appeared in between us."

"Hmm...I think we better get you all the hell out of here quick and call it a day." The pilot did a final search again for the flares on the ground but this time with no luck. "Hey! Where you want me to land?"

"Right down here on the flares."

"Better light another one—the others must have gone out."

When the pilot descended to about fifty yards, he was perplexed to notice the landing signal now came from a few hundred yards away instead. He changed course abruptly. *Weird! Why are these guys so far away from the previous position? That's some wicked cross-wind...that I didn't feel.*

Unbeknownst to everyone, refraction separated the two different spatial dimensions.

Just as the pilot prepared for the landing, the serescopter's engine released some dynamically inconsistent, unusual sounds. Fearing malfunction of his machine, he advised, "Hey listen, Professor Roc! I can't land. Please stay put where you are and we'll send someone to get you out of here as...soon...a...s p...oss...ible."

"Hello?...Can...you...he......ar...me...e?......"

The communication cut off abruptly. Thick fog and strong winds gushed in to cut off instantly both the ff-connection and visibility between the serescopter and the people on the ground.

Reflexively, the pilot ascended at the serescopter's quickest speed; he only felt relief when it finally reached an altitude covered by dark canopy; simultaneously, all communication networks functioned again.

"Funny, why the hell was that place still under bright daylight at this time of evening?" the engineer asked his comrade after the bizarre encounter.

# 4

# Searching for the Lost Expedition Team

The world famous cryptozoologist Dr. Goldie Dallas arrived in Kingsville on her own mission upon hearing from a reliable source that no volunteer dared to embark on a risky search and rescue for Professor Rochester's team, who disappeared within an odd phenomenon in the South Texas woods a few days ago. She suspected, based upon the information she'd heard, Rochester's group was caught in one of the zones she called a primitive navigational vault, subject of her life's work. Of course, rescuing the lost men was important, but the chance to study a PNV directly—and on her home soil—was irresistible.

Before she departed for her expedition, she paid a visit to the SAR serescopter pilot and engineer that reported the bizarre incident of their aborted rendezvous.

At the Kingsville seresport, Dallas chatted with the two men. "You mean when the serescopter started descending and getting closer to the ground, the landing position shifted?" She wondered how far out she would need to land and hike in to avoid a similar issue.

"Yes, it was refracted a hundred yards away from what MPPS detected at the higher altitude," Captain Mark Lee said.

"We followed the MPPS strictly during descent," the engineer added.

"By the time we received the SOS, sunset had begun to fade. Anyhow, we had to fly there to have a look. Upon reaching the vicinity, after descending to 250 yards, we soon encountered turbulence. For unknown reasons, the heat and fog reduction gadget went haywire, followed by the rest of communication networks. However, when we dropped another 50 yards, we began to encounter something we'd never seen before—we saw unusual chevrons of scintillating lights reflecting in the sky, like aurora borealis, and the ground brightening up like broad daylight, and that encouraged us to linger for the search."

"That's poetic, Captain, and yes, very unusual. You were very brave." She thought they made a good decision to stay in the vicinity despite the weird encounter, as logically the ground should have been dark by then.

"But we couldn't find any trace of them, not until they launched signal flares," Captain Lee told her.

"Of course...So then what happened?" They had whetted her curiosity. Witnesses to PNV phenomena elsewhere in the world had also mentioned the aurorae and strange tricks of the light.

The engineer spoke. "Actually during descent, something uncanny happened to those people on the ground that really baffled us. Initially, only parts of their bodies were visible, and then they became increasingly visible when the serescopter came closer to the ground. When they became entirely visible, that's when I could receive Professor Roc's ff and he was as confused as we were. He said they'd experienced ghost-like looming of members of their team on the ground as well."

"Was it because the fog or cloud covered certain parts of their bodies, giving you a ghost-like illusion?" she asked.

"Oh no, the air down there looked clear to us, we could also see the trees," Captain Lee replied. "Visibility was high, even at 250 yards. We just couldn't see the people."

"Did Professor Rochester mention anything else peculiar?" she probed.

The engineer pondered for a second. "Oh yes, Professor Roc said he could hear the serescopter but couldn't see it. He also said a stray team member was invisibly and inaudibly intercalated in between them, and only after he blew his whistle, he became visible."

"I also noticed the vegetation in the area was unusually green and lush, despite it now being autumn," Captain Lee informed her.

"Yes, it's preternatural," she agreed. "I appreciate your time and information, gentlemen."

"Are you going out there? You're going to a very sinister place, ma'am, be careful," the engineer warned her.

"Thank you for your concern."

"Please call us if you need any help," Captain Lee offered.

"You bet! Thanks for your information and your time." She gave them both a handshake and turned to leave.

The engineer called her from behind. "Dr. Dallas, wait a minute!" She turned around looking at him wonderingly. "Oh, just to let you know that it took us more than an hour to find them but Professor Roc thought we'd found them in a matter of minutes."

"Thank you again."

They couldn't get their eyes off Dr. Dallas' retreating figure. Both men waited silently until she had disappeared from their sight, then they whistled at the same time and gave each other a wink.

\* \* \* \* \* \*

Rodriguez Ranch

The ten-day International Cockfighting Festival held illegally in Kingsville, Texas had attracted participants from as far away as the oriental islands of Borneo, Mindanao and Taiwan.

Worldwide cockfighting competitions and fighting-cock trading activities could boost the local business indirectly, so Rodriguez continued to risk hosting it as long as no animal rights activist's demonstrations happened to attract media and none of those hooligans, outlaws or racketeers created outrageous illegal operations to endanger the general public and attract the authorities. Texas had made cockfighting illegal early in the century, pressured by animal rights groups, but the criminal element had little incentive to obey.

Word of this underworld event was leaked to the public and hit a national tabloid headline only when the giant owl unexpectedly preyed on the champion rooster, stolen from Professor Rochester when he went off for the SAR expedition.

Out in the field stood Mr. Rodriguez, the underworld's "King of Cocks." Generally, he appeared handsome, prominent or even nice, but when his contrasting foul temperament leaked through his sneaky sparkling glance during his outbursts—his subconscious bitterness, hatred and anger selectively redistributed to another ill-fated victim.

He was now growling menacingly at his careless right hand man. "Damn it! It's a TEN million dollar cock, why would you just leave it out there alone on the open ground?"

"I let Billy have some fresh worms as a reward for swelling our pockets. I thought he'd be too tired after all that sex and fighting," he replied.

"Damn you, it's a god damn bird, not a human being! ..... Shit! Even the fucking owl wanted to fuck it! It's gone now, you better go fuck those hens now!" he yelled angrily but actually his voice sounded desperate.

"Ahem..." *Fuck you, boss...if it's just a bird then why give it a human name? Why don't you give your dick a name too?* "Daddy Rod, good news for you! Our chicken pen was very noisy over the past few days and nights. I think those fertilized hens will soon hatch a basketful of eggs to produce at least a dozen of equal potential—future champion 'snowballs' just like their dad."

"Damn! Can you count those dozens of little 'snowballs' before the eggs hatch? Which ones are going to grow up as hens or cocks? You better show me then!"

Hmmm, boss...Actually you could employ such a specialist from China but it would cost quite a lot.

"Got that? I want you to show me as soon as possible!"

The man's neck was suddenly strangled by a necktie but soon it was released by his mad boss.

\* \* \* \* \* \*

Dallas wandered in the Texas woods around King Ranch, attempting to trace the lost SAR team's trail to the serescopter pilot's reported coordinates. She had little luck over three successive days in locating anything resembling a PNV zone. Her maps and MPPS were useless in stirring up mythical or extinct creatures that would point the way. She saw no sign of an over-large owl and no sign of any strange mist.

She received an unexpected ff-call from President Churchill.

"Where are you now, young lady? Are you feeling okay today?"

"Oh hey, Dr. Churchill," she greeted her godfather, foregoing the formality of his official title. "I am out here somewhere in Kingsville's back country. I'm fine!"

"Oh, that sounds great! Alone again?" he asked in concern.

"Yes."

"That's sounds dangerous to me."

"Don't worry, I have a gun."

"Listen, young lady! I have just ordered a special rescue unit flown into Texas today from Capitol Hill to combine forces with the state fish and game and local law enforcement to search for the giant owl," he informed her.

"You want me to join them?"

"No, no—no! They're too macho for you! You can continue your search alone. Let me see whether you or those macho men can find them first," he challenged her, "but if you find them, you better lead Professor Rochester's team back home as soon as possible."

"How about the giant owl, quit looking for it? That's the reason they remained out here after they recovered Baby Ruby, right?"

"Ahem—but due to their disappearance, the priority now is to get those five people back home to show their mamas they're sound and alive. After that you can team up with Professor Rochester to get the owl," he advised.

"You bet, Dr. Churchill." Not many people knew that Dallas was the very first baby delivered by the current U.S. president when he first worked as an obstetrician and gynecologist, before entering politics. Dallas usually kept that piece of trivia close to the vest. She didn't want to be accused of nepotism in her scientific work, although having a connection to the president had worked in her favor in the past.

"Hmm...This bird killed something again."

"Really? Not a child, I hope..."

"No. But when you see Professor Rochester, please inform him that his assistant discovered his pet rooster was stolen and it reappeared as an international champion during a cockfighting competition there in town. Anyhow, the giant owl turned up, snatching the 'golden cock' away from the unsuspecting felons." He laughed. "Then those idiots reported it."

"And...that 'golden cock' was Professor Rochester's pet rooster?" She cracked a big grin. *How would anyone know one chicken from the next, anyway?*

"Ahem...I guess so." He chuckled. "If my cat was as big as this owl is reported to be, it would make a mouthful of that feathery pet too!"

"He's not going to like hearing that," she said. *Especially if it's his favorite pet.*

"Unfortunately, nobody knew where the rooster was until the news got leaked. Law enforcement apparently had a field-day arresting people involved in the cockfights. Anyway, some unusual stuff has happened out there, huh? You're going to find out more and tell me later."

"How do you know about it?"

"The pilot who flew that mission is FBI. The phenomena observed made it into my daily security briefings. Finding these folks has become a matter of national security."

"No way!" Dallas flashed on an idea. "Dr. Churchill, may I make a request?"

"What can I help you with, young lady?"

"I need a serescopter with that same pilot and the same engineer." She would expedite her search with someone who had already been to the area in question.

* * * * * *

Over in the open woodland, fifty miles away from TAMUK, a joint-force group of Army Rangers and local Texas state troopers were having their campfire near a brook.

After hunting down a few wild boars, they were now preparing a big feast; at the same time, some of the rangers shared their man hunting stories with the state troopers.

They enjoyed this 'Big Hoot' mission so much it was like a treat to them. They procrastinated their duty in this carefree and serene backcountry without any enemies' threat rather than return to real enemies' territories, which required their constant vigilance or else it might cost them and many others' lives.

They didn't know this trivial matter of owl hunting was a reward, arranged and "hand-picked" by their president to let them relax in their homeland after they contributed so much on a recent, casualty-free, successful international mission.

A colonel shared a funny story—he told them how he was forced to get out of bed at oh-four hundred every morning to answer an ff-call from his boss in Miami, who absent-mindedly never thought of the time zone differences.

He told them how the same question and answer had been repeatedly asked and answered since day one, except this morning there was a new version:

"Daschund, how's your big hoot deal?"

"Not a single trace of it."

"*Nothing?* It's coming to a third day! Come on! You hounds were so good and could even burrow in caves to catch those 'rats.' Could it be a big problem just to catch a bird?"

"Yes sir! It shouldn't be a *big* problem, but the problem is that Texas is too *big.*"

"Well the owl is big too; wouldn't it be hard not to notice it?"

"You bet, sir."

As days of frustration accumulated with the unexpectedly ironic remarks from his boss, he hung up with his tightened fists and began hissing and repeated what his deceased old grandpa used to curse: "Fucking owls!—Owls?? Fuck owls-mama-bin-Latin!"

Due to sleep deprivation and being pressured by their boss, the Special Forces agents had become very frustrated after three fruitless, humid, rainy days cluelessly searching for the giant owl.

On the following day, when the weather turned fine, and since they had license to kill, they shot whatever big birds they saw, assuming that those birds were the terrorist.

Firecrackers, flares and smoke bombs were thrown at random over their covered tracks. When some cool-headed state troopers forbade them to continue shooting at protected birds, riots of name callings and fistfights broke out between the rangers and troopers.

\* \* \* \* \* \*

The biorhythm of birds and animals became confused by abnormal sound pollution over South Texas; even nocturnal animals began to flee in large groups.

A few experimental propulsive-energy transduced fighter saucercrafts passed overhead, emitting their muted sonic booms, and their echoes always trailed a beat behind yet could still irritate any ear, leading to physical discomfort like nausea or headaches from overexposure to such repulsive eerie echoes.

Subconsciously following the direction of the echoes, Roc looked up at the suddenly cleared blue sky, pondering those unique contrails, but no way could he spot any of those fighter saucercrafts. And clearly all the while, these fighter saucercrafts' echoes were the only noise that could transmit from the outside world to their current isolated habitat.

His ff phone vibrated, signaling newly received incoming messages. Could it be possible that another spatial dimension was intercalated on the earthly spatial dimension, and it happened that those fighters' sound waves could actually help to merge the two space-times temporarily, thus enabling a link of communication between two entirely different planes?

Once the echoes subsided, the atmosphere resumed its misty and deadly silence. He checked his ff; as predicted there was no more signal, but he was amazed to find out its solar energy auto-replenishment battery had speedily resumed to 100% charged, despite the lack of direct sunlight.

He retrieved the message:

Prof. Roc. Ur pet chicken got stolen. While being held "hostage" it won the international cockfighting competition. Unfortunately the giant owl stole Bilbo for a feast! Good news! A cryptozoologist is headed in to search for you guys and assist you. Adam

"Damn it!" He folded shut his ff with a snap. "I don't need a useless pseudo-zoologist partner who wastes resources searching for Bigfoot and living dinosaurs."

"What happened?" one of them dared to ask.

"My cock got stolen!" At once they turned their heads toward him—but dramatically in unison they began to descend their glances to below his belt.

He realized what they were thinking. "My pet *rooster*," he clarified.

Everyone began to laugh hysterically; this was good enough to ease their frustration and nervousness. The serescopter had not returned, and many more hours had passed in this strange, isolated, misty landscape.

"I have an idea," Roc said. "We might be here a while longer, and it's been many hours since we last ate. I have hook and line in my pack—let's see what we can catch out of that stream over there."

\* \* \* \* \* \*

Dallas finally boarded the requested serescopter to search for Professor Rochester's missing SAR expedition team. Captain Mark Lee called their route to the tower and maneuvered the serescopter out of town toward the ranch. In a short time, they reached the MPPS coordinates.

"Well, Dr. Dallas, I can't tell you if they've moved out of this specific vicinity, although last week I advised them to stay put right here. We'll get Mark to hover a bit lower, hope they can detect us, and fire some signal flares," the engineer informed her.

"Watch out, Captain Lee! Treetops," Dallas screamed. Simultaneously, the control panel also blinked and gave warning sirens. The pilot deftly adjusted their altitude to avoid the suddenly tall, verdant forest below.

"Watch out for those big birds, Captain," Dallas yelled again amidst the continuous alarm. Thousands of birds, from flocks of cranes all the way to black clouds of tiny warblers, swirled and settled beneath the hovering serescopter, or swirled alongside. "Weird! Why are flocks migrating this early? They shouldn't be gathered in such numbers here for another month yet."

When another round of unpiloted fighter saucercrafts passed overhead again, the birds' ordered flying patterns immediately turned chaotic.

Captain Lee had to make a sudden ascent to avoid collision with the birds. "This is crazy! I bet this must be something to do with those fighters that just shot by above us," Captain Lee grumbled.

\* \* \* \* \* \*

Another series of fighters' echoes now attracted Dr. Rochester to turn reflexively to the direction where only contrails remained far up in the blue sky. *Blue sky?* He looked out again—unmistakably he detected some spectacular broken spider web-like polka dot strings that appeared on and off over the distant blue sky.

He checked his ff; as expected, he found its reception inconsistently blinking on and off. He predicted soon it would be in haywire mode again when the fighters' echoes diminished to an end, and the mist would return.

He habitually hung his binoculars on his neck whenever he was out in the field; from their expensive crystal prisms, he saw an unusual phenomenon of flocks of different birds in the distant sky, but they were clearly in chaos, heading along their respective migration routes. *What went wrong to cause such early migration?* Not only were the autumn birds migrating but also non-migratory birds flocked in great numbers nearby. "Could both man-caused and nature-caused events trigger such chaos?" he murmured to himself.

Baffled, he detected something else in the distant sky, he looked out for it again, and soon he confirmed a serescopter was flying toward them. Immediately he alerted his team members to launch flares.

\* \* \* \* \* \*

Dallas hesitated whether this was a correct spot to seres-drop after she learned that refraction happened here; the MPPS over the control panel went haywire and the ground underneath looked too misty for a jump, but soon they spotted signal flares.

"Great! Dr. Dallas, please stay put! Don't jump! They probably have heard us," the engineer informed her, and at the same time, the MPPS system telescope strengthened again.

"I think we found them—the flares were detected at the previous spot," said the pilot, who didn't trust the illusion this time; he positioned the serescopter based on the MPPS's last recorded correct positioning. Soon the pilot cursed, "Oh damn—it's refracted again for another 50 yards!" The landing position had shifted again.

\* \* \* \* \* \*

As expected, the sound waves of a saucercraft or serescopter could somehow temporarily activate their access with the outside world. When the serescopter descended closer to the ground, the reception strength of Roc's ff gradually increased, and the mist surrounding them dissipated quickly.

Soon he saw a figure on the serescopter prepared to seres-drop; daring from 30 yards up. "Folks, if anything unusual happens again, launch more flares—and Bloodhound?" he looked around.

"Here, Doc," Bloodhound replied, coming out from behind a tree still zipping his pants.

"If anything strange happens, please get ready to blow your whistle continuously."

"Sure, Doc."

# 5

# Trespassers in the PNV Enclave

While looking out from the descending serescopter, Dallas was truly bewildered to see the unusual phenomenon reported earlier. At first, she could only see looming human heads and then more of their body parts became visible.

"See, Doc, now you know what we told you about," The engineer's voice made her hesitate about whether she should join those "ghosts" below. A risk existed they were permanently stuck. Yet this was the opportunity of a lifetime, an open PNV she could study from the inside.

"Do you still want to seres-drop?" he asked.

"YES, please, I just saw those ghosts turn into whole human beings. You better wait for me up here for about twenty minutes or until I call, just in case anything happens—that way you can still escape," she said. "I'll go down and discuss with them a way to get out of here."

\* \* \* \* \* \*

On the ground, they were curiously staring at the newcomer seres-dropping from the serescopter, and Roc waited ready to assist him at any time. As the newcomer grew closer, Roc realized their rescuer was a woman, although she was tall and athletically built.

The newcomer began to unbuckle the belt and take off the safety helmet, revealing full, blonde hair, a narrow waist, shapely long legs and a substantial bust. Like the rest of the team members, Roc couldn't resist staring at her.

He dropped his gaze to her G-letter branded transparent nano boots, then he saw through her left boot an ankle bracelet with silver, skull-like sonorous bells and some red ornamental pendant beads, dangling like a gypsy that beckoned an exotic seduction. But soon his curious glance narrowed to one of suspicion, then abruptly changed into one of condemnation, sure those red beads were made from the red crowns of the nearly extinct rhinoceros giant hornbill of Borneo. But his male inquisitiveness still prevailed; his eyes continued to ascend, and then he was more shocked to see a big canine tooth pendent of a fierce tiger right above the cleavage of her full bosom.

Dr. Dallas was used to seeing either men's admiration or their lustful glances, so she was not surprised to see all these men standing there quietly staring at her from head to toe; except this familiar face from the recent missing-persons news did it in contrary motion. She was glad her "Barbie-legs" could provoke Professor Rochester's fussy glance to ascend.

His lush blond hair over his six-foot-tall frame and perfect, handsome, forty-ish face put him on par with Hollywood A-list stars; she hadn't expected that. He was giving an unwelcome and disapproving glance at her anklet's protected bird's crown. Maybe she'd tell him how she'd been gifted this token by a Dayak tribal chief of Borneo, if he was nice. He caught her eye and his face returned to neutral as he shouted over the rotor noise. "Are you it? The cryptozoologist?"

"It?..." With disappointment, she wondered why he had never heard of her. Then another thought stopped her cold; he thought she couldn't be "it" because of her hair color, her boobs, and her sex. *Great, a chauvinist.* Pressing her lips together, she straightened her posture and shook his hand. "Sorry to disappoint you. I'm Dr. Dallas, born in Dallas. Howdy."

"We didn't expect an angel dropped from the sky to rescue us all by herself, right, guys?" He turned around, looking at the younger men; they stared at him full of anticipation of something. "Ah ha...I'm Rochester, born in Rochester, pleased to meet you."

"Rochester, Texas? What a sweet little cow town, bless its heart."

"I'm from Rochester, New York, not Texas," he corrected gently.

"I sort of figured that, with your Yankee accent and your outfit. Cowboys may not have much, but they usually invest in a decent pair of jeans." She winked and smiled.

Chuckling, Roc eyed her lush blonde hair, paired up with a faultless completion neither caked in makeup nor fake-tanned, rarely seen in a Texas girl. Okay, he was interested. If she was clever enough to get them out of here, he might find out himself later whether her blonde was natural or dyed.

Dr. Dallas dug one of her hands into an oversized backpack and produced foil packs of vacuum-sealed food; she kindly offered these to them. "Are you guys starving?"

"No!" All of them looked at the space-foods with disinterest. Roc wondered why she brought instant foods and supplies. Weren't they going to ascend to the waiting serescopter? He glanced back up toward the receding rotor noise but the copter had disappeared from view again. "We aren't that hungry." He turned to the rest of the people to confirm. "We still have lots of energy, right folks?"

"Yes!" they replied together.

"Oh great! In that case we'll be hiking out of here on foot, gentlemen," she informed them. "Y'all may have noted that sound waves from passing copters and saucers affect your navigation and ff signals."

"Yes, I have been suspecting those hypersonic, transduced impulse waves emanating from those unpiloted fighter saucercraft have something to do with this anomaly. The training route goes right past us here." Professor Rochester pointed upward to show Dallas the training route. "Whenever they passed above us, our ffs became activated temporarily."

"Well...No city dwellers could stand the noise; that's why the airspace was allocated in the remote zone here. Nonetheless, we have no idea when such testing will be overhead, and this is definitely not an ideal place for us to linger. I'm attempting to follow the serescopter's sound waves to lead our way out," Dallas said. "Maybe it's not as strong as a fighter's hypersonic waves, but from our previous experience, I think it could work to a certain extent."

"No harm to give it a try anyway," Professor Rochester consented.

"Oops... I've almost forgotten to return a call to the pilot."

After she asked Captain Lee to lead them out by keeping the serescopter as close to them as possible to maintain position and prevent refraction, she informed them, "Right now, we're in a zone of fluctuation. I can explain more later."

Soon after Roc introduced her to the rest of the team, she hoisted the pack onto her back, gestured which direction they should head and began walking. Rochester fell into step with her and the others trailed behind.

"Did y'all hunt for food during your long stay here?" Dr. Dallas asked.

Roc wondered what she was talking about. "It's only been twelve hours."

"Huh," she said, noncommittally.

"Hunt?...No, no. I prefer fishing." Rochester pointed toward her nine o'clock direction. "There are plenty of fish over in the stream there."

"Did y'all find some unusual fish?" she asked.

"Yeah, we caught some weird-looking fish and some of them were huge," one of the other men informed her, holding his hands wide to demonstrate size.

"They could be a prehistoric species. You should have kept them for research."

Annoyed, Roc lifted his eyebrows. "Well, I'm not a cryptozoologist. I would be more interested if there was a *Pelagornis sandersi* or an *ichthyornis*."

"Sorry, I forgot you're a bird specialist, er—"

"Ornithologist," they blurted the same word at once.

"Ahem...So regarding those prehistoric fish, did y'all spot any remarkable differences from modern fish?" Dr. Dallas asked.

"Yeah......" one of the younger men lazily replied, unwilling to pull his gaze from Dr. Dallas's ass. "They were boney and heavy, mostly head. Kinda like catfish on steroids."

"We haven't need to drink much either, but who knows, it could be due to the refreshing and cooling weather. It's heavenly here except that it's misty and out of touch from the rest of the world." He actually quite enjoyed staying in this unknown place.

"And all of y'all ate those unknown fish?"

"Yes, why not? We cooked them well. I prefer sashimi, but even I'm not that adventurous with freshwater fish I can't freeze first."

"Man, that's so gross. How can you eat raw fish?" one of the young men asked, shuddering.

"Once you try it, you understand the appeal." Professor Rochester again looked provocatively into Dallas' eyes.

Dallas had never tried sashimi, but she felt she had become a piece of sashimi to someone. She moistened her lips with a quick dart of her tongue. Maybe when they got out of here, she and the handsome professor could visit a sushi bar.

Anyway, past experience had taught her to stay professional; whenever she was the only female among a group of men, initially they could act hostile, even awkward, but soon she would earn their respect with her unique abilities and expertise.

Dallas began turning her head around, carefully surveying her surroundings for anything unusual. Clearly, the green, primordial forest around them did not belong in South Texas. She wanted to know what else was in the area. "Did y'all encounter any problems while stranded here?"

"Yeah, earlier on one of our guys disappeared within a few yards from us; we were shouting his name. It's unbelievable he couldn't see or hear us," one of the team members said.

"Come on, guys, none of y'all could hear or see me either," he retorted. Bloodhound came forward to introduce himself to Dallas. "Everyone calls me Bloodhound, nice to meet you."

She tried to figure out which part of his body made him look like a hound dog. He didn't have an unusually large nose, or a pair of larger ears—no dog wore three earrings on the left and looked so dashing. At last she gave his hand a firm shake. "It's nice to meet you, Bloodhound."

"I think after visiting the driest, the coldest, the most humid equatorial regions and the wildest jungle basins, I'd name this place as the most mysterious place on Earth I've ever encountered. Although we're still standing on the same planet, this particular strange place seems to suck up, dent or bar our communication," Bloodhound informed her.

Someone else said, "It's also amazed me, as my ff solar energy auto-replenishment battery still has 100% even though it's always foggy here. I wonder if there's some unknown catalyzed energy enhancing its recharging speed."

Soon everyone confirmed the same also happened to their auto-replenishment batteries.

"Yes, such catalyzed energy may exist here," Dallas agreed.

"Uhh…Besides the sky, earth and water, from this particular weird place that we're standing now, I suspect most probably there's another undiscovered dimensional entity on this planet," Professor Rochester suggested.

"Now, how about if I say it does exist?…And now we've accidentally trespassed within it and gotten stranded. Imagine that when Earth was a newly formed planet, a vault of atmosphere with a network of navigational channels similar to latitude and longitude we use today was built by an all-powerful alien technology but on a different astral plane or dimension. As the Earth biome we know developed, the aliens abandoned their vault and left Earth. Over millennia and through multiple catastrophic events, this atmospheric vault broke up into small pieces. Some of those pieces remain like bubbles throughout our planet and atmosphere, but on a plane we can't normally access. Special circumstances cause doorways to open in these PNV zones. We're currently inside a suspected remnant of the PNV, inside a time anomaly," Dallas said to them seriously. "You've been trapped here for nearly a week. From outside observation, I might have joined you days ago, now."

There was an instant stillness as everyone tried to hide his involuntary goose bumps.

An enquiry broke the silence, "Dr. Dallas, by the way, what does PNV stand for?"

"It stands for Primitive Navigational Vault," she informed them. "Primitive because it was here first, navigation for the pathways within them by which we can still locate such zones, and vault for the locked nature of the precious resource of atmosphere. PNV represents the earliest primordial labyrinth-like navigation and migratory pathways, with a central dwelling or base built by a particular almighty alien-host as his earthly station. The enclosed vault was enveloped and protected by primordial atmosphere with its own space-time, with minimum time elapsed inside that the aliens could shuttle within but stay well camouflaged all over the earth and also its outer space stations."

"You mean our earliest Earth was occupied by aliens?" one of them asked, with a hostile tone and a look of disagreement.

"Well what do you think?—If the initial earth was formless, void and without light, it'd be unbearable for any physical being's existence, thus initially it'd have to undergo a series of celestial ecological evolution and colonization. Different forms of luminous living energies from hyperspace would visit such a world at its primordial stage and with additional aliens from different galaxies at its intermediate stage. Such evolution would take billions of years before the earth's turn to undergo its own planetary ecological evolution and for its own earthly beings to govern their own Earth. At last when human beings began to flourish and dominate the earth, the remaining aliens were forced to leave or perish, as the new tertiary climatic and environmental changes might not help them to thrive soundly anymore here."

She glanced back at their stunned or suspicious faces. What a pity, she thought, that students in schools were taught only with limited Darwinian theories of evolution and humanity, consequently these limited theories taken as fact had barred them from interest and growing acceptance for pursuing other theories of the ancient earth. On top of that, Texas was part of the Bible Belt; most people here thought belief in the existence of aliens countered religious teaching. But Alibaba Ma's theory merged the aliens and true geological time scale with God. In Dallas' mind, it was beautiful.

"How did people decide these mystic zones existed on Earth on the first place?" Professor Rochester asked.

"Well it all started from our expedition teams' frustrating experiences in pursuing the silhouette of mystic creatures, as they could be only reached out at a limited point and from that unattained point onward we began to mark the zone as a PNV enclave. What frustrated us was that those creatures would just disappear suddenly within a visible range but in two shakes, thick fog or torrid storms always covered the whole vicinity, forcing us to withdraw and give up searching immediately. And more disappointments followed. Usually our photos or videos that captured the silhouette of mystical creatures under retreat were blurry or blank. Furthermore, occasionally some unknown or rare prehistoric sea creatures get caught by fishermen or their rotten corpses wash up on shore. That's why we're quite certain there might still be some unknown cryptids living within those well-preserved PNV remnants in the ocean."

"Yes, forty years ago someone collected video evidence of mermaids in a deep remote ocean," Bloodhound said, nodding and smiling.

Dallas continued, "Also too many victims get killed or disappear without a trace in a specific zone, like the Bermuda Triangle. Eventually, such a zone is prohibited as mystical or avoided as hazardous by people, so we also marked those. Pilots, hunters, marine scientists and expedition teams who accidentally trespassed and narrowly-escaped from such a deadly zone have recounted to us their respective weird experiences, and common observances link them all—often their communication devices would go haywire or they would spot suspicious primeval creatures' traces over some remote impenetrable terrain or deep sea."

"Dr. Dallas, have you ever heard the possibility of an invisible predator trying to pursue birds midair, causing those birds to crash into skyscrapers?" Bloodhound asked.

"Yes, I've read those reports, and have investigated them. Our stranded situation now is perhaps just a tip of the proverbial iceberg for unsolved mysterious cases involving strange animal behavior. The PNV theory is derived from the work of a Chinese philosopher and theologian, Alibaba Ma, who postulated that the Book of Genesis describes the alien inhabitation of our universe, and the subsequent transformation of our galaxy, solar system, and Earth.

"Do you mind giving us a briefing regarding PNV's timelines?" Professor Rochester requested.

"Sure!" Dallas consented. "At the earliest stage, the PNV's boundary was enshrouded by near-vacuum hazy space that acted as screening to counteract constant space-time turbulence and radiation that are bad for the PNV. During the mid-PNV era, a catastrophic space-time distortion caused astronomical havoc, but eventually its space-time was stabilized and its whole astronomical outlook was renewed. Inevitably, this astronomical havoc also damaged the weakest parts of outer earth's primordial vault atmospheric fence and caused PNV's nuclear reserves to leak its structural resources to the vacuum of space, thus a subsidiary atmospheric vault with its own space-time was inflated. Eventually, such leaking was stopped by cosmic forces implemented from the newly-amalgamated constellations, including the sun and the moon. Such leakages were routinely converted, monitored and regulated by cosmic forces to exhaust hostile constituents from the PNV to its wilderness atmosphere and intake vital constituents from the wilderness. However, not long after Rest Day Seven, the alien host decided to abandon parts of the PNV for certain reasons. These partially-abandoned PNV space-times gradually amalgamated with the wilderness space-time and an incipient earthly time commenced. After the flood talked about in the Noah's Ark story, the completely abandoned amalgamation of PNV space-time and wilderness space-time resulted in our regenerated Earth. Subsequently, some of those resilient PNV remnants regenerated into smaller independent PNV enclaves through its auto-repair mode and hovered within the regenerated atmospheric vault."

"Whew! Weren't these PNV enclaves regenerated like decapitated earthworms?" someone exclaimed.

"That doesn't actually happen," Rochester pointed out. Dallas shot him a glance, amused he had stolen the words out of her head. This SAR team was obviously not filled with biologists. She feared she'd been talking over their heads this whole time.

"I always considered Genesis a compilation of fairy stories," a team member disclosed, "but your interesting explanation would make me reconsider reading Genesis with new eyes."

"Thank you!" Dallas said. At least one of these men got something out of her blathering. "Actually these regenerated PNV enclaves wouldn't be able to grow unless two PNV enclaves merged, then its area might increase; however, when both the collapsed PNV and subsidiary vault merged and regenerated during Noah's flood, a regenerated counterpart just as potent did inflate," Dallas informed them. "You can read more information about the antediluvian eon on my website. I also discuss how Creation Day One-to-Day Three's source of light was not the sun."

"Wow!" someone exclaimed. Dallas was pleased to see the same respect aimed her way as when they talked or listened to Professor Rochester.

She returned a sweet smile before resuming her lecture. "Long ago, before the end of the PNV happened, the cosmic forces from the earth's central core could also release special signals to dispatch certain species of giant creatures from their confined PNV space-time vault to temporary wilderness-merged space-time zones to act as spies, calamity-forecasters, or predators for their alien-host and other alien inhabitants staying in the PNV. In our age, when constructive interference forms between cosmic signals and man-made waves, the amplified powerful surges prolong the opening of some of the most remote, impenetrable, ancient PNV enclaves to merge temporarily but unpredictably with our earthly space-time, thus both borders of the PNV enclave and Earth temporarily become a neutral ground for access and mislead some of those primitive creatures to enter our habitat and vice versa. That's why we're here now and that giant owl is in Texas,"

"Wow! We're your new fans now!" Professor Rochester jokingly proposed.

"Hear, hear," Bloodhound teasingly seconded.

"Professor Roc, our MPPS has been activated!" Bloodhound informed them.

"Okay, note our current position before it goes haywire again. It's probably working because the serescopter is still hovering right above us," Professor Rochester reminded him.

Dallas shook her head. "But we should still doubt its accuracy, even if the MPPS works. Remember now we're standing right inside another atmosphere. Refraction happened inconsistently, according to the pilot."

# 6

# Mystical Space-time Warp

A momentary deathly silence within the atmosphere promptly alerted Dallas; the thin mist amidst them was getting thicker. She had acquired a high survival instinct from her experiences—they needed to get out this unknown place as fast as possible.

Dallas took a look at everyone; obviously they didn't notice such a little change. The lack of awareness shared by the optimistic laymen worried the expert. She had expected that in order to rescue them, she would trespass into this PNV enclave, but now she doubted if she was able to lead them out of this PNV enclave successfully. They must withdraw as soon as possible.

"Are y'all ready to move a little faster?"

"Aren't we just fine inside here?" Roc quipped; he liked the weather here—*just right!* And everywhere looked green and lush despite the autumnal season.

"For the moment, but I'm not sure how this specific PNV enclave's capabilities function, as we also don't possess bi-senses like an owl to detect all kinds of signals like they do. Let's hurry up!" she hastened them. *I don't have bi-senses but I have gut instinct.* Promptly she called to the pilot on her ff, "Captain Lee, this place down here has started getting weird. If any unforeseen circumstances happen later, don't worry about us. You retreat immediately."

While trekking their way out under the serescopter's guard, Roc asked Dallas eagerly, "What was that bi-senses you mentioned just now?"

She realized Roc was a critical listener who could discretely figure out something different and unheard of from a conversation. Mischievously, she gave him a condition,

"Okay, you must answer some questions I ask before you can earn your answer."

"Why not?" He gestured for her to go ahead.

"Okay, where do frogs or crocodiles live?"

"Water and land."

"Okay, ignoring the term 'reptile' for a moment, the creatures which roam between the two habitats of water and land we call amphibians. In what two habitats do birds live?"

"The land and the sky," he replied.

One of the other men disagreed with the answer. "Hey, Professor Roc, some birds like ducks, swans and geese spent a lot of their time in water too."

Roc nodded. "Ducks, swans and geese are from the family of birds called *anatidae*. They evolved secondarily to swim and even dive."

"You know what?" Bloodhound asked.

"What?" the obviously annoyed low voice asked.

Bemused, Dallas watched everyone lean their ears toward Bloodhound. In his playful mischievous voice, he started to entertain them, "This *anatidae's* earliest ancestors were able to talk and sing like parrots, instead they also evolved to become mute. If you don't believe me, pull a feather out of a drake's tail and listen to its muted husky timbre—don't you think it hisses like a snake too? That's because this *anatidae's* ancestor helped the serpent trick Eve into eating the forbidden apple." Before he could continue his view, some of the team members began to guffaw.

"Baloney, Bloodhound! Huh, you thought ducks were punished by God to become mute? You're the biggest tale-teller. Aesop wrote a better version!"

Bloodhound just shrugged, self-amused, and still retained his cool-headed poise.

"Ahem!" Dallas was as amused as Roc, but she managed to resume her conversation with Roc after the small interruption.

"...So if reptiles, amphibians and birds are nesting and finding their food by traveling between two habitats—or three—have you thought of some creatures that once upon an ancient time could access and cohabite between PNV and its outbound zone?" she asked him.

"No," he replied.

"Water is denser than air; have you ever thought our air could be denser than another unfound entity on Earth?" she questioned.

"No."

"Eons ago, some the most primitive creatures first appeared on Earth, before any human existence. I call them amphisensus creatures. They possessed bi-sense capacities and orientations that enabled them to access and travel in either habitat and they were able to detect all kinds of signals in both the PNV and its outbound zones," Dallas told him.

"Aha, I see...in this case the giant killer owl could be an amphisensus creature."

"In our age, these giant amphisensus creatures couldn't navigate deeper into our habitat, even if they were misled by confusing signals and got stranded in our habitat. Just as frogs never stray far from water, they would be limited to roam at the earthly border zones situated near their respective PNV enclaves, as their daily navigation and seasonal migration pathways under the regenerated atmospheric space-time drastically becomes narrower with respect to their extended distance."

"Initially I surmised the giant owl's food chain was probably disturbed by environmental disaster, otherwise it wouldn't end up somewhere that normally it shouldn't appear," Roc admitted.

"Yes, it did appear somewhere odd," Dallas quipped. "Unfortunately, its ancient signal with fixed designations has misled it to our current regenerated atmosphere. Owls of its size became extinct long ago, thus it won't be able to survive on a long-run basis in our current habitat with our different food chain."

"In my understanding, its final destination was actually blocked by the narrow navigation path ahead, right?"

"Yes, it just couldn't proceed too far into our regenerated habitat from its habitat," she told him. "Actually, different PNV enclaves were repaired at different degrees; the best preserved enclaves were those least damaged ones with their respective auto-repair capacities and food chains still conserved within. Those lucky amphisensus creatures like the giant owl could stay confined and survive in there for generations."

As an ornithologist, Roc thought of the giant owl now as a refugee who got stuck in the middle of nowhere, barred from continuing to his desired destination but also barred from returning his own country. "Generally, owls only fight when extremely pressed; more often they choose to run rather than attacking. It carried off three children but made no move to eat any of them. These attacks seem more like a contemporary owl's defense of nesting territory. Obviously, this stuck giant owl's biorhythm was disturbed, thus it turned restless, agitated and unhappy."

"Yes, these highly intelligent amphisensus creatures won't eat human flesh if they have a better choice," she agreed.

"We have to find it as soon as possible and help it to return its own natural habitat. It won't be able to survive and adapt well on a long term basis in our habitat with smaller prey. Any prey large enough could put up enough of a fight to be a danger to it."

Suddenly lightning flashed in front of them. Their communications with the pilot cut off instantly. A strange phenomenon of heavy spiraling clouds began to gush in from all directions and they had only trekked for about five minutes, according to their watches.

"Don't trust your watches or ffs," Dallas reminded them. "Our common sense now perhaps could judge better than our watches if any time warp has occurred."

Besides experiencing time warp inside the PNV enclave, they also experienced a very brief on and off elapse of "time leak." This "time leak" happened during the moment when PNV enclave's space-time merged with earthly space-time, thus a PNV enclave experienced elapsed earthly time during such an amalgamated moment.

\* \* \* \* \* \*

The pilot finally reached a calm altitude after he swiftly ascended the serescopter out of the sudden turbulence. Clear air revealed no reason for the baffling winds. As suggested by Dr. Dallas earlier on, after several unsuccessful attempts to contact her or the lost SAR team, Captain Lee returned to base at last.

The team was again left stranded amidst the continuous sight of unusual spiraling clouds, and soon they noticed spiraling mists ejecting from the ground. They decided to continue trekking the same direction the serescopter had guided them toward earlier on.

After walking for some time slowly within the spiraling clouds, this strange phenomenon gradually subsided; they could see their misty surrounding scene had also turned clearer, to their relief.

"Damn, the MPPS has gone haywire again; we're lost in the middle of nowhere again!" Greyhound's complaint came immediately after.

"Hurry up, Bloodhound," one of the team members called out as Bloodhound lagged behind them. "Bloodhound, look at those dark cumulonimbus clouds? TORNADO!"

Bloodhound lazily took a second look at the fast moving, low dark clouds. "Bullshit! Heavy downpour only, but...I think we better move quickly out of this stormy epicenter," he suggested confidently and knowledgeably. Soon he made a roughly twenty-degree left turn and began to walk off quickly from everyone.

"Hey, Bloodhound, where are you heading?" someone yelled after him. Soon his best friend, Melvin, began to trail behind him.

*Where is this weird hound heading to?* Roc was puzzled to see Bloodhound deliberately walk away from them, given what happened the last time they separated in these mists.

"I think we better follow this wise hound. Maybe our trail deviated," Dr. Dallas whispered to him.

He promptly called, "Okay, let's follow Bloodhound!"

This time everyone followed Bloodhound without protest, as they finally were convinced he had an unusual sense of orientation and was also a genius in weather watching. After some time, Bloodhound finally turned his head around to confirm everyone had trailed behind him. He threw them a winning smile before instructing them what to prepare for next.

Soon they reached a slope and began to set up tents to prepare for the approaching storm. While everybody was busy, nobody noticed Dr. Dallas had sneaked a small distance from the group. A few minutes later, they heard a series of rapid shots.

"What the hell is going on out there?" Roc ran toward the bombardment source immediately. From a distance away, he saw several wild pigeons and quail dropping simultaneously to the bottom of the valley. Dallas was preparing to fire another round into the sky. "Hey, GOLDIE! Stop killing those birds!" he shouted out angrily.

This was first time she heard him calling her first name; it sounded odd to her, as all her friends had called her Dallas since she was young. Although this showed that he was greatly annoyed, she simply returned a sweet smile. He reminded her that her dad used to call her name just as loudly when he got angry at her.

Soon a herd of rabbits was approaching. Ignoring what he had just demanded, she raised her gun again and promptly fired several more rapid shots.

*Wow! Don't mess with Texas!* He took a deep breath after being stunned for a moment. To his amazement, Dr. Dallas was an excellent shot.

She turned around and sauntered toward him, holstering a pistol. She threw him a most alluring smile and then asked him so sweetly while pointing to the valley, "Can you find some guys to pick them up before the valley gets flooded? These animals obviously received signals of impending heavy storms, or something else catastrophic has changed to their natural habitat that they're evading. We may not be able to hunt anything for the next few days, and we have no way of knowing how long we'll be in this enclave."

"Sure." He thought this was the best way to reply to a Texas-grown virago who knew Texas much better than him.

Most of the team had grown up hunting small game, and soon the birds and rabbits were dressed and spitted over a hot fire. They enjoyed the feast, with one Michelin Star standard, Roc assessed, in spite of the heavy rain.

After a long, heavy, overnight downpour, Professor Rochester and Dr. Dallas woke up earlier than anyone. They sneaked off quietly from their camp and looked out at the beautiful horizon—the sun had just started to rise and the sky finally had turned clear.

"This looks more like Texas that I used to see, with birds flying in the clear sky," he murmured. He was glad they had moved to higher ground. He took a look over the valley, down by the impetuous rapids of the flash flood, where they had dragged three rabbits, nine pigeons and twelve quail to the camp's current elevation for last night's feast. He was surprised to learn his team members possessed some formidable skills to make this expedition interesting.

When he looked out the horizon again, his senses had finally returned to fully awake after a good night's sleep. *Why are so many birds high up in the sky so early in the morning?* he pondered. After careful observation, he was perplexed why flocks of different species of birds were migrating in their respective directions much earlier than their usual time of year.

He turned around, seeking confirmation. "Hey, Dallas! Have you noticed this strange phenomenon since yesterday?"

he called out for her. Dallas stood a short distance away watching the beautiful sunrise. In a great concern, he pointed up at the sky to show her the swarming clouds of birds.

She shaded her eyes and squinted toward the horizon. "Yes, what do you think?" Turning, she pointed out another new phenomenon. "The hue of these trees is different. We seem to be among the autumnal Texas scrub again."

They were standing right outside the periphery of the newly-shifted PNV enclave. Those evading animals that Dallas shot for food had been signaled to migrate suddenly under an unusual circumstance due to their natural habitat's space-time being immersed within the PNV enclave's space-time. Such displacement of PNV enclave's warped and jiggled space-time superimposed over earthly space-time also shortened their returning journey, as during the moment when such displacement stopped, coincidently both space-times' borders merged temporarily. Simultaneously it happened that they were crossing a neutral zone and this enabled them to successfully return to the earthly border.

"We should check if those birds have appeared all over Texas or just within this area...Have we gotten out of the PNV yet?" Roc called out, "Bloodhound! Wake up! I need to check our position. Bring my ff."

Soon Bloodhound yelled happily, and that woke up everyone as well. "Hey! It's working! It's working...After a night of good sleep, everything functions now!"

Everyone excitedly took out their ffs to check for a signal—the folding fan-like ff gradually unfolded and converted into one of their chosen screen mode sizes.

"Bloodhound, hurry up! Give me my ff!" Roc eagerly wanted to know what was going on with the world they had been isolated from for some time, according to Dr. Dallas.

"My ff is unusable for the time being," Dallas said. Roc threw her a questioning glance. "It dropped into the water during the storm."

"I'll let you use mine soon, but just give me a minute," Roc kindly offered her. While waiting quietly for her turn, Dallas was gracefully waving the dead, half-opened ff with its end still clicked together to imitate a Chinese lady waving her folding fan. Rock chuckled, smiling at her antics.

Roc first retrieved his messages before making some important ff-calls.

The first message read:

Prof. Roc. Birds got all confused and annoyed due to bombardment of team RG. It sounded like 4th of July! Serescopter blades hit some birds and it crashed to the ground; luckily no casualties and heavy rain stopped a brush fire.

After Roc read the message, he angrily showed it to Dallas. "What does this team RG have to do with our search?"

"Oh, it's a troop of special force rangers sent by President Churchill to join forces with local Texas Fish and Game helping to search for the giant owl."

"You mean he sent some guys who were trained to find *Homo sapiens* enemies just to kill a giant owl?"

"It's as tall as a human being, is there something wrong with that?"

"Nothing, at least he did the right thing by asking you to search for me instead of asking you to join the wrong team searching for the owl," he mocked sardonically.

"So what should we do now?"

"You call the president, tell him that if he still wants any quail hunting next summer in his Texas range, then command those troopers to stop killing any birds and triggering any type of loud disturbing noise. Ask him to send in the latest Serescopter CN888 Super Dragonfly available, as we have to search for the owl within the migration trains of birds."

Overhead, a school of black geese flew over, honking in agony.

"Shit!" He grimaced in anger. "Order them to pull out NOW! Those idiots will kill the owl instead of just tranquillizing it."

"We might have a problem requesting another serescopter because of the crash," she worried.

"It's not all our fault; the crash was indirectly caused by some laymen they wrongly deployed.

"Look up right here and down over there"—Roc pointed out birds and animals to Dallas—"even nocturnal animals and birds are getting badly disturbed. Look at them—some of them flee in chaos rather than in flocks," he complained.

"Do you think the giant owl will follow them?"

"I think so. No animal or household pet with ears can stand noise like that for long. It's like the Fourth of July down there."

Once the arrangement of a Serescopter CN888 Super Dragonfly was confirmed and dispatched, Roc dismissed the rest of the team members to return home by using the country roads over the ranches.

"If you guys are friendly and able to talk nicely to people, you might be able to catch someone who's willing to give you a free ride back to town on their pickup," he advised them.

# Lassoing the Giant Owl

An hour later, the most advanced Serescopter CN888 Super Dragonfly, fully equipped with the most advanced navigational sensors and gadgets, picked up both Professor Rochester and Dr. Dallas.

The pilot immediately complained in a southern drawl, "Hi folks. I've really got cold feet to fly out here with those crazy birds."

"Don't worry! Your MPPS's ACAS will warn you, and we'll watch out for you with our two extra MPPS and binoculars," Dallas replied in a sweet voice.

The pilot sighed and continued the risky mission.

The bird watch and search had gone on monotonously for quite some time, with occasional alarm warning sounds from the ACAS and simultaneously Dallas's anxious warning calls from watching her MPPS.

Eventually, Roc detected an obvious suspicious moving spot on MPPS; he then proceeded with his binoculars to confirm visually the silhouette of a gigantic, low-flying creature. "Yeah, I think I've spotted it," he informed Dallas. It looked obscure from far away but Roc was quite certain of what he had just spotted. Repeatedly, it would disappear beneath the foliage and then it would re-emerge just above the treetops; shortly after, he was able to mark its specific flying patterns from the MPPS.

"Are you sure it's the giant owl?" Dallas asked excitedly.

"Unmistakably. It's big and flying alone, while the rest of the birds are moving with their flocks." He pointed it out to her on the ff screen.

Presently, Roc beckoned the pilot to fly nearer to the giant owl, to enable better aim. He missed a few shots until Dallas snatched the tranquillizer gun from him.

"Let me do it, I think I can do better than you," she told him confidently.

The missed shots probably had scared off the giant owl and it ended up perching on a tall tree. "Captain, can you hover the serescopter level with that tree?" Dallas requested.

When the Super Dragonfly began to descend, Dallas asked the pilot to open its door partially. The moment she pulled the trigger, the giant owl swooped toward the Super Dragonfly's windshield with its thrashing wings and talons ready to attack. Luckily, the pilot reacted promptly, zooming away from the impact as soon as the MPPS's ACAS pre-collision warning alarm activated.

The abrupt zooming caused Dallas's lower body to fall out the slanting Super Dragonfly through the half-opened door. She would have fallen to her death if she hadn't tightened her grip on the door handle. Dr. Rochester grasped a side of her waist in time to stop her upper body from slipping through the door before he could drag her on board again.

After the bird's unsuccessful attack on the Super Dragonfly, the giant owl quickly shifted its target by flying from underneath to pursue Dr. Dallas. "Watch out! It's coming after you now!" he alerted her. Although both human beings and owls had large, forward-facing eyes to give them excellent binocular vision, the owl had an advantage of being able to turn its neck around 270 degrees, enabling a faster orientation to its prey.

With a hand still grasping the Super Dragonfly door handle, Dallas used the other hand, trying to aim the tranquillizer gun at the approaching owl.

The instinct of the owl probably could tell that the gun was its most fatal enemy; it attacked the barrel using its pecking beak but its deafening screeching sound was more threatening to them.

Dallas aimlessly triggered the tranquillizer gun a few times; the beak of the owl was so strong it began to overpower Dallas's grasp of the gun. When she used all her might to pull it back again, a tug of war began.

Hastily, Roc threw firecrackers right in front of the owl. The sudden loud bombardment caused both Dr. Dallas and giant owl to lose their respective grasps in the fight of the gun; instantly the rifle dropped straight down to the lush undergrowth below.

"Close the door, zoom another few yards away from the owl, then ascend to higher altitude. We can't let the serescopter blades kill the bird!" Professor instructed the pilot while at the same time helping Dallas to stay away from the closing cabin door. In less than five seconds, the serescopter started to zoom away from the owl and then ascended at its fastest speed. This most advanced Super Dragonfly from the U.S. Navy functioned and maneuvered flexibly, different from the old model they'd flown on more recently.

The giant owl finally gave up its attack with an agitated, eerie shriek and then flapped its wings a few times before flying off to rest on a giant tree trunk some distance away.

In contrast to its pursuers, it leisurely started to preen its feathers over the tail as one of the Super Dragonfly blades had accidentally chopped off some plumage.

Dr. Rochester looked at the owl with his teeth grinding. It'd be easier to kill you than to try to keep you tranquilized, alive and unharmed!

"Gosh, I am so sorry! I dropped your expensive gun!" Dallas puckered her eyebrows in apology, her eyes wide.

This was her first response after her life and death ordeal? Roc hastened to reassure her where his priorities lay. "It's all right! You're more important." He cautioned her, "Look over there—that hungry, red-eyed raptor is perching on the trunk, watching us. You never know when it will attack us again.

"Please come over here with me," Roc called while he opened a cabin compartment his assistants had geared up for this new expedition.

"Here you go!" He gave her another gun and also a new set of binoculars.

Instinctively they both took a glance toward the resting place of the giant owl, but it had disappeared.

"Oh, it's gone!"

An enquiry came from the front cabin. "Now what should we do? Go back home?"

Without any pause, both replied in unison, "NO. Please stay!"

"We need to take a rest. Let's go down," Dallas suggested.

"Are you sure that down there is safe?" The uncertainly in the pilot's low bass southern drawl showed his concern.

"Let's check then," Dallas replied.

After confirming from both their MPPS thermo-imaging cameras that there was no trace of an owl hiding in the surrounding woods, Roc finally decided, "It seems okay to me. Let's go down there now."

While the Super Dragonfly hovered in the air to generate a laser-cut landing pad ready for its landing, Dallas asked herself, *How did it just slip through our fingers...that quick?* When she stole a glance at Roc, his face looked puzzled as well.

He was still cautiously checking out all directions with the binoculars for any sight of the giant bird, and he only quit looking around when the serescopter began to land.

Once the serescopter landed, Dr. Dallas was the first person to touch one of her hesitating feet to the ground. She paused in the open cabin door. At once, a gentle, welcoming breeze caressed her face and trickled through her hair. She inhaled deeply; the refreshing air at last helped her gather enough courage to put her next foot on the ground.

The beautiful autumn view enchanted her to embrace it so deceivingly that she totally neglected the danger hidden around them.

Suddenly a bloody, furry creature ran across her foot that caused her to swear, followed by many of its fellows. The four-letter word promptly raised Roc's vigilance. Emerging from the "stirrup-high" grasses that had evaded the serescopter's landing laser, dozens of over-large voles scurried wildly across the clearing. They looked as if they were trying to escape from a predator.

Owls loved to hunt voles. The giant owl could be hidden somewhere nearby.

When the engineer stepped down from the Super Dragonfly, Roc stopped him immediately. "Wait a moment, let me check first to make sure it's safe."

"But I need to pee now!" he protested.

"I need to pee too," the pilot's voice followed from inside the cabin.

"All right then." Roc relented but he still cautioned them, "Don't go too far away. If you see anything unusual, run first rather than pulling up your zipper."

"Wait for me," the pilot called after the engineer.

The two men disappeared to the other side of the serescopter, out of deference to the lady present. As they were urinating, movement in the brush caught the pilot's attention. After taking another curious glance, both men were momentarily stunned as they saw uncountable owls staring back at them with sinister eyes.

Their sudden running and yelling alarmed Dallas and Roc, although the sight of the two anxious men running and struggling to zip up their pants at the same time was comical. "OWLS! There're thousands of owls over there!" They pointed to show the direction.

Dallas strode around the serescopter and promptly focused her binoculars the direction they had just pointed. "Gosh!" Chills ran down her spine, as never before in her life had she encountered an overwhelming number of owls gathered at one place.

After taking a deep breath, she bravely took another more careful glance through the lens, but this time she saw something obviously flying and fluttering. "Oh wow—this is the largest flock of giant owls that I ever encountered in my life," she murmured, smiling in relief. "It's okay, guys. They're just giant owl butterflies."

"What?" Roc said.

"Butterflies!—I meant there is a very large flock of rare giant owl butterflies. I want to go over there have a look now." Dallas got all excited like a little girl, bouncing in place on her toes. Without hesitation, she ran off.

"Hold on, take your gun and don't go too far away," Roc advised.

She turned around reluctantly and accepted his offer.

Roc had been in a state of vigilance since the "exodus" of the voles, and these voles had been on and off emerging from the same direction Dallas was heading to now. After a second thought, he made an abrupt decision to follow her in order to keep close to her.

While Dallas was engrossed in her studies, taking photos of the giant owl butterflies as close as possible, Roc stood a distance behind her not at all at ease. He glanced all around the clearing, the grasses and the scrub woods beyond, wondering where the giant owl could possibly hide.

When another bloody vole ran over one of his feet, he homed in on a particular area on the ground nearby to where Dallas was squatting. At that spot, the butterflies were scurrying in the air more chaotically than they were anywhere else, and his glance continued moving down, observing those dancing butterflies.

After some time, he began to suspect the grass-covered ground had an enormously big hole underneath it. To find that out, he picked stones from the ground and threw them directly onto the suspected ground. A few more voles began to crawl out of the grass right on the spot where his stones had dropped.

"Stop doing that, you're scaring off the butterflies!" Dallas finally rose and turned her head toward him in protest.

"No, I just scared out a few voles."

She threw him a disapproving glance then resumed her observation.

Roc suspected that if it was not a snake then another predator was hidden in that big hole, and soon it would weed out the whole colony of voles. To reconfirm his suspicion, this time he gathered much bigger stones from the ground, and then he behaved no different from a naughty boy, throwing the stones one after another into the hole. Soon after, something unmistakably like a bird's wings fluttered amidst the butterflies.

When Dallas heard the rattling sound, she didn't even raise her head. Instead, she hissed, "Hey, please stop disturbing those cute voles." Despite her disapproval, Roc continued to throw the rest of the stones one after another into the hole. He had to drive the predator out where they could see it.

Not long after, a familiar eerie screeching sound came out from the ground. Reflexively, Dallas got up, running with all her might toward Roc. "Gosh! Do you think the giant owl is hiding down in the ground?"

"Yes, darling! Now, do you want to catch the butterfly, catch the owl, or go back home?" he teased her.

She frowned with determination. "We're staying and we're gonna get it this time around. We can't let it slip through our fingers anymore."

"Obviously, there is a big hole on the ground, concealed by the tall grass." He indicated the area with a wave of one hand.

"We should have also turned on the ground penetrating system on the MPPS! I never imagined it would prey on those little voles in a hole," she gasped.

"Well neither did I suspect it would hide under the ground; it didn't look like a burrowing species. I also noticed that these voles are actually larger than regular voles." They watched another vole scurry past.

"Maybe due to living next to a PNV enclave."

"Okay now, are you ready for another fight?"

"Sure," she replied.

"We'll keep throwing firecrackers into the hole until the bird is forced out of the ground by the noise."

"Those pebbles wouldn't help?"

"No, they're too small to bother its feast. The owl won't simply come out without any great annoyance."

"Do you think it's too dangerous for us to fight on open ground like this?"

"Remember the fight up in the air was unsuccessful. We're land inhabitants—by right, we are at an advantage to fight with it on the ground." He winked, using her own reasoning to reassure her. "Now let's see what we should do." Roc began to survey the vast open ground. Soon he spotted a segment of stone fence, similar to countless stone fences crisscrossing Inisheer in Ireland. Rough stone blades and boulders had been piled about four feet tall and roughly fifteen feet long, a remnant of someone's effort to clear a field. "Let's move to the 'Inisheer-fence' there." He pointed at it.

* * * * * *

Between them, they decided to send the serescopter away and remain on foot; the whine of the engines could be disturbing the bird, encouraging it to continue hiding. The pilot promised to stay within ff-range and took off. Dallas and Roc headed to the abandoned stone piles.

While they crouched behind the stone fence discussing how to capture the giant owl, a few strange, agitated calls promptly distracted them. Curiously, they peeked over the fence toward the sounds; standing by the vole burrow, a pair of three-foot-tall owls hovered above the hole with raised, ruffling plumage, barking like angry dogs and at times hissing like aggravated cats.

Roc rubbed his eyes disbelievingly. "Oh gosh!" he exclaimed, aghast. "These should be... *Ornimegalonyx!* They're an extinct giant burrowing owl species that existed in the Pleistocene in the Caribbean and Mediterranean areas between 10,000 and 30,000 years ago. Once they even terrorized the night sky of Cuba."

"Wow, what a surprise! It seems more prehistoric creatures have been barred from returning to their PNV habitat," said Dallas. Her voice betrayed no sarcasm, for which Roc was grateful. An "I told you so" would rub him the wrong way, even if he deserved to hear it.

"Do you know how serious the consequences could be to our natural habitat when these trapped gigantic primitive species begin to threaten our food chain?"

"Yes. I hope there are only just these three giant *lechuzas*! Anyway, reciprocally, there shouldn't be many such prehistoric giant creatures within their own little conservation," she speculated. "Their numbers would be self-limiting within the confines of available food sources."

"I think after many unsuccessful attempts to enter their natural habitat, they could have been roaming near its border. This current hunting ground is monopolized by these two *Ornimegalonyx*...Look out! I guess a territorial fight has just begun." Roc nodded toward the owls and raised his binoculars.

Amidst the warnings and attacking from the two defenders, the disturbed giant owl finally emerged from the hole. An instant later, their tensed up, defensive postures made the two *Ornimegalonyx* look bigger and fiercer, with their raised and ruffling body plumage. Soon the three massive birds were involved in an intense territorial fight.

"Gee!...This is like a duel between a six-foot-tall adult and two three-foot-tall little boys. What shall we do now?" Dallas asked.

"It's the most ideal moment to tranquilize all of them."

"Didn't you notice our tranquilizer guns are not powerful enough for that thick-skinned and heavy-plumage-covered giant? Those shots merely bounced off like arrows hitting a stone wall." Dallas complained, incapably frustrated.

"Hmm...try to shoot the regions with thinner skin, such as the armpit under the wing, or right into its mouth when it opens its beak," Roc suggested.

"Hmmm—both are hard targets from a distance away. How I wish we had a truck now," Dallas said.

"Come on, if we couldn't get it on the serescopter do you think we would be able to get it with a truck?"

The agitated unworldly calls reverberating in the air told them the owls' fight was getting more intense. "I think this is the best moment to get them, while they are still concerned with attacking among themselves."

Following Roc's plausible suggestion, Dallas began to aim her gun sights at the giant owl, but he stopped her at once. "Hold on! I think it's better to dart the *Ornis* first, lest they escape from or be killed by the giant owl."

"No, dart the giant owl first so it won't kill the two *Orni* while they're down," she argued.

Suddenly, before their opened mouths and astonished eyes, the giant owl gave a few shrieking loud cries. It swiftly led off in a straight line, with legs held back, swooping their direction, just five feet above their heads, with the two *Ornimegalonyx* still pursuing it.

It promptly swung its legs forward and spread its talons in a broad pattern, and with lightning speed it pounced on a deer. A moment ago, the deer had emerged from behind a canopy of shrubs to graze on the fresh grass; now its head was gripped within a massive owl talon.

A split second later, the breathless deer had its head crushed under the giant owl's razor sharp talons. The owl gobbled down the new meal as fast as possible, its neck rotating with great speed and angles during frequent pauses to look around.

Dallas watched its behavior in awe. Roc explained, "This is called kleptoparasitism; it tries to rush its meal in order to prevent potential rivals or other predators from stealing its hard-won food."

The two *Ornimegalonyx* kept circling on the air anxiously, but each of their rotations was actually tactically getting closer to the deer's carcass. "Now look closer at those *Orni*, watch how they try to steal their rival's meal," Roc pointed out.

Halfway through eating, the giant owl tried to chase off an *Ornimegalonyx* who had just began to steal its food. It flew off with some deer meat still sticking on its beak. Simultaneously, on the other end, the other *Ornimegalonyx* began to gobble up as much deer meat as possible; the giant owl returned and took some bites on its meal, then it tried to chase off the second *Ornimegalonyx* eating its meal. In that instant, the first *Ornimegalonyx* returned to steal the food again, and the process repeatedly occurred until half of the deer carcass had disappeared with the three owls sharing it.

All of a sudden, the giant owl grabbed the remaining half deer carcass under its talons and flew back into the voles' communal burrow. As the vole hole was just big enough for the giant owl to crouch inside, the two frustrated angry *Ornimegalonyx* were forced to mantle the hole, hissing and snapping their beaks, with their tails spread and raised.

"Oh my...! What a sly and clever giant owl," Dallas exclaimed.

Very soon the giant owl finished its meal inside the hole, and with its insatiable appetite, it resumed devouring voles. More bloodstained or injured voles escaped from the hole, but once they reached outside the hole, the two *Ornimegalonyx* gobbled them up immediately. However, this situation didn't last long, as in a flash the two angry *Ornimegalonyx* swooped down the hole and began to attack the giant owl instead.

A series of loud cries issued out of the hole; soon the giant owl was forced to rise from the hole to continue the territorial fight, and feathers either fell all over the ground or flew on the nearby air carried by the breeze.

When the giant owl attacked the first *Ornimegalonyx*, the second *Ornimegalonyx* would take revenge by pecking at the giant owl's back. Whenever the giant owl got hurt, it would turn to attack the nearest attacker. Then the first *Ornimegalonyx* would take its revenge by pecking at the giant owl's turned body, and the whole process would repeat over and over.

"Whoa! These two *Ornimegalonyx* are the most cooperative pair I've ever seen." Dallas was flabbergasted. While concentrating too much on observing the birds' fight, one of her knees slipped forward from where she crouched and landed heavily on a sharp stone. She suppressed her cry of pain, but the bloodstain on her jeans drew Roc's attention.

"Isn't it painful?" he asked.

"What do you think?" Dallas replied coldly.

An idea spontaneously popped into Roc's mind. Ignoring her retort, he aimed his tranquilizer gun to target specific lesions on an *Ornimegalonyx*. Soon arrays of darts were flying out, with some hitting precisely on those wounds.

The struggling *Ornimegalonyx* gradually slowed down its movements and it tipped forward on the ground first before being fully tranquilized. Dallas realized what Roc was doing; immediately she lifted her gun to target the other two owls' open wounds.

When the second *Ornimegalonyx* fell on the ground, the giant owl finally became alerted to the new the invaders' assault; it defensively tensed up.

Roc alerted Dallas, "Watch out! It may attack us!"

"Gosh, its wounds received at least three darts just now. How come it still didn't fall?" Dallas was bewildered.

The giant owl took off without any delay. Right before it swooped toward them, Roc promptly called out, "RUN! Let's split to confuse it—you run to the left, I run to the right, we meet at the front side of this fence."

As the giant owl swooped down on its prey, the two human beings separated and ran toward opposite directions, which instantly confused the almost-drugged and obviously slowed-down giant owl about which prey it should target. Shortly after, a few firecrackers were set off loudly right in front of its face.

Both Dallas and Roc obeyed each other's good advice, instinct and ideas; however, during the dangerous ordeal neither of them could predict what their next respective spontaneous act would be.

While the giant owl hesitated, its wounded lesions received more darts. It gave a few angry painful cries but a lariat soon reached up, winding and tightening its giant beak. Another array of darts flew out from Roc's gun.

"Okay, it's enough, stop it or else you'll kill it!" Dallas called out.

As the giant owl sensed the danger of being captured, it started flapping its wings to escape, pulling its face awkwardly with tension on the rope. As it paused its panicked wingbeats to tug on that rope with a talon, another, bigger ring of flying lariat cast down its way past its neck to lasso its wings and body together before it could take off.

The lightning speed lasso was totally out of Roc's experience. He whistled in obvious astonishment. "Wow!...What a cowgirl! I was wondering what those ropes were used for. Are you going to lasso a man for yourself like this one day?"

With sweat still dripping down her forehead, Dallas threw him a cross, cold stare. "Ha ha. I don't think that's funny...But be prepared." She stuck her tongue out at him, but he already turned away, walking toward the struggling giant owl.

The giant owl tried with its last strength to free itself but without much help, the tranquillizer had started working and shortly after, it succumbed, lying motionless on the ground.

"Gee, how long did it take us to defeat them? What's the time now?" she asked, and then she moved next to Roc and drew his Seiko wristwatch closer to her eyes.

Roc took a glance at the cloudy sky. "It looks like we're going to have another storm soon. Can you call the base to inform them we need another serescopter as soon as possible? I'll call the one we rode out on now." Then he handed Dallas a signed visitor's pass. "You go with the giant owl first. My assistants will be waiting to assist you upon your arrival. I'll wait for the next flight to go with the two *Orni.* Every password in the lab is NEWYORK, one word."

# Who's the Troublemaker?

Forty-five minutes later, the serescopter that carried the giant owl with Dr. Dallas finally landed at the Kingsville Air Force Base. Despite the sudden heavy popcorn rain, two of Professor Rochester's graduate assistants still waited eagerly in the rain for their arrival. The two twenty-somethings introduced themselves as Adam and Cindy.

When they finally saw the tranquilized giant owl, they were stunned by its colossal size. "Gee, it is taller than me," Adam, the shorter assistant, exclaimed.

"If I'm not careful, I'll be dinner!" Cindy joked.

"Hoo-hoo-hoo-hoo—hoo-hoo-hoo-hoo here's the Kobe steak," Adam jeered. He imitated the barred owl call that sounded like "Who cooks for you? Who cooks for you?"

"Let's hurry up! I worry that it may revive soon. We need to lock it up as soon as possible," Dallas hastened them.

At once, they moved the giant owl into a big truck and soon they were on the way to Roc's research laboratory in TAMUK.

Twenty minutes later, upon entering Roc's research laboratory entrance, Dallas was stunned temporarily by arrays of greetings and swearing in different languages. "*Ciao!...Salve!...Buenos dias!...Bella signora!...*Hi, pretty!...Sexy!...Sexy!...Fuck you!...Cholera!...*Chinchin!*"

"Oh my...What's all that?" she asked the two grad students. They merely returned embarrassed smiles, then gestured her to follow them into a hall where dozens of exotic colorful birds were kept.

"Oh, I see! They really can talk." Dallas was surprised but also truly impressed by the array of birds.

"Yes, sometimes they can be very obnoxious, talk and swear too much," Cindy complained as she threw her shorter colleague a condemning look. "Adam was the one who taught them all those foul words in different languages and he even fed the mynah with *chili padi*. Although the mynah can't taste, Adam still believes that the smallest and hottest chilies could make them talk more."

"But sometimes they can be really adorable," Adam argued.

"I'll get you a dry shirt, Dr. Dallas," Cindy said.

"Thank you. That will be welcome." Dallas plucked the fabric of her soggy T-shirt away from her chest. Adam's eyes goggled briefly before he looked away, toward the birds.

Then the birds spoke again, "You're pretty! You're cute! You're gorgeous! Lovely! Lovely!"

"You hear that, Dr. Dallas?"

She couldn't stop giggling after hearing what the birds said. "Okay! Enough, enough—let's go lock up the owl." She still giggled when she left the hall. Cindy rejoined them, a T-shirt slung over her shoulder.

Soon they led her into another hall, where a big steel cage dominated the space. "This is the largest cage available. It's an old cage but it's made of stainless steel," Adam informed her.

Following Roc's strict instructions, the two assistants successfully transferred and locked the giant owl in the cage before it could regain consciousness.

After the two assistants left, Dallas took off her wet cotton shirt, hanging it on a chair next to a ventilator. Her bra was soaked too, so she wanted to give it some time to dry before putting on the oversized T-shirt Cindy had found for her. While resting and waiting for Roc, she heard some talking sounds. Curiously, she began to search for it and soon she figured out the noise was from a smaller room annexed to the main lab.

Upon opening its door, to her surprise she saw a beautiful albino mynah bird perched on a small tree top locked inside a big steel cage. "Oh! My poor dear friend! Why did they lock you in there all alone from the rest of your friends? I wonder if you've been abused by your 'owner.'" She frowned, hating to see captive birds that were otherwise healthy. Active, curious birds, mynah needed to be kept "busy" with others of their kind to thrive. "I'm going to set you free from this jail sentence now." She stepped forward to attempt opening its door then she realized its touch screen keypad lock needed a password. She remembered Roc told her that every password was "NEWYORK."

She looked at the numbered keypad in disappointment, then she explained it to mynah, "Look, this password obviously uses numbers not letters. Sorry, I can't help you!"

Then she unmistakably heard the mynah speak. "Six three nine—nine six seven five."

"Gee, are you really that smart?" She was truly astonished and amazed. "Let me try the numbers you just said."

With the correct password, the mynah was soon released from the locked cage and to her disbelief, it flew toward her and perched itself atop her shoulder.

"Are you hungry?" Dallas asked.

It said, "Hungry! Apple please!"

"All right, I'll go find an apple for you. I saw a refrigerator in the other room. For the time being, you go back to your cage." Obediently it left her shoulder to return the cage.

"You good bird! Great! Stay right there and wait for your apple, I shall return soon." She locked the cage before leaving the room.

Soon Dallas returned to the room in the borrowed T-shirt that reached her knees and carrying an apple in her hand; however, she couldn't find the mynah in the room anymore.

She started to look for it in other rooms, but to no avail. Eventually, she went into the hall where the giant owl was caged; to her astonishment, the cage door was open and the owl was not inside.

Frantically, she continued her search for the missing giant owl.

She soon found a side door that stood open. *How did Roc get back here so fast?* Curiously she walked through the door just in time to hear the mynah calling frantically and loudly from a tree top outside the building. A chill ran down her spine. *OMG, it knows how to enter the password for the access control system?*

"Hey! Am I a predator to your bird-friends?" Dallas asked ironically. "Where is the owl?"

"Owl ... *Au revoir.*" It took some times for Dallas to finally grasp the intonation of the French words that meant goodbye.

"Did you release the giant owl? ...Yes?" she asked sternly.

"Yes," it admitted.

Promptly Dallas's face turned green. "You?...You naughty bird! You're going back to your cage NOW! Now I know why you were locked in there!"

However, it simply refused to come down from the tree top even though she offered it the apple sitting now on her hand. "Gosh, how could I get hold of Adam to catch you?" She thought the mynah probably would listen to him.

Ironically, soon she heard the mynah began to sing, "Catch me if you can."

She felt so helpless. How was she ever going to explain this?

\* \* \* \* \* \*

Kingsville Air Force Base

Roc was cornered by a group of heavily armed DEA agents upon arrival. "Am I a Snowden, a chain murderer or a spy who sells our top national secrets?" he asked them, perplexed. Why had they come in so heavily armed just to take the two owls?

"Very sorry, Professor Rochester, I think we have to take these two *chickcharney* with us. This is something to do with national security." The leader gave him a shrug. "Orders from our big boss."

"I wonder if his name is Blackbeard?" Roc asked sarcastically, without any sign of backing off.

Roc's ff kept buzzing. He threw a cold icy stare at the DEA guys before answering it. "I got caught up with a few of Blackbeard's subordinate pirates. You wait right there for me." Without giving any chance for Dallas to respond, he turned off his ff and continued his bargaining with the DEA.

"Why didn't you guys go catch them yourselves instead of waiting for this moment after my life and death ordeal... you can't just steal them off me like this,"

"We apologize for this. Our men did go out there trying to catch them, but they weren't as good as you."

"You'll receive compensation," another agent added.

"I'm not interested in receiving peanuts that would require more than an hour to fill out the forms and more than six months to claim! I have plenty of money in my New York and Swiss banks. If I wanted dirty money I wouldn't have given up everything for backwater Texas to catch feathery things, where at any time I could get bitten by a rattlesnake." Keeping his posture upright, he squared his shoulders to the leader, blocking their access to the serescopter door, behind which lay the two trussed and drugged *Ornimegalonyx*.

"Very sorry, Professor, but we have to take them."

"Oh yeah...on a holy order from your big boss Blackbeard." He gritted his teeth angrily. "I need a convincing reason why you guys insist on taking them. What have they got to do with national security?"

An agent approached whispered closely in his ear, "Professor...we suspect there's 'yayo' inside their tummies. We need them to lead us to the head smuggler, who has a compound to the east of here."

Roc took a moment to digest that. What an idiotic theory. Balloons of drugs in the digestive tract would be far more deadly to a bird than a human mule. The owls' natural reaction of coughing up pellets of compacted indigestible matter could not be predicted well enough to benefit smugglers. "Fine. You take them then," Roc reluctantly agreed, "on the condition I only lend them to you. Once you have completed the investigation, I want them back *alive* and as soon as possible."

\* \* \* \* \* \*

Dallas tried several times to contact Roc but without any further success. Revealing her unspeakable frustration, she sat right on the floor at the side door, licking and eating the apple with deliberate slowness, facing the mynah bird, which still stayed high up on the tree top.

"Hmm—I wish I was that apple." Roc's voice came from behind her.

Her heartbeat raced suddenly and she felt really embarrassed at being caught . *Oh gosh, I must be so frustrated and mad at this singing mynah that I didn't notice he walked in!* She jumped to her feet, brushing her hands across the enormous T-shirt. Then she registered what he'd said. "Hey! That's sexual harassment!"

"Well, didn't you initiate it with sexual provocation?" Without any warning, he pulled her toward him and kissed her on her lips.

Dallas pushed him away and then slapped him across the face. "Hey! Don't you know I have four kids already?"

He looked at her in shock. "Sorry! I thought you were still single like me."

Dallas smiled a "gotcha" smile. "Huh! My mama was right. She taught me I had to lie to a man first before letting him get any chance, that way I could provoke an honest answer."

Roc rubbed his cheek where she had slapped him. "Are you happy to learn I'm not married?"

"Are you happier? Didn't your mama teach you that you shouldn't kiss any girl without knowing her well enough?"

He shrugged, trying to recall his mom's teaching on that point.

She flipped her blonde hair off her shoulder. "Where did you put the *Ornimegalonyx*?"

Before he could give her a reply, a few frantic urgent knockings on the entrance door interrupted. Roc opened the door to reveal a deputy sheriff.

"Yes, sir, how I can help you?"

"Professor Rochester?"

"Yes. I am."

"May I come in?"

Roc took a glance at noisy reporters and camera people standing a distance away, barred by state troopers. "Sure, please come in."

Once the door was closed, the man reported to them anxiously, "About thirty minutes ago, a pet bulldog near campus area got snatched and taken away by a giant owl. The sheriff wondered if your giant owl has escaped. As far as that lot outside knows, it's still here."

Roc looked questioningly at Dallas. She guiltily eyed him and replied softly, "Yes, it escaped about forty-five minutes ago."

"WHAT? WHY DIDN'T YOU TELL ME AS SOON AS IT HAPPENED?"

"Can you stop screaming? When I called to tell you, you told me something about the Pirate Blackbeard, which I really didn't understand what you were talking about, then you just turned off your ff and when did you allow me a chance to talk since you stepped in here just now?"

"You did?" he accused.

"Yeah, I did," she rebuked. "Before I could tell you, my mouth—" With a blushing face, she promptly shifted to focus on the urgent matter. "So what should we do now?"

The deputy sheriff said, "My boss asked if you could follow me back to talk to the dog's owner. He thought it'd be better to keep the incident quiet for the moment while we come up with a better solution."

"Sure! Dallas, you better tell me exactly what happened before we reach the sheriff's office."

Dallas told him the sequence of events. Roc furrowed his brow then snapped his fingers. "No worries—we have surveillance cameras in the lab."

All became clear as they re-watched the video from the unfolded larger mode ff screen.

Roc shrugged. "It's okay. It has just learned how to open the touchscreen padlock with its beak dexterity. Did you enter the touchscreen padlock in front of it?"

"Yes, but how would I know a mynah could open a padlock like a human being?"

"Normally we didn't let it see how we opened this new touchscreen padlock."

"I'm sorry, I didn't know. It was short-sighted of me." Dallas wrung her hands. "I can't stand seeing caged creatures."

"Well, it's my fault to underestimate this unusual mynah's intelligence to use just one password for all access. I'm simply dumbfounded about how and when it has mutated and evolved with cognitive understanding of the language— or were all these events merely coincidental?"

"Why it was locked alone?"

"Well, you believe it didn't want out of its cage to make mischief, for some reason?" Roc asked, eyebrow raised, mouth quirked sideways into a half-smile.

"No."

"Actually we kept it isolated in a separate room with a new touchscreen padlock because it has already mastered other voice-activated locks and motion-sensor doors in the hall and exits. Twice it opened those locks to let its bird-friends escape, but luckily once they heard Adam's voice, they all returned to the cage obediently."

"Wow, I'm truly impressed by his animal training and taming skills. Is he a modern-age Noah?"

Roc laughed out loud, proud of his assistant.

"You're not mad at me?" she asked.

"I would rather have returned to find our injured giant owl in a confined space where we could help it heal, and I'm glad the mynah didn't play any mischief or get wolfed down by the owl while she was loose, but no, I'm not angry."

Dallas breathed a sigh of relief; he had every right to be angry, and now someone's pet had probably died because of her carelessness. "You can't show that video to anyone, though!" Dallas protested, red-faced, thinking of her shirtless scene.

"We have to."

"No!"

"Trust me. Okay, just give me another minute!" Roc's fingers scurried over the touchscreen on his ff, editing and saving the video with his ff and they headed to the sheriff's office.

On the way there, Roc shared the incident with the DEA operatives taking control of the *Ornis*. As they approached the sheriff's office inside the building, they heard Sheriff Shih pronouncing a word with exaggerated slowness. "A—mour."

"*Non!* No R...You do not roll your R after the U," the lady tried to correct his pronunciation.

In order to keep the angry lady waiting in the office, the sheriff even let her teach him how to speak French without any protest. When Dallas and Roc arrived in his office, he looked like his saviors had arrived. "Gee! This is one of the most tongue-twisting languages, but luckily I don't have a French wife. I thought Mandarin was difficult; now I think French is a lot harder to speak," he complained.

Roc then muttered some Mandarin words to deliberately aggravate Sheriff Shih.

The sheriff smirked. "'Banana' is a Chinese American who can't speak Mandarin, whereas 'eating banana' is a polite way of describing eating shit. Be careful which one you say."

"Aha, obviously you did your homework." Roc never stopped teasing Sheriff Shih whenever they met. "So you're a useless banana-eating banana who can't even speak his own mother tongue."

"Ahem..." Dallas called for their attention. "Ma'am, do you mind telling us exactly what happened?" Dallas asked the French lady.

She spoke with heavily-accented English. They had to listen attentively when she started talking. "An hour ago, while my Metro was playing at the backyard, I hear him yelping in an unusual fearful voice. When I open my back door, I find a massive owl pounce on him. I was in panic as everything happen in a flash—I couldn't do anything to stop it."

"I am so sorry to hear what happened," Roc said. "Actually the giant owl was locked up by Dr. Dallas and my assistants in a cage, but it was accidentally released a while ago."

"Why didn't you lock it up properly?" the lady condemned Dallas in obvious dislike of the other lady's presence.

Dallas folded her arms across her front, defiantly. "We did lock it up properly in a cage with a padlock! But nobody would expect what allowed it to escape."

"I want to sue the culprit who caused the negligence!" the lady screamed hysterically at Dallas. "Wasn't it you who did it?" She threw Dallas a killing glance.

Immediately Sheriff Shih soothed her. "Please calm down, ma'am. You can file a complaint if you want, and a judge can decide whether the 'culprit' who accidentally caused the owl to escape should be jailed or fined, but that could take up to two months before you get a court date. I understand you're upset about the loss of your dog. You should keep this incident to yourself at the moment. I don't want the whole community to fall into a panic. For all we know, this was just an ordinary owl. It's your word against theirs.

"If you prefer, as sheriff, I can arbitrate here, listen to the evidence, and decide if we need to make an arrest. If nothing else, it will save you court fees."

The lady agreed the deal at last but she still glanced coldly toward Dallas.

Eddie ushered the whole group to a conference room and asked a deputy to attend the arbitration hearing to take notes. After everyone was seated, he asked Roc where his careless staff member was.

"Sure, just a minute, I have to ask someone to bring 'her' here." Roc made a quick call on his ff. About ten minutes later, there was a knock outside the conference room's entrance. Everyone turned their heads toward the sound; they were curious who the troublemaker was. Soon a cage was brought in with a mynah perching in it, looking as curious as those people looking suspiciously at it.

Roc gestured to the cage. "Sheriff, this is my 'staff' who released the owl by opening a password-protected padlock."

The French lady protested. "I object! It is an albino crow!"

The sheriff gestured everyone to keep quiet, then he gave the French lady a stern glance that intimidated her, and then corrected her. "It's an albino mynah, ma'am." Then he asked Roc. "Do you have any proof that 'she' did it?"

Dallas poked Roc in the ribs and glared at him.

"How about if I can't show any proof, Sheriff?"

"Well, if there is no proof the mynah did it, the only human being present in your lab during the incident will likely get the blame, as no one probably would believe a mynah can unlock a padlock with a password."

"You mean if we can produce convincing evidence that the cage was really opened by a mynah bird, Dr. Dallas will not be accused?"

"Yes." Sheriff Shih turned to everyone in the room, "Do you all agree with me?" Everyone nodded. "Any objection?" Sheriff Shih asked again, but there was only silence in the air.

Roc looked at Dallas—her face had turned red. "Hey, are you all right?" He whispered into her ear, in a rather persiflage manner, "I can also lick an apple in front of you and not give you any of it."

"Shut up! I am not a 'crow,'" she whispered back ironically.

"Well, you have to talk to me nicely if you want me to help you out of this trouble, so whatever question I ask you next, you have to reply 'yes.'"

Dallas stared at him coldly. "Are you threatening me?"

"No, it's a barter trade." He threw her an equally cold but calculative glance. "Are you prepared to say 'yes'?"

"Why, would it be difficult to say 'yes'?" she challenged.

"Hmmm—will you go out with me, Dr. Dallas?"

Dallas felt embarrassed when everyone started turning their heads and staring at her. "Yes!" she reluctantly replied under everyone's curious stares.

"Professor, where is your proof?" After waiting for some time, Sheriff Shih began to question.

"Sheriff, may I talk to you privately for a minute?"

"Approach."

Roc moved closer to the sheriff and then whispered something while transferring the edited video file from his ff to Sheriff Shih's ff.

"Hmmm—in such a case, we have no choice but to reveal it," Eddie decided. Then he gestured his deputy to pass his ff to a technician to get ready to show everyone the video.

"Hey, I object!" Dallas protested at once. "There's private and confidential stuff on that!"

"Pardon me, ma'am, what's your problem?" the sheriff asked with his eyebrows raised.

"Please trust me, Dr. Dallas. Sorry, Sheriff, it's all right," Roc assured Sheriff Shih with an "okay" gesture, and then he turned to the technicians. "Please go ahead."

While they waited, he whispered in Dallas's ear, "Don't worry, I won't let anyone see your six times six double-Ds!"

Her eyes narrowed and she wondered what he was talking about.

"Aren't six times six equal to 36, Dr. D?"

"Hello—sexual harassment?" she hissed at him in an undertone. "Can't you paraphrase it to something more reserved, cultivated or refined? What's wrong with you today? Is it because you haven't had sex for too long?"

"You bet, DD. I think it's a compliment, as money can only buy artificial boobs and I believe yours must be genuine..." He wiggled his eyebrows at her and leered.

"Can you shut up? I want an apology!" Her aggravated and heated face was turning darker with the dimming room; soon the recording appeared on the largest mode ff screen.

The record showed in the first scene Professor Rochester's assistants and Dr. Dallas locking the giant owl inside a cage.

The next scene showed Dallas interacting with the mynah outside its cage, soon it returned to the cage and Dr. Dallas locked it up, but the view without her shirt on and nasty words said were blurred out or excluded. Dallas still squirmed uncomfortably in her seat. She tried to recall when Roc had time to alter the video.

Then scene three showed Dallas leaving the room to look for the mynah's food. The mynah used its beak to unlock the touchscreen keypad lock, fled and found the locked up giant owl.

Scene four showed the mynah opening the motion-sensor side door then it returned to use its voice to open the voice-activated lock on the giant owl cage. The giant owl instinctively escaped through the opened gate and through the side door.

The final scene showed the giant owl taking flight. While the mynah began to call out loudly to alarm the owl that Dallas was coming, soon Dallas emerged from the side door with a worried face.

Everyone was still stunned when the lights turned back on again, then Eddie announced, "I have no choice but to disclose this incident of the giant owl's escape and taking of a pet. Please don't spread harmful gossip; if it really threatens us again then we will put the whole community on a giant owl alert."

"Objection! What about my poor dog?" The sobbing French lady protested.

Sheriff Shih gave her a pathetic glance, and then turned to Roc.

"Is the mynah property of the university?"

"No, it's my personal property, courtesy of the government of Indonesia."

"Would you personally be able to find this woman another dog of the same breed and be willing to pay for this dog?"

"Sure."

Then Eddie turned to comfort the lady. "Sorry, ma'am! Nobody expected such a tragic thing to happen. We sympathize with you and your loss. What this man can do to compensate you fairly is to replace your dog with a new one of equal value. You'll need to prove the purchase price of the lost dog."

"He wouldn't be the same."

"Any more objections?" Eddie turned to ask everyone.

After a short silence, he proclaimed, "Case closed," then he dismissed them.

# 9

# Terror in a Nursery School

Roc grew increasingly worried about when the escaped giant owl would bring another threat to the community; he needed to conduct a search immediately with Dr. Dallas.

Abruptly he stopped walking in the busy corridor and began looking for Dallas, who had left the room ahead of him. A moment later, he finally spotted her headed into the lobby. He called out, "Hey, I think we better figure out how to catch it as soon as possible, before it stalks the next forbidden prey."

"Sorry, I can't work with low IQ riff-raff who has no better way to get what he wants than to blackmail me. That's illegal, you know. And really—talking about my bra size in the middle of an arbitration? You could be sued by some women for such harassment," she warned him. "I have a concert to attend tonight in Corpus Christi, performed by the KIPC winners with the Corpus Christi Symphony Orchestra. Excuse me!" She pushed past him and headed off directly toward the exit.

"I'm sorry." He quickened his steps to keep up with her. "I apologize for my loss of control. I assure you that it won't happen again, and I really need your help."

Dallas crossed her arms and refused to look at Roc. "Fine."

"After we catch the owl again, tend its wounds, and release it back to its PNV confinement, I promise to take you to a concert in Carnegie Hall, New York." Only now he began to look into her eyes seriously and considered she was definitely not the usual type of girl he fooled around with.

"But I wanted to listen to that Mimi Mao piano concerto." She hesitated if she could trust his words, then something suddenly struck her; instead she asked him, "Are you my boss or am I my own boss?"

"We're *partners*," he told her firmly.

At the moment they stepped out of Kleberg county sheriff office's exit door, Roc's ff rang. "Yes—speaking—what?—hmmm, in this case please keep everyone indoors and don't let the children see what is happening outside. I'll go over right now," Roc advised.

He turned around to search for Sheriff Shih and spotted Sheriff Shih also looking for him. "Let's hurry up!" Roc said. "We'll go in my Land Rover. I have the full array of necessary weapons in there." He also signaled Dallas to come along with them.

While on their way, Dallas was eager to hear what was going on, so she asked Sheriff Shih, "What has happened?"

"I was told they spotted a giant owl flying periodically in the sky above the nursery school and perching on big trees right outside the school compound. The principal described it as a giant ugly bird bigger than a man. I guessed it must be the giant owl," he told her.

Dallas was not so optimistic. "I think we won't be able to catch it as easily as last time, 'once bitten twice shy.' We have no choice but to issue a community giant owl watch alert. What do you think?" She wanted to hear opinions from both men sitting in front of her.

"Hmm... let me handle the public relations part. You both think of a way to get that owl." Sheriff Shih lifted his ff and gave some orders to his staff.

\* \* \* \* \* \*

Alpha Nursery School

After all the kids were locked in with their respective classmates, Tom and Jerry, in Einstein Classroom, began their routine daily fistfights before turning into the two best friends again. When the teacher's back was turned, one of them managed to open the lock. The boys zoomed toward the playground.

"No! Tom and Jerry! Stop running at once—you can't go out there. A giant bird out there is going to eat you," one of the running teachers warned them; soon the principal also joined in shouting and chasing after the boys.

When the trio of Roc, Dallas and Sheriff Shih reached the nursery school, they found it quite amusing seeing two fat women one after another running after and trying to stop the two fast-running little boys.

Tom shouted toward the adults, "You're telling us lies. How could a bird eat us?"

"My mom said both giants and giant birds don't exist!" Jerry argued, chin thrust out defiantly.

Roc called out sternly at once in his commanding voice, "Look up at the sky! This hungry giant bird is stalking you. If you don't run back to class now, it'll be too late to escape." He turned to the teachers and principal. "Quit chasing after the boys, and go hide inside the building immediately. We'll deal with the owl."

The boys obviously were more used to obeying the authority in a lower male voice. When they looked up, the giant owl was visible high up in the sky.

"Naw, it's just a small bird." Little Tom refused to budge.

"Why don't you look up again?" Roc gave them a stern command. Again, they looked up in the sky, but in awe, they realized the giant owl had moved swiftly nearer and it looked immense to them now.

"Run! Jerry, run! No joke, it's a giant owl!" Tom said.

Jerry could see clearly that the giant owl had already dived toward him; he panicked for a moment, but luckily his friend Tom dragged him along.

"Now, hide in the playhouse next to you and close the door, and no matter what, don't come out until I say so," Roc instructed them.

The nervous teachers also started to call out, asking them to hide in the toy house. Tom dragged Jerry into the playhouse in time, but the giant owl was just as fast. It was too big to fit through the door, but one talon began to penetrate the door and grabbed at one of Jerry's little boots.

"Take off the other boot and throw it out as far as possible," Roc instructed.

As Roc predicted, the giant owl moved off to grab the thrown out boot. "Now, block the little door from the inside," he told them. With the owl no longer attacking it, the boys were able to block the playhouse door securely.

As the door closed behind them, the owl picked up the small red boot; it looked like a little worm holding onto the owl's beak. The owl walked a step away then dropped the boot on the ground and started pecking at it curiously, but after a bit, it quit pecking at the inedible boot. Once more, it turned to the playhouse, emitting hair-rising, loud, agitated cries.

Once it reached the miniature house, it started scratching on its closed door furiously. After a few unsuccessful trials, it jumped on top of the little house and flipped its wings.

As its body size was massive enough to cover the whole toy house, soon it started rocking the toy house until it almost toppled, but then it flicked back onto the ground again. Amidst the screams, the owl pushed and pulled the toy house on the playground.

"Should we use the tranquillizer gun?" Dallas crinkled her brow in worry.

"No, not at this moment. We can't take any risk when there are kids around," Sheriff Shih advised.

"I wish I'd brought my lariat."

"I know something that may work!" Roc snapped his fingers. "If the owl forces through the door, target its wounds," he instructed Sheriff Shih. "I'll be right back."

Roc ran to the nursery school's entrance hall. He looked around and quickly found a big aquarium, well over 1,000 gallons, full of flashing, palm-sized tropical fish. The owl may not be a fish-eater, but motion that would attract its attention was his goal. Without hesitation, he pulled one of indoor palm trees out of its big rattan planter for netting fish and grabbed a big plastic garbage bin for holding the fish.

Soon, he tugged a garbage bin full of jumping fish out of the hall. Dallas ran toward him. He directed her, "Hurry up! Go catch as many fish as possible from the entrance hall aquarium!"

Once he reached the playground, he threw the jumping fish to its center, which was a distance off from the playhouse. Then he began to mimic an array of hooting. Soon, the giant owl became attracted to the calls; it paused first then began to turn its head toward Roc's calling direction. It bobbed its head, analyzing the motion of the flopping fish.

Under all the nervous, watchful eyes, the hungry owl finally was persuaded and walked suspiciously toward those jumping fish. When a fish jumped toward it, the owl wolfed down the whole fish as if it was a small anchovy. It would take longer to catch the jumping fish than to eat them, giving Dallas and Sheriff Shih time to bring more fish.

They sacrificed at least fifty big fish out of the school aquarium to feed the giant owl, but even after wolfing down all those fish, insatiably it still wanted to get back the playhouse. Roc came from the Land Rover with a handful of assorted firecrackers.

"Now, boys, you're going to hear some loud firecrackers, but stay inside the playhouse—don't come out until I say so," Roc warned the boys.

In order to stop the giant owl from approaching the toy house, they started throwing firecrackers and spinning, sparking Jumping Jacks toward it. One of the firecrackers hit right on its wounds. The owl gave an obviously annoyed cry and stopped approaching. When more firecrackers were thrown toward it, it wisely flapped its wings a few times then fled, to everyone's relief.

In front of the toy house, Dallas tried her best to sweet talk the kids to unbar the door, but they were obviously still panicked.

Roc called to them, "Now you can come out."

Eventually they opened the door but refused to come out. Dallas had to keep talking and persuading them until Roc repeated his order, "Come out!" Upon hearing the repeated order, they finally peeked toward the sky from the door.

"It's all right now, boys, see? It's gone!" While she said it, her heart was still pounding hard and she roamed her gaze over the sky, expecting the owl to return.

After confirming that the two little boys were unharmed physically, they left them to the teachers. Sheriff Shih returned to town with one of his deputies. Roc and Dallas were about to leave when children's faint wails from the entry hall halted them. Roc remembered what those kids might cry about.

Promptly he called one of his assistants. "Adam! This is urgent; please call the largest pet shop in town, have them bring whatever big fish they have to fill up the saltwater aquarium of the Alpha Nursery School, pronto. Put it on my bill." And he was so pleased to hear from Adam that the fish truck was already on its way now to the nursery school. This was because Adam could hear and see what his boss did from his ff's Rochester Office Assistant Spyware.

He then entered the hall to where the big aquarium stood, virtually empty of fish. "Sorry, angels! Thank you for letting me borrow some of your fish. I'll bring you some even bigger, nicer and more colorful fish soon. So there's no reason for you to cry anymore, right?"

Amid sniffles, the children agreeably nodded their heads.

He was glad their teachers had locked these children in classrooms; they were as yet unaware of what had happened to those assorted fish during the past hour. Tom and Jerry may not have seen, either, so he hoped the trauma of the school pets being eaten would be minimized.

"Professor Rochester, a group of TV crews and reporters has just shown up. I've barred them from entering the school grounds, but beware they are now waiting outside the gate," the principal warned them kindly.

When Roc reached the nursery gate, he couldn't move his car anymore in the clamor of people. When these media people saw him, they framed his car immediately and started to knock on the windscreen demanding interviews.

"Huh! They're more aggressive than the giant owl." Roc felt annoyed by them, and when he wound down the window, immediately the variety of questions overwhelmed him, so he just picked what he wanted but answered in a tongue-in-cheek, silly manner.

"Professor Rochester, can this giant owl eat people?"

"Sure! If it gets provoked, hungry and if there is no other choice."

"What should people do?"

"Stay inside your house, don't come out. Tie a big fat goat in your front yard and an overweight lamb in your backyard."

Beside him, Dallas snorted.

"We heard that a pet dog was already killed by the giant owl. Is it true?"

"Yes! So don't let your cat out to poop in your neighbor's flowerbeds and your dog to pee in the backyard to attract it."

"Where is this giant owl from? Are there more of them?"

"Sorry, I don't know yet. Why don't you all interview Cryptozoologist Dr. Dallas?"

"Where is he now?" they asked him.

"Sorry, I have no idea." Clearly they didn't know who Dr. Dallas was. When he used the corner of his left eye to look at Dallas, he found she had disguised herself with one of his hats and sunglasses. She gave him a cheeky smile.

"Hey, Professor Rochester, the giant owl watch alert has just been released in the community. How you are going to solve this problem?"

"We are on our way to catch it now. Time is ticking to save lives. Can you all kindly give parents who are arriving to fetch their children a space to move their cars as well as give me a space to move my car, so I can leave here to solve this critical problem?"

But none of them was moving still and instead suddenly they all turned to look the opposite direction. A truck with a pet shop logo approached them with non-stop honking; obviously, the driver was annoyed with the jam by news media crews. Soon the hive of curious reporters rushed to talk to the driver, but very soon they rushed back again, stranding Roc's moving car and demanding to talk to him again. "The driver of the truck said you had ordered his pet shop to replace the missing fish. What was all that about?"

Roc finally lost his temper. "Hey, guys! There is a very high risk that one of you might become prey for the giant owl if you all persist on standing out here on open ground. Give me space to get out of here and I'll give you the answers you asked for."

They still refused to move. Then he saw a car was coming behind him; he cheated them without a second thought. "Oh, that's Dr. Dallas's car coming behind me." Finally they gave him a space just enough to move his car as they began to rush behind, trying to stop the car approaching them.

Just before he zoomed off, he turned back to them. "Tell everyone if there aren't enough goats and lambs to tie up in the front and back yards of their houses, fish will be a good alternative...I think the giant owl might have a special appetite for paparazzi too. Be careful of standing out here too long." Before they had a chance to unravel his sarcasm, he had already zoomed off with the smelly emissions trail behind the Land Rover.

* * * * * *

Despite the community watch giant owl alert, many people believed that the giant owl could only be a threat to children and pets, not to adults.

Sheriff Shih received a very angry call from Roc when he happened to pass by a park still filled with joggers on promenade. "Many ignorant idiots are hanging out in the park. You better send some of your men down here with riot weapons that won't hurt the bird, just in case the giant owl attacks any of them."

One couple kept their teenage kids in the house with their pets, but still took their early evening stroll and jog in a park on the outskirts of town. After jogging, the couple trailed back toward the parking lot. Suddenly a violent, unearthly scream exploded from what sounded like inches behind their heads. They both screamed and dropped automatically to the ground in a state of sheer panic.

After holding their breaths, they spun around. A giant owl perched on a branch fifteen feet above, staring directly into their eyes.

The devil-like giant owl's scream also alerted a newly arrived troop of men armed with salt pellets and rubber bullets, ordered by Sheriff Shih to protect the ignorant joggers in the park just in case the giant owl got interested in preying on any of them.

When the park wardens and state troopers rushed nearer to the vicinity, they saw a muddy couple crawling on the ground from one tree to another tree, slowly making their way back to their car. Once the couple reached their car, they shouted to the officers, "There is a giant owl perching fifteen feet up in a tall tree over there." Then they pointed to a specific tree.

"Are you all right?"

"Yes! But it scared the shit out of us. Its eyes are red. It looks like a devil. I didn't dare to give it a second glance," the woman replied with a shaky voice. "I thought it would only attack kids and pets, but I didn't know it was so huge!"

When they finally located the tree with the giant owl perching above, they were stunned to see that this bird was truly huge. And it seemed to know that they were going after it; cunningly it gave a few unearthly loud screeches, which freaked everyone out for a moment. By the time the troopers regained their composure, it had already fled.

\* \* \* \* \* \*

After awareness spread that the giant owl's threat also extended to adults, although no one had spotted it during the rest of the week, people in the community didn't feel at ease or relaxed.

Armed state troopers and local police vigilantly patrolled South Texas counties at all hours; in spite of warnings by law enforcement and the fish and game officials, every nut with a gun camped in his front yard hoping for a chance to take a shot at the winged menace. Roc sincerely hoped no one would find success in shooting the magnificent bird, which as an owl was protected under the same laws as normal-sized owls and other raptors.

Most people still played safe and acted unbelievably cooperative. Interviewees on the news said they would rather stay at home after work or only continue their indoor activities. What they didn't know was that the giant owl had long left their vicinity and moved on to an isolated, rich feeding ground.

## Silent Aerial Ambushes

Somewhere along the freeway on the outskirts of Kingsville, a magnificent hedgerow of tall pines camouflaged the massive Chinese retrograde-styled quadrangle architecture within, making it difficult for public eyes to pry or trespassers to intrude.

Over this tightly secured, vast compound, the quadrangle was linked by almost a mile of labyrinthine winding lanes from the entrance gate. Armed guards rotated their twenty-four hour routine surveillance duty throughout the mini zoo.

During the past few nights, whenever darkness veiled the compound, a nocturnal visitor would descend silently from the sky and perch on one of the giant conifers near a huge, high tech, artificial lake.

For many nights, it had been enjoying the feast of big fishes and sharks from the estuarine lake, but no one in the compound noticed the fish numbers decreasing daily. Eventually, the population was wiped out entirely.

The loss was only discovered one morning after a few divers prepared to use some sharks again for another drug trafficking journey; in awe they found not a single trace of those big fish in the water.

The owner of this massive property was a Chinese immigrant. He converted to become a protestant after he married a Chinese-American Christian wife. Every Sunday he fervently went with his wife to her old Methodist Church in Corpus Christi, and he seldom missed the monthly Holy Communion.

In the public's eyes, he successfully portrayed a rich businessman that owned several successfully-run, nationwide Chinese chain restaurants, exotic pet stores and globally-linked shipping companies, but they didn't know these companies were just veils of money laundering for the accumulated wealth through his immensely prolific chain of illegal operations from Monday to Saturday. Although the FBI and CIA both had long suspected his illegal operations were associated with his pets, they had yet to find any hard evidence.

Being creative and lack of clear misconduct were never offences the law could pin on an underworld syndicate; for the past two decades, Mr. Mau's unique ways of transporting his customers' "shipment" had successfully escaped the authorities' scrutiny and investigation in multiple countries.

His major trade included helping the drug dealers to deliver their drugs, or gemstone dealers to smuggle diamonds and precious stones to their destinies all over the world.

His converted methods of deliveries were much more innovative than most international courier service companies. Usually, the shark's and big fishes' stomachs would be filled with smuggled items and relocated to an underwater, high-tech, invisible compartment mounted in a ship, tugboat or submarine. Pigeons and eagles were regularly trained to fly certain routes for trafficking smaller parcels.

Recently, two of his "777 carriers," loaded with high grade heroine, had somehow lost their way during the return route. He began to worry when recalling how once a Chinese *feng shui* master warned him in his coming age of fifty he might face a crisis, and he was also cautioned by the master that any business relating to "water" was a taboo for him.

Actually, the master had hinted to him not to get involved in any more illegal business, as *shui huo*, "water stocks," is a Mandarin slang for smuggling goods, but somehow in his mind he never perceived its actual meaning. Ironically, when his wealth increased, his attitude had "evolved" more arrogantly, yet his vigilance had "retrograded" quickly, even after his two *chickcharney* were missing due to "detainment" by the DEA, yet he had still no awareness that adversity had just begun to creep upon his doorstep.

A prominent *feng shui* master from Hong Kong was giving a consultation to Mr. Mau in a study. Suddenly there were a few hasty knocks on the door and Mr. Mau's most trusted personal assistant entered without permission to whisper something into his ear. His face turned red, but he suppressed his anger in front of his guest.

His guest could sense from his client that something had gone wrong. Wisely, he stood, gathered his *feng shui* compass *luopan*, ff and few other belongings into his briefcase and was ready to depart. Nevertheless, he kindly gave his client a final piece of advice, "It's okay, Mr. Mau, if you are busy, please go ahead. You can call me anytime, as I will still be here in town for another week, but at the moment—I think it is better for you to go overseas. The best is to retreat to a remote island as soon as possible." The modern-day Cassandra indirectly hinted to his client that he might run into trouble.

"Sure, thank you." Mr. Mau gave a distracted, perfunctory bow to the *feng shui* master. "Ah Ho…ask the driver to send Master Chan back to the hotel," he ordered his assistant then left the study in an obvious rush.

In modern times, Cassandra's prophecy again met the same ignored fate; the advice by the *feng shui* master was quickly cast out of Mr. Mau's mind once he walked directly toward the scene where it was rumored his toothless sharks and big fish had all disappeared.

Right before he reached the lake, a Chinese man approached him with a bow. "*Lau Ban*, our shipments to Miami supposedly should leave this evening, what should we do now?" he asked.

Everyone waited nervously for Mr. Mau's instructions. "Prepare those St. Bernard instead. Feed them and be ready to leave by midnight—we use land transportation instead. Anyway, the shipments will still reach there on time, though it will cost a bit more," he calculated.

After he received the reports and inspected the site, he suddenly recalled the advice of his *feng shui* master not to involve himself in any activity to do with water. He immediately ordered his men, "I want this empty lake filled up with soil today; after that, move some big trees here." *To canopy my bad lucks*, he decided.

Often, he would practice as his own *feng shui* master; he would only accept ear-pleasing advice from *feng shui* masters, and none of his employees dared to contradict Mr. Mau, lest they risk themselves ending up as fertilizer for plants. They all knew that even with his kind, friendly, smiley mask on all the time, no one could tell what he would do to his enemies or betrayers behind closed doors.

* * * * * *

Mr. Mau's night visitor had noticed that just within last two nights of absence, its hunting area had been restocked with another kind of vital prey.

Its preying eyes were now observing a roll of steel cages offering different choices for its feast, but unfortunately, they were kept in the cages.

After some time of prying, its eyes finally came to focus on a prey that it was ready to ambush. Abruptly its body tensed up then it dove toward the nearest cage.

When the security guards from the mini zoo entrance heard a cacophony of chilling cries and growls, they rushed to the scene, but only discovered some dead dogs with crushed heads that still remained inside their cages. They couldn't find any trace of an intruder possibly hidden at the scene.

As the bloody scene looked too disgusting and gruesome to them, a chill ran down their spines; they quickly opened the cage, pulled out the carcasses and dumped them aside and left the scene immediately. They decided to report the incident in the morning, as it was already past midnight. Mr. Mau did not like to be awakened.

High above their heads, a pair of prying red eyes looked at these security guards and dogs' copses back and forth mischievously. It waited until they were gone to resume a second tactical ambush, and more dog heads were crushed.

Another succession of cacophony of chilling cries and growls called back the security guards. They found this time even some puppies had been massacred. After carefully checking everywhere—except they carelessly omitted the sky—and finding no obvious intrusion sign, again they pulled out the carcasses, piled them up on other carcasses, and left again.

At an hour before dawn, after the forth ambush by the unknown element during that restless night, Mr. Mau was called up from his bed; he came personally to inspect the scene.

He gave a rare pathetic glance to the carcasses and some fatherly pats to the surviving pets and then he ordered the nervous men to guard next to the cages of the few remaining pets until sunrise.

Though deprived of sleep, his deceptive, smiling, and kind face was still on, a contrast to the creature perched right above his head. The red-eyed primitive mammoth had a true devilish look; but at least its true dangerous nature was not concealed.

Perhaps due to an animal's instinct, it chose not to feast on the pile of drug-filled dead pets or attack any of those armed men. Silently, it flew off.

When some twigs and leaves dropped on the piles of dead dogs, it promptly reminded the guards that although they had checked everywhere on the ground, they had neglected to check upward—among those big trees.

Later that morning, a group of insurance company agents arrived at Mr. Mau's mini zoo for evaluation of the dead pets for the insurance claim, but Mr. Mau was informed that the claims couldn't be processed without launching a police report. Mr. Mau began to think how to settle his mess by bribing his Chinese fellowman Sheriff Eddie Shih.

But Sheriff Shih brought along two uninvited, unwelcome white guests instead.

A group of scientists from the CIA DS&T branch were tracking the flight of the two *Ornimegalonyx* that they and the DEA released the day before.

A few days ago, they scanned the *Ornimegalonyx* but didn't find any trace of drugs or micro GPS, so they affixed their own micro GPS chips on them instead. The birds flew southward from Kingsville toward its outskirts then registered as stationary within Mr. Mau's property.

Once the CIA confirmed their findings, they contacted Sheriff Shih but were informed that he had just left a few minutes ago with Roc and Dallas to the same suspected place that the DEA planned to raid.

Thus early in the morning, both Dallas and Roc respectively had received a call from Sheriff Shih concerning a mini zoo terror attack The report had been of "an unknown predator," but they all worried it could be an ambush from the giant owl.

When Roc, Dallas, and Sheriff Shih showed up at the mini zoo, the soft-spoken Mr. Mau seemed friendly enough. In brief, Roc explained to Mr. Mau about the six-foot owl they were attempting to capture. Suddenly Mr. Mau's mood swung abruptly and he began to swear loudly and scream at the newcomers for mismanagement of this dangerous predator.

"In this case I am quite sure your escaped giant owl slaughtered my beloved pets. Now, I want you all to get out of here as soon as possible so that I can put up a net on this zoo!"

He led them to the site of the carnage. Dallas tried not to gag at the stench of dismembered dog bodies and the sight of headless puppies.

While inspecting the pile of carcasses, Roc quietly looked at those St. Bernard's heads, which were obviously crushed under the giant owl talons. He also noticed some trees were obviously newly planted. To confirm his suspicions, he asked,

"Mr. Mau, can I speak to those security guards who looked after this place last night?"

"No, I don't think so, they have to return home to sleep now!" Mau objected, then he began to gesture for them to leave the zoo, but an innocent security guard moved forward.

"Excuse me, are you looking for a security guard on duty last night? I am still here."

"Did you check those tree trunks for any suspicious culprits last night?"

"No," the guards whispered softly, worriedly turning his frightened face toward Mr. Mau, but luckily he already moved to the exit gate.

"Your boss is right; these pets were attacked by a giant owl. If you had reported it immediately last night, the scene might not look as bad as this." Again, the guard took a worried peek toward Mr. Mau's direction and he looked relieved, seeing him talking to Sheriff Shih.

Roc never liked dogs, never mind piles of dog and puppy carcasses. While Mr. Mau talked to Eddie, Roc took a stick and began poking at some torn carcasses. All a sudden, some fine white powder leaked out from a perforated stomach wound of a St. Bernard. He called out, "Sheriff, you'll want to take a look at this."

About three steps away, Mr. Mau rapidly took up his latest laser rifle and signaled the rest of his security guards on scene. In a flash, over twenty of the latest laser pistols and assault rifles targeted the temples of Roc, Dallas and Sheriff Shih.

"Sorry, I think you have poked your nose too much into our business. You will be buried together with those dead dogs and no one will know that you have become the fertilizer for these newly planted trees." Mr. Mau pointed to the newly transplanted firs, while throwing Dallas a lusty glance, lamenting of what a waste for her to die so young.

"Remove the angel dust from all the tummies at once before sending this latest stock to our 'guests.'" he ordered his staff, and then he waved one of his assistants over, whispering something into his ear. His assistants nodded obediently; soon, at gunpoint, they were forced to move out of the zoo.

* * * * * *

A remote house outside of public areas was easier to raid rather than one in a busy residential area; Mr. Mau's quadrant was a good example. As the guard dogs had been killed by the giant owl during the night, the security was instantly loosened for the vast compound, so now a group of armored DEA agents and police SWAT teams surrounded it easily with tear gas and necessary weapons, prepared to raid the house once an assault signal was given.

After a crouching DEA agent tried several times unsuccessfully to get a hold of Sheriff Shih, Professor Rochester and Dr. Dallas on ff, he alerted his boss.

"I can't get hold of any of them; their lines are all dead!"

"Let's check the movement inside." Danger prevailed with all three ffs being unreachable .

After spying behind the canopy of lush foliage for some time, at last with their binoculars they spotted the three handcuffed hostages walked on a winding pebble path at gunpoint.

"Continue to trail after them along the fence; try to get the three of them when you find a feasible chance. I will go with the vice-squad to the front and try to talk to Mr. Mau; he is a member of my previous church in Corpus," one of the agent told his comrades.

* * * * * *

The winding path seemed endless; suddenly Dallas called out the armed men, "I need to pee!"

"You can pee, but please don't try acting funny, lady."

"I can't pee with my handcuffs on. Come on! How can I fight six armed men by myself?"

"Sorry, you have to think of a way to pee."

Another man with a heavy Mexican accent threatened Dallas with a cold-hearted chuckle. "Don't need to keep looking at your handcuffs or try to enter different password,

112

*gringa*! Only Mr. Mau knows the password for these custom-made handcuffs from Germany. I know your fingers are long enough to reach the numbers, but once you enter the wrong password, it will lock up permanently."

Suddenly they heard some noises in the bushes—like stones dropping. These armed guards obviously were very experienced; they were not fooled by the DEA agents' "cheap parlor tricks" to distract and confuse them. Promptly, one of the armed men moved away to make a call.

After he returned, he ordered half of his men to join other armed guards to inspect the mansion's compound.

"Now, move quickly!" he ordered.

"Hey, I told you I need to pee," Dallas reminded him.

"No," he refused sternly.

After walking for another two hundred yards, they finally reached a place with fewer trees. The sound of a waterfall smacking into standing water somewhere nearby reminded Dallas she wasn't bluffing about needing to pee.

The man cruelly announced, "Now we are going to tie you up here under the trees to feed the giant owl and our two *chickcharney*. Our boss has been so gracious to you; otherwise you'd be thrown like the other men into the kiln."

"Oh yeah, this is gracious," Dallas replied sarcastically. "Our fates will be the same as those poor dead dogs?"

"Shut up! Or else I will shoot you now," he threatened Dallas. He turned his rifle on Roc and Sheriff Shih in turn.

He threw them a devilish glance before calling to order a delivery of the two *chickcharney* to the site. After the order, they prepared to leave the scene.

"Hey! Who are the other men being thrown to the kiln?" Dallas asked them.

The man coldly turned his head to inform her. "Since you are going to die anyway, I am going to tell you. They are your friends from the DEA."

"I don't think being eaten alive by the big owls is less brutal than being thrown into a kiln," Dallas angrily shouted at him. Roc attempted to shush her; Eddie said nothing. The man shrugged, ignored her and continued to depart.

As soon as the three armed men moved out of their sight, Dallas suggested at once, "Quick! We have to get out of here, or else it'll be no joke that we'll get crushed, torn to pieces and eaten by those owls."

Sheriff Shih asked, "But don't owls hunt at night? We have lots of time before dark."

"*Ornimegalonyx* are diurnal—they hunt during the daylight hours, just like modern burrowing owls," Roc filled in. "Once night sets in, we have the other giant to worry about as well."

Dallas turned their attention to the cuffs. "We're lucky. I've been noticing this looking at the cuffs on both of you. There are dirty stains on three specific numbers, six, eight and two on each of our handcuffs."

The two men took a careful look over their handcuffs and both nodded.

"Let's see if our luck stretches. We have three handcuffs; hopefully they all have the same identical password."

Both Roc and Sheriff Shih signaled Dallas, "Ladies first."

She rolled her eyes before preparing to test her luck, "Six, two, eight."

"Hold on! I think the password is MAU..." Roc said.

"Isn't that same as six, two, eight?" She raised her eyebrow.

"I'd have to look at my ff keypad," Eddie admitted sheepishly. "Let's pray it's the right combination."

She carefully turned the numbers. The cuffs unlocked with a soft *click*. "Bingo! I got it!" She quickly untangled herself and then helped the others.

# 11

# Escape of the Hostages

Sheriff Shih was frowning and wondering why his deputy hadn't come to rescue them, as he had been gone without checking in for nearly a half day already. He started to nag Dallas and Roc. "Now what should we do?...We have no firearms—how far can we go before anyone discovers that we've attempted an escape?...Not to mention the two *Ornimegalonyx* will arrive any minute."

Only tens of yards away from where they were now, the two *Ornimegalonyx* had arrived on the site on a truck with two armed guards and an animal trainer.

When one of the armed guards confirmed that their captives had fled, he hissed angrily, "Oh, those motherfuckers have escaped. They shouldn't be far out; let's find them and just shoot them to save the trouble."

"Stop running. Do you know which direction they went?" the animal trainer asked him. "Now quick, help me to release these two *chickcharney*. They can trace and pursue prey and kill it even better than a dog, as they can fly. We just stand here, no sweat and no fight—why waste our energy to go after them? I'm very sure soon we will hear them screaming and being tortured under the talons."

The two *Ornimegalonyx* were released from the cage, and placed on a mobile perch. The animal trainer removed their hoods and blew his whistle, with his fingers snapping and pointing toward a particular direction. The two *Ornimegalonyx* gave a few very devilish cries, then bounced into the air on broad owl wings before orienting toward the noise of their human prey.

A few minutes later the armed guards faintly heard Dallas's screaming and calling out from far away, "Watch out! *Orni* are diving toward us!"

"I don't enjoy listening to the sounds of death. Let's go," the driver pestered them to leave. The rest of them hopped into the truck reluctantly. The driver put on loud Mariachi music to drown the noise.

The music and the faint owl silhouettes alerted the three escaped prisoners. "Jump into the waterfall pond," Roc suggested.

"We'll be trapped! What if we have no way out of there?" Dallas said.

Roc swiftly looked around for alternate hiding places. "Run toward three o'clock—there is a big hole under the tree, you can get in there."

Dallas hesitated. "A rattlesnake might be hiding in there. Or spiders."

"Come on, there's no snake! But there could be spiders. You better run now."

She suddenly stopped running instead, panicked.

He turned and grabbed one of her arms. "Now, you come with me!"

They reached the waterfall, which plunged into the converted artificial lake surrounded by resplendent exotic tropical palms and orchids. He shoved her into the water and then dived in.

A moment later, the two pursuing *Ornimegalonyx* arrived at the lake, circling and hovering above the water, ready to dive into the water and attack their prey.

In the water, Roc grabbed Dallas's hair without mercy to dive down and forward until he found Sheriff Shih.

They needed air but they also faced the deadly silent hunters from above. From underneath the lake, they could see parts of *Ornimegalonyx* talons already immersing in the water, but the talons soon disappeared again.

Unexpectedly, they heard a familiar giant owl screeching sound. Roc signaled Dallas they could be safe, as he knew that a territorial fight had just commenced above them.

Quickly, they emerged from underwater to take a few quick breaths while the territorial fight happened not too far from them. Again, they dived in the water to avoid being found by enemies, but soon Roc lost his grasp of Dallas. He searched for her to no avail.

Sheriff Shih had been hiding and waiting anxiously inside the bushes on the opposite bank of the lake until he finally saw a head emerge right beside the bank, gasping for air in obvious exhaustion.

He ran out the bush to the bank to reach out a helping hand, but Roc gestured that he would remain in the water to wait for Dallas.

"Where is she?" Sheriff Shih asked worriedly and they both stared at the lake anticipating her emergence.

"She struggled and then I lost hold of her."

"Hey y'all, I'm over here." A familiar soft call came from behind a little slope. While they wondered how she managed to escape from drowning, she ran toward them.

"What happened? Did you turn into an eel?" Roc smiled in obvious relief.

"No, I got sucked off by a very strong current and found myself sitting right on a platform at the back of the artificial waterfall. I crawled through its underground tunnel and I found that I had reached the opposite side of this hilly slope."

"Gosh! You're so lucky," Sheriff Shih told her.

"Let's get out of here now before they find us again," Dallas suggested.

They scrambled away from the lake. From the distance they saw the three owls still fighting next to the waterfall; the loud unearthly screeches could chill anyone's blood. "You know what?...I think we better run before these creatures change their minds." Roc's years of research had concluded that both birds and girls' emotions were as unpredictable as the weather.

\* \* \* \* \* \*

After they'd run another two hundred yards, a piece of barren land opened in front of them, revealing a serespad with a serescopter and a few uniformed mechanics refueling and checking the engines. Sheriff Shih suggested, "We better fly it off before someone else does."

They looked at each other and blurted out the same question at once, "Who knows how to fly?"

"I learned how to fly many years ago, but not since I came to Texas," Roc informed them with a shrug.

"You learned to fly a serescopter or an antique airplane?" Dallas raised one of her eyebrows, doubtful at his hesitation.

He paused for a moment and his reply really surprised them. "I learned both."

"Then why wait?" Sheriff Shih gestured. "We better jump up there before any of those guys discover us here. And obviously while these guys here are unarmed."

"We better wait until they're gone," Roc suggested.

"No, we shouldn't wait. There have four men." Dallas threw a doubtful glance to both men who stood beside her. "Are you guys ready to use your fists to fight?" They gave an equally arrogant challenging glance in return to each other.

"I'll take that small and skinny Chinese mechanic." Dallas picked her victim first. "Finally, I can practice my Chinese *kung fu*." She warmed up with a few excited *kung fu* fists and kicks.

"Then we take the rest of the three." Sheriff Shih glanced at the three other large mechanics and then he looked back at Roc, who appeared as tall as him, but he was unsure whether the academic could carry his weight in a fight.

"We are as big as them, why not? I learned karate." Roc accepted the challenge. But as they started running to ambush those mechanics, Roc noticed a driver in a solar, electricity and gas refilling truck they had carelessly overlooked.

Without a second thought, he ran as fast as possible to get into the SEG truck instead. The driver alertly ignited its engine. They both tried to reach out at once for a gun on the backseat. The driver had only one hand to fight for the gun but he was obviously not an untrained guard, easily to defeat. Immediately, he swung the truck in such a way that could force the backseat passenger to get thrown out the window.

The driver found his ponytail tangled and pulled by a strong force from behind; suddenly he applied the brakes and to everyone's astonishment, the truck stopped just an inch away from the serescopter tail. The driver gave a breath of relief but at the same moment, his neck received a karate chop.

When Roc hopped down from the truck with a gun on his hands, he watched the six other people still fighting.

With the gun in ready position, he called out warning, "I'll blow your heads off in a minute if you don't stop now." The two teams separated at once. He told Dallas, "Now, quickly get in the serescopter. Ignite its engine first." Then he looked at her in doubt. "Do you know how to do it?"

"I probably can start its engine but I can't fly it. I saw my uncle doing it when I was young."

"An antique helicopter?" he raised one of his eyebrows, asking sarcastically, but chuckled softly. "Then hurry up!"

When Roc still didn't hear any ignition sound, he inquired, "Are you okay?"

"I'm still figuring this thing out...I can't find the key."

"Get out, let me do it!" Roc handed her the gun. "I think you can handle this better than me."

Dallas called out for Sheriff Shih, "Sheriff! Can you see if there's a serescopter key left in the truck?" Then she called out again but louder this time, with more urgency, "Quick, Sheriff, I think I heard some vehicles are on the way."

After some time, Sheriff Shih shouted, "I got it! I got it!"

"Run! Get in the serescopter—the vehicles are coming toward us now."

Dallas stood near the serescopter door; she yelled sternly to the unarmed men, "Stop moving! If y'all take another step, I'll blow your brains out."

Sheriff Shih managed to pass the key to Roc as he climbed aboard, but the serescopter engine had turned on already. "Do you still need the key?"

"I wonder what that key is for? Who told you this serescopter needs a key?"

Sheriff Shih turned his head to stare at Dallas as she crouched inside the still open door with the gun they'd taken from the truck.

"Sorry, Sheriff, I think I was too nervous and forgot. Modern serescopters only use a password."

"Hmm...What was the password?" Sheriff Shih looked toward the front again.

"MAU!" they replied in unison.

"Huh!...What a typical narcissism," Sheriff Shih mocked.

When the first three vehicles approached the serespad, the serescopter had just started to ascend. Immediately Mr. Mau ordered the guards to shoot down the escaped hostages.

Sheriff Shih said, "Hurry up! Shoot them before they get us."

A moment later, a loud explosion announced the vehicles at the front and rear were both detonated.

"Ha!...Killed two birds with one stone," she happily chuckled.

The explosion temporarily cautioned the enemies to withdraw a distance away.

Roc looked amusedly from the serescopter's MPPS at the blown up vehicles. "Babe! You're getting better at this kind of warfare."

Sheriff Shih also found that amusing; he said, tongue-in-cheek, "Wow, what a Valkyrie!

She ignored the two men's cheeky remarks and gave another lethal shot to the luxury car convoy. Two Escalades at its front and back soon exploded one after another.

"Wow, I love this powerful 3-D digital gun." She blew it a kiss.

Roc quickly adapted to maneuvering the latest model high tech serescopter, and had ascended high above and flew far away from the enemies' assault.

"Gosh, we finally made it." Sheriff Shih expressed their shared relief from this life and dead ordeal.

Over Mr. Mau's property compound, the demolished Chinese garden looked like a torrid hurricane or tornado had been through. Broken glasses hit by bullets and the smell of cordite and burning shrapnel still lingered and scattered all over the house and its compound.

The living room was almost impassable under the rubble, with remnants of ruined Baccarat crystal chandeliers, blood-stained Pozzoli sofas, dented custom-made Chinese furniture and smashed Qing Dynasty smuggled antiques—this was the mess that greeted the newly-arrived agents.

Right after Roc, Dallas and Sheriff Shih were taken hostage, a severe gunfire fight broke out in the courtyard of Mr. Mau's grand four-winged house, and the bloody mayhem continued for the next few hours.

In their own familiar terrain, Mr. Mau's well-armed men outnumbered the federal agents, and finally won their fight against the DEA agents and vice-squad team both inside the house and outside the compound.

The authorities had underestimated Mr. Mau's capabilities; they were doomed before they got a chance to discover Mr. Mau even had an elite armed troop. They were surrounded and handcuffed by Mr. Mau's men before they could call for backup.

# 12

# Escape From the Criminals

For the entire morning after Sheriff Shih left the station for his duty, no one could get a hold of him or any vice-squad members via ff. One of his deputies began to feel restlessly nervous and started to smoke in his office while contemplating. When his ff signaled a call from his Chinese-Vietnamese girlfriend, he received some unexpected clues from her.

His girlfriend worked as an assistant chef at one of Mr. Mau's Chinese restaurants. She reported to him worriedly of what she had seen in Mr. Mau's mansion. Since very early morning, she had been in the mansion kitchen to assist a chef preparing some Chinese moon cakes for the mid-autumn festival.

She informed him that not long after she started to work, she heard an array of gunshots from within the mansion. No one else seemed bothered by this, and at first, she guessed that there was a shooting practice going on in the front wing of the house. The gunshots continued periodically over several hours.

Later, after she entered the other secluded wing's unoccupied toilet, she heard someone approaching her direction; soon she heard name-callings and cursing.

Out of curiosity, she peeked through a keyhole. She saw at least twenty handcuffed men, some with navy jackets that read "DEA" on the back in big yellow letters, being forced along under gunpoint by a group of Mr. Mau's armed bodyguards.

Something unusual had happened in Mr. Mau's house. She managed to find an excuse of menstrual cramps and left her work as soon as possible, trying to get ahold of her deputy sheriff boyfriend.

Without delay, the deputy promptly contacted the DEA office and reported to them what his girlfriend had seen and heard. He learned from them that they had also lost their comrades' communication under Mr. Mau's roof. The deputy was informed that local, county, and state law enforcement could step aside for this raid; a siege team consisting of not only more DEA agents but also FBI, ATF and CIA agents headed to Mr. Mau's house.

* * * * * *

Before Mr. Mau sent out his order to turn their stubborn, tricky and resilient DEA and vice-squad hostages into traceless ashes, he had an important meeting with his closest aids in an underground cell.

None of them was aware of another, larger group of silent intruders during the last half an hour that gradually drew nearer until finally it crept or crouched right under their noses.

By the time they discovered the second siege, some of Mau's armed men were already fallen and his compound was engulfed with tear gas fumes that enabled the trained armed agents to infiltrate and invade further into the premises.

Mr. Mau got worried when he saw what had happened via the CCTV, as obviously this time the well-prepared intruders were fully geared with latest weapons and ammunition, in greater numbers, and their combat skills were obviously well trained, well planned and systematic.

He also noticed that most of his guards started to show their exhaustion in facing another mean fight. In the midst of the gradual defeating combat, he began to digest what his *feng shui* master just had hinted to him.

Immediately he made a hasty decision, planning an escape to a remote island somewhere in South East Asia with his closest aides.

They only had enough time to escape with limited personal belongings, fake third world countries' passports, diamonds and cash through the secret underground pathway linked to the cell.

Once they escaped through the underground tunnel, a convoy of vehicles and elite coups right in the exit waited to deliver them to the secret hideout serespad.

After a few turns in the winding path, just before they reached the serespad, Mr. Mau saw their serescopter was already in midair. Someone had hijacked the serescopter. Looking closer, Mau saw that woman crouched in the doorway of the serescopter, aiming a weapon at the convoy. He ground his teeth—the escaped hostages were supposed to be in his owls' stomachs.

An instant later, he helplessly witnessed their vehicles detonating one after another. Most of his loyal guards couldn't escape from their exploded vehicles on time.

The loud explosions of these vehicles' reserve fuel tanks reached Mr. Mau's mansion to alert those agents still in combat; immediately they ordered a surveillance serescopter to investigate the remote bombardment site.

Not long after Roc flew off with Mr. Mau's serescopter, the navy base received a request from Sheriff Shih for a surveillance serescopter to pursue the escaped criminals.

\* \* \* \* \* \*

The ballistic Mr. Mau was still screaming and scolding his useless employees and closest aides near the bombardment site, until they heard an approaching surveillance serescopter. "Fuck! Run into the woods before they discover us down here," ordered Mr. Mau, unaware that the agents on the serescopter had already detected their traces and direction of their escape route through MPPS thermal imaging camera.

"Fuck! The fucking 'scopter keeps following and hovering above us. Shoot them!" Mr. Mau commanded his aides to aim at their target.

Due to the serescopter hovering so low, when the pilot and agents received an MPPS collision alarm, they found their serescopter's reserve fuel tank was already on fire, and they had just enough time to escape.

"Hooray! We got those sons of bitches!" They were cheering when the serescopter started to swirl and drop.

Very soon deafening explosions erupted that probably could be heard from miles away.

\* \* \* \* \* \*

Meanwhile, in Mr. Mau's house, nobody seemed to care about another series of loud explosions, as by now they were in the climax of their life and death combat. Mau's resilient elite gunmen approached the agents mechanically—without any trace of mercy or emotion.

Eventually, the well-prepared agents tactically defeated the toughest bullet showers and barriers. The ransack led them into the labyrinthine underground, where Mau's death penalty chamber was located. They heard screams for help from their fellow agents locked within the stainless steel gate.

When the rescue team forced through the door, the heat blew directly to their faces. If they hadn't ambushed the house thirty minutes ago, the hostages would have already been thrown in the kiln and burned to ashes. Instead, Mau's guards left abruptly to join their exhausted comrades to defend themselves against the unexpected intruders, leaving the trapped agents in relative safety.

\* \* \* \* \* \*

The two wounded *Ornimegalonyx* were still fighting for their territory with the equally injured giant owl next to the waterfalls. During intervals they would perch and rest on trees before one of them provoked a next round fight.

Suddenly the two *Ornimegalonyx* erected their postures to give a few loud happy hoots, and ceased their fight by flying off toward a direction in the wood where familiar voices echoed. Almost an instant later, the giant owl pursued them but in a rather uncertain, curious manner.

Mr. Mau and his aides were by then hiding in a nearby ranch; they were discussing how to cross the border from Brownsville into Mexico by using their counterfeit passports.

They planned to hijack two cars to reach the border as soon as possible and also steal a few ffs to avoid detection. Their plans also enabled them to receive help from other triad members during and after the border crossing.

Just as the moment they prepared to depart, they heard certain "swishing" noise and the familiar excited cries of the two *Ornimegalonyx*. After a few "ceremonial circles of dance" the two owls perched on the ground a short distance away.

"Shit! Kill these noisy brats! They can't follow us!" Mr. Mau ordered his animal trainer.

"Okay, I'll try to ask them to go away."

The two *Ornimegalonyx* cried very anxiously. The animal trainer moved himself closer to them; then he noticed they were both injured. "What happened, babies?" He snapped his fingers, signaling the two *Ornimegalonyx* to perch next to him on the ground. Instead their plumage suddenly ruffled. They ducked their heads, clacking their beaks, and opened their wings, enlarging themselves to look more massive.

Some unearthly hissing cries soon followed from the sky. The animal trainer saw a massive flying assailant dive toward him. "Hide behind the trees," he yelled to alert the others of the approaching danger.

The giant owl never got its chance to attack the animal trainer, as the two *Ornimegalonyx* coincidentally blocked their master from any harm. Territorial fights started all over again.

"We better move on, before it's getting too late. Let those noisy and annoying bastards fight!" Mr. Mau ordered.

The animal trainer protested, "Mr. Mau, I think we better shoot that giant creature, then I'll ask our two big owls to go back home."

The word "home" touched Mr. Mau's nerve; he growled fiercely, "There won't be a home for them anymore; I don't need their service anymore. God dammit! They were the main culprits to lead those sons of the bitch to us. Let's go!"

Without uttering another word, he picked up the latest laser gun, recklessly targeting the *Ornimegalonyx*; brutally he gave the prehistoric creatures a few rounds of burning light.

Some eerie cries were followed by a silence in the atmosphere; all the owls ended up perching weakly on the ground; obviously, their wounds were exacerbated, thus they stopped their fighting.

The animals' trainer stood with an open mouth, but he didn't dare to go against Mr. Mau, lest he get executed like those ill-fated owls.

The sinister moment wound down with the quietest transition of the last sunset twilight to the fall of darkness.

\* \* \* \* \* \*

Every living thing drowned into invisibility in the increasingly darker canopy, but once the horizon began receiving the sun's reflection from the moon, another kingdom of nocturnal insects and creatures woke from their daytime sleep, soon emerging actively in their own visible realm.

A pack of wolves, like its cousins all over the world, roamed the Texas wilderness; one generation after another, under harsh and extreme climate, they survived with their unique wits.

Their howling intimidated their prey, gave goose pimples to hunters and alerted nearby ranchers the possibility of invasion hazard from a canine family.

In the dimly illuminated sky floated a layer of forever-moving, grayish chiffon clouds beneath a looming crescent moon that synchronized time to time with the wolves' howling.

One old farmer still broke out in a sweat whenever he heard the chilling cries of wolves that came close to his ranch. Though he maintained an electric fence surrounded the paddock, these wolves never gave up their interest in pursuing his deer.

Infiltration was not likely, but once in a blue moon, they would threaten and harass the eighty-two-year-old man's herds. A frightful night like this always prompted him to inspect and double check, ensuring that there was no broken fencing first thing in the early morning right after sunrise.

A few years ago, he faced financial loss and exhaustion when his deer were ambushed every night. Whenever he heard any sound during those nights he checked his deer but there were no casualties, merely minor wolves' bites on different parts on a deer's body.

This situation repeated for almost a week. Those bitten deer soon got weaker day after day, caused by exacerbated wounds, and one morning, he found all those wounded deer had been killed and eaten overnight during his sleep.

After the incident, his grandson Max had visited him, explaining to him the hunting behavior of a pack of wolves: A small pack of wolves would run through a herd of deer; the deer thus would get scared and scatter. From the chaos, the wolves would detect the weakest ones and bite them, but they would leave the wounded deer alive before retreating.

The preying period would continue for a week or so; the wolves would repeatedly inflict more wounds on those injured deer until they became too weak to flee. Badly injured deer wouldn't be able to defend themselves and eventually they would get eaten by the pack.

"These bastards really never quit hounding after me," The old man murmured. He gave a sigh and began to pray. Miraculously, the howls stopped, then his dogs' barking and growling toward the north diminished.

The old farmer sighed in relief; he was thinking to retire finally, as recently he had earned a lucrative profit out of selling stocks and real estate properties. But he planned to remain on his farm until he died.

He smiled fondly, thinking of his genius grandson who had taught him a valuable financial lesson: Don't be greedy for an immediate profit overturn. Act like wolves; slowly demoralize your prey until they get weak and crippled, then swallow them up overnight.

After leaving those fat and juicy deer inside the unapproachable fence, the hungry wolves' eyes sparkled excitedly when they found bloodstains they had detected by smell earlier.

These blood trails eventually led them to their prey; carefully and curiously, they observed their unfamiliarity from a distance, as these three strange creatures were the biggest of any bird they had ever pursued. Though they were wounded and perched on the ground, they were still alive.

Soon the ambush commenced. The wolves howled menacingly out of a silent atmosphere. The owls, in distress, began to move apart from each other a little distance. With flashing speed, the wolves again zoomed in between the owls to further scare and scatter the owls away from each other. The injured, weak owls just flapped their wings and made ugly cries of protest.

The wolves soon retreated and observed their prey quietly with sinister glances. After some time, the wolves reappeared and zoomed in between the owls, separating and splitting each of them even further from each other. Before the owls could attack the wolves, the wolves cleverly retreated again.

Obviously, the owls were not just hungry; they were tired after the long territorial fight and critically wounded after receiving several lethal laser gunshots respectively. The fatal threats from the wolves drained their energy. This cycle repeated until the owls were fatigued. The bloodthirsty wolves had been waiting for such a moment to instinctively frame and jump on the weakest *Ornimegalonyx*, biting first on its infected wounds. The bird had fallen to its back, panting, in a final effort to defend itself with its talons, but to no avail.

The giant owl was much bigger and taller than the two *Ornimegalonyx*; facing the group of fierce, jumpy wolves trying to attack its wounds, it managed to stand up on its feet. However, the two severely wounded, smaller and shorter *Ornimegalonyx* had suffered merciless attacks from the hungry canines.

The greediest and fiercest wolves never gave up threatening the giant owl. Unexpectedly, the spark in its red eyes rekindled and it counterattacked the fearless, annoying predators. In a flash, its talons reached out, slashing a few wolves' sides, and that superior violence prompted the rest of the intimidated wolves to retreat, with fur bristling along their spines. They retreated with mourning howls and useless snarls before joining other wolves attacking the two now motionless *Ornimegalonyx*.

Just before sunrise, the patient tactics of the wolves succeeded; the two resilient *Ornimegalonyx* had finally lost their last breaths. The whole pack of wolves joined one after another enjoying the morsels, but the big feast didn't last long.

The giant owl began to move closer to a carcass; some of the wolves gradually withdrew in helpless yips and snarls when facing the ferocious giant enemy.

The giant owl soon crushed one of the *Ornimegalonyx's* heads with its strong talons. It gave a satisfied cry and with its strong hooked bill began to nibble the brain. After it finished, it went on to open the *Ornimegalonyx's* abdomen to eat its kidneys, liver and other organs.

The growling wolves obviously were not happy, but they patiently waited nearby. They only began to rush for their meal when the giant owl shifted its interest by moving on to crush the skull of the second *Ornimegalonyx*.

# 13

## A Clue from a Giant Feather

Just as he had for the past sixty-odd years, the old farmer got up before dawn. After taking breakfast, he pulled the pickup out from the garage. Automatically some of his old dogs jumped to the bed, happily wagging their tails, moved to the front and gave their master some affable, affectionate barking that sounded to him like "Good morning."

But this morning, the old farmer looked a bit more anxious; he also drove a little faster than usual.

Once he reached the suspected location, after he parked his pickup, he went off to check the deer paddock fence.

Every day, he would count his deer carefully, until he counted to the last number in satisfaction. And his obedient dogs would faithfully look up for him and then trail after him from one place to another during his work.

But today his dogs were barking way more than usual, and one of them oddly even disappeared for a short while into the brush, but when it returned, it held a giant feather in its mouth. When the old man saw the giant feather, immediately he thought his grandson might be interested in it.

For the whole morning, almost compulsively, he inspected every section of the fence and mended any possibility of broken wire. When his shadow became a circle under his own feet, this reminded him to quit for lunch and also that he must contact his grandson Max, whom he hadn't heard from for a while.

\* \* \* \* \* \*

For the past three hours, Roc had been sitting restlessly in his office filled with frustration; he had no clue where those owls were, not until around lunchtime when he received a call from his grandfather.

While he exchanged pleasantries with his papa, his mind was still wandering around until Papa told him what had happened in his deer paddock during the night. "You said a group of wolves approached your ranch last night but they left abruptly?" He paused to listen attentively again.

Suddenly something his papa casually mentioned made him sit erect, "What?—A giant feather?—How long is it?—What color?" He got all excited, sure it was the clue to where those missing owls could be.

"Thanks, Papa. I think I need to borrow Ruble and Zloty later. I'll be able to reach the ranch after your siesta. Bye!"

Roc promptly made an ff call to Dallas.

"Hey, beautiful. I suspected those owls ran into their deadly predators last night. I need to go to the valley now to take a look. Do you want to come along with me?"

"Sure. But ... Mr. Mau's property is still under investigation; we won't be able to go in there without a permit."

"Don't worry, we won't be going there searching for the owls. I'll pick you up from your house within fifteen minutes."

\* \* \* \* \* \*

Fifteen minutes later, after Roc picked up Dallas from her home in Bishop, Dallas wondered why Roc was still driving toward Mr. Mau's ranch.

Once they reached Mr. Mau's ranch entrance, the few troopers who recognized them just waved them through.

"Did you manage to get a pass?" Dallas asked.

"No, but I still have Sheriff Shih's search warrant somewhere in the glove box."

Their conversation was interrupted when a guard called out to them loudly from behind, "Do you know those felons got caught near Matamoros check-point?"

"Great!" Roc responded. Dallas also cheered.

Out of curiosity, he backed up his Land Rover to move closer to the guard. "How'd they get them?"

"They nearly got through the checkpoint with their counterfeit passports, but one of the checkpoint officers is a Chinese food fan who recognized Mr. Mau from those big blow-up newspaper cuttings posted all over his Chinese chain-restaurants."

"Huh, that serves him right for being a high-profile show-off."

In relief, he drove off again, and few minutes later he pulled up his old Land Rover right in front of Mr. Mau's four-wing quadrant entrance door.

"You said we weren't coming here," Dallas reminded him, confused.

"Just wait. There's a method to my madness."

Soon a group of agents walked over suspiciously to check why the newcomers had remained seated in the Land Rover for quite some time without coming out of it.

"Huh...we're lucky—Blackbeard's crew is finally coming." Roc recognized among the group the two agents who took away the two *Ornimegalonyx* in Kingsville Air Force Base.

When the agents approached the Land Rover, one of them recognized Roc and hesitated a step. Red-faced, he politely greeted Roc. "Oh, it's you! What's up, Professor Roc?"

"Hi, guys, I need your help. Can you go with us to the valley to search for the lost *Orni*? You took them away but never returned them to me as promised. I need them back for my research."

"Couldn't be helped, man. Both of the owls were mounted with micro GPS, but our lead agent in charge of it is on leave in Thailand."

"I can't wait for your fearless leader to return from his vacation," Roc said, cracking his knuckles. "Please bring your full gear, ammo and weapons, and follow after my Land Rover. I think I roughly know where the owls could be."

Roc could tell these agents were slightly hesitant, but due to their broken promise, they were forced by their conscience to accompany him. He was glad he didn't need to show them the order in his pocket from their director—a permit that he could bring a half-dozen of them to conduct the owl search. Two would be plenty.

A short while later, Roc reemerged at Mr. Mau's ranch entrance but this time he got a convoy of two cars with logos following behind that would enable him to access other private ranch roads without any prohibition; this cut short the route to his intended destination.

"Where are we headed?" Dallas asked.

"To see an old man," he replied casually.

\* \* \* \* \* \*

Forty minutes later, Roc drove into a small ranch and stopped right in front of a big, country-style cottage. He honked a few times before hopping down from the Land Rover. Two hounds ran toward him, barking and circling him excitingly.

Watching from inside the Land Rover, Dallas saw an old man come out of the cottage with a giant feather. He and Roc gave each other a big hug and exchanged some pleasantries before they bid goodbye.

"Jump, Ruble!...Jump, Zloty!" Roc ordered.

The two dogs obediently followed his command; they jumped and sat right in the trunk of his Land Rover. Roc climbed into the cab and started the engine.

"Who is the old guy?"

"My grandfather."

She spun in her seat to crane her neck toward the small ranch. "I didn't know you had relatives in the area, Mr. New York."

"Yeah, my mom is from here."

"Will wonders never cease?" She wanted to ask him more but hesitated to pry too much.

They resumed their journey. After driving for some time on a remote winding country road, Roc finally signaled the cars behind him to stop next to the roadside.

After he hopped down from the Land Rover, he let each dog sniff at the giant feather, then ordered them, "Now, help me find the owls."

The two smart hounds seemed to understand what Roc was saying. They promptly jumped down from the truck and began sniffing the ground outside the deer paddock then barking and trailing excitedly northward to the most remote corner of the paddock.

At one place, the dogs stopped abruptly, waved their tails anxiously and started to growl, finding some bloodstains on the ground.

A whistle for the dogs came from behind. "Come here, Ruble!—Zloty!—" Roc then produced a few pieces of clothes and more feathers to let the two hounds sniff them, and they got even more excited.

"Now show us the way. Go!" he ordered the barking dogs. "Prepare for a hike now," he told everyone.

They had trekked for perhaps thirty minutes when the dogs stopped abruptly with cringing tails, growling menacingly. They refused to go further. After leashing them, Roc dragged the two protesting dogs toward Dallas. "Tie them under the tree and stay with them there." He gestured a direction to her. "I'll go with the agents to take a closer look over here."

With extra help from the MPPS odor sensor, they trailed after some suspected objects on the ff screen and they also could smell increasing odd, nauseating odors carried by the breeze when such targets were getting closer.

When they grew closer to the ff target, small birds got frightened away by them, and that tipped off Roc that believing the owls to be alive might be optimistic.

Not long later, he and the two agents began to run into torn feathers and bones. The scattered, broken carcasses evidently had been attacked by several kinds of scavengers. Not just mammalian carrion-eaters, but also vultures were joining in the big feast.

Roc mischievously called out, "Doc. Have you had your lunch?"

"No, why?" She distrusted the mischievous tone to his voice.

"Come over here, then. There's a buffet over here."

Dallas crossed through the brush to him. Immediately, she recoiled at the carnage, yet the biologist in her was fascinated at the killing power on display. "Oh, gosh...! What did that to them? Aren't these the two *Ornimegalonyx's* crushed skulls? Where is the giant owl?"

"Obviously these *Ornimegalonyx* skulls were crushed by the giant owl's talons, and I guess it won't be too far off."

After searching for some time in vain, they still couldn't find any obvious trace of the giant owl. "We better get those two dogs to assist us again," Roc suggested.

A sudden conjecture popped up in Dallas's mind. "Hmm...the dogs were cringing, looking utterly frightened and barking continuously when I tied them under the tree. Do you think the giant owl might be somewhere near them? We can use the MPPS to locate it."

"Nope, I think the dogs can do a faster job."

"Let's go!"

When the barking dogs were unleashed, at once they rushed toward their target; obviously, they had detected something over there. The dogs led them directly up to a point; after that, they started to growl but simply refused to proceed any further.

"The giant owl should be in front there. Let's go find that out," Roc suggested.

After they moved forward about ten steps, Roc and Dallas began to hear some familiar weak shrieking. From the sound, they soon found out the giant owl's wings had gotten tangled up between the trees and vines, and they also noticed the new wounds on its body.

"Don't you think these exacerbated wounds and some new wounds were hit by guns?" Dallas asked.

"I think so. Can you tie its beak before we untangle it from these vines?" Roc asked.

"Sure." She turned her head and asked the panicking agents for help. "Agents, can you call for a serescopter to take this giant creature back to Professor Roc's lab?"

"Gee! You mean this is an owl?" one of the agents asked with doubt in his voice.

"Do you think it's a dinosaur?" another agent sarcastically replied to his comrade.

"It is one of the most primitive legendary mammoth owls," Roc informed them. After that he threw his Land Rover's sensor-key to one of the agents. "Can you drive my Land Rover back to TAMUK? This time round, I won't trust anyone else to keep an eye on the giant owl anymore. Last time, she carelessly let the giant owl escape, and"—he first threw Dallas a narrow-eyed look then he turned his face to give those agents a condemning glance—"right under my nose, you guys snatched my two *Ornimegalonyx* at gunpoint. And now they're dead and I can't even get any decent samples from them." He would never forgive those agents for breaking an ornithologist's dream to successfully conduct research on such legendary birds.

"And the giant owl is half dead now," Dallas deliberately aggravated the situation, but in her heart she really worried if the giant owl could make it to the lab.

"Did you know that a snake, even when it's half dead, can still crawl and escape?" Roc asked. Then he murmured something to console himself. "Usually primeval creatures are very resilient."

Hearing the promptly approaching serescopter finally gave them a sigh of relief.

"What time is it now?" Dallas moved Roc's wrist to look at his wristwatch. Her presumption bothered him, yet her closeness tickled his primitive desires. He regretted that he had no time at the moment to act like an animal.

Twenty minutes later, the serescopter airlifted the injured giant owl to Roc's laboratory with the utmost discretion, secrecy and secure supervision, personally provided by Roc.

# 14

## Absence Made the Heart Grow Fonder

At last, Dallas finished recording her most recent ordeal—a successful rescue of the SAR expedition team from a time-warped PNV enclave and the subsequent capture of an amphisensus creature, and she felt those three days had just passed exactly like being trapped in a time-warped PNV enclave.

Their lucky escape and empirical experience could be the preliminary convincing evidence she needed that the PNV did exist once upon a time, even if the zone they'd stumbled across was just the tip of an iceberg. She recalled her past frustration when scientists and scholars merely considered those impenetrable PNV enclaves to be just a myth.

Once she turned idle, she began to feel a little odd that she had not heard a word from Roc since they parted. He hadn't even cashed in on the promised date. Finally, on the fourth day, she decided to pay Professor Rochester a surprise visit; she had an urge to figure out if he was genuinely interested in her or if his flirtation was just a typical playboy act or if it was merely because she was the only female confined among all those men.

\* \* \* \* \* \*

Early in the morning, an overworked Roc bent and stretched his four limbs for relief. After sipping his Jamaican blue mountain coffee, he still yawned sleepily; despite the tiredness he felt rewarded, as the giant owl would screech at him whenever it saw him coming.

Even though a team of vets worked routinely to give injections and wound dressings for the post-surgical care of the injured giant owl, he still stayed awake most of the past three consecutive days to babysit the wounded giant owl.

Luckily, the laser gun wounds didn't penetrate too deeply into the skin; only a few festering burn wounds on top of some old wounds were critical. However, under the magical laser, strong dosage of elixirantigen and vitamins, the giant owl was recovering sooner than expected.

The early autumn cooling winds sifting through his open windows carried along the aroma of his coffee mixed with a familiar voice arguing with the new shift of state trooper guards. He instantly felt heart-lightened, and he finally comprehended the famous proverb: *Absence makes the heart grow fonder.*

His lips turned into a mischievous, sardonic crescent. He stood automatically, still gripping his coffee cup, and then promptly stepped out his office and headed to the entrance, calling out the guards, "Hey there! Let her in, she is Dr. Dallas, President Churchill's supporter."

"Hey! I'm not a Republican," she declared, whipping her head around guiltily in the university setting.

"Then you're anti-government," he said, pulling her leg. He'd learned from his Far East friends that some third world countries' political ruling party considered their opposition party as anti-government instead as just a rival.

"Let's just keep that quiet, shall we?" she asked, stepping inside.

The entrance door shut a little bit heavier with some faint laughter still echoing from behind them, yet he gave her annoyed look a light-hearted, amused smile.

"What brings you by?" he asked.

"What, not interested in a date anymore?" Then spontaneously, she gave a playful, flirtatious caress of his hair. "I've been wanting to ask, is this real or transplanted?"

He dodged away from her hand, surprised at her violation of personal space but pleased she would reach for him. When she smiled widely at her own joke, he gave a snap with two of his fingers on the enamel of her perfect set of teeth in retaliation. "I've wondered, is this real or implanted?"

Dallas' smile morphed from a friendly greeting to a genuine grin. She did not retreat but held her ground. This girl could give as good as she got, and she could take a joke. Who knew? He'd worried over the prior three days if he'd imagined his attraction to her. It all came rushing back in the intimate, flirtatious exchange.

Today she was dressed differently than he'd seen in their earlier meetings, no longer outfitted to go into the wild. He peered curiously at what new accessories and outfit Dallas put on to come see him. He was fascinated to see how she was able to dress up and present herself with great character and distinction, even with a simple pair of jeans and a cotton blouse. She seemed taller, too. Her hair didn't seem any bigger, but she'd pulled it back to reveal dangling earrings, and she was wearing a touch of eye makeup and lip gloss. He wondered whether her bra today was sheer lace, and what color.

Dallas raised her eyebrows; she had the clear sensation he was undressing her with his gaze. "Enough?" she asked him suddenly. He met her gaze and gave an "I'm caught" smile. He reminded her of her naughty little nephew whom she hadn't seen for a while; whenever he saw her, his little eyes would wander all over her body before he gave her a hug. But at least when her nephew did it, she didn't have a tingling anticipation that he might see her naked.

"How is the owl doing?" she asked. "How soon can we expect to release it?"

"Oh, it's doing fine and healing speedily. I was just about to call you and here you are. Were you missing me?" Roc was obviously still in a flirtatious mood. Together, they walked to his lab.

She started to get a little annoyed by his one-note answers; she wondered if he was no different from those men who would try to cross her either by their eyes or by their words if they couldn't get her into bed.

"I think we have to release it before it gets strong enough to escape and endanger someone again," she suggested.

"Are you sure it's not from our habitat?"

"Come on, Professor Roc. It's not your dead pet rooster from Kikicoo Island or an albino mynah from the Borneo jungle." Perhaps he was trying to rationalize keeping the giant owl as another of his rare, unique specimens. "The giant owl and the *Orni* most certainly originated from an exclusively confined PNV remnant hovering near our area. You know very well that our food chain could be completely destroyed by them if they live continuously within our zone. Can you afford to feed just one of them?" she challenged him. "Probably like feeding three extra adults?"

His eyes followed her when she slowly walked over the cage where the Mynah was eating an apple on the floor. Dallas bent at the waist and got closer to it and began to sing the nursery rhythm Song of Freedom.

Roc knew his smart little friend would understand when someone was heckling it. He frowned at Dallas. "Don't be so mean. Who knows—one day if you get kidnapped and locked up somewhere remote, it might come to recue you," he joked.

She threw him a fierce glance. "It treated me as a predator for its bird-friends!"

"But you don't look like a cat to me."

"How did you come by having a mynah, anyway?" Dallas asked, ignoring his jibe.

"I brought it back from Sumatra about a year ago when she was merely a little bird. She was as badly injured as the giant owl when I picked her up from fairway, then the Indonesian government presented her to me as a gift." He sighed. "It took me a lot more effort to get the bird admitted to the United States."

"That might be best for it. Poor thing."

"Yeah…" Dr. Rochester barely listened to what Dallas was saying, as his eyes had been trailing behind her since the moment she bent over. He eyes narrowed when he saw the deep ravine of her bottom revealed from her low-rise V-cut jeans. He was amused that the latest V-back jean fashion was a mimic of a V-neck shirt. The deep ravine right above her butt cleavage acted as a "switch" for any normal straight man to raise sinful fantasies. He tucked both hands into his trouser pockets and adjusted himself, enjoying the view.

His cynical eyes moved lower and he figured her four-inch heel boots were the most expensive thing on her entire body, aside from that anklet with the dangling hornbill beads. Then his glance began to ascend; her blue, backless T-shirt reminded him of a toucan's beak. He clenched his hands inside his pockets to still the impulse to touch the smooth skin of her back.

Dallas soon lost interest when the mynah simply treated her as an invisible object. She straightened and turned to face him again. The brooch pinned on her chest was a flower made of peacock feathers, and on her earlobes hung some more red beads made of red-crowned Rhinoceros hornbill. He looked at the ornaments disapprovingly but secretly he admitted they looked elegant on her. "I think we were very lucky to escape from the PNV remnant. We knew we had experienced time warp, but without much awareness of how much earthly time elapsed. Obviously, such a time warp could also cause memory lapse, but how could we remember then?" She shrugged uncertainly but chuckled.

"Did we really experience time warp?"

"Have you checked your watch or ff time and date since your return?"

"Of course, but I found both were slow, way behind the current time."

"No, I think both your watch and ff-time are accurate for the time you experienced inside the PNV. You just need to adjust them forward to our present 'earthly' time again. The lagged time was the overall on and off time warp y'all experienced during your expedition. Bloodhound called me to discuss the time warp matter after he couldn't get ahold of you," she informed him.

"I turned my ff off."

"Oh, no wonder. I told him you were probably busy with the critically injured giant owl. Instead, I asked him to figure it out. He called back the next day and told me the time was warped for around 459 hours in PNV. You were there nineteen days total, give or take."

"Jeez...felt like being there for just a day and overnight."

"That's why one creation day was likely one day of God's space-time in his earthly dwelling vault, but not a day of what we observe of geological time out here on the earthly plane," Dallas said.

"That makes sense." He took a sip of the coffee in his hand, gone cold since Dallas arrived. "Do you want a cup of coffee?"

"Sure, why not?"

"Right this way." He gestured for her to precede him to the office kitchen. The path reminded her of the day she tried to look for an apple, only to have the mynah let the giant owl loose. This also reminded her that she should not just lock the cage but also should close the room's door; guilt colored her cheeks.

Roc grumbled upon finding the coffeepot empty. "You'd think grad students could make coffee and not just drink it." He dug in a cupboard and pulled out a paper sack of coffee beans labeled from Jamaica. "I really didn't feel like we stayed in there for more than a day, although the place was always foggy." He reached for the coffee grinder. "Darkness never fell and we didn't feel that hungry either. Our metabolic rate was either suppressed or we really were trapped in a warp of space-time that carried us past Earth-time."

Dallas leaned against the counter, impressed at his practiced motions in making coffee, and that he used the real stuff rather than canned, pre-ground drek. "I stayed there too short a time to notice anything odd."

"Too short?" He gave a throaty chuckle. "Don't you usually eat over three days?"

She ignored his jab. "I have long suspected there are unusual, *noctilucent* clouds in the PNV that can store and reserve solar energy but release it during the earthly night.

This scintillating atmosphere actually would enhance growth and restore health for all living things thriving within it."

"Yes, none of us were sick or tired while we were there," he observed, while he began to brew the coffee. "I've been reading your website since we got back, and I have lots of questions about the PNV. But first, tell me what interested you in finding a zone of origin for cryptozoologic creatures in the first place. How does a biologist meld with a Biblical scholar to become you?"

"I..." Dallas wondered if she should tell Roc something that troubled her since she was very young. "You know what?..." She got tongue-tied and abruptly stopped.

"Go ahead," Roc encouraged.

"When I was young, whenever I heard Sunday school teachers' repeated Bible stories about Adam and Eve's banishment from the Garden of Eden, so many questions would pop into my mind about what kind of place they went to after God banished them to work the ground from which they had been taken. Obviously, there was an immediate land attached outside the Garden of Eden, where Cain was born. Then after Cain murdered his brother Abel, Cain begged God, saying that if once he got driven out of the land, he would be hidden from God's presence. This verse showed that the Garden of Eden and this attached land were both God's territories. Was it just the strip of land between the Tigris and Euphrates, like we're told in school, or something more special? Cain begged God that whosoever found him would kill him, and I always wondered who those deadly enemies were outside their confinement. Very obviously, Adam's family was well-protected inside their land. Why did they need to be protected by God himself? Wasn't Adam's family the only people God had created on Earth?"

"Your doubts were solved when you came out with these PNV theories?"

"Yes, sort of." Dallas nodded.

"To solve unsolved puzzles, one should first try to figure out some convincing hypothesis rather than to evade those hidden doubts in the mind," Roc suggested. "I understand how you came to the field of science to look for answers."

"Many devout Christians and Biblical scholars dare not make any assumption due to the warning at the end of the Revelation verse 22:18, 'I warn everyone who hears the words of the prophecy of this book: If anyone adds anything to them, God will add to him the plagues described in this book.'"

"It meant nobody should add anything to the prophecy of Revelation, it didn't apply for the whole Bible that many have wrongly interpreted." Roc crossed his arms. "Remember how many translations and re-translations there have been of the Bible over two millennia."

"According to the Bible, a serpent who could talk prompted Eve to eat the forbidden fruit." Dallas shifted her stance, leaning forward to express her passion in the origins of her research. "I could understand why there were so many atheists, those who needed proof, such as evidence that once in an ancient time, serpents could literally talk. I set out to find creatures of legend, those animals found in myth all over the world, to find the proof. What I found was PNV. I think that snake could be a humanoid reptilian, perhaps a very intelligent subspecies among those aliens."

"Or an alien's pet?" Roc suggested. "Here's your coffee." After pouring two mugs, Roc gave one to Dallas.

She took an exploratory sip and then made a face of pleasure at the quality. "Oh, thank you!"

"It's Blue Mountain coffee that Bloodhound gave me; some of his relatives are from Jamaica."

"Yeah...what happened to Bloodhound exactly?" she asked. "Captain Lee told me you'd experienced something weird involving him."

"Well, when we both lost sight of each other in the fog, he made a U-turn, running toward us merely by guessing where he last saw us. At the same time, we were searching for him the direction we last saw him go. Soon we heard shrill whistling, then Bloodhound suddenly appeared standing in between us and then he bumped into Melvin's back and panicked. Obviously, he couldn't see us initially. We were actually walking arm-in-arm in a line. When he quit blowing his whistle, we observed each other turning into ghost-like floating amputated limbs or dismantled figures and our words were partially muted."

"Did he say something?"

"Yes. Now something has intrigued me. Bloodhound blamed us that we took so long to find him, but we started to look for him immediately when we discovered he'd disappeared, but I felt it actually didn't take us long to find him."

"Hmm...time warp. His whistle merged the two entities or two space-times temporarily. Now you know when you step into a super quiet room, if you feel goose pimples you deliberately sing and walk loudly, subconsciously thinking the sounds might be able to scare off ghosts."

"True enough, Bloodhound told us he whistled because he got panicked suddenly."

"Most probably he could sense there was another entity intercalated in the space-time that he walked through, although he couldn't see anything when he entered through that space-time."

"That sounds logical. When we found him, I noticed there were goose pimples all over his arms."

"Professor Roc, Sunny finally learned how to sing *Mary Had a Little Lamb*," Cindy announcing happily, entering the staff kitchen. "Oops...sorry for the interruption, you have a guest." She retreated a step.

"It's okay, Cindy, this is Dr. Dallas."

Cindy did a double-take. "I didn't recognize you, Dr. Dallas. Welcome back." She glanced at Dallas' outfit. "I love your boots."

"Thanks," Dallas said.

"Marvelous job you have done teaching Sunny," Roc said. "Do you mind bringing her over my office to entertain Dr. Dallas?"

"Sure, I'd be delighted."

"Thank you."

After she left, Roc gestured to Dallas. "Let's go to my office."

"I thought those birds only spoke foul words." Dallas chuckled as they left the kitchen.

"One time when our university president walked in the hall looking for his daughters, he was surprised to hear all those four-letter words greeting him. He wasn't pleased."

"Oh, that's hilarious! And that also happened when I first came here."

"Luckily, they only do that to adult-strangers," he told her. Upon reaching the office, Roc rolled out a typist chair for Dallas to sit next to him before he sank comfortably into his swivel chair. After a sip of his coffee, he thought it would be a great idea to share a question with Dallas and find out her take on it.

"As I said, I've been reading your website, and noticed parallels between a couple of sources you cite. You seem to use 'God' interchangeably with these alien-host beings that came to Earth before our own biome began to flourish. Some people refuted Zecharia Sitchin's implication that the alien beings from Nibiru were actually the Gods that human beings worshipped, yet others remained mute about it. Do you know why such revolutionary concepts weren't universally condemned?"

"Yes, because some people only believe in monotheism, and only in the God that stayed inside the Garden of Eden. But those human slaves cloned by alien-beings believed in polytheism. They worshipped every one of their alien-being masters as their idols and their descendants and believers did the same," Dallas explained. "Not everyone on the planet is Christian, Jewish, or Islamic."

Rochester's finger was flipping on his ff screen; sheepishly he told her, "I'm reading Genesis again after twenty years...There were a few speculations about those 'sons of God' in Genesis 6:2—some said they were actually the planetary beings from Nibiru that Sitchin wrote about, some suspected that they were the rejected watchers banished by God from heaven since eons ago and thus they were considered to be the devils that went against God."

"Actually, Sitchin was mocked badly as a member of the illuminati for the book he wrote, but I think he actually contributed in revealing some antediluvian eon facts of aliens' presence on Earth that we wouldn't be able to read from our history and science books. I'd rather appreciate than condemn the writer, whether some facts are partially true or untrue." She sipped her coffee. "I'm surprised you're familiar with his work."

"I did a bit of light reading after we returned from the PNV zone. I found the reference in your bibliography."

For a moment, they both grew quiet. Roc watched Dallas sip her coffee, the soft movements of her throat as she swallowed. He thanked his lucky stars he'd answered that late-night plea to find Baby Ruby that night. His adventure brought him in contact with the most intelligent woman he'd ever met, one who was dead sexy as well. Everything about her was perfect, from her tousled blonde hair to the tips of her booted feet—especially the middle portions. Proportions. His mind flashed again the view of her in just a bra he'd seen on the video monitor. Physical arousal flared briefly.

But her willingness to discuss her theories and engage in academic discourse made him want more from her mind, which was a completely new experience for him.

A knock called for attention from the office door. "Are y'all free now to listen to Sunny singing?" Cindy brought a cockatiel and was now standing outside the office.

"Oh great, please come in."

"Wow, what a pretty girl you are." Dallas started to talk, caress and play with the cockatiel. "Now, sing for me." The shy bird refused to sing but rather wanted to play.

They had to continuously feed the cockatiel pine nuts and talk and play with it; after two minutes it was finally willing to sing for them. Dallas was amazed that while it sang, it even danced. The song ended perfectly; amazingly, there was no note out of tune or beat.

"Bravo!...Encore!" Everyone cheered but the bird refused to sing anymore.

"Ha, ha...obviously it won't sing without the expensive pine nuts." Dallas chuckled.

"Yes, Sunny is an esurient bird. Okay, Sunny, say goodbye," Cindy instructed it.

"Goodbye," it bid them farewell obediently.

"What a good bird you are," Dallas flattered.

"Thank you for bringing her to entertain us. You've done a marvelous job," Roc praised Cindy.

"Shit, chin chin, fuck, cholera..." The bird swore right after leaving the office.

"Gee...Bipolar cockatiel! Make sure you bar any baby who just started talking from getting near those birds." Dallas couldn't help giggling.

"Don't worry, my lab is not a zoo," Roc quipped.

A picture of phoenix hanged behind Roc's back caught Dallas' attention. It was a Chinese silk painting of a phoenix in a frame of equatorial ironwood.

Dallas bristled. What a hypocrite that man was! "That's a nice painting. Where did you get the belian frame from?"

# Discovery of Amphisensus Creatures

"How do you know it's made from belian?" His eyebrows shot to his hairline.

She crossed her arms and set her jaw. "Don't tell me you're unaware of its endangered classification?"

"I'm well aware of its rarity. But you're thinking of darker color belian species *Eusideroxylon zwageri.* This belian frame is the lighter color and less durable species *Potoxylon malagangai.*"

"And is just as rare and just as endangered. I can't believe you have this on display in your office—that's almost blasphemy, considering what you do for a living."

He narrowed his eyes. "What about those poor birds who had to die for your jewelry, missy? Do you have any concept of how hard I and others have worked to conserve rhinoceros hornbills in the wild?"

Dallas smirked and jiggled her head to make her earrings swing. "My great grandparents used to work as diplomats in Malaysia, this set of antique jewelry was a gift presented by a Dayak chief from her Sarawak state and it was carved long before the birds were endangered. I thought you might be the only person in Texas who could appreciate their origins, so I wore them just for you." She laughed. "I'm sorry—I didn't stop to think how that would look to an ornithologist. Believe me, I didn't kill the birds. I certainly don't condone poaching."

Roc smirked. "As well this antique framed picture was a gift from a Chinese-Malaysian businessman friend back in New York. I didn't cut down the tree."

Dallas looked more closely at the painting within. "Usually a Chinese person would give a phoenix to a girl but a dragon to a boy. He probably knows you like birds, so he gave you this phoenix."

"Maybe..." Roc sat back in his chair, face softened again.

"Could you accept the idea that once upon a time phoenix really existed on Earth?"

"Now that I'm learning about PNV zones, I think so. It must be one of the earliest creatures God created and would burn itself to ashes before resurrecting or reproducing itself," he replied.

"Most primitive vegetation also propagated in such a manner—only after intense heat exposure would their seeds germinate. Many plants we can still find today operate under this same requirement in areas where fire is an annual event, such as the Australian outback. But how could people gather evidence after millions of years if those creatures burnt themselves to ashes upon dying? I have always been amazed by the ability of painters to imitate legendary creatures with such vivid features, description and appearance. Could human imagination, creativity and aesthetic taste enable them to draw and paint a non-existent bird that lifelike? The legend of the phoenix is found in nine distinct cultures worldwide, and it amazes me that painters don't modify its features even now."

"So do you think it lived inside the PNV or its outbound zone?"

"I think it lived inside the Garden of Eden even earlier than Adam and Eve. According to legend, the holy bird was rarely seen by people and it appeared only once every five hundred years. After the PNV was abandoned, just like salmon, it still would return with uncanny precision to its natal ground where it was born, died and was reborn before flying off again back to the Garden of Eden. That's why it was hardly spotted by people unless it returned to its PNV natal ground."

He nodded, seemingly quite satisfied with her reply.

"In Genesis's Creation Day 5, I believe that God was actually creating some of the earliest amphisensus creatures for sky and water, and that could include this legendary phoenix.

"Other than amphisensus creatures, God kept most living things inside his own vault. Whereas the incipient subsidiary vault superimposed over its primordial vault was permeated with thin dusty air and sulfuric stink from Earth's volcanism, it was considered wilderness by God and where extraterrestrial drought-tolerant creatures like dinosaurs could flourish."

"That's interesting. So you believe dinosaurs did not evolve on Earth?"

"No, I think God didn't create dinosaurs for Earth initially, but at the later stage he probably had to clone some predatory dinosaurs, releasing them into the wilderness to hold down populations of burgeoning herbivorous species. Remember, no other tetrapod on Earth has a perforate acetabulum. I think the Jurassic dinosaurs could originate from other planets but were propagated to Earth during a close inter-planetary collision that happened during a transitional period when Earth's nuclear reserves were sending out its auto-defensive buffered water and auto-repaired oxygen, while the primordial vault was on its way to inflate a subsidiary space-time vault to the wilderness space. Those eggs could be protected inside the half-dead female dinosaurs, and the creation day's light could indirectly help those dinosaurs' eggs to revive under favorable conditions."

"Hmm—that goes against everything I've learned about the origins of birds from the fossil record."

"I know—it makes your head spin. But if you can be open-minded, the idea of PNV makes perfect sense alongside our fossil record and geological findings from our perspective."

There was a light knock on the door; when they turned their heads they saw two young girls smiling brightly at them. Dallas guessed them to be around seven to ten years old.

"Oh, come in, honeys, this is Dr. Dallas." Roc wore a big smile, obviously delighted to see them.

"How do you do, ma'am?" Both girls bobbed a brief curtsey.

"These are the daughters of our university president," Roc introduced the girls to Dallas. "They're the regular visitors to the lab due to their love of birds."

"Oh, hey, pleased to meet you two beautiful young ladies."

"We won't take much of your time, but please teach us something new again," they politely requested.

"Sure," Roc fondly agreed. "Okay, let me think first of what new exciting thing I can teach you today while Dr. Dallas is here."

He rose up from his seat and crossed to a poster of a frog and stopped next to it.

He asked the girls, "Can you name this amphibian?" while pointing his index finger toward it.

"It's an anura."

That the older girl replied with the scientific order name for frog really impressed Dallas. "Wow, what a smart girl!"

"Okay, anura lives happily either in water or on land, so can you name any living thing that catches insects in the air and on the ground?" Roc asked.

"Aves!"

Dallas was truly impressed when the younger girl could also give the scientific order name for the bird, and she whistled and gave the girls a thumb up. "Bravo!"

"Have you ever thought there could be another order of living thing in this world that lives in our realm but at the same time can detect another coexisting realm that we cannot see, smell or hear?" Roc asked them.

"Hmm...I never thought of that," the two girls replied simultaneously; they paused a second to digest it.

"Now, imagine that if one day a deep sea fish got caught by a fisherman. From inside the net, it saw many fishermen standing in the air. The big fish made a leap from the net, into the air, and returned to the deep sea, telling its fish-friends what it saw and encountered during the narrow escape. Do you think those fish would believe it?"

"No. Only frogs would believe it," the older girl replied playfully.

"Okay, good. Many living things on land have access to hunt the fish in the sea, but most fish won't be able to come ashore hunting for their food. Conversely, if there was a hyperspace with some kind of superior luminous energies' existence, they could access our dimension easily, yet we human beings could barely get to its fringe. Actually, most of us are unable to access it or even sense its existence."

Dallas added, "If people returned from dead trying to tell us what heaven is like, surely nobody would believe them. It would be just like the fish trying to convince his fish-friends about the existence of human beings and other air-breathers above them."

"Can you name some double-sense living things that that live in our land habitat, yet their senses are capable of roaming on other realms at will?" Roc asked the girls again.

"Cats, dogs, owls, falcons, snakes?..." The younger girl blurted out these animals while she looked into Roc's eyes without blinking.

"I think God must have created these animals for certain purposes since ancient times. Do double-sense living things that can see dimensions that we can't have a name?" the older girl asked curiously.

"Dr. Dallas calls them amphisensus," Roc informed them. Now both girls turned to look at Dallas. "Dr. Dallas is the person who discovered the possible existence of amphisensus creatures. I'll let her explain it to you now."

Dallas preferred to explain to children using an easy shortcut. "Have y'all been to Sunday School?"

"Yes," both the girls replied.

"Okay, then it is easier for me to explain it to you," she told them. "Think about the creation story at the beginning of Genesis. Amphisensus creatures are believed to be the

155

earliest living things that God created before human beings. They were deployed by God to guard the Garden of Eden and also set out as spies or predators to kill alien-enemies in the wilderness. They had bi-senses and special strength that enabled them to navigate back and forth from the Garden of Eden to Earth's wilderness zones during specific times. They also had the highest survival instinct and could give warning of trouble. They could even lead their human masters to a safe place during cataclysms or their masters could observe their unusual behavior to know of impending disaster."

"Wow, that's interesting. Thank you. My mom said we could only stay and talk to you for five minutes. Bye!" The two girls scurried from the room like the wind.

Dallas chuckled and wiped her brow with her sleeve. "Whew—did I chase them off?"

"Their IQ is over 130, and at least once a week they pop into the lab, talking to those birds first before coming here to talk to me, but every time they stay for no more than five minutes. They run out after I explain things too, so it's not just you," Roc told her with a laugh, "and those birds never say any foul words to them."

"Hmm...What a surprise." Dallas's pupils were dilated so wide they appeared purple. Roc felt he could fall right through them into her soul.

# 16

# Evolution of Earth's Atmosphere

"Hang on a sec," Dallas began flicking her fingers over her ff screen to drop down certain ideas that suddenly popped into her mind. After a few seconds, she asked, "Can I hear some your opinions regarding some of my hypotheses?" she asked him while flipping her fingers over her ff screen, searching for something she had written before.

"Sure, why not?"

"Let me show you something." Dallas rolled her chair closer to Roc and then placed her ff screen right in front of him. He saw it displayed her most recent PNV report. "You can have a quick read through; at least you know I'm not a stupid pseudo-zoologist who chases after Bigfoot and dinosaurs." She said it sarcastically.

*Those jealous boys must have told her that.* He stared at the ff screen and pretended he didn't hear the jibe.

*During the antediluvian eon, primordial amphisensus creatures in the ocean, on land and in the air traveled respectively in their daily navigations or seasonal migratory routes either inside the PNV atmosphere or outside its subsidiary atmosphere. These illuminated orientation signals were directed by nuclear reserves from hollow earth rectified by cosmic forces, unfortunately these signals are undetectable by our human eye pigmentation.*

*After Creation Day 7, as outer earth's PNV was abandoned and left to deteriorate by its creation host, the damaged PNV fragments could either merge with its subsidiary vault's space-time or embed as independent self-reliant enclaves, thus in the late antediluvian eon assimilation could happen between both original and subsidiary vaults' inhabitants at such merged lands.*

Dallas pointed her index finger at the bottom of the ff screen to cue Roc. "Here I mentioned that primordial amphisensus living things could detect illuminating orientation signals."

"Yes. Would these orientation signals be ruined or distorted when the PNV was abandoned?" he asked.

"No, proto-orientation signals had already been inflated and extended into the subsidiary vault," she replied. "I don't think PNV orientation routes could be easily ruined by man. Even after the PNV collapsed during the postdiluvian era, these orientation routes could still inflate and extend along with the structural frame of the regenerated earthly atmosphere. The new earthly canopy expanded, and a new succession of living things gradually devolved to smaller sizes.

"Old PNV remnants still exist because of their auto-recovery facilities. Primitive giant creatures adapt and propagate through millions of years inside conservatories situated at the crossroads of suitable climate and abundant food, and their orientation routes are repaired by the nuclear reserves from hollow earth through remote rendering.

"The orientation routes gradually contracted and become narrower as they radiated and extended toward higher altitudes with the expanded atmosphere. This stabilized a few generations postdiluvian. Eventually, most of the routes became impassable for creatures with large body mass, and this was one of their extinction factors. These gigantic creatures could only survive if they happened to return to the safe zone of their old habitats during space-time regeneration and encryption.

"The regenerated orientation routes remain today, but they only allow the smaller migratory birds and creatures to migrate faithfully subject to seasonal changes and to navigate for their daily livelihood."

"Wow! Scientists have released different theories trying to convince us of how birds know their respective destinations during migration even under starless skies, but now I'm totally convinced by your theories of pre-existing orientation routes. Can I also hear your opinion why certain birds fly thousands of miles, crossing oceans for days during migration, yet they eat sparingly or go without food at all and where they get such stamina and energy?

"Did you feel hungry when you got trapped?" she countered. "Obviously time warp happened. These birds probably only felt they were flying for a day."

"But we could track those birds."

"Theoretically, if a bird flew timelessly, it could disappear from our tracking, but if the migration route OTS—their visual spectrum—was not in function or if its time warp occurred on and off inconsistently, we could still track the birds."

"Hmm... sounds logical. Okay, then how about the orientation routes in the oceans?"

"I think those were the least destroyed orientation routes during past global catastrophic destruction; however, from time to time we still encounter heartbreaking sights of a pod of whales or dolphins that stray off course and strand themselves on the beach. In the past, scientists and animal behaviorists have had no clear explanation for this. My theory explains it clearly."

"What's the cause?" he asked.

"Just like a shifting railroad track, when a dormant oceanic orientation route is activated by an ancient migration signal that detours to a shore, it also misleads migratory marine creatures into a deathtrap. Vibration frequency differences account for only one species at a time being affected."

"Would you like some more coffee?" Roc asked, and then he rose abruptly from his seat, and wandered back to the lab kitchen.

When he returned he refreshed the cup of coffee in front of Dallas and set down a plate of chocolate chip cookies too. "I baked them. You better try."

"Oh, thank you!"

He took a sip of his fresh cup of coffee before resuming their conversation. "So what happened to those old PNV enclaves that intercalated in the regenerated earthly atmosphere after Noah's deluge?"

"Actually those enclaves were intercalated and camouflaged everywhere on Earth within the newly inflated earthly atmosphere," she informed him. "Some enclaves float like bubbles in the air, but the most harmful ones, containing heavier toxic metals ions, get stuck in between basins or stagnant zones on the ground, and frequent earthquakes also periodically bury or compress some enclaves in subterranean strata or in the seabed."

"And in some cases, earthquakes could resurface those buried enclaves on the ground or in the air?" Roc added.

"Yes," Dallas agreed. "We could walk within some of these enclaves every day unknowingly, but some enclaves only open to access once in a blue moon. Usually, the living resources of smaller PNV enclaves corroded faster than bigger enclaves, as bigger enclaves possess higher resilience of the auto repair mechanism. Good PNV enclaves promote health for any living things that dwell within or beside them. They eliminate and neutralize any harmful articles, radiation or electronic interferences, but harmful PNV enclaves drain any living things' energies, cripple their metabolic rates or distort their hormonal productions, etc."

"I've heard of trapped underground water and subterranean water veins that brought geopathic stress. They've been known to cause fatigue, unknown sicknesses or depression and terminal illness to those people who dwell above them or have prolonged exposure to them, although they live healthily and eat healthy foods."

"All good or harmful PNV enclaves can be found all over our environment, but they appear invisible to us, as they're effectively blocked by a layer of PNV primitive color spectrum I called OTS for Original Tint Spectrum, and our evolved human eye pigmentation can't perceive OTS. Imagine if there was actually a phoenix flying overhead inside a PNV enclave but we couldn't see it, as its fence was protected by the OTS undetected by our eyes."

"Well, unless someone discovers OTS through another kind of prism or crystal ball," Roc quipped.

"Perhaps it would be again another accidental discovery by scientists." She laughed. "...Scattered PNV enclaves with their peripherals surrounded by sucker particles and OTS in different strengths and compressions could be hidden everywhere in our environment. There have been cases like when a saucer accidentally intruded into a contended PNV enclave, a tug of war occurred between both parties' forces, and the saucer soon vanished from the radar. Highly skilled and experienced pilots allow themselves to swirl for a while just like a bird would do when encountering strong winds. Or some pilots enter a swirling funnel, and then they wait for an opportunity to escape. These trespassers usually reappear mysteriously far away from the saucer's original course within a very short time. They experience time warp starting from the time their saucers disappeared from the radar screen. Some victims and vehicles have been spiraled into PNV enclaves but became senselessly or timelessly preserved. But I always suspect that if one day these enclaves finally dissipate to merge with our habitat, these missing persons could still revive and find out the world has passed three decades, and their children have become as old as them, just as Einstein says in his relativity theory."

"It may possibly happen; some animals are known to revive themselves after hibernating for long periods of time." Roc shrugged unsurely.

Dallas paused a moment when Roc uncontrollably gave a yawn, "Sorry, you're not boring; this was caused by three sleepless nights, but I can't go to sleep while this giant owl is still here."

She took a sip of the remaining coffee. "Hmm—this coffee tastes great even as it cools down."

"Do you need another cup?" he asked.

"Oh no, thank you."

He looked at the empty cookie plate. "So how are my cookies?"

She looked at the empty plate. "My action already said it, right?" she replied with a killing sweet smile.

Their conversation diverted when something on Dallas's wrists provoked Roc's curiosity. "Is there a watch on one of those?" He moved forward to take a closer look at her two-inch, sculpted silver bracelets on both wrists.

"No." She showed him both bracelets. "You know there's a risk of being kidnapped by aliens due to wearing a watch with those jumping digits that look familiar to them." She joked while stealing a glance at his digital watch. Actually, her TAG accidentally dropped to the floor, its crystal cracked and the replacement would cost almost half the value of the watch, so she had left it in a drawer since then.

"Okay, I wonder if any of such stupid aliens could ever manage to land on Earth," he sniggered. "No wonder you always asked people what the time was. You could check your ff."

"Naw, I'm more used to checking the time directly from a watch or a clock." Dallas glanced at the antique wall clock. "Am I taking too much of your time?" she asked.

He shook his head and smiled to reply to her indirect question whether he wanted to continue their conversation or not; he could talk to her all day. One pressing subject had not yet been covered, so he asked, "How does one move in or out of a PNV zone on purpose? How do we send our owl home?"

# Riddles Hidden in the Lunar Calendar

"I'll have to answer that with a bit more background," Dallas said. "According to the Bible, after God drove Adam and Eve from the Garden of Eden, to bar trespassers he sealed the Garden of Eden's east side access with cherubim and the tree of life's access path with a flaming sword. Let's presume that the forbidden fruit tree was actually cultivated by God for those godly amphisensus spy-birds to revitalize their double-senses for free access in and out of the PNV to collect information needed for God.

"According to what I read from an early 20th century true account of a Norwegian sailor who trespassed into and narrowly escaped from the hollow earth—I suspect those creatures and the abandoned Garden of Eden were still situated inside the hollow earth's encrypted enclave, segregated from the outer earth," Dallas guessed. "So many archaeologists have tried to establish the true location of the Garden of Eden on the outer earth based on the source of the four rivers the Euphrates, the Pison, the Gihon, and the Hiddekel, but they couldn't find anything."

"Excuse me, why not Tigris?" Roc wondered.

"Hiddekel is Tigris in Hebrew," Dallas informed him. "I'm a firm believer that their source was the mighty artesian fountain of the hollow earth, but unfortunately the Norwegian sailor's account was just another modern Cassandra version; most people would consider him a lunatic, as modern science has told us the earth's core is so hot that it's in a molten state.

"More related reports of hollow earth have been published in recent days compared to thirty years ago. If hollow earth really exists—with those aliens really inhabiting it, they would know the universe, the earth's structure and Earth's history more than any of our outer earth's human beings.

"Clearly only very few human beings have been lucky enough to trespass into the hollow earth's enclave and return safely to the outer earth. The frigid temperatures at the poles and hazardous icebergs are natural obstacles to reach any such openings," Dallas remarked. "I surmise most auto-recovered PNV enclaves still manage their respective ecosystems in a self-reliant manner, as they still receive signals from the nuclear reserves from the hollow earth through an auto-remote function. Their individual enclave-borders still block trespassers, and their intake and exhaust holes still interchange oxygen or carbon dioxide with their immediate vault—the regenerated earthly atmosphere."

"Do these PNV enclaves work reciprocally with their immediate earthly habitat as well?" Roc asked.

"Yes, as there are more inhabitable lands and plant biomass concentrated in the northern hemisphere, thus more PNV enclaves exist there as well. In summertime, these remnants discharge more $CO_2$ to their immediate earthly habitat in exchange for more $O_2$ over an extended time."

"And this high dose of $CO_2$ helps vegetation thrive during the summertime."

"Yes, actually over such a long daylight, photosynthesis could release an equally high dose of $O_2$, but global climate change has threatened this ecosystem's balance. Thus, toward the end of summer and early fall, if highly critical $CO_2$ accumulation arises at particular times over certain stagnant zones, some people might experience fatigue or more serious symptoms such as hallucinations, and also under this situation normally inhibited OTS could possibly be strengthened to trigger ghost-like illusions. Yet this phenomenon won't emerge in other seasons when PNV enclaves interchange good and bad air with their earthly habitat worked differently. And Chinese would consider this phenomenon as the Ghost month! My Chinese classmates told me that some Chinese employees refuse to work overtime during that time of year, especially during the night of lunar mid-July; they believe their chances of running into ghosts will be highest during this particular night. During the ghost month, according to Chinese legend, it is believed that the hell-gate is opened widely. The hungry ghosts and spirits come out from the lower world to visit our Earth..."

"We caught a hungry owl in this case," Roc quipped. "Luckily we only have one night of Halloween."

"Huh! Fourteen hours of darkness has always created enough social problems and troubles for the police. Often the trouble is more human beings than mischievous ghosts on Halloween," she complained.

"Do you think the giant owl was misled into our habitat during this 'ghost month'?"

Dallas shrugged. "No, I'm not sure."

"Anyhow if it really emerged to our habitat during ghost month, it's too late now to send it back during the same window. What's your suggestion?" Roc asked.

"Hmm—I think we can try to release it on the lunar calendar's next auspicious time, as I believe during auspicious moments well-preserved PNV enclaves routinely release oxygen to our habitat. There should be a limited time that could last from a few minutes to a few hours for both borders' space-time to merge," Dallas said. "That could explain how y'all got trapped there."

"What if finding an auspicious time doesn't work out? Or the giant owl doesn't know how to return?"

"Well we could choose a day with a longer auspicious time, and also prove if your giant owl is really an amphisensus creature or not. If its habitat really is inside the PNV, do you think it won't know when and where to return home if we place it somewhere next to the gate?" Dallas challenged him. "Surely the PNV's returning signal will hasten the owl to return in time."

"No harm in giving it a try," Roc agreed.

The old antique clock on the wall struck ten times, interrupting their conversation, and this reminded Roc to set his watch to an accurate time.

"Let's go. It's time to give the owl an injection," he told her.

She followed behind him to the lab where she had assisted Adam and Cindy in housing the giant owl. Within the steel-barred cage, the owl was perched upright, looking much healthier than the last time she saw it. The feathers were clean and smooth, and its eyes were bright. It observed her coolly as she approached the cage.

Professor Rochester took out a big syringe and filled it with a measure of elixirantigen. After that he approached the giant owl cage and opened its gate. The owl clapped its beak and danced away across its perch, but did not flap or attempt to escape.

Dallas thought Roc looked comically small next to the owl. She wouldn't be brave enough to go into the enclosure that near to the owl and its weapons. At any time, it could strike at Roc with one foot and kill him instantly. She chewed her bottom lip as he raised the syringe toward the owl's chest and lifted feathers aside to find the skin.

The owl looked down to watch but did not interfere as Roc jabbed the needle in, pushed the plunger, then retreated, rubbing the spot with his other hand. He stepped back out of the cage and re-locked the door. The owl suddenly grew twice as big, raising all its feathers in a rouse, then shook all over like a dog. The feathers lay back down flat and the owl turned its head away from them, as though banishing them from thought.

Roc opened a refrigerator door on the other side of the lab and pulled out a limp rabbit. "It isn't much, but I can't keep whole deer in here." He tossed the rabbit into the cage. The owl continued to ignore them.

"I'm glad to see the owl recovering. Do you have any idea if it's male or female?" Dallas asked.

"No way to tell without two of them side-by-side. Females are larger, in birds of prey."

He led her back to the other end of the lab and opened the door to the mynah's room. She looked at him and gave a loud, raucous greeting. He pulled out a plastic sack full of giant biscuits. Dallas guessed them to be dog biscuits or pet cookies of some kind, but they were round and fist-sized like topless muffins, with a design of some sort stamped on one end. Roc gave the mynah one to eat. "Here you go, a special treat for you!"

Dallas asked, "Where did you order these enormous pet cookies from?"

"I got them freshly baked from Mr. Mau's kitchen."

"He also made and sold pet food?"

Roc chuckled softly and his face turned puckish. "No. These were specially made for his family."

"You mean for his dogs?"

"No...These special 'pet cookies' are for someone who behaved ruthlessly, like an animal." Then he chuckled mischievously. "...or talked innocently like a pet."

"What a sicko."

"I'm joking. It's people food." He took another one out of the sack, placed it on the empty cookie plate, and cut out a slice to hand to her. "Try this."

She stared at it. The outer pastry shell looked overcooked and spongy, and the filling had a greasy look to it, like hardened pudding. She gave him a disgusted gesture. "No, thank you."

"Come on! This is a Chinese double-yolk moon cake—or you want to try a bird nest moon cake?"

"Oh," she cried excitedly. "I've heard about Chinese moon cakes—they're for the Mid-Autumn Festival. I want to try both."

"Are you sure? Bird nest is an excretion of swift birds' saliva." He grinned at her again.

"It's okay. I heard that the bird nest is good to balance a lady's hormones and can help to improve a lady's complexion."

"Do you need it?" He looked at her faultless skin.

She laughed. "Can't hurt, might help. I'll try anything once."

"Some food scientists think bird nest is not really a super food except its amino acid is more difficult to digest."

"And therefore you burn more calories digesting it, sure." She nibbled at the filling of the moon cake slice. "This isn't that bad. It's not like an American pastry or something European like we're used to. The texture is weird."

"Don't eat too many moon cakes, or you're going to gain fat like a pig. That's the Chinese's description. Traditional moon cakes are made with lard, but I think these have a different oil in them."

She finished her slice of the moon cake and swallowed. "In that case, you better keep me away from moon cakes. You already stuffed me with cookies."

Dallas eyeballed the plastic sack of moon cakes. "How many moon cakes did you collect?"

"I filled a whole big garbage sack."

"No one wanted them?"

"Nope...There was not a single Chinese agent besides Sheriff Shih and he said he's on a diet. Some agents came in later and wondered if there were drugs inside the moon cakes. I simply bluffed to them that these were the special baked bird-nutrient cakes for Mr. Mau's two *Ornimegalonyx*, so they let me take every single piece."

Dallas shook her head at his duplicity.

"So will the giant owl be fit enough to be released soon?" she asked. "The next auspicious day when we're likely to access the PNV zone will be three days from now, and there will be a time in the late afternoon that lasts longest within this month."

"Yup...I think so, it's recovering pretty fast," he replied. "It might devour me right here if it becomes too strong. Can you be responsible for logistics and transport? We'll need to return it as close to the PNV zone as possible, of course."

"I'll take care of it. Thank you very much...I mean for the coffee, cookies, moon cakes, and the conversation." She felt tempted to take a few more pieces of bird nests-filling moon cakes. "I'm glad the owl is doing so well."

Roc stood as she did and gestured her out of the lab back toward the door she entered by. They walked together down the short hall.

Before Dallas stepped out the door, suddenly she slipped her hand into her big tote. She pulled out a box and then opened it to show something to Roc. "An archeologist friend gave me this artifact after returning from one of his most perilous expeditions." It was an odd, antenna-like metal prong shaped vaguely like prayer hands.

"Is it an antenna?" he asked suspiciously.

"That's what everyone who sees it thinks, but somehow nobody can tell me what metal this mysterious antique is made of. I'm particularly curious if it models that we should pray with our hands with palms together and all fingers straight and pointed upward to the sky so God can receive telepathic transmission effectively."

He looked at it curiously. "Perhaps engineers should consider it for their current antennas' design. And I think I'll try to pray this way tonight—maybe God will grant my wish."

Dallas met his gaze and smiled warmly. "And what would that wish be, Professor?"

"Can't tell, or it won't come true." He chuckled while bidding her goodbye.

# 18

## An Unexpected Hawaiian Trip

As soon as Dallas stepped in her downtown Alice office after returning from visiting Roc, she received an urgent call from Michael Hudson, a former high school classmate of hers, who was now working as the head of a marine research center based in Hawaii.

He was particularly worried when a whole pod of dolphins, despite being rescued and hauled back to the sea, kept returning during high tide to get stranded along a remote beach. He said after he read the most recent article of her report about the PNV, he decided to call her for advice. He believed someone like her might have a better idea how to solve this kind of mystery.

"Okay, I'll fly there as soon as possible today, but I have to get back to Texas on the earliest flight on the day after tomorrow," she informed him. Dallas started to get excited; she had been waiting for an opportunity to dive into the sea to take a look at any suspected oceanic PNV remnants.

This was a very unusual year, perhaps due to a certain distant primordial cosmic trajectory aligned with the earth activating obsolete signals. Secretly she hoped that once she had collected enough existing PNV remnant sites, she would be able to create her own software simulator called PNV Labyrinth Puzzles to help her figure out other unfound possible enclaves. Perhaps one day she could confirm the greatest mysteries—where the Garden of Eden was once located, whether the PNV had any co-existing relationships with the ley lines, and if earthquakes were actually triggered by the big bangs' incidental inflation, gravitation structural waves or cosmic force' trajectories, but they all had to be rectified by the earth's nuclear reserves and atmosphere before Earth's tectonic crusts were adjusted.

There was a knock on her office door. Her assistant entered at once and alerted her of a high priority ff-mail from another marine specialist from Borneo, seeking for her advice on an unusual phenomenon of a large scale of starfish being washed onshore continuously for several days on a remote coastal shoreline facing the South China Sea.

Dallas read it through quickly from her ff. "Hmm...he said there is no pollution, not a single trace of other dead marine creatures, neither was there a disturbance of the starfish breeding ground nor was there construction going on, and it happened on an isolated beach."

She felt like rushing to observe both remote sites; she looked up the clock on the wall, thinking of her priority and duty. She instantly made a quick decision.

She instructed her assistant how to reply to an ff-mail from the marine specialist from Borneo. "Ask him to update with my website's reports continuously, and explain to him perhaps the shoreline actually has been overlapped by a dormant PNV oceanic enclave. Once in a blue moon, when its orientation signals are activated by an obsolete primordial cosmic trajectory, if a group of starfish happen to pass by its opening, they might be able to perceive specific migratory signals but that would mislead them into a deathtrap. Usually the situation will stop after a few days, once the obsolete trajectory has shifted. Tell him I'll visit him as soon as possible right after my two commitments here in the United States, maybe four days from now."

While busy packing, Dallas reminded her assistant, "Please don't forget to inform Professor Rochester that I'll be going to Hawaii for two days to help Dr. Hudson, but I'll be back in time to help him to release the giant owl."

"Sure," her assistant replied; at the same time, she corrected the words that transferred from Dr. Dallas's recorded voice data on the replied ff-mail to the marine specialist from Borneo.

While reading the saucers' flight schedule to Hawaii, Dallas figured out if she chose to fly on a normal commercial saucer, she wouldn't be able to reach the scene before sunset. She rarely felt like bothering her influential Air Force friend for a favor, but when it came to her work, she tended to break this inhibition. Without any hesitation, she picked up the ff to enter the numbers she hardly used.

She was lucky; one of the fastest and most advanced saucers fetching a governor and his entourage was in transit, stopped now in Corpus Christi, and they would be ready to fly to Hawaii within an hour's time.

Her friend even kindly told her that he could arrange to delay the saucer's departure if she couldn't reach there on time, and once she landed in Honolulu, there would be a surveillance serescopter to pick her up right away to deliver her right to the beach where she needed to go. "Thank you. I think there is sufficient time for me to reach the Air Force base on time."

He actually had a bet that someday, due to his formidable designation in the U.S. Air Force, he might in turn require her expertise to assist him.

\* \* \* \* \* \*

When the serescopter descended on the remote Hawaiian beach a few hours later, it attracted a crowd of curious onlookers. Dr. Dallas seresdropped from the serescopter. Once she had landed safely on the beach, she gave a thumb-up sign and waved goodbye to the pilot and then she watched the serescopter flying off again.

At last, she turned to greet the curious crowd then walked past them. "Hey!" Her voice attracted Dr. Hudson's attention; he turned his head curiously to the sound. He smiled, called out her name excitedly and then ran toward her.

He gave her a big hug. "Gee, I can't believe my eyes! When I couldn't get hold of you through ff, I was wondering when you would be arriving."

"Sorry, in the rush I left my ff on my office desk," she told him. "I need to borrow your ff later."

"Sure. I thought you must be on the way in a great hurry. But I never dreamt you'd be dropping down from the sky like this."

Then he looked doubtfully at her diving suit and oxygen tank.

"I plan to dive and take a look down there. Is it possible?"

"Sure, why not? Do you want me to accompany you?"

"Sure, but it'll be at your own risk," she kindly warned him. She and Michael used to be infamous daredevils during their high school days. "Do you have any assistant to check the next four hours' weather conditions and level of tides? Are they flexible and alert enough to handle any unforeseen accidents or incidents?"

"Yes. My crew members are very well trained and all of them are professional divers."

"Sounds great. We have to hurry up before darkness falls. Are we able to leave the shore now?"

"Sure, but hold on a second." He pointed to a group of rescue workers. "They're your fans and some of them are my students from graduate school. Can you spend some time talking to them about PNV?"

"Sure why not? But just briefly," she agreed.

They approached the gathered college students, enabling her to a get closer look at the stranded dolphins. Their cries really could spear ones' heart. Dallas finally understood why these compassionate rescue workers were tirelessly trying their best to haul the big intelligent creatures back to the deeper sea.

"I can't believe the most intelligent mammals after human beings continuously get themselves stranded onshore," Dr. Hudson lamented. "We had some stranded whales and dolphins in the past years, but this year the number of casualties have increased and also the days of occurrence have lasted longer than before. They're keen to know the possible reasons."

Dallas decided if no one mentioned the giant owl, she wouldn't talk about it. "Howdy!" Dallas greeted them in the Texans' way.

"Aloha!" The enthusiastic crowd cheered back in the Hawaiians' way.

"...Hmm...Let's cut it short, as we all have limited time...Probably y'all have heard of ley lines but not PNV right?"

"Yes."

"No."

"Yes...We actually learned about ley lines from your website," one of them yelled back.

Dallas gave them a sweet smile before continuing. "But not every one of y'all has read my website, right? Right now, I'm still doing my research to figure out which cosmic trajectories would align with the earth on auspicious and inauspicious days. Ancient civilizations' astrological markers, especially Chinese, would mark them down precisely on the lunar calendar, which is altered yearly. And I suspect there is another obsolete primordial cosmic trajectory that could also align periodically with the earth, but it would enable temporary amalgamation of our habitat with the mysterious, abandoned ancient PNV enclaves. PNV stands for Primitive Navigational Vault, and PNV enclaves are their shuttered encrypted remnants that hover inside our atmospheric space-time. That's why we must protect our environment, as all environmental abuses and pollution could exacerbate or confusingly prolong space-time merging between our Earth and PNV enclaves—such as unpiloted hypersonic saucers' vibrations combined with the ozone layer's erosion, which could intensify ultrasonic cosmic rays' penetration to infiltrate deeper and longer into the PNV enclaves. Even some previously inaccessible dormant PNV enclaves could be merged with Earth under this abnormality."

A woman in the crowd interrupted her, "So what has this PNV got to do with the stranded dolphins?"

"Let's assume that there was a dormant strip of PNV oceanic migratory route remnant that happened to be shifting and thus overlapping inshore from the ocean..." She looked at their blank stares; quickly she paraphrased and simplified, "Imagine during an earthquake, if there was a straight, ten-mile stretch of highway that was shifted and broken off abruptly from a hundred-mile highway. All those drivers who were trapped on the broken fragment could drive straight into an ocean from a cliff. Especially right after the earthquake, if there was no warning sign of a ruined highway."

One of the students argued in a hostile tone, "But MPPS in the car should be able to detect danger ahead and warn the drivers in time."

Dr. Hudson said, "But most of the time, drivers turn off MPPS when they know their way. MPPS can be noisy and annoying." He looked at his students; they all kept quiet, so he continued, "Y'all know dolphins are able to communicate among themselves, similar to how we communicate with our ff."

Dallas added, "The dolphins use sonar to hunt. Certain cosmic ultrasonic or infrasonic waves could intercept dolphins' infrasonic communication waves. The successful interference could result in either deafening amplified constructive waves to cause them to go crazy or soundless neutralized destructive waves to cause them loss of communication with each other. Normally, the dormant PNV migratory or navigational routes are inaccessible, but some obsolete primordial cosmic trajectories have successfully activated certain PNV enclaves' primitive orientation signals due to successful interference. Reactivated migratory signals usually just mislead a specific species of marine life, but successfully intercepted navigational signals might lure different species and sometimes even certain unknown prehistoric creatures to reappear within our habitat."

"So the released dolphins kept returning? What can you explain about the suicidal behavior?" one of them asked.

"If those unlucky dolphins happened to swim close by the entrance of the suddenly activated access, they would receive obsolete primordial signals to migrate into such access. They're controlled by signals within a transmitting range and specific time to migrate into a deadly trap. Imagine if a migratory communication signal reception range is within a mile width but ten-mile length, in that case you have to haul the dolphins far away from such transmitting range. Just like if we got lost in a PNV remnant, we'd be like a bird that accidentally flew in a room through one of its windows. The bird would lose its orientation. If we just move it to another room, it'd probably return again to the first room unless we release it outside the house or it gets lucky enough to find a way out through one of the many windows of the house on its own." Dallas explained.

Dr. Hudson was impressed by Dallas's explanation and he noticed that her charm had also begun to attract more curious crowds. Soon they heard someone calling out loudly from the beach in obvious frustration, "Dr. Dallas, can you predict how long this situation will go on?"

She projected her voice over the crowd. "I think this tragedy won't persist for too long; usually this uncertainty can be blocked by very thick clouds, outer space dust clouds or we may just need to wait until its trajectory shifts. This unusual situation could occur for fifteen minutes once or twice daily and last three to five days or sometimes it could even occur once or twice daily for a few minutes at a time for a week or so. We have no way of knowing."

She glanced at the sad face of her high school classmate. "So what's your plan now?"

"I think the best way is to use large fishing nets to toll them back to the deep sea far away from the vicinity. Luckily, it's not whole pods of whales coming ashore. If those gigantic mammals were out of the water, their great weight could literally crush them to death."

"I don't have any idea how vast an area this overlapped PNV strait covers. Tolling the stranded dolphins away from the coast sounds logical and workable, but this time round, I brought along a newly-invented device that may stop the tragedy. We soon will figure out if it works or not."

Someone called to them from the boat, "Dr. Hudson, everything is set. Are we ready to go now?"

"Sure." Dr. Hudson gestured for Dallas to move toward the boat, and they marched up the gangplank.

# On Board with a Hostile Captain

Upon boarding the boat, Dallas introduced herself to everyone. She found that they were courteous, greeting her politely, but soon resumed their respective chores. Presently, one of Dr. Hudson's crew passed her a list of information that she requested earlier on. She gave the data a quick study; soon plans had already set in her mind.

"Attention please, gentlemen," she called. "First of all, we have to search for a suspected PNV remnant."

"What's that? The sea is so vast where do we find it?" The boat's captain gestured with a sweep of one massive arm, a scowl on his weather-hardened face.

"Oh, sorry, Captain, you were obviously not in the crowd just now. A PNV remnant is a special place in the ocean where we may be able to find creatures of myth such as mermaids. How do we find it? Just a minute." She typed something on her ff; soon a heading of "How to Find a Possible PNV Enclave's Entrance on Water" appeared on the ff screen.

She read it out aloud for everyone: "We're looking for anomalies on the water surface like unusual ripples, vortices and swirls. On occasion all gadgets onboard may go haywire; unpredicted sudden squalls will fall frequently just on that particular area. The area will remain misty longer than other areas..."

She stopped abruptly when she noticed the captain had turned his attention elsewhere. The crew was still busy on their chores and obviously, Dr. Hudson was the only one listening to her.

She saw Dr. Hudson blink to hint her to leave them alone, then he gestured her to take a look at MPPS where the dolphins got stranded. To reconfirm, she looked out of the boat; she saw a dozen dead dolphins on the shore headed toward the north, then she keyed in something to the MPPS.

After that she pointed out those dead dolphins to Dr. Hudson. "We'll go to the south following those dead bodies' alignment; I suspected that's where those dead dolphins are coming from.

"Captain, let's go now toward the south now," she told him.

The boat headed south for the next forty-five minutes. Even with the help from MPPS, Dallas could find nothing unusual on the sea surface. "Can we take a break a little bit further there?" Dallas pointed for the captain to an area where she saw no seagulls flying, thus she got curious.

After the pilot took a look at her pointed direction, he shook his head. "No, I won't go there. No local fisherman here wants to get any nearer to that little risky 'Bermuda Triangle.' Before they get any fish their compasses go haywire. Often their boats are almost capsized by strong underwater currents. Sometimes sudden storms or sudden thick fog covers that ghostly area particularly. No fish can be found there, either, that's why there's no seagulls there," he told her.

Dallas raised her hands in exasperation. "Captain Jones, why didn't you tell me earlier? That's the unusual place I was talking about and have been trying to look for during the last forty-five minutes after we traveled offshore for twenty nautical miles." His hostility toward her pissed her off.

He simply shrugged. "Sorry, lady. Okay, I'll take you there now, but I'm the captain of this boat. For everyone's safety on board, I'll only stop somewhere near it."

Soon they anchored the boat in a calm place to refresh themselves. After peeling off the tangerine skins, the old pilot tossed them out to the sea; though he detected some disapproving glances, he simply ignored them. The fish and other marine critters would eat the orange peels. When he came across a rotten orange, he simply treated it as a softball; he threw it out as far as possible. Everyone's glances followed the tossed orange and after it splashed in and bobbed back to the surface, to everyone's amazement, it swirled in circles.

"Oh gosh, there is a swirl bigger than our boat not so far from us," she cried out. She wondered if she could ask the captain to move the boat a little nearer to it, so she could take a dive, but soon she refuted such an idea. *No, something must be down there!*

"If you want to dive in there, I won't be able to get you out later," the pilot warned her, as if he could read her mind.

"I want more oranges."

One after another, she threw all the oranges to that particular southward direction. "There are two big swirls and the water in between the two swirls is quiet. We're going down there to take a look, but let me confirm it from MPPS first."

"The swirls will stop soon," the captain revealed to her.

"How you know?" She saw the pilot shrug again with an unmistakably cheeky grin. She finally realized he was trying to make a fool out of her.

"Every fisherman here knows that it will swirl for five minutes after every sixty-minute interval."

"According to your information, we better go down as soon as the swirls stop and come out before it starts again. Dr. Hudson, let's get ready."

"Do you want this rope to guide you back here just in case?" the captain offered to Dallas.

She looked at the useless stern rope—she thought if she was on ground, she might be able to use it to lasso a wild horse. "Nope, thanks."

He offered it to Dr. Hudson instead, who told her, "This type of rope is commonly used by divers for underwater cave diving, it guides a diver to return if he loses his way, but sometimes it accidentally gets tangled, which could endanger a diver's life if it doesn't get cut off promptly. Yes, Captain, we'll use it, thanks."

As soon as the swirls stopped, the old pilot cautioned them, "Remember, try to avoid getting closer to any of the two vortexes, even if they stop swirling. We'll wait up here for an hour. It's getting dark and soon there will be high tides."

He worriedly looked out the sea and the sky; they looked so far so fine. He had never stayed out this late at this particular "Bermuda triangle" before.

Dallas and Dr. Hudson merely gave the captain a nod; without delay, they both dived in the water.

Just few yards underwater, they discovered that the indirect cause of the swirls was arrays of crumbled underwater ruins, somehow undetectable by MPPS; obviously it was an ancient site.

Just like what the captain told them before—they couldn't find any sign of life down here. No fish, no coral and no plankton, which should supposedly thrive in this rocky undersea habitat.

Dallas began to suspect they were now actually diving inside a ruined oceanic PNV migration track. Suddenly she recalled something; she grabbed the wrist of Dr. Hudson to check his watch. She kept staring at the watch for a while but she couldn't figure out if it had been moving faster or slower than normal. Unable to determine the answer, she released his wrist.

She continued to scrutinize the surroundings for any anomalies. Despite its lifelessness, her main aim was trying to find this ruined PNV migration track entrance, but it was a hard task, as she found big holes and small holes everywhere.

Sudden, loud, strange sounds caused them to turn their heads to locate the source. Small rocks were falling down beside a hole which was just big enough for a person to swim through; soon a dolphin was struggling and penetrating the hole. Then one after another, more dolphins began to enter through the hole and started swimming toward them.

They had actually witnessed a transitional moment of a reactivated oceanic PNV enclave that overlapped onshore. The migratory signal had begun to mislead dolphins toward their deathtrap.

In order to stop the dolphins from continuing to enter through the hole, Dallas signaled the still stunned Dr. Hudson. They quickly swam toward the entrance hole, where Dallas placed a small, experimental sonic device that could tune itself automatically to neutralize incoming ultrasonic cosmic waves.

While they waited for its self-tuning to take effect, they couldn't know their scheduled rendezvous had passed more than an hour ago for those on board the boat who nervously anticipated their return.

They were so focused on observing the success of the newly invented device that they overlooked the end of Hudson's guide rope being sucked up accidentally from the very fringe of the swirl. An accelerating force gradually moved Dr. Hudson toward one of the largest vortices.

It continued to suck up more rope, and when the speed accelerated, Dr. Hudson began to feel his body being dragged toward the big swirl. When Dallas saw what had happened, she took out a knife to cut off the guide rope without a second thought.

The cut-off actually generated a force that ejected him to within a foot of the swirl; Dallas quickly caught one of his arms to drag him back to a safe position.

Up on the boat, when the two divers didn't appear at their appointed time, the worried pilot and assistants decided to wait a little longer.

Soon they noticed the boat had a tug-of-war between the anchor and the dangerous swirls.

"Shit, something is wrong. Should we cut off the stern rope?" An anxious assistant hesitated to cut off the guide rope, lest his boss got lost underwater.

"No! Don't do it. They'll cut it off if anything happens to them," one of them objected, and the rest of them seemed hesitant too.

When the boat started shaking violently, and the old captain noticed they couldn't make a decision, without their approval he suddenly released the anchor and maneuvered the boat toward the shore at its highest speed against the pulling force caused by the stern rope.

The four assistants almost fell overboard. One of them shouted angrily to the captain after stabilized himself, "Damn! Stop it now, Captain! You could have killed us and maybe the one down there too. I need to check the stern now."

When the assistant pulled the stern rope, his spine chilled when he didn't feel any weight on it; he predicted that there was nothing on its end. "Can you move the boat back to where we anchored before? Two of my colleagues are going to dive down there to check out what happened."

They waited a while until the swirl stopped. Two more divers were just about to take a dive under everyone's worried glances when to their great relief they saw two heads pop out from the surface not far from them.

Immediately, the two scientists swam toward the boat. After they were assisted aboard, Dr. Hudson quickly instructed, "Inform the dolphin rescue workers that at least five more dolphins are on their way to the shore now. Tell them not to travel into this hazardous PNV remnant zone, to avoid unforeseen or unnecessary risk, but to release those dolphins maybe ten miles away from this coast. We already placed the auto tuning sonar device on the PNV activated entrance spot; hopefully, it will work until everything returns to normal."

"I hope those confused dolphins that got suddenly barred from the ruined PNV entrance were okay." Dr. Hudson's assistant showed his concern.

"Don't worry," Dallas answered, "soon the gadget will neutralize the migratory signal and they'll choose to follow the signals that radiate from one of their normal daily navigation routes."

"Yeah, you know what? I think those confused dolphins will yelp like crazy bitches who can't find mates when they're in season," The old pilot interrupted sarcastically.

Dallas ignored his vague provocation; he probably found her attractive but couldn't rationalize that with either her intelligence or being in charge. "You're right, Captain Jones. Their outrageous behavior is being controlled by a kind of hormone triggered by a signal, sight or smell." She gave him a killing sweet smile. "We could even see those zealous dolphins; one by one they followed each other tightly and emerged by twisting and rushing through the compact, tunnel-like entrance hole." She then winked flirtatiously at him.

"Can I take you out for a beer after this?"

Immediate protest came from the two assistants. "We want to come too."

The old pilot stared at them murderously. "I should have moved the boat in such a way that you all got thrown off to feed those jaws."

Dr. Hudson gave a throaty chuckle; he had long missed Dallas's flirtatiousness since their high school days. Few could resist Dallas back then, and clearly, she still "had it."

He cleared his throat, calling back Dallas's attention. "My watch is slow according to this ff, what happened?" He remembered her trying to drag his wrist to read the time.

"Hmm...time warp happened. Let's check the differences. I need the record."

"Should we go home now? It's getting dark and misty," Captain Jones asked.

"Sure," Dr. Hudson replied.

# A Day Off in Hawaii

The continuous wake-up alarm had finally created enough annoyance to awaken the still sleepy Dallas; reflexively she glared at the digital alarm clock mounted on the bedside table that showed 09:00. She wondered why she still felt tired, lethargic and fatigued despite after an eight-hour sleep; instinctively, her hand reached out to check her forehead, but after checking, she thought she was in perfect health.

Perhaps she needed some fresh morning air. Reluctantly, she got out of bed and walked toward a transparent glass window panel; simultaneously, a flashy red Ferrari now drove toward the hotel entrance. The driver braked abruptly to avoid a collision with a pedestrian.

For a moment, she was as stunned as both the pedestrian and the Ferrari driver. After regaining her composure, she noticed she had slept overnight in a T-junction room.

She started to do some stretching exercises as though in a trance. Fifteen minutes later she suddenly remembered she had an appointment with Dr. Hudson. She rushed through a shower and went down to the hotel lounge for breakfast.

Thirty minutes later, Dr. Hudson picked her up from the hotel. He stared at her pale look in concern. "How are you Dallas?"

"I feel a bit sleepy still. Even a cup of strong coffee hasn't yet revived me." Then she told him what she had seen with the near accident.

"Hmm...luckily the pedestrian didn't get knocked down. A few years ago, a Chinese *feng shui* master friend of mine checked out of this hotel immediately after only a one-night stay. He told me our bodies act as a sponge to stale poisoned air, radioactive positive ions or bad energies that likely get trapped in the stagnant zone of a T-junction. In the short term it can cause fatigue, depression, lethargy and aches, pains and complaints, and for long term it can cause certain chronic illnesses."

"Perhaps these harmful metallic particles in the PNV clustered-bubbles tend to accumulate in T-zones due to being heavier," she speculated. "What do you know of *feng shui*? Is that a thing, living in Hawaii?"

"Ah—it's my newest hobby." He pulled his car past the hotel T-junction.

"Hmm..." Dallas yawned and stretched. "Last night when I checked in here late, I didn't see my room was situated in the T-junction...Your *feng shui* master friend could be right. I feel my vitality being drained or sucked up by something despite a whole long night's sleep. I doubt it's just saucer-lag or a holdover from our dive yesterday. We weren't under that long or deep."

"However, my *feng shui* master friend told me for anyone born on a specific time of the tiger, dragon or snake year, bad energies won't be a serious threat," Dr. Hudson said.

"We are the year of the horse, unfortunately." She sighed. "I wonder if during the years of tiger, dragon and snake, there was a specific cosmic emission infused in the atmosphere during a specific time of a day that promoted defensive cells or antibodies developing in the fetuses for them to reflect bad energy in their later days."

"You've studied Eastern Philosophy and Chinese astrology, and I read your references to it on your website. Let me tell you something interesting—the Chinese consider a newborn baby to be a year old, as they count that the new life began on the first day of conception, yet they count their birth date based on the zodiac."

"That's why many people don't believe in astrology, as it doesn't have conformity," she chuckled.

"The Chinese also only choose an auspicious timing for a baby to arrive in this world—especially when they only get to have one. In order to produce lucky babies, some Chinese women prefer induction or C-section to make sure their babies are delivered during a specific auspicious time and date."

"If there really was such a thing as a cosmic ray brain scan on a fetus that could produce a baby-genius, then I would also calculate the Chinese auspicious date and time of the fifth week embryonic period when the brain begins to form," Dallas pointed out. "Long ago, I read an article from a group of scientists at Germany's Max Planck Institute for Demographic Research. They reported that the highest achievers in school usually were born in September. I speculate it's because their fifth week of embryonic development more likely fell into the auspicious Chinese New Year, the very early spring. And this article also reported that those who struggled at school and scored substantially lower in national achievement tests were the August babies, and coincidentally, the Chinese lunar calendar's Ghost Month is more likely to fall around August. This report also announced that people born in autumn live longer than those born in spring, and they're less likely to become as ill in old age. Do you know that for babies born in early spring, their first trimester period falls more likely into the Chinese Ghost Month?"

Dr. Hudson chuckled. "Very interesting, but I hope such research has adjusted and taken into account the facts that due to age cutoffs for school registration, kids with September birthdates are older than all the other students and therefore have more developed brains. I read that only the imperial household in ancient China would emphasize the importance of such *feng shui* calculation, discretely based on both conception and birth date and time, to produce a future king. And another secret is July babies have higher probability to turn into a great leader; the Biblical Joseph was believed to be born in midsummer, and the month of July itself was named for Julius Caesar."

"In my experience, ordinary people see astrology as bunk," Dallas remarked. "By the way, do you know that both Adolf Hitler and Saddam Hussein were born in April? The fifth week of their embryonic periods could have fallen during Ghost Month."

"Hmm...no, could it be coincidence?" he wondered. "*Feng shui* calculating is subject to change every hour, every day and every year. It's a complicated esoteric knowledge. Let me tell you something interesting—once my *feng shui* master friend calculated my son's time and date of birth, he predicted my son would be a genius."

"Wow, isn't he?"

He shrugged and replied uncertainly, "Hmm...he has photographic memory. You think it's genetic or because his fetus brain was 'scanned' by an alien cosmic ray from outer space?"

"Of course most parents would like to hear that their kids have inherited their high IQ. Aren't you smart?" Dallas winked at him. He smiled sheepishly; she remembered he only studied the night before exams yet he scored straight A's.

"Ahem..." He gave a throaty chuckle then smartly slipped off to discuss other topics with her.

Twenty minutes later, they reached a compound with rolls of modern architectural buildings. Dallas immediately spotted the marine laboratory; the block was built architecturally in shape of a dolphin.

After Dr. Hudson parked his car under one of its "fins," he led her to enter the "mouth," which was the reception area. Upon entering the building, Dallas inhaled a refreshing smell in contrast to most marine laboratories' specific fishy odors. An impressive display of colorful fish swam in various large and small aquariums.

"These are some uncommon types of fish I've collected from all over the world."

"How many of them altogether?"

"Seven hundred and seventy-seven."

"Seven-seven-seven! That's your license plate digits too!"

"Yes."

Then he led her to a small aquarium where he showed her the tiniest fish in the world, which he collected from Malaysia few years ago. "I only brought two back to the States, but you see I have a whole school now." He wore a proud smile.

"Wow! What kind are they?"

"*Paedocyris progenetica*. Okay. Let's go check the results first." Dr. Hudson gestured for her to follow him to the laboratory.

Within the lab, several technicians and assistants were busy examining the digital microscope slides smeared with the collected water droplets taken from the ruined PNV migration track.

"Any result?" Dr. Hudson asked them.

"Sorry, Doc. We haven't found anything yet. Now we're looking at the last water sample. Here are the previous samples' results..." One of his assistants showed them the reports on ff-screen.

Another assistant called her over, "Dr. Dallas, please take a look of these slides here. I'm eager to hear your opinion of the lifelessness over this oceanic PNV remnant." Dallas noticed this girl had been among the audience yesterday.

Dallas expected to see no life, but she still moved over to take a look at the slides. "Obviously, this underwater lifeless PNV remnant wouldn't even allow any photosynthesis to take place. Probably the *noctilucent* light functioned by the OTS Ray Spectrum could never promote any propagation on any non-primeval organisms or could never germinate any non-primordial spores thus disabling the most basic thriving of living organisms or plankton to dwell in there."

"Aha—are some PNV enclaves not barren?" the assistant asked.

"Yes, if there were some primeval spores or primeval organisms that accidentally entered such a PNV enclave, somehow they possess such capacity to collect limited sunlight to radiate as *noctilucent* light through the OTS Ray Spectrum, thus eventually they would be able to germinate, thrive and form a colony there. Such vegetation would have duo-capacities to receive both limited solar light and radiation such as *noctilucent* light through the OTS Ray Spectrum in order to let photosynthesis take place. We call the kind of ancient vegetation that thrives in PNV amphisensus vegetation," Dallas informed her.

"Excuse me, Dr. Dallas, this is your coffee," a secretary offered her.

"Oh, thank you very much." She sipped the coffee but discovered she didn't feel as tired anymore. "Michael, what's that refreshing smell in here? I think it's something that has just refreshed and revived me," she asked.

"It's the latest zionizer, upgraded by one of my brothers from conventional ionizers. He found a few kinds of healthy negative ions top up with conventionally found negative ions to invigorate our vital energy and support general health. Ahem...are you suspecting the hotel T-junction's stagnant harmful positive ions or sucker particles possibly sucked your body's good ions away to cause your tiredness?"

"Oh yeah, maybe that's fact. When the PNV was abandoned, its shattered remnants were exposed under different level of destruction and recovery modes, thus the densities of sucker components and OTS were varied in different PNV remnants. Some of those tossed out floating cluster-bubbles with heavy matter and positive ions could be most harmful due to their auto-repair recovery particles being absent. They would usually accumulate over stagnant zones without winds," she informed him.

"Let's go to my office." Dr. Hudson waved her out the lab door. "My office is just next door to the lab."

Upon stepping in Dr. Hudson's office, she saw many *feng shui* books displayed on the bookshelves.

Dr. Hudson told her, "Well, when talking about *feng shui*, probably a few thousand years ago, Chinese *feng shui* masters discovered that our living environment consisted of bad energy, they called it *sha qi*, killing *qi*, and good energy, *sheng qi*, growing *qi*, co-existing in us. *Feng shui* masters believe that houses with good *feng shui* can trap and generate good energy to augur in all good prospects, money, luck, power and health. From overpopulated China, *Feng shui* masters talk about bad and good particles likely to accumulate in certain areas, discovered through empirical experience. To improve a bad *feng shui* in a bedroom, they find ways to trap '*Yan Qi*,' solar air, and eliminate '*Sha qi*,' killing air, or balance them."

"Hmm ....obviously they are helping and advising people how to trap the good negative ions but eliminate harmful positive ions in order to promote good health in their living environment. But the old Chinese pseudoscience practices and herbal medicines are still not accepted by many scientists and Western doctors, even practices and herbal medicines based on personal experiences and empirical knowledge gathered for the past five thousand years."

"Pseudoscience is like wind that we can't see, but we only can see its aftermath," Dr. Hudson remarked.

"Actually, do you know why those Biblical figures could live such long lives?" Dallas asked.

"How?"

"Because they dwelled in the PNV. It was once an almost timeless, secluded canopy on Earth before it was abandoned by the creation-host." Then she told him about the existence of the giant owl she and Roc had been chasing and the government's interest in it.

"Really—it's more than six feet tall?" He shook his head, stunned for a moment.

"Sure. Do you believe giant creatures once lived on Earth?"

"Hmm...food chain theory. If there were giant humans, surely there would have been other giant creatures and vegetation too," he reasoned. "But they're extinct now."

"So what happened?" He realized time had passed too fast; they had not chatted like this for more than ten years.

"Well, we caught the giant owl again, but it was badly injured and now it's locked in Professor Rochester's lab."

"Good gracious, giant owl! Now should I add another new hobby to become an avid follower of PNV enclaves?" he joked.

"When the creation-host abandoned his PNV, some of those shattered PNV fragments recovered under their own respective auto-repair capacity and turned independently into self-reliant enclaves. If PNV enclaves with larger terrain still carry their own inflated navigation and migration signals with sufficient essentials and elements reserved within the enclaves protected from trespassers by a sucker fence, the living things confined in there would not be endangered. These incredibly fitted amphisensus creatures that possess the highest survival instinct with intrinsic altruism would be able to thrive, breed and adapt through millions of years in this crossroad zone of fine climate and abundant food."

"How would the sucker fence give warning to trespassers?"

"The PNV fence on the land would possess sucker particles and OTS. They either produce frequencies that repel any earthly living things and human trespassers or render them visionless before they get any nearer to its border. Then the fence on the air either produces heavy turbulence or triggers strong digital and electronic interference to aircraft that try to fly any nearer to it. The forbidden fence in the ocean always produces deadly water spouts, giant tides and strong underwater currents that spiral a ship to traceless destinations. It also triggers strong interference or causes any digital or electronic mechanism to go haywire, which makes a ship instantly lose its direction, control and selected functions."

"Hmm...Dangerous invisible traps of nature. My friends all talk about dragon lines and ley lines—you think they're associated with this PNV?" he asked.

"Yes," she replied. "I presume they were the original residues of PNV tracks, although their original foundations, structures and components had already been cast out, destroyed or shifted. However, their residues still could emanate energy periodically when they intersect with primordial cosmic trajectories."

"Sounds very interesting."

The screensaver of Dr. Hudson's ff suddenly attracted Dallas's attention; shimmering green aurorae across the arctic star field. "Awesome! You know where auroras originated from?" she asked him.

"Yes, of course...They're from PNV." Dr. Hudson was pulling her leg; he gave her a cheeky smile and gestured for her to continue.

"Come on, it's not funny. Without PNV, our Earth might still look like any of those unlivable planets." She lifted her eyebrows and shrugged slightly. "When PNV started to deteriorate, the *noctilucent* particles also gradually inflated to the poles where there was less sunlight. This aurora actually was the proto *noctilucent* particles originating from the PNV atmospheric fence to store light when available and release it when the light was absent. When tertiary atmospheric vault was inflated, *noctilucent* particles shifted almost entirely to the north and south poles would store both sunlight and nuclear reserves' light from hollow earth and radiate them as magnificent streamers of colored light over their horizons during the night to promote general growth and health for living things there."

"North and South Poles, including Antarctica, and parts of that two poles' open oceans are the regions with the least intense sunlight on Earth and also where lightning doesn't strike, that's why they really need aurorae."

"Yes. Wow, you are very knowledgeable." She was really impressed. "Do you know why there were no rainbows before the flood?"

"Are you testing my general knowledge?" He raised one eyebrow.

"No, I want to test your Bible knowledge."

"Genesis 2:5b: '...for the Lord God had not caused it to rain upon the earth.' Genesis 2:6: 'But there went up a mist from the earth, and watered the whole face of the ground.'"

"Oh gosh, you can even recite from memory, bravo!"

"According to what I learned from you, I guess that during the antediluvian eon, vapors went upward from the ground, as the ground was closed to PNV atmosphere. Its situation was actually like when we walk in the clouds on the top of a mountain, there was no rain due to not enough water droplets reaching the upper atmosphere, but after the Antediluvian, more water from lower fountains of the deep and the upper expanse's floodgates remained in the tertiary atmosphere. The global water had increased, thus there was rain. When the sunlight and raindrops interacted, rainbows formed and the rainbow also benefited mankind as a great sterilizer to replace aurorae, especially for the equatorial and tropic regions."

Dallas nodded. "During the age right before the flood, a decrease of vapors went upward, but thickened atmosphere on the wilderness Earth was either partially perforated or eroded due to anthropogenic disasters. There were frequent series of droughts and famines; the water in rivers and inside PNV remnants was running low. The flood also marked the complete collapse of abandoned PNV zones on Earth. I suspect those antediluvians were not just highly corrupt, immoral and promiscuous but they also abused their environments with their high tech lethal weapons."

Dr. Hudson suggested, "From the downfall of ancient antediluvian civilization, we learn that any highly assimilated civilization with advanced technologies that begins to gear up with highly lethal weapons and deploy espionage surely also begins to head for its doom. Think about Rome, or the Soviet Union. These activities denoted the incoming major social uprising or warfare caused mainly by military strength competitions, religious and racial conflicts. I highly suspect antediluvian civilization was geared up with the highest advancement of ammunition and technology, including laser beam guns and nuclear bombs. It was the civilization when our earthly humans were actually under the supervision and manipulation of those callous, inhuman, predatory alien-outlaws, and good aliens rivaled them constantly."

Dallas thought he really could read her mind; just like those old days, very often he would help her express what she wished to say. She wondered if she would ever reach that stage with Roc. Some of the things that came out of his mouth she would never think in a million years. Maybe they were too different.

The antique Black Forest cuckoo clock on the wall struck once.

"Let's go for a quick lunch. There's a five-star Chinese restaurant nearby, owned by local Chinese-Americans," Dr. Hudson proposed.

"Sure, sounds good to me," she accepted happily.

# From Hawaii Back to the Texas Outback

A big trademark of a phoenix hung outside the Chinese restaurant next to the trade name. Hudson remarked, "I came across some articles that said the phoenix was an asexual creature."

"Yes, usually the most primitive living things on Earth were asexual and they were also ultra-resilient," Dallas agreed.

"Ha...I think the name of the restaurant also reflects its owner, Mary," he said amusedly.

Dallas returned a perplexed glance.

"You'll understand soon." He gave her a wink.

Upon entering the Chinese restaurant, a Chinese man promptly approached them with a warm greeting and welcome. He seemed to know Dr. Hudson, who Dallas gathered was a regular at this establishment. He called the man "Mary," which puzzled her. Dallas could feel that Mary eyed her attentively while ushering them to their table.

Once he left, Dallas asked Dr. Hudson in a hush, "His name is Mary?"

He cued her to look at the Chinese man's throat and then she began to realize that "he" was actually a woman; she finally understood why Hudson had winked at her just before they entered the restaurant.

Mary was listening to a waitress attentively. Dallas whispered back to Dr. Hudson, "I think that's her girlfriend."

They immediately hushed and turned their smiles toward an elderly Chinese man who waved and walked toward them. Dr. Hudson stood up to greet him affectionately. "Hey, Dr. Pui, how are you? May I introduce you my friend Dr. Dallas from Texas?" Hudson indicated Dallas with a wave. "Dr. Dallas, Dr. Pui is Mary's father."

She extended her hand to give him a handshake and they exchanged pleasantries while Hudson resumed his seat.

"I read from a magazine that your daughter once even worked for Paris's Maxim. How did she end up opening a Chinese restaurant instead?" Dr. Hudson asked.

"Ha...because she wants her Chinese restaurant to win some Michelin stars."

"One day she'll win many stars for sure—the food here is fabulous," Hudson said. "Is she running this alone or with her friend or...husband?"

Dallas thought that was a bit nosy, even for a regular.

"No, she is not married, and actually I am helping her right now to entertain her guests," Dr. Pui joked. "When she was young, I calculated her fate and realized that she has no *Yuan* with men."

Most Chinese-Americans were still conservative, but this Chinese man hinted to them very subtly that his daughter was a lesbian, and he was okay with that. Dallas was impressed by his open-mindedness. "Can you read my fate?"

"Sure. You write down your birth date and birth time; I need those details. In the art of *feng shui*, a combination of the five elements can help to foster good energies. Thus, a person's birth place, time, date and season would be calculated, for an example if he born lacking of water among the five, he should introduce water into his living environment. By combining the productive cycle of the five elements, good fortune would be taken into his lives. Please excuse me a moment, I need to go collecting some tools from the office."

Soon he reemerged with a small plate of Chinese rice cakes and an ff. "Are you surprised? In this mid-twenty-first era, all Chinese *feng shui* masters are actually using modern gadgets to calculate ones' fate and different kinds of *feng shui* new software also have been kept releasing."

He then showed them something after taking a seat across from Dallas. "Look at this *feng shui* software; it works a lot faster compared to my grandpa's days." He keyed in the necessary information and waited for the result. "It saves *feng shui* masters' probably ten times' less time and accuracies."

"Where did you learn all these...?" Dallas asked.

"I learned it from my grandfather while none of my ten siblings was interested, and I only become more interested in *feng shui* after my son released a series of the world fastest *feng shui* reading intelligent software. Up to date, it has sold more than three million copies and it was also his gift for my 70th birthday," he told them with a soft chuckle in obvious pride of his son.

Then he informed them, "About sixty years ago after my grandfather read my fate. He said that I would be destined to work as a *feng shui* master, but I went into medical school instead. Only after I retired as a surgeon from John Hopkins then I decided coming here to Hawaii staying with my daughter. After I noticed many *feng shui* masters couldn't calculate convincingly, I began to give some free *feng shui* master classes and consultations as pastime. My forefathers were the *feng shui* masters cum Chinese doctors working for imperial and servicing royal households. Their jobs, besides consulting ones' fates either by palm reading, face reading or calculation based of time and date of birth, they also helped to locate dragon lines for their kings or emperors to build their palaces and graveyards.

"Now please show me your right palm." After he read her palm for some time, he read her left palm. "Hmm...Dr. Dallas, do you have any boyfriend?" Before she could give him an answer, he continued, "I think you are going to get married soon and more likely your husband will be a smart, prominent or a rich man. Your facial feature has fate of a phoenix like Jacqueline Kennedy but you will have a faithful husband."

*Who doesn't like to hear that kind of smooth talk?* Dallas thought. Anyhow, she was amused; she giggled happily like a little girl. "Wow! If someone rich or prominent asks me to marry him, I'll definitely invite you for my wedding." She immediately thought of the poor yet smart Roc, who had made a scene in the sheriff's office asking her out. But whenever they were alone, he would never express outright if he liked her romantically. "Anyway, do you think phoenix really lived on this earth at one time?"

"Sure, but I bet you phoenix from Chinese painters would look a lot prettiest and most vivid." He laughed. "There were more phoenix paintings drawn by Chinese than any other races. About thirty years ago, I met a schoolteacher who possesses rare *Yin Yang* eyes; in the West, we often call it as 'third eye,' clairvoyant eyes or spiritual eyes. One day he even spotted a dragon on the sky when he was driving home from work. He thought he was dreaming, so he even pinched himself to make sure he didn't see a dragon kite instead. He told me it looked exactly like those dragons in Chinese paintings."

"Other people might think he hallucinated instead." Dr. Hudson chuckled.

"Amazing!" Dallas exclaimed. She wondered if the man's vision happened during an ephemeral occasion when the OTS Ray Spectrum of the PNV fence in the air was neutralized by cosmic #XZ-rays. She wondered if a creature present at that particular instant at that particular PNV enclave spot appeared visible to any naked eyes, or if it would only appear visible to those extremely limited people born with primitive eye pigmentation.

The old man then added, "Chinese believe that if a person sees a dragon, it will bring him the peace and luck."

Dallas suspected if anyone witnessed such a dragon, surely he wouldn't be able to escape from neutralized rays of the OTS Spectrum and cosmic #XZ-rays that shone upon him as well. She wondered if such a neutralizing ray could benefit one's physical and mental health to promote positive thinking, increase IQ and self-confidence.

\* \* \* \* \* \*

Back in Alice, Texas, Dallas's secretary had been acting as a busybody, trying to match up her single young boss with the eligible Professor Rochester. She deliberately didn't tell Professor Rochester what Dallas had asked her to convey, especially after she noticed that Dallas had left behind her ff on her office desk.

Just as she had predicted, the next day when Professor Rochester couldn't get hold of Dallas by ff, he called Dallas's office.

"DD's office. May I help you?"

After a slight hesitation, a man asked, "Where's DD?"

The assistant recognized Professor Rochester's unique Yankee voice; she touched on the speaker button mode, and she winked to beckon the rest of Dallas's assistants to come closer to the ff-phone.

"What's the matter, Professor Rochester?" She deliberately gave a long southern drawl.

"I can't get hold of her, where is she?"

"Is it something important?"

"No. I just want to make sure she remembers that tomorrow we have to release the giant owl."

"Oh, she left for Hawaii yesterday."

"Why did she go to Hawaii in such a great hurry?"

"She went there to meet her old high school classmate."

"Who's that? A man or a woman?

The secretary thought that distinction might have outraged him. She replied lazily, "Dr. Michael Hudson is a man, why?"

"Because...I'm her boyfriend," he announced sheepishly.

"Oh, wow! I thought Dr. Dallas was just one of your girlfriends," she teased him.

"Listen, now she is my only girlfriend," he declared to her impatiently. Obviously, he was aggravated by her intentional stupid act. What he didn't know was on the other end, a group of older women surrounded her desk, with both their hands covering their mouths, who could hardly stand for laughing.

"What's that funny noise?"

She gestured a hush signal to the women.

"Nothing," she lied. "Okay, if she calls I'll relay your message to her."

"Ask her to give me a buzz."

"Okie dokie!"

However, the secretary decided not to inform Dallas that Professor Rochester was looking for her. Instead, on the next afternoon, upon seeing Dallas's arrival in the parking lot, she promptly gave a buzz to Professor Rochester informing him of Dallas's return; secretly, the whole office staff anticipated a scene.

When Dallas entered her office, the old secretary crooked her mouth with amusement at Dallas' exposed, tanned back. "Wow, Doc! I like your *provocative* sexy summer dress; it's so pretty. If I were slim like you, I'd wear it every day to flaunt my rear and back in front of every man I could find."

"Oh really?...Good! I bought everyone an equally 'provocative' summer dress, but since I was rushing, I left them inside the car trunk just now. I'll bring them tomorrow," she promised.

Forty minutes later, the secretary was not surprised to see Professor Rochester pop into the office, obviously in a great hurry. She was amused to see a big bundle of red roses in his right hand and a big sack of Dunkin Donuts in his left. *Oh gosh, this bouquet has at least fifty roses,* she thought.

"This should be enough for everyone," he told the secretary while placing the paper sack on her desk—it was a little surprise for her. She felt slightly guilty but quickly recovered her composure.

"Oh thanks a lot, Professor Roc! This is so sweet of you. Dr. Dallas is in her office. I'll send in two coffees right away." She didn't expect him to try to please and bribe an old crow like her.

Roc crept into Dallas's office without her awareness; when a bundle of roses appeared in front of her nose, she turned. When she saw Roc standing at her back, she got all excited and bounced like a teenager.

"Now, give me a kiss." Her little red, floral bareback dress revealing her faultless skin and perfect curves made him suddenly jealous of the company she'd been keeping. "Why you didn't take your ff?"

She politely gave him a light peck on his cheek. "Could you believe it? When I left in such a great rush, I left it on my office desk."

Taking the bouquet, she sought a container to put them in water. "What's the matter that you've been looking for me? Didn't we already agree to meet at three this afternoon at your lab?" She raised her eyebrows while questioning him with her innocent big eyes.

He hesitated for a second; then he finally revealed indirectly, "Wouldn't you miss me if you didn't call me every day?"

"Gosh, what are you saying? It's been less than three days. When I didn't call you for three days while you nursed the wounded giant owl, did you miss me as much? You didn't call me either, that time."

"So are you really jealous of that bird?" If she was like all the rest of the women he knew before, she would dig out all the dirt from the past to make a fuss when she couldn't get her way.

"When you were busy with the wounded owl you'd forgotten me, so you must have been very free for the past two days. Kiss some frogs, did you?"

"No," he denied flatly.

They weren't aware that the secretary had been standing outside the office to eavesdrop.

The smart old lady decided to act as a busybody again to help Dallas; she knocked and entered with a tray of donuts and two cups of freshly brewed coffee. "Hmm...Dr. Dallas, Professor Roc stopped into the office looking for you yesterday," she lied; actually he only called the office.

She ignored Dallas' confused glance and Professor Rochester's furious eyes seemingly wanting to swallow her up; she continued to provoke him. "I heard that your old friend Dr. Hudson is a smart, famous marine specialist and handsome too, right?"

"Huh!" Roc grunted. "Oh, yeah, he's happily married with two kids, unless you're blind. I think I'm a better choice."

Neither woman expected him to go to such an extent in checking the marine specialist's details.

"Professor Roc. Remember, love is blind!" the secretary teased him again.

"Oh yeah...then I'm blind to fall in love with a woman who is blind as well." He gritted his teeth while he spoke.

"Hey, Professor Roc, you just said you're in love with Dr. Dallas."

"Did I tell you yesterday?" He looked accusingly at the secretary.

"No. You told us...she's your only girlfriend. That doesn't mean you're her only boyfriend." The secretary left them with a cheeky wink and shut the door behind her deliberately a bit louder to indicate the door was closed.

He held his anger and stepped forward to Dallas to question her. "Am I your only boyfriend?"

She really thought the conversation had turned childish. "Prove to me I'm your only girlfriend first, and then I'll give you my answer. By the way, thanks for the nice roses." She took a look at the clock on the wall. "Professor Rochester, I think it's time to get ready to release the owl."

In the reception area, the secretary touched her forehead, screaming in frustration when she saw Dallas' young nephew enter from outside with flowers and leaves collected in his overturned cap held on his hands. "Oh no! My chrysanthemums!" She rushed out the office and saw that the flower patch looked to have been munched up by a herd of hungry goats.

When she reentered reception, the four-year-old boy was already sitting on the floor arranging and counting the flowers and leaves tossed all over the floor. She said to herself, "It's better that you count this way than doing your alien math homework on my desktop calendar and documents."

Soon Dallas and Roc stepped out of her office and saw the messy arrangement of numbers made by flowers on the reception floor. "Sorry for the mess," Dallas said. "This is my nephew, Amazon. His parents went to San Francisco in a great hurry for a funeral. As soon as I got down from the saucer, they threw me their car sensor key and their son without giving me any chance to say no before they ran off to board their flight."

Dallas crouched near the boy and addressed him. "Darling, can you stay with Aunty Julie, as I have to work somewhere else today?"

"No. Mommy said I shouldn't talk to any strangers."

"Well, my mission may be too dangerous for you."

"No! No! No!" the boy protested. He simply enjoyed following his exciting and interesting aunty.

The secretary had a few bad experiences in babysitting this little rascal; she suggested cunningly to avoid an extra chore, "DD, I don't see that he'll be a problem."

"I think it could be an educational trip for him, since he is so active. He may like some outdoor activities," Roc suggested. "How many opportunities does a kid get to fly on a serescopter?"

"Do you think your 'educational trip' may be a bit too dangerous for a little boy like that?" Dallas pointed to the boy, who was tearing petals one by one from the flowers.

"Don't worry. Let me take care of him. You take care of the owl and getting us to the gate of the PNV."

\* \* \* \* \* \*

In contrast to the hot and humid summer, the Texas early autumn was pleasant in between hurricanes or tropical storms, and the temperature gradually cooled down from late afternoon into the early morning.

Despite walking on the beautiful campus promenade, neither of the two hurried people paid any attention to maple leaves that had just started to turn flaming hues. The little boy who trailed behind them randomly plucked flowers that he fancied along the way.

Once they reached the lab, the mynah in the cage got all excited seeing a little boy walking toward it. Dallas also came along from behind and she noticed there was a new member added to the cage. "Hi, are you going to sing for us today?" she asked the mynah.

But the mynah kept repeatedly telling them, "Turkey! Turkey!" Actually the moment the tom turkey saw them approaching, it started to display its beautiful plumage.

"Wow! A beautiful turkey," Amazon looked at it, impressed.

Suddenly it got aggressive, trying to attack Dallas with its beak from inside the cage. "Oh gosh!" Dallas tried to stay away from the cage.

"What are you trying to do?" She heard Roc talking sternly to the turkey.

"Can you change your colorful dress? Tom turkey feels threatened and challenged whenever it sees colorful fabric. It's not suitable for this mission either." Roc stared at her dress disapprovingly. "Your wet jeans and shirt that you left here a month ago have been cleaned and I brought them here." He was thinking if she didn't strip the dress off, he might do it.

"That's a good idea, thanks. I lost my opportunity to stop at the house and change before we left. Someone dropped by my office and interrupted my plan." She looked pointedly at Roc.

A few minutes later, Dallas emerged from the lab in the jeans and T-shirt. Her nephew was holding a smaller cage with the mynah inside; she stared questioningly at Roc. He shrugged.

"He insisted the mynah must come along with him or else he wants to stay back here with the mynah."

"You spoil him," she complained.

"Anyway it's no harm to bring the mynah. I think if it's an amphisensus bird, it might alarm us of unforeseen danger that we couldn't sense or see with our naked eyes," Roc suggested.

\* \* \* \* \* \*

Thirty minutes later when they reached Kingsville Air Force Base, Roc saw the same old engineer but was surprised to meet the first pilot that he talked to but never met before. "Hi, Captain Lee, nice to meet you! I thought you were scared to fly after the crash."

"Come on, Professor Roc! If you get bitten by a bird once, are you afraid to chase after it again?"

Roc chuckled, and glanced at Dallas, who was now helping Amazon to board the serescopter. "No. Getting bitten would challenge me more to get it into my cage as soon as possible."

The captain chuckled too; he seemed to understand the crossed meaning.

"Hey guys! Hurry up," Dallas called after them. "The tranquilizer for the giant owl will last only for about an hour." She wondered if there were no women in this world to monitor or to help behind straight men, would they be able to accomplish their duties as efficiently?

As she took her seat in the serescopter cabin, she was ambivalent when she saw her hyperactive nephew sitting quietly playing his games on Roc's ff-screen, despite it producing all sorts of disturbing noises. "Hmm..." *Perhaps this boy receives a man's lower voice tone better than a woman's higher pitched voice, so he responds better to men?*

\* \* \* \* \* \*

In the later afternoon, a group of children playing in an open field saw a serescopter flying overhead and they waved excitedly and stared at the serescopter until it disappeared over the horizon.

# Farewell to the Giant Owl

The smooth passage under the bright sunny weather had temporarily eased everyone's initial anxiety, but the moment when MPPS began to blink to remind them that there would be just thirty more miles before reaching the previously recorded PNV enclave's boundary, they became uneasy.

Sure enough, startling clear air turbulence started to make them felt like they were galloping on horseback. Without a skilled pilot to maneuver the serescopter, it might have gotten spiraled and tossed off course. Simultaneously, webs of eerie lightning sparkled and circled outside the serescopter.

"Captain Lee...Withdraw now! I think this enclave has shifted again. The serescopter obviously has just trespassed into its border."

While Dallas yelled, the experienced pilot had already escaped by ascending the serescopter and backing off promptly. As fast as a human's alarm instinct, the serescopter MPPS sensor had detected its potential risk; it released a warning alarm before the serescopter was rejected like aluminum foil inside a microwave oven.

"Obviously this PNV enclave's peripheral fence has shifted about thirty miles closer," the captain informed them.

"As we don't know the exact moment for the enclave border to merge with our habitat, we better wait on the ground for the right time," Dallas suggested.

While Captain Lee was generating a laser landing pad, both of them took out their digital binoculars, searching and figuring out a possible PNV enclave entrance.

After searching for some time, Dallas looked at the remaining twilight over the western horizon with a frown, and she asked Roc, "Do you know how Dr. Hudson and I figured out the PNV entrance in the sea?"

"How?" he wondered. "MPPS didn't work?"

"Nope, MPPS would go haywire whenever we approached the PNV...We had to figure it out using our naked eyes and brains. One of the crew threw a rotten orange to the open sea, and it got 'sucked' and spiraled by a swirl. We tossed out a whole bag of oranges and watched the currents swirling on the surface. Finally, I predicted the ultra-calm place in between the two large swirls was the entrance. So what do you think the differences could be of PNV in the air and on the ground? It won't work on the ground if we throw an orange, unless we have a kite? I think it might work."

Roc pondered for a moment with her; suddenly he held up the binoculars hanging around his neck and took another look at a particular direction and its surroundings again. "When there is wind or current, the fog won't stay in a place. At this hour of the earlier evening there's supposedly no fog yet."

"Yes, no fog."

He then pointed to a certain direction. "Could it be there? It's misty in that particular area."

Dallas took her binoculars, looking toward the pointed direction, but she hesitated.

"Look there," Roc called out.

She looked toward the direction he still pointed; aghast, she saw a huge swarm—probably thousands of rats, as she had never seen in her entire life, migrating.

Dallas excitedly yelled, "Yes! Yes! Apparently, they're heading to that misty area, right? But do you dare to enter the PNV with the rats' exodus?"

"Nah, we won't go in there, we'll bring the owl closest to it. If its habitat is really in there, it'll instinctively know how to get back inside. At least, that's your theory. Let's hurry up."

Once the serescopter landed on the ground, they quickly moved the tranquilized giant owl out of the serescopter and laid it on a length of netting. "Gosh, this owl is so light for such a big animal," Dallas remarked.

"They have to be light to fly."

While they carried the net over the stirrup-long grass, the closer they moved toward the misty ground, the stronger the headwind blew toward them.

"Should we leave it here?" Dallas was growing tired of fighting the wind and the grass stems slicing at her sandaled feet.

"Let's move it just another few more yards closer. Do you feel the headwind is getting even stronger now?"

"Yes, let's hurry up." They pushed onward against the wind, checking the owl to be sure it wouldn't come-to and begin struggling in the net. "Okay, let's stop here, I feel needles pinching on my face," Dallas complained. At last, they stopped moving and set the large bird gently on the ground.

"The giant owl will revive any time; we better leave it here now," Roc decided. "I think we don't have much time left. Let's hurry up now," he told her. Hastily, they untied the net from the giant owl and ran back to the serescopter.

When Dallas entered the cabin, she heard the mynah's loud distress call that cautioned her of an unknown danger and she saw her nephew had looked up from the ff screen to watch the activity outside. All of a sudden the boy started to cringe and scream in obvious terror while he pointed out something on the ff screen to his aunty. Instinctively, Dallas glanced toward it.

At a swoop, she ran toward the serescopter entrance and with her greatest might, grabbed and pulled Roc into the serescopter.

"Hey! What are you doing?" he protested while he struggled to balance his body.

Dallas had to drag Roc fully into the serescopter to close the cabin auto door.

"Hey what's happening?" he yelled.

Just a few seconds ago, the captain wondered why the serescopter's MPPS directed him to ascend instantly to avoid a collision and soon its ACAS began to give out its loudest warning alarm to indicate severity. The experienced pilot instinctively followed its instruction for the unforeseen circumstances rather than trust his naked eyes. The instant the cabin door was shut, the serescopter descended immediately. "Buckle up," the captain ordered.

Under the confusion, Roc hissed angrily, "Hey! What's the hell's going on?"

All hands pointed at once toward the window; the boy finally stuttered a word, "Ka...a!"

Roc was perplexed. "Kaa?" He turned to where they all pointed.

He finally spotted it. He shouted loudly to the pilot, "Captain! Hurry up! Or else we'll be swallowed up by a giant viper!"

The pilot was glad this latest model of serescopter— which was also dubbed the King Cobra—could ascend as quickly as an elevator. From the front panel deck, the pilot finally could see with his naked eyes that an erect giant king cobra was trying to attack the serescopter.

His sweat evaporated all over his body. The engineer beside him shook badly and finally was able to utter some words after a moment of panic, "Damn! I hate snakes. Luckily I didn't go down to pee right away after the serescopter landed, or else I'd be its dinner."

"You're just a little hotdog for Nagini." Just as the pilot said it, venom spat out from the snake's gaping mouth and spread over the front panel of the serescopter, blurring the vision of the pilot. "Oh shit, sly devil," the pilot cursed. The serescopter kept ascending and soon its wipers cleared off the disgusting venom in time for the serescopter to reach cruising altitude.

Roc worriedly looked through the serescopter window panel. "Do you think it's going to eat that owl on the ground?"

"That's my worry too," Dallas said. "Captain Lee, can we circle for a while to see what'll happen to the owl?"

"You bet, Doc."

"Captain, please watch out, don't hit the tree tops," she warned.

"Sure. Or else we might all end up as hotdogs for that Nagini."

The giant snake finally gave up spitting its venom and lowered its body, as the serescopter had already flown beyond attacking range. Once it retreated to the ground, under their worried glances it started to crawl toward the giant owl.

"Damn! The big owl is not going to get killed like this," Roc yelled helplessly.

"Should we shoot it from the air?" Dallas suggested.

"No, not a snake—the injured snake's tail could sweep the whole area like a cyclone and that could include sweeping that owl away from the gate."

"Gosh...what should we do?" Dallas suddenly felt indecisive.

It happened that the peak moment of an auspicious time had just begun; the atmosphere on Earth was receiving its highest doses of good air, negative ions and living essences from this well preserved PNV remnant-enclave. This was also a very brief moment that both boundaries were temporarily amalgamated for incoming and outgoing creatures from both space-times to access.

The moon was camouflaged upon the bright sunset sky; cosmic rays' reflection, interception and rectification went on between the earth's central reserves. This phenomenon couldn't be detected by the naked eye, but soon the misty patch of fog near the PNV entrance dispersed and cleared off.

Under everyone's helpless anxious gaze, the giant snake began to erect its attacking pose toward the semi-conscious giant owl, which had begun to twitch and sit up. Just at that critical instant another bigger giant owl emerged from the PNV entrance with lighting speed to give a peck on one of the snake's eyes. The cobra struggled and wriggled before retreating to the ground and trying to escape with its life.

However, the giant owl fearlessly continued trailing after the giant snake in midair. A moment later, the giant owl struck again, following an unexpected swift drop, and this time its talons precisely landed on the snake's head.

The snake's head now had been partially crushed, but with lightning speed, it retaliated with a sweep of its tail and struck body of the giant owl. The unexpected impact of the giant snake's tail caused the giant owl to fall down to a nearby understory.

The half-dead giant snake's movement obviously had slowed down but the preying instinct was still there; now came its turn to counterattack its predator.

From the air, they saw the giant snake start to crawl toward the dropped giant owl. "Gee! Captain, can you hover a bit lower, I think I want to kill that bastard," Roc said.

"Stop that suggestion. Our serescopter might drop like the owl—obviously its mighty tail can still move," Dallas warned. "Usually, a reptile's tail has greater precision to hit its predator before its last breath."

Luckily, the owl dropped into a thick pile of foliage that consisted of dried grass and dead leaves, thus it was not injured despite the unexpected impact and fall, but it got tangled up by thorny scrub. When the wriggling snake moved closer toward it, it also struggled harder and shrieked louder.

When the injured giant snake erected its pose ready to attack the desperate giant owl, from the PNV enclave entrance suddenly emerged four smaller giant owls, shrieking agitatedly and flying hurriedly toward the giant snake. The half-blinded snake now changed to defense when these little giant owls ferociously started pecking on its body. After a while it decided to escape with its life, but these fierce little giant owls never gave up pursuing it.

While everyone's attention was on the life-and-death battle of the prehistoric creatures' fight, the tranquilized giant owl had just regained full consciousness. The shrieking sounds of its brood instantly provoked its parental and preying instinct. It gave a few flicks of its wings then began to fly and dive to peck the escaping snake's remaining eye.

The snake struggled with obvious pain. The giant owl dived again; in a flash, its talons completely crushed the snake's head. While struggling to escape, its tail was still powerful enough to whip the giant owl and cause it to drop into the nearby bush.

The four trailing little giant owls never gave up attacking the escaping blind dead snake; they continued to peck at the snake's body. Soon the two stranded giant owls got themselves untangled from the bush; they joined their brood to trail and to attack the escaping snake until it could hardly move.

"Look at them! They're preening each other now. Are they a pair and those are their chicks?" Dallas looked at the resting owls.

"If they are a pair, the one we caught was the male, and the bigger one that we just encountered should be the female. This phenomenon is known as reverse sexual size dimorphism, common in most birds of prey so that it has enough energy to produce and protect the eggs and chicks. I think these chicks are still very young, although clearly they're mature enough to fly. Apparently these prehistoric primitive mammoth creatures are braver and smarter than most creatures living in our habitat." Roc was greatly impressed by their protective instincts and hunting capabilities.

"Of course, or else how could they still survive up until this current millennia? Anyhow, does reverse sexual size dimorphism factor happen to human beings?"

"Hmm... no?...yes?...Women get fatter after they have babies, right?

"Usually they gain a bit more weight after each baby. Hormones trigger it...so they can protect their babies in many different ways.

213

"Oh my...Look!" Everyone saw Dallas' aghast open mouth and followed her pointed finger.

The owls had picked up the dead snake body and started to fly toward the newly-covered, thin misty fume of the PNV entrance.

"What a happy family," Dallas said, admiring them. "I hope the female is not hurt due to the drop."

"I don't think so, look at them. Or else they wouldn't be able to carry the snake altogether."

"A big feast when they reach their nest."

Without any warning, clear air turbulence shook the serescopter once again. Instinctively, they looked down to see the foggy mist gushing in had already covered almost the entire area.

"We better get out of here now," the experienced captain decided wisely.

# Return from a Successful Mission

On the serescopter on their way back, Roc asked Dallas, "While you were on the descending serescopter—can you explain why initially you couldn't see us, then you saw us as a collection of detached body parts, but that illusion didn't happen to those trees?"

"It is likely that because human beings possess both dormant and invisible ethereal energies, if the primitive spectrum of light shines upon them, the primeval light would be absorbed by the ethereal energies, thus they appear invisible to our evolved naked eyes from the PNV enclave's periphery. The descending serescopter probably dispersed some of the primeval lights, so when your bodies were only partially exposed to primeval light, your body parts appeared to be floating as separated parts of a whole. Perhaps people who have recessive primitive eye pigmentation could see such invisible parts as grey," Dallas explained.

"So obviously a tree doesn't possess the ethereal energies?"

"Yes, unless a tree possesses a 'ghost' or particular form of invisible ethereal energy."

Just before the last twilight disappeared from the horizon, to everyone's relief, the serescopter finally touched down peacefully at Kingsville Air Force Base.

They were glad that they could accomplish their arduous mission within a quarter day, without the necessity to enter the PNV enclave yet able to witness the giant owl returning safely with its family to its PNV habitat. It was an ordeal with many cold sweating moments, but they felt grateful that everyone had finally returned home safely.

Secretly Roc touched his forearms to check if any goose pimples remained; he felt lucky his expedition team didn't encounter any those primitive giant snakes or predatory creatures when they got trapped inside the PNV enclave.

A long absence of a young voice in the cabin suddenly reminded him of something. He looked around the cabin. "Where's the little rascal?"

"He covered himself all over and hid inside a blanket." Dallas pointed toward the back of the cabin.

"Enough unexpected terrors for him in such a short time."

"I hope after this exciting ordeal, he'll grow up and act a little more mature."

"But I think first of all he needs some counseling sessions."

"Let's go get him."

When Dallas pulled off the blanket that covered him, immediately the boy covered his face with both his hands. "Honey, look at me." After hearing his aunt's voice, reluctantly he took his hands from his face.

She looked at her nephew's pale and still astonished face; her sister would never trust her to babysit him again. "Mammoth creatures are definitely not as lovely and cute as those Disney animals, right, boy?"

"But you told me they're braver and smarter than children."

His retaliation made her frown and stunned her to wordlessness for a moment.

It took them some time to convince the panicked boy to come out of the blanket completely. They all felt relieved when he started to talk. "I'm hungry...I want fish and chips, apple strudel and ice-cream..."

"Okay, let's get out of here then I'll take you to dinner," Roc promised him.

Once they stepped out of the serescopter, under the cool autumn breeze, the rest of the party realized they were also as hungry as the little boy.

Most of them were thinking of the nearest available fast food outlet, but Roc suggested, "Shall we go to The Texas Maxim?"

"Why not?" the captain agreed first. "To celebrate that we are back alive."

Soon the rest of them confirmed.

Fifteen minutes later, they were sitting at a posh restaurant waiting to be served. While waiting, a familiar discussion was broadcast on the captain's ff screen.

"...Should we confine the giant owl in the zoo or release it to its natural habitat?" a talk show hostess asked one of her guests.

"I think since Baby Ruby was unharmed, and the giant owl didn't kill her, there is no reason that we should keep it in the zoo. It would be like a jail sentence for that glorious animal."

Another guest immediately refuted, "How could we be so sure that that it didn't kill any of those missing babies? I mean it could have killed a baby, but nothing was spotted and reported to the authorities. I heard gossip from the valley that an undocumented Mexican's baby went missing just before that giant owl killed the dog."

Roc watched the broadcast with great disapproval and his eyes narrowed in displeasure. "Gosh, I bet if we all got killed during the mission, this entertainment industry could make even more money on the topic."

Everyone's eyes followed Roc when he stopped talking and began looking out at the parking lot—a familiar figure from Texas society page and an attractive girl in a blue dress stepped out of a white Porsche that parked right in front of the restaurant. Roc's eyes narrowed when the couple entered the restaurant.

When the girl passed by their table, she blushed and greeted him. "Howdy, Professor Rochester."

"Howdy," he replied coldly and gave the flamboyant Dr. Dick Fisher a polite nod; simultaneously he tried to reach out for a menu, pretending to read it while they walked off.

Dallas threw a glance at Roc's sudden solemn mood change. Her sixth sense told her the lady was his ex-girlfriend, and this prompted her to provoke him. Cheekily, she asked him, "Gee—isn't he the rich and famous Dr. Dick Fisher that your gorgeous ex-girlfriend is dating now?"

"Yes," he replied without any sign of emotion or regret.

"Aptly named. She ditched you for him, right?"

"Oh yeah, Dr. 'Dick'!" Roc snorted.

"Don't worry, I like you better than her." She gave his arm a flirtatious caress.

"Really?" He lifted one of his eyebrows and looked at her funny.

Her glance then came to linger on his torn jeans and faded TAMUK T-shirt. She cooed, "Oh sure, I prefer this," while she used her index finger to poke some of those opened holes on his torn jeans. "I think that classic Armani suit that Dicky wore could cost your whole month's salary."

Roc ignored Dallas' deliberate provocation and silent flirtation; seeing that woman hanging off Dick's arm, flaunting his money, stung him deeper than it should have. Again he resumed reading the menu and soon he beckoned an attending waiter.

*Dr. Dick is rich? Huh! Let me feed some pine nuts to these innocent birds today.* "Hey, give everyone..." Without seeking approval, he pointed at one of the most expensive champagnes on the wine list. "Two bottles of this Brangelina purple, please."

Spontaneously, he closed the menu and ordered a full course dinner for everyone. "Four orders of caviar on lobsters, French bread, Tuscany salad, American Wagyu tenderloin steak—medium rare, with assorted berries, pine nuts, cheesecake and coffee."

Abruptly he reached out to open the menu again, "...And this Canadian wild salmon fish 'n chips entree with Persian salad, orange juice and the vanilla ice-cream on apple strudel for the little boy."

The waiter soon returned with the champagne and glasses. Everyone had turned quiet; they probably were hiding their great disapproval of his ordering for all of them. To camouflage his guilt, he simply shrugged. "Don't worry, it's on my bill." The other men muttered protests at his overly-generous act; this was not cheap food. "To celebrate we're back alive and thank you!" He raised his champagne to give everyone a toast.

Dallas gave him an odd stare. "Aren't you showing off just a little more than you can afford to? She's all the way on the other side of the restaurant."

He chose to ignore her barb; Dallas couldn't know money truly was no object. It probably did look bad, in her eyes. But he didn't dare tell her the truth.

Not long after, the waiter approached them again. "Sorry, Professor Rochester, our American Wagyu has run out today. Can we offer you Texas grown organic grass-fed?"

He raised one of his eyebrows, surprised that the waiter recognized him. "Sure."

"Excellent."

Dallas eyed him doubtfully, but not one person at the table refused the free food after more than a token protest. The waiter happily repeated the confirmed order before he left. The men got rowdier after the champagne; more jokes shot around the table while they waited for their dinner.

Roc turned to talk to the little boy. "Look at the lady in the blue dress there." He indicated his ex. "Now tell me who is prettier, the lady in blue or your aunty?"

The little boy didn't even blink. "Aunt Goldie!"

Roc tugged the elastic of his undershorts above the waistband of his jeans. "What does this say? Tell your aunt loudly, what is this word?"

The boy spelled one letter after another; finally he declared, "Oh! It's...ARMANI! Aunt Goldie, you like that, right?"

The other two men began to move their heads over curiously to confirm Professor Roc's underwear's logo while Dallas blushed. He deliberately aimed his sarcasm at her.

The captain whispered heavily in Dallas's ear. "Dr. Dallas, let me tell you something—I think what you need to look for in a man is something inside him, not something that's on him."

She didn't disagree. Did Roc understand that?

Twenty minutes later, the dinner was served. Dallas learned from their conversation that Roc would quit his teaching from TAMUK at the end of the year.

"So what are you going to do next?"

He shrugged and simply rolled along more white lies to her. "I'll return to New York, but I wonder how soon I could find another teaching job in a university. It depends on what research project I get involved in. And how about you?" *Oh yeah, that doesn't mean I'll be jobless.* But he still kept calm in his composure.

"Actually I'm leaving the day after tomorrow to Borneo to take a look at a remote seashore there. I was told schools of starfish have washed on shore continuously for more than a week already. After that, I'll search for a rare Borneo birdwing endemic to the island and also a giant centipede spotted by a friend. I'm planning to be there awhile, but just on my own time, not on a research grant."

"Why don't you go to New York with me?" His heart pounded in his chest. This was first time in his life he'd had the incredible courage to propose to a girl, even indirectly.

She gave him a tight smile and turned her shoulders away slightly. "Not now, it wouldn't be a good idea. Until you find yourself a new job—or else two of us will both be jobless and it's easier to starve there in a big city than staying out here in the country. I don't mind that you're poor, because I prefer a handsome man." She gave him a playful wink. "But for the moment, I'll only think of going to New York after I spot a new butterfly species longer than birdwing or a centipede longer than just a twelve-foot."

Obviously, she didn't comprehend his casual proposal.

"Don't you think I'm a better one to pursue?" he proposed now to her more directly. "Come live with me, Dallas."

She hesitated a bit before replying. "Sorry, I don't know. Please give me some time to think about it. If I start to miss you very much, right after my Borneo trip, I'll fly directly to New York. I'll meet you there."

\* \* \* \* \* \*

Despite his wish to renew the terminated contract with TAMUK in mid-December, Roc still lingered and remained in Texas for a while to keep his old grandfather company, and that really pleased the elderly man. He tried calling Dallas multiple times, but the ff-calls never rang through to her, just to a message line.

She didn't return any of his messages.

Through Christmas, Roc prepared meals for his grandfather, helped him as an extra farm hand and helped him buy and sell some stocks to make some quick money—he admitted he was too old for this kind of nerve-wracking stock exchange game. The exchanges would only happen when Roc's mother was not around—as this kind of gambling was not permitted in the Rochester family.

Finally, Roc left Texas, only after his mother's continuous pestering calls to remind him it was time for him to return to New York to take over his dad's designation. Unwillingly, just ahead of New Years, he left the Lone Star State, with his heart still wondering where Dallas was now.

# 24

# Love Arrives Timely

Since Maximilian's return to New York a week ago, his mother started to get busy in organizing a ball for her son's homecoming. In her mind, she planned to invite over a hundred of those pretty, eligible single ladies and handsome bachelors from those affluent families she knew of. It was high time the boy married and started making grandbabies.

On the day of ball, starting in early morning, everyone in the mansion was busy preparing for the upcoming evening function, but Mrs. Rochester didn't spot a single trace of her son around the house.

She was very curious why her extrovert, outgoing son spent most of his time in the bedroom since his return from Texas. No one had forced the boy to come home; he said himself his grant project was finished and he had no tenure at TAMUK. He said he had no ties there. So right after the antique clock struck nine times in the morning, she decided to creep into his bedroom suite.

She found him hugging and sleeping with a photo on the bed. The photo showed her son with a beautiful blonde woman and the giant owl he'd told her about. Could that woman be the infamous Dr. Dallas, the cryptozoologist? Maximilian had said she argued with everything he said and was way too smart for him, as though that was a bad thing. She smiled; her playboy son must have fallen in love with this gorgeous girl in the picture.

She carefully pulled the photo out of his hands, intending to take a closer peep at the girl, but it awakened him.

"Where is this angel?" she whispered to his ear.

"What do you mean?" he grumped at her in a sleepy voice with still closed eyes.

"Don't act stupid. I said where is she? Who's this pretty girl in the photo here?"

Roc cracked his eyes as his mother flashed Dallas's face past them.

"She's gone."

"What are you talking about? Son...Get her back here at once!"

He rolled to turn his back to her and pulled the blanket back up to his ear. "I have no idea where she is now. I haven't heard from her for quite a while since she left Texas. She told me she'd only come to New York if there was more than a foot-long butterfly or more than a twelve-foot-long giant centipede for her to catch." *Actually, she said if she missed me a lot she would come to meet me here in New York. As soon as possible, she said, which would have been more than a month ago.*

"Okay, so you know her very well, obviously. Come on, son! Remember you're more than six feet long and definitely you're much stronger than that twelve-foot long centi—pede?" She shoved at his shoulders, rocking him back and forth under the covers. "MAXIMILIAN MCCOMBS ROCHESTER, YOU USE A HOOK OR CROOK TO GET HER BACK NOW—I WANT A WELL-ROUNDED DAUGHTER-IN-LAW LIKE HER!"

He finally eyed his vibrant Texan mother with his fully-awakened eyes.

After a knock on the entrance door, an old butler interrupted their conversation. "Excuse me, Roc, there was a call from Tokyo at one in the morning by a lady..." Then he noticed Mrs. Rochester was in her son's bedroom, too. "Oh, sorry, am I interrupting your conversation?"

"No, don't worry, please go ahead," Mrs. Rochester told him, interest clear on her face.

The butler paused a moment, looking into his note. "...Dr. Dallas—I guess you know her, right?" He raised one of his eyebrows. "She wanted me to inform you that she has finally spotted her one-foot long butterfly in Borneo but unfortunately not a trace of the giant centipede. She said she will be reaching Rochester International Saucerport in the late morning." Then the butler handed him a note with the written details of flight number and the arrival time before leaving the bedroom suite. Roc wondered how Dallas had gotten ahold of their unlisted and guarded private ff-number—but he was glad she had.

After the butler left, Mrs. Rochester immediately pestered her son again. "Hey! So please tell her that you are surely longer than that butterfly and stronger than that centipede and you need more of her attention." She gave him a wink before walking off happily.

"Come on, Mom! You're silly," he complained.

His mother's voice from outside his bedroom suite now reached his ears, "Hurry up and get up now. Or else you'll be late to pick her up from the saucerport."

The unexpected news of Dallas coming to New York had revitalized him; he thought finally in her heart there was a place for him. *Wow what a relief.* For a while, a hole had sat in his heart, wrenching when he couldn't see her or talk to her. He missed their adventure in the Texas wilderness, and her passion as she explained PNV theory. He missed being around a woman who understood and shared his interest in studying birds, and who was okay with simple academic life.

Mrs. Rochester left her son's bedroom with a relief sigh. *Somebody has finally woken up from hibernation.* The tabloids could always trace out her son's whereabouts faster than her, but she wondered why this girl, Dr. Dallas, had never appeared in any of those tabloids until her old dad told her about how lovely the girl was. She amusedly thought, perhaps she always hung out with him in Texas's back country—out of the reach of those nosy paparazzi.

About a year ago—a big photo appeared, big enough to fill half the page of the biggest size tabloid magazine, with one of her son's arms holding a rooster while the other was holding a sexy black beauty, and the headline read:

# PLAYBOY ROCHESTER WITH TWO HANDS FULL OF CHICKS

She muttered and shook her head with an amused smile; he was confident to play as a dashing playboy but so inexperienced to act as somebody's good boyfriend.

\* \* \* \* \* \*

Roc anxiously watched passenger after passenger come through the security gate where he and others waited for them to disembark the international saucer and customs check. The blonde he waited for finally appeared. She wore a straw hat, and was tucked into a brightly-colored, body-hugging tube top... *wow, she has nice big boobs*...matched tastefully with a simple batik sarong skirt. Her carry-on was a woven rattan, log-shaped tote-bag. She looked like an exotic wildcat. Certainly she wasn't prepared for a New York winter in that outfit.

By the look on her face, Dallas was totally unprepared to see a dashing Roc an Armani suit come to the airport to pick her up with a chauffeured limousine.

"Hey, when did you accept a seven-figure job?" she asked, teasing with the smile he'd missed while she was away.

"Come on, darling, it's not the year 2020 anymore. Can someone with a seven-figure job afford a chauffeured limousine?" he retorted. "Why don't you give me a hug or kiss before asking me such a silly question?"

She promptly gave him a hug and a peck on both cheeks, clutching her straw hat to keep it on her head. "Hmmm......I missed you so much!"

*Hmm...this is something I like to hear,* Roc thought. "Luckily you still remember me after the long distance saucer travel!" After extensive saucertravel, many passengers would experience both saucerlag and some temporary short term memory slips for unknown reasons.

Reluctantly he pushed her back to arm's length, disallowing any further PDA, as was proper. He wrapped his wool coat around her bare shoulders and escorted her out of the terminal.

By the time her luggage had been taken and put into the car trunk by two hunky body guards and she and Roc were tucked into the warmth of the limousine interior, she clearly realized that his aura had changed to more a serious, prominent and respectful one then she knew from him in Texas.

She quickly figured out the differences. "Hmmm—you're actually from a rich family, right? That means you've fooled everyone in Texas, including me?"

"No...Not my old grandpa there," he denied. Because the old man kept his wise mouth shut all the time.

"Oh yes, actually I called Papa twice from Borneo to check how he got on, did he tell you that?"

Hmm...when did she start to call my papa as her papa? Why, Papa never told me she called him. "No." Obviously, the old man kept his mouth too tight sometimes. Perhaps he is unhappy that I left him alone now with his busy sons and farm hands.

"When I was in Borneo, my old ff accidentally dropped into a stream I crossed. I could only remember your papa's ff-phone's last four digits, which is the same as my birth date. That's how I got your house ff-phone number from him."

That explained why he couldn't get ahold of her through her old ff.

"He told me that you have a new ff but he has no idea what's your new number, so he finally gave me your house ff-phone number."

Oh yeah...I just added another ff phone. This old man deliberately wanted me to experience "longing makes the heart grow fonder."

"I didn't change my ff number, it's still good. I just added another new ff number." He doubtfully stared at Dallas now—he wondered if ever such a wild cat would willingly be confined in a cage-like marriage like they would find in New York, surrounded by his parents' society friends. "Baby, you look even more gorgeous after I haven't seen or heard from you for a while." Even though he was quite unhappy that she had ignored him for so long, he still couldn't stop staring from her feet up to her radiant face and tanned complexion.

He was attracted to her physically but also mentally. He admired her charming outlook and their intellectual sharing conversations were always filled with excitement and jokes. Even if they argued, soon their ire was buffered by an interesting compromise. He'd never met another woman like her, and doubted he would ever meet anyone else like her again.

When she admired his meticulously-cut Armani shirt again, she noticed he wore it tieless with open neck that really made him looked sexy in a city-boy way, but that also made her a bit uneasy and insecure—she wondered if ever such a wild bird could be confined happily into a cage-like married life. Why couldn't he have stayed free in Texas?

"Oh my, you look...so handsome and sexy." Anyhow, she flattered him while looking into his eyes to find any old familiarity or mutual sparks.

An hour later, Dallas was even more stunned when she was ushered into a grand mansion owed by the Rochester family, contrary to her old worry if Roc might be broke and jobless when returning to New York.

"Gee, I was worried about you. I kept asking Papa if you have found a job yet back in New York. Both you and Papa have been fooling me all the while!"

He shrugged, a sly grin tugging at the corners of his mouth. "Too many girls were going after my money, but I needed a girl who loved me before my money. I'm hoping that's you."

Dallas was speechless. She couldn't decide if Roc looked different to her now that she knew he came from old money. Could he still be her sexy, rough professor?

Soon a butler and two maids came to greet them and introduced themselves to Dallas.

"They'll take you to your bedroom," Roc said. "You rest first. Pablo will be at your door at 3:00 p.m. later to escort you to afternoon tea, and I'll see you there then."

At 3:00 p.m. sharp, Dallas was led by Butler Pablo to meet Mrs. Rochester in a chaise lounge for afternoon tea. After they exchanged pleasantries, they began to chat and at last Mrs. Rochester even told Dallas how she met her husband fifty years before.

"I was born and raised in Texas too. I met Maximilan's dad when I was a teenage girl. He chased after the quail during game hunting season on our property, year after year, until one day when I was twenty-two he asked me to marry him without a single date yet." She chuckled fondly.

"Maximilian?"

"That's the name I gave him the day he was born. Lord knows why he prefers 'Roc.'" She sipped more tea and set her cup aside. "We only have a short time before tonight's formal party, dear—you'd best get dressed up now."

Dallas' heart sank, mentally inventorying the clothes she had brought. "Sorry, I am unprepared at all for all these—"

"You can wear this batik dress again for the evening." Roc showed up silently from behind her and eyed the sexy silk outfit she wore for the afternoon tea.

Mrs. Rochester threw him a reproachful glance. "Please don't listen to the naughty boy! Let me take you to try on a gown you can borrow." She stood up, ready to lead Dallas out of the lounge.

"Hold on, I have something for you," Roc said. Both ladies looked suspiciously at him.

He pulled out a box from his pocket and gave it to Dallas. "Open it."

"Wow...Phillip Patek!"

"Patek Phillip," he corrected her. "From now onward, I don't think I can have any more 'Texas kind of time' to let you 'twist my arm' asking me for the time again." He helped her put the watch on and unexpectedly gave her a passionate kiss on the lips. Then he turned to give his mom a winning grin before walking off.

Once the watch was on her wrist, Dallas had a strange mixed feeling; she felt she had gained something yet she also felt she had lost that little something.

Usually a man liked to show his love practically, but a woman expecting another kind of service from a man might often confuse a courtesy as an act of love. For example—a girl would think that a man loved her if he always opened the car door for her. But if he was in rush and wasn't able to give this kind of service to a girl, should she get disappointed?

* * * * * *

Three Months Later

Wedding music rang through a Rochester church. The guests became bewildered to see an albino mynah bird was perching on the ring bearer, Amazon's shoulder with its neck tied with a ring as they moved down the aisle toward the altar. And only when they heard Wagner's "Bridal March" begin did they stand and turn their heads behind to look at the beautiful bride and her father getting ready to march down the aisle.

Most women were excited to finally able to see one of the most talked about and allegedly one of the most expensive designer wedding gowns of the season. It was indeed spectacular; giant owl butterflies with eyes of imported hambergite crystals were embroidered beautifully all over the sheer silk gown.

Soon the bride's father gave the bride's hand to the bridegroom, but when the bridegroom whispered some words seriously to the bride, most well-wishers were fallen into momentary doubt if the pair would call off the wedding. They couldn't know the bridegroom was belatedly asking his bride an unrelated question.

"Where do you think those thousands of rats ran to in their exodus?" He was actually in the mood to pull her leg, and also he kept forgetting to ask her this question during the past few months.

She looked embarrassedly at the preacher. "Please excuse us," she apologized. Then she joked to Roc, "Maybe they were trying to attend our wedding." She looked again at the preacher and wondered if she could answer Roc's random question during this serious occasion. He seemed so sincere, and so nervous; if it would calm him to know, she would answer.

The preacher gave her a consenting nod so she quickly explained. "During the flood, when both the damaged PNV and its outer vault regenerated into an amalgamated renewed space-time vault, some of those old PNV fragmented ruins could superimpose and merge with the renewed vault, which resulted in open lands. We could even build houses and plant crops on them. However, their dormant, existing PNV orientation routes aren't obsolete forever; perhaps once in a blue moon when cosmic XZ-rays intercept one of those primitive dormant communication signals, it could activate a migration signal for rats."

"So if such a migration signal leads the rats to an old well, would all of them jump into it?"

"I think so."

The preacher interrupted with his asceticism, "Just like if somebody you loved jumped into a well, you would likely jump in as well to rescue him or her, right?"

Dallas and Rochester laughed, squeezing each other's hands.

"Shall we proceed to the ceremony now?" the preacher asked.

"You bet, darlin'," Dallas said, before Roc could squirm out of it.

\* \* \* \* \* \*

New York Times

ROCHESTER: The most prominent Rochester Real Estate, Banking and Technology Dynasty's only heir, the "Diamond" bachelor Maximilian Rochester, also well-known in the financial world as a shrewd investor that earned him the nickname "King Falcon," is a bachelor no more.

He has also gained notoriety as an ornithologist, based on his recently-published book, *The Giant Owl*, with thirty millions copies sold worldwide to date.

However, not many Texans knew of his noble identity while he worked under the alias Professor Roc. Our diamond bachelor successfully disguised himself as a sloppy, underpaid professor in torn shirts, faded rugged jeans, old cowboy boots and hats while teaching and conducting wildlife research at Texas A&M University-Kingsville.

Professor Rochester was finally lassoed last Saturday by a career diplomat's only daughter—gorgeous former Texas lasso champion, Dr. Goldie Dallas. President Churchill himself was rumored to have matched them up, and our reliable resources have learned the president has been her godfather since the day she was born.

Dr. Dallas is the author of several internationally-famed cryptozoological books, and she is also a government-authorized cryptozoologist conducting controversial research, rediscovering and collecting data that she claims proves the existence of an ancient Primitive Navigational Vault (PNV)

Both of the couple currently work part-time as Professors-in-Residence for the University of Rochester, and the graduate dean there revealed to us that their limited courses on International Investment Studies and The Hollow Earth Theories were over-packed by zealous graduate students, setting a new precedent in those hallowed halls.

Their return to New York has been fully embraced, especially by Rochesterians. So many low-profile bigwigs are crouching in this quiet tech capital of New York State, indeed it needs a lovely golden couple such as this to embellish their social events.

The latest PNV information by Dr. Dallas can be read at her website: dr_dallas_cryptozoological.com, released in conjunction with her wedding.

E.F. Geller

# APPENDIX A

Genesis of Life on Earth Theory, explained in seven parts by theological scholar Alibaba Ma, Ph.Ds.—Cosmology, Theology, Evolution, Astronomy.

Chinese translation provided by Sin Yee Wong
French translation provided by Andre Roux
German translation provided by Wilhelm Gelb
Italian translation provided by Andrea Tarabella
Japanese translation provided by Yumi Kaku
Polish translation provided by Dorota Lewinsky

## Part I

## From Pre-Planck Hyperspace Void to Formation of the Multiverse

The untimely fusion between different forms of superluminal primordial energies in their hyperspace-void ultimately induced an overflow of energies.

Under continuous fusion, these energies further mutated into different forms of intelligent living energies to enable competition for their respective capacities and establish a hierarchy for their respective existences.

Their aggression led to an inter-hyperspace cataclysm, triggering a pre-Planck time inferno. Eventually, it ruptured in a proto big bang to fissure a new dimensional realm's void—the very first—but a mock universe was formed.

Almost nothing existed in this mock universe, but from this fissured void, its super-force fissured uncountable distorted, timeless worm-vein webs in a continuum linking hyperspace with its future physical universe; in turn, these worm-vein webs lay an impeccable, strong foundation.

Almost immediately after, a second big bang erupted; its super-force ruptured an auxiliary mock universe, but from its incidental force, the proto mock universe ruptured a proto space dimension that soon kept up the pace and intercalated the worm-vein web continuum to form a formidable foundational structural frame for its entire future universe. This superluminal structural trajectory dilated faster than light or any other kind of plasma.

Subsequently, the proto universe's lagging helix-time trajectory began to levitate and gradually coalesce along the structural trajectory to establish incipient space-time. Whereas the frontier of the structural trajectory continued to radiate at its superluminal speed until a variable of space expansion known as Space Lapse Rate (SLR) occurred, phenomena of increasing matter coalescing on the structural trajectory decreased its inflation rate and distorted as warped and jiggled swirling pits, especially in the frontier region.

Under this situation, the helix-time trajectory was able to maintain its pace and began to condense along these proto structural trajectory's eddies as proto gas clouds.

Lagging plasma from the helix-time trajectory that immersed subsequently into this swirling caldron eventually caused overloading, expanding and increasing pressure to the worm-vein webs, triggering an auxiliary third big bang.

The subsequent auxiliary third big bang took longer to rupture than its forerunner, and the occurrence of each and every consecutive big bang in the future was variably prolonged, subject to space-time expanding continuously.

This inflation again inflated an auxiliary mock universe of void, and its incidental force fissured within its precedent mock universe a second physical universe that was younger, more energetic and denser than the proto physical universe.

From then onward, the proto universe was not "fleeing" alone, thus the intensity and speed of any future auxiliary big bang's super-force and incidental forces that inflated its variable older universes variably decreased, and their variable space-time distortions during the SLR stagnant phase also decreased with the increase of variable, younger universes.

In order to modulate a balanced space-time, every universe's original, uniform distribution of matter, energy and fundamental forces, especially structural gravitational force, consistently altered after each space-time expansion and subsequent distortion. As a result, the more irregular and distant the galactic distributions appeared in space-time, the older a universe would be and vice versa.

The immersion of a younger universe's expanded space-time to the proto universe also expedited proto universe's displacement to its Natal Space-time Belt's stagnant phase. Here at this distorted space-time frontier, another stage of great condensation occurred—water molecule clouds began to form, and attracted by the spiraling eddies flowed toward gravitational collapse.

When some precocious stars—the proto comets—began to form, they streaked through dense clouds of water molecules along their warped orbits, successively regulating nebular gas clouds' circumferences. They also acted as interstellar shower spouts and propagators to cool down incunabular planets and to shower primordial minerals, dust molecules and building blocks of life along their trails.

At this final phase of the proto universe's Natal Space-time Belt, small proto galaxies had begun to conglomerate amidst nebular and primordial clouds; although its space was still opaque at this stage, deionization was already in progress to clear the space.

Concurrently, space-time distortion occurred again to link up both the hyperspace and proto universe through temporary distribution worm veins and wormholes; this interlink also modulated, stabilized and kept the proto universe from overload or shortage of any cosmic forces, matters or energies.

Subsequently, the earliest series of proto intelligent living energies also started to emerge from their hyperspace voids, traveling to the earliest incunabular planets, and they left the planets just before another big bang was triggered.

The auxiliary fourth big bang inflated a fourth new mock universe and also incidentally inflated the proto universe into the Creation Space-time Belt.

The big bang's super-force brought variable incidental displacement and turbulence to its immediate and two other pre-existing older physical universes. The hyperspace linked again to these universes to extend and distribute its worm veins webs, and another round of intelligent living energies was dispatched or retreated.

When the proto universe's inflation rate decreased toward a stagnant phase, space-time distortion happened again. At this stage, an alternate way emerged to modulate a balanced regional space-time inter-universally through connecting throats of wormhole funnels between each and respective immediate universes. This interlink between universes enabled inter-transfer of variable fundamental forces, matters and energies.

In between stages of space-time distortion, whenever old worm-vein webs multiplied their new worm-vein webs, uncountable wormholes temporarily opened to interlink both hyperspace and universes. If an incipient star or stars were trapped at one or both sides of connected wormhole funnel throats of two space-times, certain pressures were exerted on the surrounding worm-veins.

If continuous stretching of such space-time happened, their respective throats were eventually torn and touched the veins of the wormholes. If such tearing was beyond repair, the throats' connection collapsed to become a permanent wormhole where two different space-time dimensions amalgamated.

Consequently, bigger and more accumulated permanent wormholes swirled in the older universes than the younger universes, which helped transfer an older universe's rarer-attracting matter to a younger universe.

When an auxiliary fifth big bang inflated a fifth mock universe, its incidental super-force resonated with other older incidental forces to accelerate the proto universe's displacement into the Living Space-time Belt.

These amplified mega-waves brought unprecedented, serious space-time abrupt expansion and subsequent serious distortion, especially over the Living Space-time Belt. The space-warps or space-blankets arose in different space-time regions to impel catastrophic collision and galactic cannibalism among celestial bodies. Millions of galaxy clusters superimposed and agglomerated with each other to form super-clusters.

Along this star-pervaded space-time belt, more comets than ever collided and collapsed with derailed planets and stars to form distinguished asteroid belts. Eventually, a newer version of the astronomical map set the stars into their respective accords and positioned them in the stabilized space-time, now more stationary than ever.

When an auxiliary sixth big bang occurred, the sixth young mock universe's inflation drastically decreased, as it had to levitate and distribute its incidental forces over its immediate universe and the four other older physical universes, thus the incidental force reached the proto physical universe at the very last and at the slowest rate among all other younger universes. Subsequently, it helped the Living Space-time Belt displace into the Flourishing Space-time Belt but without serious space-time distortion at this frontier region.

This space-time region had well-balanced, distributed regular matter throughout it, such as celestial bodies and living things. However, if its particular space-time region was over-expanded by immersion of denser, repelling dark energies from younger universes, to achieve a balanced space-time between universes, such immersion transferred an older universe's overflowing, rarer-attracting dark matters through black holes to a younger universe's particular regional space-time. If the dark energy immersion was overwhelming, it caused a supernova explosion; its trajectory range's space-time distortion depended on how sturdy a universe's foundation had been established. These supernovae's aftermaths would incur a Great Exposition Phase (GEP) to its surrounding space-time, especially where planets with living things freed from star clouds and abused planetary atmospheres would be seriously mutated under radiation.

During the seventh auxiliary big bang, while the Flourishing Space-time Belt was displacing into the Grace Space-time Belt, the seventh mock universe's super-force reached a point of resonance with other older incidental inflation forces. Another round of abrupt space-time expansion and serious distortion occurred; however, its aftermath was not as serious due to a space-time structure firmer than the earlier era's astronomical havoc.

When a catastrophic mega-wave trajectory inflated directly toward those stars and planets, and that included the unprotected Earth, this regional astronomical calamity recycled the primary and subsidiary damaged earthly atmospheric vaults once more.

A global protecting atmosphere with its own space-time vault was inflated from its central core of resources. Its regenerated gravities also were adjusted and thus continents drifted further apart and shaped the earth's topography that accordingly reflected universal astronomical morphology. Once this regenerated atmosphere completed its inflation, any alien's willful intrusions to the earth had to break through its extended radius's thicker layers of obstruction.

And through each and respective space-time mega turbulences, the earth would be repaired by gaining additional atmospheric space and also have its space-time rectified with the multiverse's inflated space-time.

After the beginning phase of the Grace Space-time Belt, its regional space-time finally tempered and achieved structural stability. This was a most peaceful era after the six Creation Days, a Rest Day compared to all other restless eras before and after. The planetary living things and beings living along this expanded space-time region were free from frequent aliens' visitation, invasion and control, due to the intergalactic distances.

At this stage, when space-time was under expansion, any structural forces from worm-webs and densities of helix-time trajectory from any consecutive big bang were always stronger and higher than its variable precedents. Thus they formed their own respective void of density, gravitational field, matter, energy and space-time to intercalate among hyperspace to frame an impeccably strong structural support inter-universally. As a result, this separated all living energies and physical living things into their respective dimensional realms and prevented infiltration from one to another.

If there were any transference of unparalleled dark attracting matter from older universes to the younger universes, they acted as an absorbent filter. If there were any immersion of incompatible dark repelling energies from younger universes to this proto universe, they acted as an insulator to protect the fragile living things and beings living along this space-time range.

The Eighth big bang moved the Grace Space-time Belt to the Stagnant Space-time Belt, where all galaxies and celestial bodies began to stretch further from each other, overwhelmed by variable forces of dark energies from an array of six younger universes' inter-immersion.

Eventually, when the incessant incompatible forces of dark energies within the Stagnant Space-time Belt started to compress on the hyperspaces and other universes' peripherals to cause expansion and acceleration more than ever before, it began to weaken the inter-galaxies' gravitational forces, and subsequently galaxies began to drift further away from each other.

Those drifted stellar systems were easily attracted to and annihilated by oversized and growing numbers of wormholes, thus galaxies collapsed one after another within the Stagnant Space-time Belt until a catastrophic space-time imbalance arose.

Again GEP happened at the Stagnant Space-time Belt's distorted space-time phase. Here most living beings were condemned, hence most planets' atmospheres eroded and aliens again invaded their planets of interest through highly distorted space-time, but this only happened among those surviving galaxies free from heavy dust clouds. However, their breakdown did not last long, as the increasingly deteriorating, collapsing and shrinking space-time accelerated a subsequent auxiliary big bang.

When the ninth big bang expedited, its incidental inflation prompted astronomical havoc to the proto universe's Doom Space-time Belt whilst on its displacement from the Stagnant Space-time Belt. Over the extent of time, due to serious deterioration of inter-galaxy gravitational forces, substantial masses and lives had been annihilated within black holes. However, this serious space-time distortion shortened intergalactic distance, thus aiding the most resilient celestial beings and highly evolved planetary beings to continuously migrate to those limited favorable planets until everything collapsed at the end, unless they successfully trespassed to one of the most compatible younger auxiliary universe's phases to endure and sustain their lives.

During this dying era, the dooming-comets became as active as their Inflating Space-time Belt's equivalents, but now their passing trajectories only brought annihilation to any surviving celestial bodies and remaining ill-fated lives. Along their way, these doomed icy-comets collected specimens from drifting proto celestial bodies liable to have fallen into their worm-drain circumferences and transported them through distribution wormholes and worm-veins to other new and younger auxiliary universes.

A big crunch occurred to this Doom Space-time Belt's end phase as more celestial bodies were annihilated. Eventually all the remaining stars, planets and celestial matters were obliterated until there were only wormholes in the quickly shrinking remaining space-dimension.

And these vanished stellar systems were transferred through wormholes to distributing worm-veins to end up as coils of conserved primordial crucial information, forces, energies and matter in the hyper-rotating conservatory vaults all over the periphery of hyperspace. Conversely, the overloaded conservatory vault and their distributing veins webs were dilated and compressed to reach their ultimate peak of capacities, densities and pressures.

Abrupt contraction of the space-dimension started when the bigger wormholes began to swallow smaller wormholes to increase their respective sizes until all wormholes coalesced to form a mega compressed wormhole, and all matter, light and energy drained in it was transferred through worm-veins to a conservatory void. After the contracted space-dimension was withdrawn into the mega wormhole, finally even the strongest worm-vein webs could not escape this mega wormhole's gravity.

It took another pre-Planck epoch for a compressed mega wormhole to mature as a mega white wormhole before an auxiliary tenth big bang occurred to form a timeless inferno void, commencing an auxiliary new multiverse.

Before advancement of any auxiliary multiverse's first big bang, the intergalactic forces of its primitive multiverse decrease to its weakest, especially its Doom Space-time Belt, but the hyperspace forces increase at its strongest, and the expanded hyperspace compresses on the periphery of the multiverse.

When the ultra-forces and vortexes eject the first big bang of an auxiliary multiverse's worm-vein webs, the compressed space-dimension will soon be transferred through the throat of the mega-compressed wormhole and in time through another auxiliary big bang to inflate and to intercalate its mock universe's inflating worm-veins to form the first physical universe of an auxiliary multiverse.

Commencement of a new multiverse only happens when its last multiverse's Doom Space-time Belt is completely immersed and replaced by an auxiliary multiverse's Doom Space-time Belt. Each Doom Space-time Belt's demise also indicates the birth of an auxiliary multiverse in the near future, and this continuum keeps the multiverse infinite.

The continuum of a new big bang to inflate a younger physical universe, gradually replacing a doomed physical universe, maintains and halts any hyperspace-realm from getting any chance to deform the physical space-realm, and a whole multiverse commences whenever an auxiliary tenth big bang is triggered.

# Part II

# In the Beginning

The hyperspace's host of all hosts and its proto intelligent living energies of various forms were the main contributors to evolution of various primordial inter-planetary ecologies or procreation and creation of intelligent living things or living beings from primordial essences and resources available on any habitable primordial planets.

Within the physical multiverse, subject to their positions in varied space-time belts within different universes, these living energies with varied abilities transformed to their respective adapted features, and their respective longevities or duration to remain as a physical entity varied according to their respective presented space-time intrinsic superiorities and missions.

Periodically different forms of living energies, with their individually-assigned missions, traveled from hyperspace through worm-veins to emerge at routinely opened-up wormholes to reach their respective planets located in different universes. Once they completed their duties, inferior forms of living energies usually perished, their possessed or transformed physical entities with their living energies extinguished. The superior forms either departed a planet, continuing to another new destination for their next respective tasks, or returned to their respective hyperspace-domains.

Thus any incoming cataclysm to threaten their living energy levels was avoided by leaving the doomed planets to other less hazardous destinations, and these living energies could only rejuvenate and stay in optimum eternal bliss if they returned periodically to their respective hyperspace dormant realms.

Under the deployments within highly radiated space-time, weaker and more willful forms of living energies would mutate to evolve a physical world's consciousness, greed and lusts to indulge in worldly activities but rebel against their endowing roles.

However, between the non-substantial hyperspace and physical universes lay certain laws of nature's decree; if any of these living energies overstayed, unbridled or abused their endowed creating ability and numinous prowess in any other alienated entities other than their own realm, their living energies would be reduced according to the level of power they misused.

Their insufficient living energies might get them trapped in a physical form and thus they had to remain sojourning in different universes; eventually they would either perish physically on one of the planets, with their living energies instantly extinguished, or with their insufficient living energies become trapped and tormented in an incompatible state of realm-less abyss.

During the course of creation of the multiverse, even the highest forms of living energies could become mutated, corrupted or evolved. Thus beginning eons ago, some of them either were cast out by their host of hosts to sojourn at different planets or some of them simply refused to return to their hyperspace-homes by evading their duties to hide on different planets in various disguises of transformed physical features. But if chance permitted, they preferred to sojourn on their favorable planets to transform into their most captivating, most indulgent and most glorifying planetary beings' features.

Eventually, due to their overstaying in a physical realm, their respective transfigured features' living energies ended up too weak and too corrupted to transform back into a living-energy state for wormhole travel, thus they invented spacecraft for intergalactic travel.

These tainted, fallen living energies normally lived up to a thousand Earth years as transformed physical beings;

therefore, in order to sustain their longevity in a physical world, they usually chose to stay in an invisible, powerless, dormant living energy state until a breakthrough time—when they learned that some planetary living-beings' sacrifices could be used to refill their living energies and to resume their formidable prowess in performing some of their specific supernatural feats.

As these intelligent living energies were corrupt, they also manifested as equally corrupt transfigured celestial beings on any planets over any physical universe.

Gifted by their supernatural intelligence and specific abilities to possess other physical beings or transform their physical features accordingly to cater to their needs, their disguise features usually helped them exercise their authority, gain control over various planetary living beings and reign over different planets.

* * * * * *

Although living things and planetary beings emerging on different planets were adaptable and evolved through an eon of generations along different space-time belts, they only experienced longer and better life if they happened to live at a calmer phase of a space-time belt or on the most stabilized Grace Space-time Belt freed from major astronomical havoc or camouflaged from dust clouds. This they could do without being discovered, invaded, interbred and corrupted by any ambitious celestial being outlaws or curious alien planetary beings.

Whenever space-time distortion arose, certain intergalactic routes could be shortened. This encouraged different aliens from older, advanced planets or doomed planets for intergalactic traveling with mechanical means of transport to touch down on their favorable planets. These aliens' invasion or visitation unavoidably happened to some of those planets that floated along the Natal, Creation, Living, Stagnant and Doom Space-time Belts.

During the earliest generations, some alien-outlaws used spacecraft for intergalactic travel to do reconnaissance and later they invaded those primitive planets with rich primordial resources of minerals and gemstones to commit themselves as intergalactic criminals by transporting those minerals back to their own respective dwelling planets.

During their subsequent successive returns to Earth, some of these outrageous alien-outlaws began to conduct genetic engineering experiments to clone successful living beings as local slaves to work and mine for them, and from time to time they even kidnapped and maneuvered some of these slaves to other planets.

* * * * * *

Just like all habitable planets throughout different galaxies, Planet Earth had its own scheduled wormhole openings and access times to link up intergalactic zones and even the hyperspace realm.

As nature decreed, during the final phase of the Natal Space-time Belt, it called forth the earliest presence from the mightiest host of all living energies of hyperspace to Earth.

Subsequently, through those undetected abysses connected by worm-veins, a series of different living-energy forms penetrated the wormholes with their varied inherent missions disposed and dispatched. They reached the young Earth one after another over elapsed space-time, but again they found they were neither the first nor the last comers.

To date back among those proto preternatural living energies, one form among them hailed as the oldest, mightiest and the most intelligent, resilient and formidable among other secondary, tertiary and inferior living energies.

They were immortal in hyperspace, as they were not bound by time, space and matter. They possessed abilities to transform themselves into different forms of luminous living-energy states that enabled them to surf superluminally with traceless ease through varying dimensional worm-veins and wormholes to reach their desired destinations faster than any weaker living energies.

In order to cope with their respective sojourns, usually upon reaching each individual planet, as they possessed such great capabilities, their luminous living-energy states transformed accordingly into respective ideal states or transfigured to living physical features to cater to a planet's favorable environment.

These living energies deflected foreign interference better than other, weaker living energies. When they manifested in their co-existing physical and living-energy states in their present new entity, they co-exhibited certain features, which were incompatible, unfathomed and unattained by many weaker living energies and planetary living beings' limited capacities of intelligence, imagination and understanding.

The most divine and the very first intelligent living-energy induced in this earliest existing hyperspace colony was their *Omni*-host. Out of respect, love and according to *etis* original luminous features, *et* was called *Albha* by those earthly humans and their descendants that *et* created.

In order to halt the chaos, turbulence and instability among overflow surging living energies in the unsubstantial dimensional void, *Albha* masterminded and dispatched different forms of living energies in continuum to the physical dimension's continuum.

But *et* restricted any primordial living energies from overstaying or conquering permanently any physical entities by opening and linking their inter-dimensional traveling passages in such a way that, based on laws of nature, regulated their respective designations.

If any of these living energies didn't return on time to their own dimensional homes after their respective missions or if they evaded their obligations, then they were cast out from their dimensional home and eventually exterminated.

What other primeval living energies didn't possess, other than *Albha*, was *etis* omnipotence with intrinsic resilience, backup reactions and filtering capacities that automatically followed up to protect *etis* perfect self by counteracting those imperfect living energies that challenged, haunted or harmed *etim* unceasingly.

*Albha* was omni-featured, as no other living energies surpassed *etis* ultimate abilities, capacities and flexibilities in transforming *etimself* unconditionally into new perfect living energies. *Et* could fissure different features and present *etis* counterparts over different realms of co-existing living states at different dimensional realms at *etis* desire.

And *Albha* was omniscient; *et* could see into the distant past or future, *et* possessed spells that could read and thus manipulate others' thoughts and actions, yet *et* seldom enforced these powers, preferring to let all other living energies and living things freely explore and choose their own destinies within certain restrictions. Inevitably, *Albha* was also omnipresent to protect those *et* created and cherished.

In physical universes, *Albha* was hailed as the fastest and earliest emerged divine deity and *et* alone executed *etis* creativity, which was unfathomed even by *etis* own form of *albhly* living energies.

*Albha's* innate mission brought forth only continuous impeccable creations, propagations, peace, unconditional love and grace along *etis* presence.

Those *albhly* inclined living-beings created by *etim* instinctively sought *etim* through telepathy when their souls and lives were in deep troubles; only if ungrateful living beings lived vulgarly would *Albha* forsake them.

*Albha's* living energies possessed such unfathomed combinations and formidable capacity that *et* wouldn't become influenced and defiled by any physical world, freshly indulgent and seductive; instead, *et* rolled continuously, accumulating, improving and mutating along each and every developmental stage of the physical realm universes.

With intrinsic, incredible, unbeatable feats and facilities, which none of the other hosts from living-energy colonies possessed, *Albha* anticipated the burning hot naked incipient Planet Earth, that could be easily mistaken as an asteroid within the Natal Space-time Belt, cooling down after it had been plunged successively by icy comets. Consequently, a sphere of dark hollow void was inflated in its core that was covered by a deep-water atmosphere enshrouded with a thick, steamy, turbulent ocean.

These icy comet tails plunged to the earth, and other planets acted as the ice dispenser. They also carried along primordial constituents of life that they collected along their trails from other regions of space, older planets and stars, and these potential lives waited for their respective favorable instant to flourish over the wilderness of Earth.

Certainly *Albha* foretold the urge and desire among spying primitive living energies; *et* thus planned to expedite the Earth's creation by constructing a vault-like earthly station and navigational routes, with impediments over its peripherals in the existing wall of primitive water resources, to link up *etis* different space-stations and hyperspace dimensional home.

Initially, many hundreds of millions of Earth years elapsed from the leaking time of this earliest creation days' enclosed earthly station, and routes were oriented while just a single hyperspace day elapsed for *Albha*.

The construction of this vault also helped to keep earthly primordial resources, precious stones and minerals hidden and protected from theft out of the earth by alien outlaws.

The primordial reserves inside the impediment enabled *Albha* to cultivate living things and create other living beings under a protected shield free from astronomical calamities.

# Part III

# Six Creation Days

To generate *etis* plans, *Albha* was way ahead and quicker than any other primeval living energies in terms of *etis* speed, plans and creations; thus earlier than any of them, *et* created communication links from *etis* dimensional realm to other planetary space-stations before *et* finally brooded over the primordial earth on the long-evo Creation Day One.

*Albha's* presence and *etis* deadly luminous *albhly* lights, as luminous living energies began to conduct reconnaissance on bubbling, water-enshrouded Earth, barred any foreign living energies' rival approach or intervention.

When *et* retreated from work, light gradually subsided from the earth and darkness displaced it; the destined icy comet tails collided with the earth periodically to wipe off the first series of primordial heat-resistant extremophiles that flourished under *albhly* light. Due to the extreme drop of temperature without an atmospheric shield, the earth's water temperature dropped.

The phenomenon of brightness brought by *albhly* lights indicating *Albha* was present at work on Earth, was considered Creation Day, and the phenomenon of darkness indicating *Albha* was at rest and absent from the earth was considered Creation Night.

At this earliest stage of primeval Earth, which still hovered within the Natal Space-time Belt and the earliest phase of the Creation Space-time Belt, its incipient space-time elapsed similarly to hyperspace-time.

On long-evo Creation Day 2, the earth began to move into the Creation Space-time Belt. With help from an auxiliary big bang's incidental forces, *Albha*, in *etis* luminous living-energy state, began to connect *etis* outer space links to the earth. Through fundamental forces executed to part the water from the newly inflated firmament, an intricate network of labyrinth-like territorial-pathways framed and concealed *etis* earthly space-station inside the subterranean hollow earth.

Soon, *Albha* left the day's work; simultaneously, darkness fell. Designated comets faithfully swept across the earth with their icy tails again. Eventually the globe of water dropped to sub-zero, declaring the doom for outbound Cambrian primordial marine life that flourished under *albhly* light.

During this long-evo creation night, an abundance of filtered and retained primordial matter and elements inside the newly inflated vault gradually converted to enrich *albhly* living air *quionz*, water *creionz*, light *xions* and soil *albhlysolz*.

On long-evo Creation Day 3, again by executing another auxiliary big bang's incidental forces, *Albha* in *etis* luminous living-energy state began to generate a series of successive air and water turbulences and folding and unfolding to create undulating scenic landscapes of continents and seas.

By now *Albha's* labyrinth-like territorial vault had successfully emerged over the prime terrains of outer Earth, immersed in the water and concealed within the subterranean span of hollow earth. The source of four ancient rivers was hollow earth's mighty subterranean artesian fountain. These rivers then divided and subdivided to link and extend all over Earth's surface. Zones excluded from *albhly* outer Earth's territory vault were wilderness, and consistently exposed to meteorite strikes.

In order to furnish the earthly station with a strong structural foundation and an established self-reliant vault, *Albha* mounted seven cornerstones at different corners of *etis* vault. Three big crystals faced the east, three big crystals faced the south, and a big stone faced the sky. These respective crystals' wavelengths triggered very powerful energies to tune the canopy space-time automatically and align it parallel with the universe's space-time inflated direction and therefore inducted a time warp. In turn, *Albha* and *albhly* living energies that dwelled inside the canopy could escape from the physical world's elapsed time, which had commenced.

Moreover, other inducted sources of energy and residues were redirected to the center of *etis* earthly station as a central source of energy to radiate fundamental forces, livelihood light and functional signals for living things.

The fundamental forces automatically regulated prevailing air and water currents to control the earth's axis tilting. In turn, this tilting helped to monitor the canopy's communications and space-time orientation, and the presence of central perpetual livelihood light helped the growth of thriving varieties of vegetation inside the canopy.

In contrast, Earth's wilderness land was almost barren, with hot mist rising from the surface immediately vaporized into space. This opaque, vacuum space was permeated by misty dust and smelled of acrid sulfur, and was where the earliest, highly heat-resistant Permian plankton began to thrive.

*Albha's* shuttling vault was linked from way above the primitive atmosphere and extended downward to the earth, where a labyrinth of pathways continued on the ground and down into the subterranean hollow earth. At an innermost prime terrain goal, *Albha* planted a garden, monitored consistently by the perpetual central source of energy's livelihood light. *Et* also placed two specially-created fruit trees for future yields and consumption. One of them was prepared as the chief source of invigorating vital health for *albhly* spy creatures after their wilderness trips, and another one was prepared as the secret source of sustaining life for physical state body features; essentially the key to eternal life. *Albha* would use its forever living fruit to rejuvenate *etis* physical state after each wilderness trip.

*Albha* finally incorporated the physical earth in creating an additional magnificent dwelling base with independent space-time on this earthly planet, and its periphery was secured by *albhly* atmospheric fence with sucker particles, which effectively kept trespassers out.

The sucker particles of the *albhly* atmospheric fence, made with unbeatable resilience, could eliminate, convert, insulate, neutralize, auto-repair or deflect any unfavorable foreign elements like living energies, external harmful cosmic radiation, poisonous air, electromagnetic interference, foreign elements, pressures or forces. If this defensive atmospheric fence was disturbed, its surroundings triggered lightning and fumes. For counteracting continuously approaching trespassers, during the day a pillar-like cloud formed, and during the night a pillar-like fire formed. Additionally, both underwater and atmospheric peripheral protective fences first ejected lightning as a warning to trespassers and later rendered the intruder visionless, senseless, disorientated, and confused or made them refrain from proceeding along that course. If any trespasser was mindlessly stubborn and would not retreat, the intruder would be exterminated, leaving no trace. The intruder's energy would recirculate and replenish the exhausted energy source of the *albhly* atmospheric fence to repair any damage done to it.

From the very first creation day, when almighty *Albha* in living-energy state planned to construct *etis* territorial base on the desolated earth, *et* had figured out that a series of incoming incidental inflations would resonate with other older incidental inflations during the transitional phase between third creation day's eve and fourth creation day's dawn, triggering a catastrophic space-time distortion. In turn, these amplified mega forces would cause space-time to expand abruptly to cause billions of celestial bodies to transfer through temporary wormholes, space-warps, space-blankets or through multiple collisions to end up in some unexpected space-time locations to agglomerate with other galaxies, clusters and super clusters. Under this havoc, millions of planets collided or were declared doomed as billions of shattered planetesimals remained in space.

After the abrupt change of astronomical outlook at the beginning phase of this Living Space-time Belt, whenever any regional space-time distortion happened again, the comet's trajectory wouldn't intercross with the shifted Planet Earth's orbit anymore; instead, they showed up periodically to intercross other planetary orbits in the solar system to demolish or collide with some of their ill-fated natural satellites, dwarf-planets, planets or planetesimals.

In turn, these shattered remnants were ejected to other nearby planetary orbits and that included the earth's orbit; nevertheless, most of these asteroids remained to travel inside their original trajectory accordingly to Bode's Law. These comets only picked up excess asteroids from intercrossed orbits and discarded them later to replenish intercrossed planetary orbits that deprived them of mass, and under this situation the mass and space of respective planetary orbits could be restored and rebalanced for generations with the expanded space-time, in turn the existing planets' well-being could be protected.

Multiple cataclysms occurred during the third creation night's long bitter ice age that coincidentally jeopardized by pro tem fourth creation day's abrupt astronomical havoc. Eruption of *albhly* outer earth's canopy eventually caused the largest mass extinction of Permian living things ever known on Earth.

That was the main reason why *Albha* didn't create any living things until Creation Day Five, as *et* knew that during such a calamity-prone era, living things wouldn't be able to survive under sudden decompression and compression when *etis* primordial vault had to inflate an incipient subsidiary vault and rectify its space-time with the outer space space-time's abrupt expansion and distortion.

The new astronomical scenes of countless solar systems, clusters and super clusters eventually incorporated a sun, a moon, planets, constellations and billions of stars seemingly stable above the earth; however, all these big and small lights were barely detectable by naked eyes, as the aftermath of galactic calamities made the vacuum of space look hazy and opaque, and even strong sunrays hardly penetrated the haze to reach the incipient secondary atmosphere of the wilderness earth, which was inflated when the outer earth's *albhly* canopy pathways were ruptured by the mega force.

This rupture caused excessive leaking of *albhly* vault's central source of energy; thus its fundamental forces, living air and other living essences were discharged to the wilderness, as well as its web-like orientation signals were also extended to the newly inflated vault.

Inflation of a subsidiary but structurally weak and unstable wilderness space-time also quickly tore the supercontinent Pangaea's foundation, creating the risk of Pangaea breaking apart at any moment. It also gradually tilted the earth's axis from perpendicular to the plane of ecliptic. This uncontrollable leakage gradually came under control when cosmic forces from the new constellations, sun and moon became fully functional around Earth. Leaking fissures along the vulnerable *albhly* atmospheric fence converted into exhaust and intake ventilation holes generated routinely by cosmic forces.

The newly set of astronomical features would function fully after the sixth creation day in prompting the new earthly day and night to commence its' own timing and bio-rhythm, and the constellations were used as signs for seasons, days and years.

From then onward, the universe's space-time had gained major stability with no major astronomical upheaval until its pre doom and doom, and the additionally inflated subsidiary atmosphere in the wilderness acted as a spare protecting shell for the outer earth's *albhly* pathways.

On the fourth creation day, under reionization of *albhly* light, the hazy wilderness-atmosphere turned clearer, and also under *albhly* living air and living light's induction, all kinds of high-resilience spores, algae and plant seeds began to germinate, thrive and propagate along hot bubbly waterways. Subsequently, resilient dormant embryos from numerous closely touched down meteorites or closely collided older planets also began to revive and give birth to successive primordial creatures, including dinosaurs.

Once *Albha* called off *etis* fourth creation day, the wilderness returned to its darkness veil. Subsequent series of comets discerningly inter-crossed to collide or demolish induced star-crossed masses on imbalanced planetary orbits in the solar system, and some ejected asteroids or asteroids carried by comets ended up discarded on Earth's orbit or on Earth, and when the earth's subsidiary atmosphere was perforated, its surface temperature lowered abruptly.

Consequently, "thermal downshock," caused by the dip of sudden coldness to the subsidiary atmosphere, caused Earth to expand abruptly. Thus supercontinent Pangaea began to break into the subcontinents of Laurasia and Gondwana. This series of calamities caused during the transition from fourth creation night's eve into the pro tem fifth creation day only brought minor mass extinction to certain species of Triassic creatures and dinosaurs, since most living things could still inter-cross the subcontinents and migrate to sunshine-prevailing belts.

On long-evo Creation Day 5, *Albha* started to create successive *albhly* mammoth sea monsters, marine creatures and birds for *etis* recovery canopy. They were designated to expedite propagation of varied vegetation to unreachable hinter zones and wilderness selectively and tactically. Some of these intelligent creatures were well trained to assist *Albha* as territory guards, as wilderness zone spies, or as forecasters of portentous weather and environmental catastrophe.

*Albha* also selected some special-featured creatures as wilderness biological pest control, especially as *et* was aware that some foreign living energies had cunningly escaped from *etis* presence of *albhly* lights by possessing either rocks, mammoth organisms or some burgeoning extraterrestrial savage creatures like dinosaurs to gain strength, size, regenerative and mutative abilities. They survived symbiotically by breathing thin dusty air and combusting toxic gases amidst the wilderness environment.

To propagate, some of the most highly adaptable primeval vegetation, birds and creatures burned themselves to traceless ashes at the end of their lives, but cyclically regenerated or were reborn after burning.

When *Albha* called off *etis* fifth working day, successive comets again discerningly collided or demolished remaining star-crossed planets that inter-crossed each other in the solar system. Their aftermath's asteroids ejected into Earth's orbit and perforated the subsidiary atmosphere, lowering Earth's temperature once more.

Both related aftermath of "thermal downshock" and abrupt expansion of subsidiary atmosphere reflected structurally on the tearing continental plates. Consequently, huge amounts of methane released from the torn ocean beds inevitably wiped out vulnerable coastal marine creatures to near extinction. However, highly resilient Triassic-Jurassic creatures evaded this and inter-crossed the parted lands to sunshine-prevailing belts in time, remaining to survive.

Conversely, those favorable *albhly* creatures that stayed in vulnerable outer earth's *albhly* canopy or roamed in the wilderness distinctively received their migrating signals right before any calamity happened and escaped into hollow earth or hollow earth's divisional or subdivisional subterranean caves.

After long-evo fifth creation night's havoc and following restoration, activities began to hasten at both the *albhly* canopy and the wilderness on the final creation day. *Albha* commenced *etis* long-evo Creation Day 6 by creating successive domestic land mammals, creatures and insects to fill up *etis* canopy.

In the subsidiary atmosphere, under radiation of *albhly* living lights, building blocks and spores carried to Earth eons ago by icy comets and meteorites started to revive one after another under their respective favorable conditions, and highly resilient vegetation and living things propagated in the water finally invaded and thrived on land.

Again, *Albha* detected increasing minuscule sparks of rivalry and malicious threats from another series of incoming secondary living energies. Whenever exposed to *albhly* lights, they would cunningly possess rocks or creatures; cataclysm made them energetic or gained them regenerative and mutative abilities.

Eventually came a time when dinosaurs burgeoned and reigned over the wilderness zone; they also began to threaten the tame *albhly* living things. This incited *Albha* to clone and release predatory creatures into the wilderness. These *albhly* wild animals could not only kill ferocious wilderness prey but could also extinguish parasitic living energies by belching out *albhly* fire when they got angry.

In order to ensure *etis* living things traveled in and out of the canopy in an orderly and peaceful manner, *Albha* also designed their respective daily navigation and seasonal migration routes systematically to cater to their different needs. These daily and seasonal communication networks were guided by the most primitive color spectrum, transmitted by the central source of energy through cosmic forces.

These various transmissions routinely emitted different signals to confine, dispatch or reallocate various *albhly* mammoth living creatures to thrive and breed best within their own range of feeding grounds, hideouts and territories. This mysterious, labyrinthine, wire-like transmission coverage was unaffected by bad weather, by other alienated frequencies or by any kind of obstacle. Instead, it effectively penetrated and conveyed underneath the subterranean hollow earth and inside and outside the canopy.

Time elapsed as *Albha* created more and more things to fill up the earth. *Et* decided there should be a superior living thing to oversee and manage those living things that *et* created. A good idea conceived in *Albha's* creative mind impelled *etim* into action.

Soon the spying, alien living-energies hidden all over the wilderness fringe pondered uncomprehendingly why *Albha* appeared on *etis* canopy's pathway transformed from *etis* luminous state to a stunning physical-being with a halo shining on *etis* heads. They tried to imitate this transformation accordingly, but in frustration they couldn't figure out why they were unable to perform such a feat. Actually, this halo was a protective shield for *Albha's* living energy physical feature state.

Initially they doubted when *Albha* picked up living *albhlysolz* moisturized by *creionz* from the ground and sculpted it according to *etis* image. The penetrating, scintillating observers' twinkles had increased in perplexity and questioned why *Albha* had to debase *etimself* for this latest creation by working manually. After they witnessed how *Albha* instantaneously transfigured into a physical-being to perform the breath-graft of living energies to *etis* creation and successfully brought forth a life out of it, they realized they had actually underestimated *Albha's* prowess. Jealous alien living-energies manifested their anger as colorful lightning and thunder flashing and rolling all over the wilderness.

At a specific space-time on a fair, habitable planet, and from its available primordial resources, *Albha* would use *etis* transformed image-being and transfigured physical-being to create an optimum new species of planetary-being, but this only happened on limited fair planets across different galactic belts. Nevertheless, on this Planet Earth, with *Albha's* specially constructed vault, the same fair result was also achieved.

*Albha* called *etis* newly propagated earthly being *Homo albha*. *Et* knew *Homo albha's* weakness, thus to avoid any harm falling upon *etis* beloved earthly being from jealous alien living energies, *Homo albha* was immediately confined into the innermost lobby of *Albha's* secret hideout.

In using the breath-graft *spiritus vitae*, a technique unknown to other alien living energies, *Albha* needed to consume plenty of living energy and vitality from *etis* transfigured physical-being state. *Albha* therefore only used *Homo albha's* tiniest living *asionz*, found in one of his ribs, and radiated it with *albhly* lights in order to clone an accompanying and assisting female partner for *Homo albha*. This work concluded *Albha's* creation upon *etis* sixth creation day.

When *albhly* twilight subsided on the sixth creation night, successive comets began to approach some planetary orbits in the solar system again. Through the past three creation nights, the inter-crossing comets had gradually redistributed and modulated most shattered excess or deprived remnants to different planetary orbits over the solar system. But on this particular creation night, a series of comets was particularly liable to inter-cross an obviously overweight orbit located between Mars and Jupiter, where a huge planet lived—once the oldest and the most wicked but smartest planetary-being in the solar system.

Eventually this habitable planet and the rest of its natural satellites in this highly distorted orbit were completely demolished to become a significant asteroid belt. Over this fateful creation night, the earth was bombarded successively by ejected extraterrestrial asteroids or asteroids brought by comets especially originating from this newly formed asteroid belt.

The damage to the subsidiary atmosphere caused by successive, massive meteorites' impacts promptly turned the wilderness into an opaque space and triggered serious "thermal downshock." Subsequently, the subsidiary atmosphere expanded abruptly, especially when the central source of energy's auto-repair mode became activated. The excessive natural disasters like meteorites strikes, a sudden dirge of extreme temperature, lack of sunlight, lack of air or land partings, extended starvation, suffocation and annihilation eventually caused mass extinction to Cretaceous animals and vegetation, and most significantly dinosaurs became extinct.

# Part IV

# A Rest Day and its Succeeding Chaotic Days

On long-evo Rest Day 7, after *Albha* had completed all *etis* creations on the earth, *et* remained at *etis* earthly station. The earth was now located at the Living Space-time Belt's Hallowed Enveloped Phase (HEP), as after reionization completed on the opaque subsidiary atmosphere, it was promptly enveloped by negative ions and living light and this helped to restore *Albha's* living energies that *et* consumed during the creation days.

For the first time the constellations over the sky of the earth started to become visible under the moonlight. The sun, the moon and the constellations were finally tempered and started to fully function. The space-time and wilderness atmosphere had structurally stabilized, thus for the time being, the living things on Earth wouldn't face major natural calamities and hostile threats from other aliens and menacing creatures. Also the wilderness atmosphere's oxidation level had abruptly increased.

*Albha* was pleased to see living things under the outer earth's canopy enjoy their sunbathing, singing and dancing under the sun and how owls hooted and lightning bugs danced under the moon. The peace, joy and order happened to all living things and nature on Earth. *Homo albha* and all living things revered *Albha's* mighty creations, thus they regarded this Rest Day as a holy day, too.

At this hallowed age, the outer earth canopy's primary atmosphere conserved the solar residues and distant celestial rays by converting and amplifying them to luminous particles in a *noctilucent* cloud. And before this happened— during the preceding creation days—*albhly* lights were conserved and converted into a *noctilucent* cloud.

This cloud would brighten up its canopy perpetually, and the level of micro luminal particles emitted during the night was dependent on the strength of solar energy collected and conserved during the day.

If micro luminal charged ions were amplified by the central resources, the intensity formed nuclei that bonded with living vapors through bombardment to cause arrays of colorful aurorae. This would further enhance catalysts for primitive vegetation to propagate, germinate or grow lushly and for all living things to rejuvenate, promote healing or growth. This phenomenon was known as aurorasynthesis. This aurorasynthesis especially benefited *albhly* living things by inhibiting their hunger and mobility during long creation nights and during long periods of outer earth's calamities.

Another special phenomenon happened in this epoch called solarnating. It worked almost like hibernating, except that hibernating happens in winter. Solarnating happened during transitional moments when darkness subsided to welcome the first morning sunlight. Under the direction of the earth's central resources the filtered receding nocturnal ions collided with astronomical dawn light to bring suppression on *albhly* giant creatures' hunger while they lay under the morning sunbath. Their inactivity while solarnating gave time to other smaller creatures and *Homo albha* to forage.

After *Albhly* Rest Day 7, the Living Space-time Belt began to displace into the Flourishing Space-time Belt. Within a Great Exposition Phase (GEP), space-time was cleared from heated gas and dust clouds. Living energies, living beings and living things that stayed on a planet without a shield of thick atmosphere to protect them inevitably were exposed under GEP's radiation to experience degeneration, mutation and rejection.

During GEP, Earth's protection was weakened by successive huge meteorites perforating its wilderness's subsidiary atmosphere, and the activated *albhly* canopy's central resources could not exhaust its repairing elements quickly enough to mend the resultant enormous ozone holes.

Consequently, this partially exposed, inhabitable Earth particularly attracted other advanced planetary alien-beings and wicked *albhly* living-energy outlaws to escape to the earth in evading their respective planetary orbit's upheaval or regional space-time's upheaval.

In an earlier time, before the earth's creation days, some ill-fated *albhly* living energies during their intergalactic sojourns radiated upon their earliest attempts of physical feature transfiguration. They slowly began to corrupt and eventually some of those unbridled recalcitrant ones simply refused to show their respective decreed designations, thus they were kicked out by *Albha* from *etis* dimension or some of them simply refused to return to their dimensional home, instead they took refuge on remote or obscure planets all over the multiverse.

Among them, *Albha's* chief assistant *Morg* had mutated and descended into the most jealous, deceitful and sly of all *Albha's* secret rivals. *Ut* led corrupted *albhly* living energies under his disposal and dispatch.

Due to dereliction of their respective duties, initially some of these guilty *albhly* living energies played hide and seek with *Albha* so they wouldn't be caught red-handed, but during GEP, if any of these *albhly* living energies outlaws dwelt along this radiated belt, they mutated quicker and thus became more defiled and corrupt than ever. Once they learned that *Albha* was physically absent from GEP space-time, they began to show up boldly on wilderness earth one after another.

After hiding for so long in the universe realm as transfigured physical beings with a variety of adaptations, most of these fallen *albhly* celestial beings' living energies had greatly reduced, until some of them were unable to transform into a living-energy state for wormhole travel or to perform other feats. They began to use spacecraft for intergalactic travel between their obscure planets and Earth.

When these alien outlaws descended on Earth during their earlier epoch's sojourns on Earth, they usually lurked in desolate wilderness to spy and steal earthly primordial resources and then transport back to their hideout planets.

But under GEP's continuous exposure, they soon mutated to become physically lazy. After they experienced hard toil on Earth, they wanted someone to work for them. This prompted them to conduct genetic engineering experiments, aiming to clone earthly beings like *albhly* beings.

Initially, they trapped different *albhly* wild animals and primates as their subjects for genetic engineering experiments, and some of those unsuccessful experiments included hybrid-beings and chimeras.

Not until the later generation, through genetic manipulation between stolen obscure planetary sterile beings and ape women cells, did they find partial success. Short, stupid and ugly imbeciles or slave-beings were cloned to finally take over their hard toil under the highly radiated wilderness earth.

*Albhly* celestial beings' genetic engineering experiments to improve slave-beings were conducted on and off through a long period of time, restricted during their successive sojourns to Earth that extended over several generations, as their safest, shortest and quickest intergalactic traveling passages between their planets and Earth were restricted by certain astronomical features arisen only during space-time distortion.

As stealing of other planetary beings' genes or cloning of any extra-planetary beings for a planet was considered against *albhly* declarations, initially these alien outlaws carried out the experiments secretly in wilderness hinterland. Whenever they were busily experimenting and creating their slave-beings, they had to keep a wary eye and stay alert to avoid detection by *albhly* ferocious giant spying-creatures. Thus they overlooked lurking foreign living energies surrounded them, as this dark ground was their territory.

Unknowingly to *albhly* celestial beings, their cloned slave-beings possessed a body with an available space that could store weak living energies. This gave an opportunity to foreign living energies with equal strength living energies to possess them before *albhly* celestial beings realized what had happened.

These slave-beings either had luminal-sensitive, over-pale skin or the reverse, skin tones that reflected the hue of wilderness soils. Most of them had low mortality rates besides being very savage, disobedient, and lazy due to being possessed by different foreign living energies, later known as "evil spirits." Their innately weak living energy level permitted other compatible foreign living-energies to possess them.

While *albhly* celestial beings were frustrated, most of these inferior parasitic foreign living energies were exhilarated because they could possess a physical body to manifest their individual characteristics and strengths through contending, fighting and brutal killing.

When irritating, ugly, eerie, triumphant laughter rolled over the air in waves of foreign interference, it sounded more like mockery to *albhly* celestial beings.

To their great disappointment, their mass production of slave-being imitations was not as perfect as they initially expected. Usually they perished prematurely, in contrast to the earliest cloned chimeras and hybrids that mutated into ferocious, crafty, monstrous living-beings—these creatures had long lifespans, could adapt soundly and flourished in the harshly-radiated wilderness. Ironically, they loved preying on the slave-beings and even attacking their creators.

These resilient hybrid-beings' primitive breathing systems and physical features were evolved to adapt to the wilderness extreme temperatures, highly radiated thin air, toxic gases like carbon, methane, sulfuric or nitric, and especially under the GEP radiation, they reproduced and multiplied in an uncontrollable rate. They even expedited continuous newer successions called *chimeragomy*—which occurred when a mutated ovum was successfully fertilized by an amalgamation of sperm from different species of animals, creatures and even slave-beings.

This *chimeragomy* eventually encouraged, evolved and selected the strongest life-resilient monster-hybrids capable of regenerating with just a small part of their body.

With all their existing innate capacities much inferior to *Albha*, these *albhly* conspirators never realized they were not equally omnipotent to rival the unfathomed *Albha*. Their overconfidence and arrogance indirectly led to overvaluing, underestimating and rating unknowingly their own flaws.

*Albhly* celestial beings then realized they shouldn't have created anything in the wilderness hinterland that inevitably would invite other foreign living energies' interference; they should have created their slave-beings inside a well-shielded atmosphere like *Albha's* concealed vault, enriched by primordial life resources.

They fretted further when they discovered their direct interaction with slave-beings was constrained by certain conditions that hindered their mutual cooperation. These earthly slave-beings could not see their masters in living-energy state unless the masters were in their transfigured physical form and the slaves could only interact with their masters' living energies if they were possessed by other foreign living energies.

Upon their subsequent returns to Earth over later generations, these fallen *albhly* celestial beings had mutated to become more defiled and more daring than ever by challenging *Albha* openly.

By then their paradigm shifted to use improved slave-beings for pursuing their other wildest ulterior motives, desires and ambitions; thus they kept trying different genetic modification technologies to continue improving for better slave-beings.

In order to enable the improved slave-beings to survive soundly and safely from some of those ferocious hybrids, they were led by their sneaky masters to dwell next to the border of the *albhly* canopy's remote periphery, where existing exhaust holes with periodic expulsion of good *albhly* living essences helped in rejuvenating their general health. These *albhly* essences also helped them in such a way to deter those hostile hybrid creature predators.

To overcome the problem of these slave-beings' living energies being possessed or "downloaded" in advance by other alien living energies, *albhly* celestial beings organized carnivals periodically to perform a living energy transference ritual and tattooing to claim their ownership of their slave-beings.

In order to dispose and control the slave-beings, *albhly* celestial beings invented the earth's first caste system based on slave-beings' different outlooks, innate abilities and intelligence levels.

Thus different kinds of body marks encoded and allocated different slave-beings for their respective designations, missions, classes and identification of their own kindred from *Homo albha* or other alien living beings.

Like their fallen masters, the slave-beings also possessed insufficient living energies, thus after their afterlife transformation, their remaining living energy level was too weak to return to their original dimensional home.

Their remaining non-perished weak living energies had to keep repeatedly reincarnating within other sick slave-beings, sick animals or sick babies on Earth as they thought that would accumulate and eventually increase their individual living energy strengths. And if they felt too tired to live again on Earth by possessing a physical being or another living thing, then they could choose to roam as weak living energies in the abysses or underworld.

But for other hybrid-beings' intermixed living energies, their incohesive living energies survived from depreciative reincarnations to gradually diminish from existence in this physical realm, never to reappear.

# Part V

## The Stealing of Female *Homo albha's* Cells

As time elapsed, the wilderness earth became more populated than ever before by a series of continuously incoming alien living energies, fallen *albhly* celestial beings and planetary beings.

Their purposes to sojourn on Earth varied, but most of them were only interested in mining and stealing as much rich earthly primordial resources as fast as possible to take back to their own planets, to evade cataclysm or doom of their planets or to colonize the earth as one of their planetary-colonies.

When these alien migrants' populations increased on Earth, they began to contend among themselves frequently. Civil wars were fought among their own alien groups or inter-alien wars were fought to exterminate weaker alien species. Usually whoever possessed the most earthly slave-being warriors and lethal weapons would claim being the strongest.

As fallen *albhly* celestial beings originated from the most superior living energies of hyperspace, even when they transfigured to celestial beings, they still reigned the wilderness earth over all other inferior living energies and planetary-alien beings.

All these hectic extraterrestrials' activities on Earth began to commence during the mid-antediluvian period. They contributed to promoting some of the earliest ancient civilizations on Earth but they also triggered non-natural environmental havoc that eventually brought the second doom to Planet Earth and razed the antediluvian civilization at its height.

At first, *albhly* celestial beings were unaware of the existence of a female sex that could be used for reproduction—not until their male slave-beings sexually mutated to become the rare sequential hermaphrodites. Their existence soon awakened *Morg* to recall how one of those two awesomely good looking *Homo albha's* physical features was obviously very different from all the rest. *Ut* at last comprehended the hidden agenda of *Albha* to create a female *Homo albha*. But to *utis* great disappointment, the sequential hermaphrodites somehow could only procreate male babies.

From then onward, *albhly* celestial beings tried hard to clone a female slave-being, but they never succeeded in cloning any true female from those sequential hermaphrodite's cells due to being unable to crack the chromosomal secret format of a female earthly being.

Their inability to produce female slave-beings finally instigated *albhly* celestial beings to steal female *Homo albha's* cells for cracking the secret code. Alongside this conspiracy, secretly executed among *albhly* outlaws, in *Morg's* defiled vicious mind, *ut* had begun to plot the earth's first genocide—*Morg* intended to exterminate *Albha's* superior earthly kindred during the act of stealing the female *Homo albha's* cells.

Earlier on, when *Morg* detected an annoying presence of other intervening foreign living energies that resulted in creating imperfect slave-beings, *ut* learned a secret that whichever living energies intervened during cloning of a slave-being and whatever went on in their mixed subconscious thoughts and behaviors, certain dominating characteristic traits might be transferred and manifested within the newly cloned slave-beings.

Besides being *Albha's* able assistant, *Morg* also had a penchant for beauty, balance and aesthetics; therefore, when *Albha* wanted to create a beautiful female partner for the male *Homo albha*, *Morg* was called forth by *Albha* to assist *etim*.

*Morg* was still unaware of the sexual differences of earthly humans. As the thought of betraying *Albha* kept haunted *etis* conscience throughout the *asionz* propagation and nurturing course, *Morg* predicted the female *Homo albha's* subconscious mind might carry domineering disloyal and betrayal traits.

As *Albha's* one-time closest assistant, *Morg* thought *ut* knew how to indirectly aggravate, manipulate and challenge *Albha* at *etis* creations but without being caught red-handed by *etim*. Hence a plot to subtly exploit the defiled female *Homo albha* as an accessory then subsequently let her corrupt the original perfect *Homo albha*. *Morg* schemed firstly to beguile the defected female *Homo albha* to eat the forbidden fruit and then let her instigate the perfect male *Homo albha* partner to eat it and thus in such a way both *Homo albha* would die.

*Morg* thought that if their living energies dissipated from eating the forbidden fruit, their luminous living energies would be extinguished and thus they would be exterminated. As *Morg* was living-energy, death in hyperspace meant their living energies got extinguished, thus *Morg* and other *albhly* celestial beings wouldn't be able to have feeling, emotion or compassion for any earthly mode of physical death.

But *Morg* didn't know both *Homo albha* were planetary beings with ample *albhly* living energies within them that kept them in a deep secular subconscious state; there was not enough room for them to possess much earthly eye pigmentation and consciousness, and such ethereal living energies also barred them from lusting after each other for any biological reproduction in an earthly manner.

As a shirked and betrayed *albhly* living energy, *Morg* knew how incompetent *ut* was to challenge almighty *Albha* directly. Normally, *Morg* avoided sneaking in *Albha's* dwelling canopy lest he be caught red-handed for any wrong doing, and most of the time *Albha* deliberately let these betrayers ostracize from *etim*.

In order to achieve a win-win result, *Morg* recklessly used different accessories to accomplish *utis* schemes but *ut* reckoned a serpent would be one of the best among them. As serpents were the slyest, wickedest and mightiest in terms of physical and mental abilities among all wild *albhly* creatures released to the wilderness, they were the great spies and bodyguards for *albhly* watchers; that's why the serpents became one of the favorite wild creatures to get hunted down, tamed and used by *albhly* defectors.

These serpents could talk and understand words better and more than any other land and sea *albhly* wild creatures could. They were also the leading masters in adapting for survival, possessing nimbleness in the water, underground, on land and in the sky.

Almighty *Albha* had long detected that *Morg*'s pet serpent with its unusual shining aura successfully gained an entry to *etis* vicinity; nevertheless, instead of stopping the shining serpent, *Albha* decided to give *etis Homo albha* unprecedented choice to choose their own destiny based on their intrinsic qualities, freewill and loyalty. *Albha* specially reminded and warned them not to consume any fruit from a specific banned tree lest that they should perish.

These inedible fruits on the giant forbidden tree were far from *Homo albha*'s reach. They were cultivated by *Albha* specifically for aggressive territorial mammoth spy-birds and water creatures to consume, to dominate and to guard its specific vicinity.

These forbidden fruits contained a *chromozyme* constituent, which activated living creatures' earthly dimensional senses of color, smell and sound in gaining orientation for an outbound adaptability and survivability.

In fact, this *chromozyme* was designed by *Albha* to use for rejuvenating and invigorating those giant birds' bi-senses, bi-breathing features and bi-adaptabilities after their outbound flights, and this *chromozyme* also eliminated any parasitic foreign living energies possessing returning *albhly* creatures from the outbound zones.

However, as the fruit was genetically modified, thus unsuitable for *Homo albha's* consumption, its *chromozymes* would react differently upon *Homo albha's* body by destroying a specific part of *Homo albha's* organ function.

Their existing living energies would be inactivated to a dormant state; conversely, their additional earthly nose and ear cilia and eye pigments would be activated and their earthly consciousness would be awakened from their deep subconsciousness.

Such consciousness would in turn awaken their physical bodies for secular wisdoms created for earthly survival of fitness, greed and lusts; eventually *Homo albha* were intended to be converted to conscious earthly physical beings.

Without corruption by this *chromozyme*, *Homo albha* could live in a highly-subconscious state created for the *albhly* canopy or the hyperspace realm. When they lived inside the earthly *albhly* canopy, they would possess abilities like those *albhly* living energies, except their limited capacity couldn't possess both living energies and highly functional earthly perception and cognition at the same time like *albhly* living energies.

*Morg's* continuous latency on *utis* accessory pet serpent in *albhly* territory but at the same time secretly bribing other *albhly* creatures as accessories had coerced *Albha* to try out earthly *Homo albha's* subconscious spontaneous inwardness and free choice, which was under *Albha's* influence but not within *etis* control.

In order to lure the *Morg*-possessed shining serpent to act upon *utis* tasks, *Albha* deliberately chose a time to leave *etis* canopy. As *Albha* expected, soon the serpent creepily burrowed out of the *albhly* subterranean vault and entered through its linked subterranean waterway to the open waterway.

While swimming on its way to approach the *chromozyme* fruit tree, it was camouflaged by flocks of its accessories, which supposedly were *albhly* spy-*anatidae*, but they were easily bribed and tricked by one of their most crafty spy-family members, the serpent, to be given plentiful *chromozyme* fruits later upon its success.

As none of the *albhly* spy-*anatidae* had given any alarm calls to alert the fierce territorial mammoth spy-birds of an intrusion, when the serpent emerged within a flash to steal one of their *chromozyme* fruits before retreating through the lush foliage with lighting speed, the spy-birds were stunned by such an unexpected theft by the most agile prey on Earth.

After the *Morg*-possessed serpent acquired a *chromozyme* fruit, it approached the friendly *Homo albha* and befriended them by offering the banned fruit. Initially, they refused to touch it, with the reason that the fruit was poisoned. The shining serpent cunningly took a mouthful of the *chromozyme* fruit to beguile the simple-minded, child-like *Homo albha* that the fruit was indeed edible and it also convinced them that after eating they could gain worldly wisdom and sight like it had.

Eventually, the serpent persuaded them to take bites of the *chromozyme* fruit. At once dizziness overwhelmed them. However, after the serpent ate the fruit, the *chromozyme* forced *Morg*'s living energies to emancipate from the serpent, thus enabling *utim* to transfigure promptly into *utis* physical being features to collect flesh and blood from the powerless, semiconscious female *Homo albha*'s heel.

After eating the *chromozyme* fruit from the forbidden tree, both *Homo albha* fell temporarily from semiconscious to unconsciousness as their earthly physical features activated. With an additional earthly palette of the color spectrum— their earthly sights were enhanced and their earthly cognitive awareness awakened, but they were not aware that the halos over their heads and upper body had dissipated.

With the newly acquired earthly consciousness, color perception and sensations, they recognized each other's nude bodies. New secular physical lust and emotional attachments also provoked their feelings and interest in the opposite sex, thus from now onward they would be able to reproduce offspring biologically according to the earthly manner designed by *Albha*.

Soon after the incident, *Albha* returned to *etis* earthly home. *Et* was not only disappointed by the just-defiled *Homo albha*, who didn't want to confess their wrongdoing, but also that they dodged his questions and refused to be accountable for their actions.

*Albha* lamented *Morg*'s assisted outcome of weakness and imperfection during cloning. *Ut* had not just grafted some recessive disloyal traits to female *Homo albha's* subconscious mind, but *utis* defiled state also would be reflected through degeneration that passed on to her and hence it would forever be inherited by her descendants.

Either undefiled subconscious mind or defiled subconscious mind bound in a physical body, although cautioned by warnings, could easily be influenced by a second party to commit any ethereal or earthly offence. Thus there must be a strong existence of conscience—an earthly highly conscious mind conditioned and governed by a set of earthly wisdoms, commandments, morals and ethical standards, imprinted deeply on an earthly being's subconscious to overcome their consciousness's temptations, curiosities and emotional weaknesses.

Thus the first male *Homo albha*, although perfectly created by *Albha*, was without both high earthly consciousness and conscience as his backup capacities. He was unprepared to counter any complicated interaction and instigation in an earthly manner. He could be easily influenced to defilement by his counterpart female *Homo albha*, and female *Homo albha* could be easily controlled to degenerate by her crafty grafter, *Morg*.

The subconscious was a very powerful mindset for the living energies, but it could only fully function within the hyperspace realm. The fully awakened earthly conscious mind could be evolved in an earthly manner through time but normally would be barred from access to the subconscious unless *Homo albha* were in deep sleep, hypnotized, physically under unbearable pain or unconsciously shifted to a subconscious state during total concentration.

Inevitably, after taking the forbidden *chromozyme*, *Homo albha's* living energies together with their subconsciousness had deactivated to half strength; their living energy states had turned dormant but their earthly features were activated. The genetically modified constituents turned them into earthly physical beings. They were not dead in a hyperspace sense; *Albha* had already intuitively prepared a backup capacity for *etis Homo albha* as future earthly beings, but this outcome was unexpected by *Morg*.

After this incident, *Albha* evolved all species of wild serpents to become dumb, wingless and legless creatures, lest any of them be used by *Morg* again as an accessory for *utis* evil plots, and eventually *et* banned all of them from entering the *albhly* canopy.

*Albha* also disintegrated all *Morg's* accessory *anatidae* and creatures' living energies to their lowest level strength; thus from then onward, when they wished to speak to humans or other species of animals, the audible sound would only be their respective unique yet undetectable mono sound of different registers and dynamics. All animals were confined to converse and understand only among their own species respectively with their own languages.

In an exception, a small population of *albhly*-inclined loyal birds' living energies was retained in higher level strengths, thus they remained able to talk and sing upon being taught, and also only specific *albhly*-inclined animals' living energies were selected and reserved for sacrificial purposes.

Since then, all descendants of *albhly*-inclined human beings, *anatidae* and creatures who were once betrayed by *Morg's* pet serpent have inherited their highest subconscious fears or enmity toward any kind of serpents, especially those descendants of *anatidae*. Territorial mammoth birds ironically crushed their major genetic material donor's descendant's heads whenever possible.

*Albha* also had decided the earthly *Homo albha* with evolved but unreliable earthly conscious mind shouldn't dwell in the innermost sanctuary filled with the most concentrated *albhly* living essences to further enhance their physical longevities. As *et* worried that another existing living tree's fruit in the *albhly* canopy with its constituent *genozym*, if taken by *Homo albha*, could create an inverse effect to decode, transform, and eventually modify and continuously rejuvenate the living cells of a physical state body to promote an everlasting life on Earth.

Under *Albha's* great compassion, *et* only expelled the two defected *Homo albha* out of the innermost sanctuary, but *et* still allowed them to dwell along *albhly* pathways from which they were created originally. This was to ensure that they could continuously receive vital *albhly* living essences for healthier faster propagation and longevity than other slave-beings that began to flourish outside their dwelling ground.

Under the expulsion, *Homo albha* began their new lives in the *albhly* pathways without *Albha's* frequent presence; they had to live their lives based on their newly acquired earthly wisdoms, hunting, gathering, planting and harvesting foods by themselves without *Albha's* direct intervention and attention.

They first suffered physical hardships, experienced emotional frustrations in their new, harsher environment and struggled to live independently for their basic needs. Life became even tougher and more hectic when they began to produce biological offspring.

# Part VI

## The Cloning of Female Slave-beings

After *Morg* obtained the female *Homo albha's* bloody flesh sample, *albhly* celestial beings finally learned the hidden secret genetic code of a female being. They lasered female *Homo albha's* cells with *albhly* lights until they successfully collected a haploid female gamete sample to clone the first successful female.

When precious cloned female beings were rare, they were well-kept by *albhly* celestial beings, and their pet serpents escorted, accompanied and guided these female beings.

Due to *Morg's* pet serpent being one of the chief contributors to the successful cloning of female-beings, which led to improving their general male beings' intelligence, height, appearance, temperament and longevity, their descendants—*morgly*-inclined humans—worshipped serpents, used serpents as an emblem, or inherited a subconscious love of serpents.

\* \* \* \* \* \*

Under the continuous radiation of GEP, the ozone layer on the subsidiary atmosphere repeatedly repaired and eroded due to frequent nuclear wars fought among aliens and ultimate SSKP Nanoweapons that *albhly* watchers used to annihilate those remaining resilient but revived alien creatures—dinosaurs.

Through *albhly* exhaust holes joined with the earthly border, harmful radioactive particles inevitably seeped into *albhly* pathways to further weaken the two *Homo albha's* reserve living energies and thus slow their procreation rate.

They begat the first two biologically born earthly offspring. But before the two new *Homo albha* reached puberty, one of the boys degenerated into a violent, brutal and jealous youngster. Envious of *Albha's* apparent favor toward his brother, the boy committed murder of his own sibling, and cunningly hid his younger brother's corpse by burying it under the marshy field that he worked in.

What the murderer didn't know was that the corpse wouldn't be able to decay under oxygen-deprived, muddy, water-logged ground, which was a vital corpse breeding-ground. The corpse absorbed *albhly* essences from the field, causing the soil to gradually collapse and become barren. As the land was situated under *albhly* canopy, the corpse's dormant living energies reactivated at their fastest rate and the body cried forth unto *Albha*. This was not expected by the murderer.

When *Albha* approached the murderer to interrogate him, he was disappointed that the murderer behaved just like his parents, who had not wanted to confess their wrongdoings.

To punish the murderer, *Albha* decided to banish him into the wilderness to live with those equally murderous slave-beings and hybrid beings. The murderer begged *Albha* for mercy, as he knew any of those savage inhabitants in the wilderness who found him would slay him.

Due to still being underage in *Albha's* eyes, he was granted another chance to live. Concurrently, *Albha* was aware of the increasing threats from the resilient meteorite-transported extraterrestrial spores and microorganisms exposed under radiation. These had revived, mutated and burgeoned into deadly parasitic organisms, leading to an outbreak of famines, pandemics and plagues across the wilderness zones that wiped out masses of livestock and slave-beings, and these hazards had begun to spread closer to the border of the *albhly* canopy.

To ensure the murderer could still live soundly and receive sufficient *albhly* living air and essence in the wilderness, *Albha* gave up repairing a part of *etis* outer earth's pathways damaged by meteorites, and this activated the central source of energy, resources and air helping to repair, strengthen and thicken the subsidiary-atmosphere at a faster rate. The wilderness atmosphere's oxygen level increased abruptly. This improved atmosphere disinfected contagious air, filtered harmful radiation and withstood astronomical collisions better than before.

Since *Albha* ceased to repair *etis* damaged pathways, other parts of pathways also began to erode, and their protective atmospheric fence's self-defense system, in response to such deterioration, periodically discharged *albhly* air to the wilderness in the form of pure oxygen, hydrogen, methane or carbon.

When these eroded pathways deteriorated beyond repair, from time to time they collapsed suddenly to amalgamate their space-time, fundamental forces and structural bonds with their immediate wilderness lands. However, this unpredicted cataclysm happened to coincide with the deadline calling for those foreign living energies, *albhly* celestial beings and alien beings to leave the newly changed, uninhabitable wilderness earth behind.

Under this cataclysm-prone generation, lucky slave-being survivors in the wilderness could only save their lives if they escaped to unaffected caves far away from the *albhly* atmospheric fence's faulty zones.

The cataclysms brought by amalgamation of abandoned *albhly* pathways with wilderness borders eventually wiped out or weakened the mortality rate of different resilient giant predators and slave-beings.

After ensuring that the most life-threatening predatory entities had gone extinct, been exterminated, become dormant, retreated to desolated regions or left the earth, *Albha* lasered a tattoo on the murderer's body according to the slave-beings' highest caste mark. This would ensure that no surviving cannibals dared to kill him.

Finally, *Albha* banished the murderer. He exited through one of the earliest collapsed canopy remnant ruins where *Homo albha* was originally created. By now it had merged with its wilderness border ruins to become an amalgamated barren land. Once this wilderness settlement was cohabited by and flourished with the most ferocious slave-beings and crafty *albhly* celestial beings.

When *Albha* abandoned parts of *etis* outer earth's canopy pathways, the pathway's auto-repair capacity mechanism promptly activated by encrypting an enclave-joint from their deteriorated parts, and this slowed down their corrosion rates. The last defense mechanism with intelligent and high-resilience auto-repair capability encrypted any open land into an enclave.

If any aliens tried to trespass in one of these enclaves, their defense mechanism retaliated with successive high levels of unfavorable air to trigger fire or other cloudy toxic fumes to directly intoxicate or burn their trespassers. Initially these enclaves were unlivable, as too many strange phenomena arose, especially their incipient earthly time vacilating, elapsing or lapsing unstably.

The day *Homo albha's* murderer was banished from his homeland was the first day incipient earthly time commenced in outer earth's abandoned *albhly* pathway, as the original was almost a timeless realm vault.

Under the direction of *Albha*, the murderer soon drifted off into desolate wilderness where more mellowed, smarter and fairer groups of primitive slave-being vagabonds dwelled. They were the defectors, once escaped and hidden from celestial beings' inhumane merciless abuse, torture and murder, but now they remained the lucky survivors.

However, some groups of controllable slave-being survivors remained, abandoned by their manipulative celestial being masters in the wilderness. They continued practicing cannibalism rituals. These slave-beings were so used to worshiping something they could see with their naked earthly eyes, that after their *albhly* celestial being masters left them alone for too long, they began to sculpt idols according to their celestial being masters' images, intentionally to remind their descendants who their creators

1

were. Eventually these carved idols became gods for their descendants to worship.

And their descendants also didn't have good judgment to discern matters rationally. They were innately avid followers attracted by equally radical leaders, and they usually worshipped many gods at the same time. Besides worshipping their ancestors' idols, some of them even worshipped inferior foreign living energies who only remained and survived on Earth by possessing compatible creatures, slave-beings or a specific kind of higher-carbon-content trees, rocks or subterranean marshes.

*Homo albha's* murderer strayed as a vagabond in the wilderness without *Albha's* presence for 500 years. Until the *albhly* celestial beings returned to Earth, *Albha* knew these more defiled and aggressive outlaws would pursue any *Homo albha* as their deadliest enemy.

Under *Albha's* granted protection, benevolence and mercy, again the murderer was allowed to return and settle at the very first amalgamated open land that once upon a time he passed by during his exile.

Bestowed with this homeland resettlement, he finally married a wife from his own *Homo albha* race and raised his family and descendants there.

Due to this particular amalgamated open land retaining remnants of *albhly* living resources, the settlers of this special land continuously enjoyed abundance of good farming harvests that made them famous for their gigantic fruits and melons, and also they lived longer lives than elsewhere among the wilderness lands.

Finally, the murderer was able to settle down, propagate his descendants, and dwell closer to the rest of his *Homo albha* kindred. *Homo albha's* most senior patriarch named his great grandson's great grandson after this new grandson, as both of them were born on the same year and *Homo albha's* babies born on the same birth year with same name would appear again in the family tree 250 years of incipient earthly time later. This customary practice helped to trace

*Homo albha's* family tree record and made their generational timeline easier to track.

Before the murderer and his descendants became fully corrupted by those fallen celestial beings, *Albha* still cherished and tolerated the murderer and his wicked descendants for seven generations, and they were even commemorated as forefathers of all musicians, master smiths and nomadic herders and recorded in *Homo albha's* family tree.

Like the murderer, from that date onward to perpetual later generations, most *albhly*-inclined humans with far superior brains and fair looks subconsciously moved, dwelled and flourished on the lands next to *albhly* enclaves or on amalgamated open lands, and here dwellers still received remnants of good *albhly* living resources.

But those less *albhly* inclined, ill-fated people subconsciously moved and dwelled in lands isolated by geographical and natural impediments. These were usually the harshest, driest, hottest and most inferior terrains on Earth, far away from any existing *albhly* pathway enclaves and open lands.

\* \* \* \* \* \*

What the increasingly corrupt, newly returned *albhly* outlaws faced in wilderness earth after 500 incipient years were groups of improved, smarter strains of earthly beings and other planetary alien beings. In order to reign over the earth once more, these celestial beings began to assimilate from one city to another to demonstrate their prowess in manipulating nature and presenting amazing knowledge regarding a variety of subjects to impress and attract an audience.

They succeeded in intervening in earthly beings' livelihoods and influencing their technological advancements and cultivations; earthly beings in turn reinstalled them as their gods, kings or lords, and soon early civilizations began to emerge on Earth, but amidst the most savage religious scarifying practices of cannibalism.

Initially, any abandoned *albhly* pathway's open lands were considered taboo and ill-fated landmarks by these *albhly* celestial beings and their superstitious slave-beings. Thus the murderer, his family members and foreign slave-being settlers lived in this amalgamated open land peacefully for quite some time until they turned stronger, prospered and flourished into the first city on Earth, which the murderer named after his son.

When the murder's descendants and their extended cities continued to flourish, prosper and radiate into a hinter zone of continuously eroded and collapsed *albhly* pathways, their booming eventually attracted the fallen *albhly* celestial beings and their slave-being settlers to slowly infiltrate, assimilate and cohabite with them until at last they invaded and reigned over *Homo albha* ancestors' land.

Highly assimilated feudal societies were overruled by their inhabitants' excessive debauchery and promiscuous behavior, but without a code of ethical standards, soon fallen *Homo albha* descendants began to copulate with female slave-beings. Their offspring were genetically enhanced; they were fairer, taller and smarter, but due to bad upbringings and influences from their corrupted single parent mothers, they usually were highly materialistic, cunning and licentious. They even seduced fallen celestial beings, causing them to unbridle heavenly decree and vows in committing sexual offences.

When *albhly* celestial beings came unto these female earthly beings, crafty and ferocious hybrid-giants were born. They were also mighty fighters, born in time to contend with and kill revived alien giant predators and resilient mammoth-creatures.

This race of hybrid-giants were known to hold great enmity toward *Albha* and any *Homo albha*, to such an extent that sometimes they even killed their own mothers if they discovered their mother's half-*Homo albha* mixed identity.

Under the influence of *albhly* celestial beings and slave-beings, they also favored cannibalism and thus they had become a great threat to those mixed and pure *Homo albha* who cohabited among slave-beings or to those pure *Homo albha* who stayed inside *albhly* pathway reserves. They believed pure *Homo albha* and *albhly* creatures possessed ample living energies, therefore they considered pure *Homo albha* to be the supreme human sacrifice for themselves, their father-gods or masters.

In time, most of *Homo albha's* descendants began to forget *Albha* and *etis* mercies granted to their forefathers; instead they were ashamed of their mixed or pure *Homo albha* identity. As instinctively they still needed a creator to worship, they converted their belief to follow popular paganism and polytheism, and such conversion also saved them from being killed by the evil hybrid-giants as human-sacrifices.

The murderer-descendants' pure *albhly* women usually emerged as the fairest and most intelligent but also the most crafty women in the amalgamated open land radiated cities due to their nurturing and the influences in a corrupted society. In the past, they would not intermarry with a new strain of mixed earthly beings, but they had been corrupted and succumbed to greed, wealth and authority by marrying fallen *albhly* celestial beings.

What they didn't know was these celestial beings considered pure *albhly* women to be trophy wives used to aggravate *Albha*. Some of them even built crystal castles for the fairest women in the amalgamated open lands in order to exhibit the pure *Homo albha* women in their possession.

These ethereal celestial beings and earthly *Homo albha* women's offspring turned out to be mighty hybrid-giants with enormous strength, super brains and great abilities. They were usually known as gods' sons and daughters by slave-beings, and these gods' sons and daughters became famous kings, great warriors and builders.

As betrayers of *Albha*, *albhly* celestial beings were also never a faithful husband or great lover to their wives; their promiscuity and frequent absence thus encouraged unfaithfulness among their wives—zoophilia and licentiousness often happened that led to frequent murder.

As fallen *albhly* celestial beings were eternal living energies from hyperspace, their original state was as living energy, not as mortals. Their transformed physical bodies were liable to defilement and insatiable lust but never adapted to reflect any earthly human or fatherly emotion, responsibility or love toward any earthly beings or even toward their hybrid-giant sons. They were not perfect like *Albha*, who expressed compassion, tolerance and love toward everything that *et* had created.

The hybrid-giants were born of living energies and mortal flesh; they were begotten in carnal blood, a mix of immortal living energies with perishable flesh. In some ways they were almighty like their celestial being fathers, except their living energies were partially dormant just like any earthly being's.

These *albhly* outlaws indulged their reprobation on Earth, as some of them had insatiable thirst of earthly beings' blood and insatiable lust of earthly beings' sex and had prolonged their transformed physical features under radiation, thus their polluted and degenerated living energies gradually dissipated, together with their ethereal abilities.

When these fallen *albhly* celestial beings' living energy strength dropped and they became unable to travel by wormholes anymore, they began to travel, sojourn and invade from one planet to another by innovative spacecraft instead of solely depending on routine space-time warps for intergalactic travel.

And if their living energies' reserve remained at the lowest level, which forever made them incapable of returning to their own hyperspace home, their alternative was to endure in everlasting physical life as long as the earth and other planets endured. Thus they chose to keep reincarnating within sick human beings or weak babies.

They continuously played hide and seek with *Albha* in the physical universes to challenge, rival and gain control of *Albha's* creation but their ultimate aim was to extinguish *Albha's* living energies

# Part VII

## Abnegation of *Albha's* Earthly Station

Since the day *Homo albha's* living energies became vulnerable and partially dormant, their remaining living energies easily leaked through as their negative emotions, bad temperaments or violent acts. Consequently, their longevity, emotions, intelligence and spiritual quotients would be determined according to their individual living energies' strength.

Hereafter *Albha* commanded *Homo albha* to perform sacrifices according to certain procedures prescribed by *etim*. They learned that through shedding of *albhly* animals' blood, their dissipated dormant living energies would be refilled, but usually these sacrificial rituals only limited empowerment to their kings, chief warriors or chief priests.

Whereas what *Morg* could never comprehend was when *Homo albha's* living energies turned partially dormant and vulnerable, all fallen *albhly* celestial beings' living energies also incidentally diminished and their slave-being sorcerers' living energies that used to converse with dead slave-beings' living energies also turned partially dormant and became even more vulnerable than any *Homo albha*.

To overcome such unexpected changes, the fallen celestial beings eventually learned *Homo albha's* secret of how to refill their living energies. They performed not just the sacrificial ritual of shedding *albhly* animals' blood but also exacerbated it by shedding as much of slave-beings or *Homo albha's* blood as possible. These killing rites were aimed at refilling their dissipated living energies as fast as possible, so that their ethereal transcending abilities and telepathic communication among themselves could be strengthened or resumed, too.

In order to deceive their slave-beings to sacrifice themselves willingly as immolation, these fallen celestial beings modified those harvest carnivals and deified them with additional animal and human sacrifice rites in the name of granting peace, blessings and good harvest for the slaves. Their sorcerers were taught to practice cults, sorcery, incantations and divination, and they were also imparted with astrology knowledge of how to choose slave-beings' babies born with the highest living energies based on astrological calculations.

In turn, slave-beings were deceived to immolate their babies' lives, honored as martyrs, and then the sorcerers raised these baby-martyrs under a set of strict rules and diets until they were fully grown before shedding their blood. Ironically, most inhabitants who lived under such earliest civilizations were deeply brainwashed to believe that martyrs would go to heaven directly, but it was for those sorcerers and celestial beings' own sakes, ensuring their living energies were replenished through periodic human sacrificial rituals.

An occasional human sacrificial rite was performed if there was a prolonged drought or other unusual calamity. Some of these fallen *albhly* celestial beings could transform back to their living energy state under special living energies' transference rituals. They manifested their individual ethereal abilities to accomplish something astonishing to impress the slave-beings; in turn they were exalted and classified by those lower intelligent slave-beings as deities based on their respective abilities. This is the origin of polytheism.

In order to continuously refill living energies to regain their abilities, the ritual of killing or even group killing was held routinely to such an extent that they promoted wars to gather enemies' living energies. However, unknowing to these fallen celestial beings, sorcerers or hybrid giants, overfilling of different foreign forms of living energies in a prolonged term caused an adverse reaction of self-destruction on their physical-state bodies and consciousness, and even polluted their original living energies. Due to some of those sacrificed enemy-victims being possessed by other predatory foreign living energies, these parasitic evil foreign living energies were more than happy to find their respective prominent hosts to repossess.

When the number of hybrid-giants on Earth finally became a threat to mankind, many of them were not only murdering earthly slave-beings or *Homo albha* for the purpose of refilling their living energies but also as food; they deeply believed eating or wearing particular martyrs' body parts would make them became stronger, braver and cleverer.

However, these hybrid-giants wouldn't be able to burgeon forever. Early on, *Albha* had foreseen the possibility of fallen *Homo albha's* descendants mixing with other planetary extraterrestrials, fallen celestial beings, slave-beings or even hybrid-giants, thus *et* encoded *Homo albha's* genome in such a way that if a female being carried an alien fetus in her uterus, its dominant blood would attack its mother's blood. Her living energies would reduce abruptly and thus her life expectancy would drop to only 120 years. Or if a female being carried an inferior alien embryo, when its mother's blood attacked it, it would be aborted immediately, thus the reproduction rate would decrease and eventually reduce to barrenness down through the generations.

This shortening life span of female earthly beings could control the reproduction rate and also directly shorten the longevity of their evil hybrid-giant sons that sired offspring with fallen celestial beings. Under this manipulation, only stolen female *Homo albha* descended genes and pure male *Homo albha* genes would be selected to survive, propagate and flourish on Earth for the future generations.

Toward the end of the antediluvian eon, due to frequent nuclear wars launched by alien or hybrid-alien kings, the wilderness environment was incessantly deteriorated and indirectly also corroded *albhly* abandoned outer earth's canopy faster than ever.

Pure *Homo albha* by now were forced to retreat to the secluded hinter zone of those *albhly* pathway reserves or dwell within the least corroded abandoned *albhly* pathways.

The instant *Albha* abandoned *etis* outer earth's canopy, *et* avoided exposing *etimself* at any amalgamated space-time zones unnecessarily and *et* retreated in *etis* reserved pathways' innermost goal. During *Albha's* long absence, devoted *Homo albha* began yearning for *etim*, and that's when they started to worship *etim* through telepathic means, in a condition that if one's living energy was in higher level than such telepathic communication, feeling and relationship with *Albha* would be possible.

In order to keep their bloodline pure without contamination from any foreign beings, for a long time these *Homo albha* practiced strict intermarriage only between pure *Homo albha's* immediate kindred. Although this caused the slower propagation rate than those foreign-beings, their offspring were born healthy and normal. Provided they retained high living energies and were born inside *albhly* living resource-filled pathways, they could live very long lives of an average of 500 years compared to those fast-propagated but shorter life span foreign-beings or fallen *Homo albha* women that lived under secondary atmosphere, who could only live up to a maximum of 120 years.

The pure *Homo albha's* practice of intermarriage between consanguinity continued for many thousands of years before *Albha* prohibited such incestuous marriages among them, as *albhly* living resources had diluted on tertiary earthly atmosphere's larger inflated circumference and *Homo albha's* living energies had sharply decreased after the collapse of the Tower of Babel.

The pure *Homo albha* practiced monotheism; they believed in *Albha* as the only living god. As pure *Homo albha* possessed more living energies, thus they were mostly born as *alieniuses* with photographic memories and ultimate emotional stability; they were awesomely good looking, handsome or beautiful with charisma and aura. They were preconceived with their individual prodigious talents of broad spectrum information and knowledge regarding philosophy, medicine, astrology, math, science, (zoology, botany, astronomy etc.), engineering, music, or the arts.

They were also innately a highly independent, resilient, disciplined and self-reliant race, and they wouldn't mix with any outbound alien-beings whom they considered evil, promiscuous and murderous. As *albhly* lands they confined themselves in continuously received plentiful food and water resources, they also enjoyed good crops harvests independently of outside lands.

But during the final generation of the antediluvian eon, the serious droughts and famines caused by environmental abuse happening to both wilderness zones and open land zones had finally attracted the overpopulated alien inhabitants to invade pure *Homo albha's* habitats and corrupt pure *Homo albha's* youngsters. Eventually, willful *Homo albha* and foreign-beings still mixed, controlled and cunningly manipulated by fallen celestial beings under *Albha's* lament.

The fallen *albhly* celestial beings had universal knowledge, but as they didn't possess any carnal compassion, conscience and emotion, they were not inclined to be creative, spontaneous and innovative like humans. They were only interested to interact and be in counsel with *alieniuses* scientifically in name for mankind's technological and constructional advancements, but deceitfully they wanted to use these *alieniuses'* aptitude as accessories.

In exchange, the celestial beings imparted *alieniuses* with unprecedented universal knowledge of how to pursue other dimensional possibilities by using unparalleled mathematical and mechanical calculations and how to unlock some divine science and esoteric teaching but subtly limited them within certain constraints.

From some *albhly* enclaves, these fallen celestial beings finally found an abundance of valuable minerals, precious stones and resources that were hidden by *Albha*, which they had been trying to find on Earth since eons past. Among these excavated treasures, they discovered that some could be extracted as catalysts to use for genetic modification, life extension and cloning of new lives.

As those hybrid-giants were not fully compatible to reincarnate in any earthly beings or living things, one of these celestial beings' ultimate aims in cooperating with *alieniuses* was to find a way to store their hybrid-giant sons' afterlife limited living energies into a genetically modified hybrid living entity. They developed an ultimate biotechnology of how to convert back and forth between living energies and physical-state, how to download or switch memory from a living being to another living being and how to revive, download or switch both living energy and its memory from a dormant state to the newly cloned compatible hybrid living entity.

Later they discovered that *albhly* primitive communication waves could be helpful for space technological development for themselves as an alternative mechanical way to reach their dimensional home. They also detected that such waves could be used to hack and manipulate *Albha's* inter-dimensional communication networks and pathways, and in such a way that *Albha* couldn't detect them and stop their unbridled activities on Earth.

Under the alien inhabitants' invasion, very soon *Homo albha's* hard toils under the sun in their ancestors' lands also turned futile due to environmental degradations. The presumptuous correlation, ingratitude and rampant behaviors between fallen celestial beings and hybrid-giants with *Homo albha* eventually haunted and annoyed *Albha* to *etis* utmost toleration.

*Albha* repented the creation of earthly beings, especially when some of *Homo albha's alieniuses* descendants began to denounce the existence of *Albha* under the influence of fallen celestial beings and their hybrid-giant descendants, and therefore their reverted overbearing arrogant wickedness and constant bloodthirsty evil notions were also enhanced.

Their frequent nuclear wars, aggravated by unbridled explorations, extractions and abuse of their habitat, not only severely disturbed the subsidiary atmosphere's ecosystem, but also quickly eroded *albhly* abandoned outer earth's canopy.

When the hollow earth's central core resources couldn't keep up to repair both the corroded outer earth's *albhly* canopy atmosphere and the badly perforated subsidiary atmosphere, *Albha* had to make a critical decision either to leave the earth's central core resources continuously leaking to its exhaustion, which would result in the whole earth being doomed as an uninhabited planet, or to save the earth. *Albha* had to abnegate *etis* earthly station in order to let the earth regenerate once more, but in turn those conscienceless alien outlaws, hybrid-beings and wicked mankind that continuously rampaged and abused the earth would be annihilated.

*Albha* lamented *etis* earthly vault was originally created as an earthly station with very strong structural foundation and protecting atmospheric-fence to protect earthly lives from any unforeseen cataclysms, but *et* relented the outer earth pathways for the sake of protecting *etis* beloved *Homo albha* murderer's exile. Now *et* had to abnegate *etis* earthly station in order to save the whole earth from being doomed as an uninhabited planet.

To ensure the future renewed earth would be maintained and managed under good reliable hands, *Albha* had to find a family of pure *Homo albha* untainted by any foreign aliens, and thus they were saved by *Albha* as the keepers for future outer earth's land, its sky and living things.

Only those lucky pure *Homo albha* and *albhly* species of animals were directed by signals from the central core resources to escape their doom by hiding in a specially-designed barge ordered by *Albha* to *etis* chief human-keeper to build upon the only safe zone on land. Some *albhly* species of creatures were also directed by cosmic signals to hibernate in another secluded safe-zone in subterranean hideouts.

Finally, a day came when the two junctions between the outer earth's vault and hollow earth's vault were both collapsed to merge with the badly-perforated subsidiary atmosphere. That directly exposed the hollow earth to outer earth's imbalanced space-time. Its central core resources of energy, fundamental forces and reserves sent out both auto-defensive retaliation and auto-repairing reactions. Simultaneously, both junctions' floodgate water on the higher expanse gushed out to circulate and hover over the periphery of its newly-inflating vault on the outer earth, and the hollow earth's subterranean crusts and mighty artesian fountain on the lower expanse broke. Thus water burst forth from springs to the outer earth to cause a flood on the earth's surface.

Due to great heat radiated by the central core resources circulating and hovering over the periphery of the inflating vault, its peripheral water began to evaporate, forming a layer of steam turbulence. When the preliminary inflation ceased, the temperature dropped and the atmosphere deflated slightly, and thus immediate condensation took place to let the overwhelming clouds rain for forty days and forty nights.

The gushing of central core resources, buffered by the primordial reserved water on both of its upper and lower expanses, promptly slowed down the outrageous inflation of the regenerated vault. This controlled the earth from spinning wildly out of its orbit, although its axis had rectified. This water-buffer also sealed any central core resources from being leaked to the vacuum of space.

When the central core resource inflated reserves finally achieved a balance with its regenerated vault, some of those very resilient old space-time remnants intercalated within the renewed space-time vault also automatically repaired themselves and became encrypted into their respective enclaves. Simultaneously, the junctions' floodgate and hollow earth's subterranean artesian fountain restored under their respective auto-repair mechanisms also gradually closed. In turn, both rain and flood gradually subsided.

This regenerated atmospheric vault's structural foundation, space-time, environment and ecosystem had regenerated and changed, especially its water exposure on Earth's surface and air, which had increased. Its atmosphere now was as potent as the previous *albhly* canopy atmosphere and reciprocally it stretched to a higher altitude and covered the entire globe after it rectified with the latest space-time inflated expanse.

After the flood, three continents became parted to barely link with the remaining narrow lands, but areas of livable open lands abruptly increased on outer earth, their landscapes transformed by another new succession of flora and fauna species. However, the earth's crust now would be constantly regulated by cosmic forces, rectified by central core resources according to space-time-topography changes.

Under the incipient space-time-vault with its new meteorology, environment and ecosystem, the lucky *Homo albha* survivors only remained decent for two generations before some of them began to damn themselves by again comingling with the returning fallen celestial beings.

By now, the returned fallen celestial beings' living energies had become so weak that they usually possessed sickly earthly beings, and they expected *Homo albha* to idolize and worship them for their ethereal abilities. In order to continue using earthly beings to refill their dissipating living energies, they taught *Homo albha* how to build a skyscraper-tower to collect *albhly* essences and resources for enhancing their lifespans and living energies. Most human sacrifice rites were held on the highest towers' offering altar.

Very soon, they started to hack into and interfere with *Albha's* communication networks again. In order to stop their presumptuous behavior, *Albha* decided to confound these fallen *Homo albha's* communications by disintegrating their remaining dormant living energies to minimum level strength. Thus their ability to understand different languages and dialects was disabled after lightning flashed across them.

As *Homo albha's* limited living energies were reduced to dim mode, their remaining ethereal abilities were thus limited, and they finally degenerated to become the fully earthly beings known as human beings, with restricted abilities and capabilities only.

Before the confusion of languages happened, *Homo albha* was never aware that their own mother tongue was different from others' mother tongues, and they understood innately what other *Homo albha* spoke and even what celestial beings spoke.

*Albha* responded to their ingratitude and wanton behavior just like long ago when *et* confounded the fallen birds and fallen animals' understanding of other living things and living-beings' communication. Now human beings were greatly confused why they heard human voices but couldn't understand other races' mother tongues.

The frustrations of human beings' communication confusion, coupled by communication failure with fallen celestial beings, eventually dispersed three major human groups to three major directions according to respective migration signals rendered subconsciously to their respective ethnic chiefs.

Shortly after that, a catastrophic continental lands parting permanently detached and separated different human ethnic groups to seven continents separated by seven seas, and this geographical isolation stopped them from easily reaching out and interacting with each other for many generations.

Concurrently, at this particular uncertain phase of the Flourishing Space-time Belt, the sky was in chaos, as its regional space-time folded and unfolded unpredictably and thus the wormholes opened and closed unpredictably.

Intergalactic space-traveling or wormhole traveling became highly unreliable. Many of those overstaying, disobedient living energies and fallen celestial beings that traveled within were exterminated, and when these chaotic astronomical phenomena reflected on the earth, inevitably both the earth and its living things ended up in chaos, too.

Under the fluctuating cosmic signals, most *Homo albha's* emotions responded with extreme swings, which caused frequent violent riots and wars among themselves. Frequent unpredicted earthquakes brought more alarming faults on their lands, and when the confounding of language happened, subsequently the most serious continental partings followed; thus many unperishable wicked celestial beings ended up buried and sealed in earthly subterranean abyss by the unexpected havoc.

Under the cosmic force's orientation again, the distance of continental partings was based on different human ethnic groups' distributions at different geographical locations on the earth. Through these cosmic signals' allocations, those least *albhly*-inclined human ethnic groups were segregated to inhabit the hardest terrains on Earth but higher-*albhly* inclined human were allocated right on those *albhly* open lands or next to *albhly* enclaves.

The absence of bad influences by too many evil celestial beings upon frustrated human beings ensured the incipient regenerated earth would restore fully and let the earthly human races spread all over the outer earth to reign the lands by themselves. Some mellower, highly-advanced and intelligent *albhly* created planetary-aliens were allowed to sojourn in hollow earth. They came out of the earth occasionally, advising the human beings' advancement and also helping the human beings as watchers of Earth, lest it be destroyed by man-caused, unrecoverable environmental havoc or invaded by other evil alien beings again.

Ever since the central core resources leaked to inflate a subsidiary-atmosphere during Creation Day 4, the earth's structural bonds had become malleable, and from then onward the lands suffered from perpetual earthquakes. The reflection from space-time expansion's cosmic forces exerted upon Earth's subsidiary vault inflation parted the lands accordingly.

After the regenerated incipient atmosphere covered the whole outer earth, its postdiluvian earth crusts continued to part due to its incipient vault still being under continuous inflation by the force from the earth's central core resources but rectified by the cosmic forces. But once the tertiary atmosphere stabilized, the earth's central core resources rectified the incoming cosmic forces.

Thus *Albha* was also aware that in the future, through unfolding and folding of continental crusts, those long locked-up, bitter living energies could escape from the subterranean lands again to reign over and take revenge upon mankind.

When the earth began to move into the Grace Space-time Belt and another series of civilizations arose on the regenerated earth, due to *Albha's* unconditional love granted to human beings that *et* created, *et* generated a living energy counterpart to be incarnated, sired and raised as a human being in order to remind mankind of *etis'* existence. *Et* died as a human being, and *etis* bloodshed worked to purify and revive human being's dormant living energies automatically if they sought *Albha* as their creator God once they died and decayed physically.

In order to continuously protecting human beings' living energies from being unknowingly consumed by those blood-thirsty fallen living energies, evil human beings and all other kinds of harm on Earth, *Albha* generated another group of *albhly* guarding living energy counterparts to remain on Earth before *et* departed the earth to prepare a new dimensional home to cater to reactivated earthly living energies.

The resurrected earthly living energies were able to gain access to *Albha's* parallel dimension, and whoever denounced *Albha* was cast out to a dimensional abyss incompatible with *etis* existing living energy state.

# APPENDIX B

Dr. Goldie Dallas' research, as listed on dr_dallas_cryptozoological.com:

## 1. Structure of the PNV

The Primitive Navigational Vault was originally a timeless space-time vault constructed by an almighty alien-host with an atmospheric protecting fence that shuttered like a labyrinth all over the primordial earth. His earthly station was hidden at its center, located in the hollow earth.

It is surmised that the hollow earth's center is also where the earth's nuclear reserves are located. Not only could it radiate lights for the PNV during the creation days, when it got threatened, it could also protect, replenish or repair the PNV atmosphere by giving defensive responses to disoriented trespassers or by giving auto-repairing responses to supply necessary missing resources or to inflate a subsidiary vault that shielded the PNV's periphery. If both original and subsidiary vaults were eroded beyond repair, the nuclear reserves inflated a regenerated space-time vault to replace them.

The PNV gradually deteriorated after a series of astronomical havoc, meteorite bombardments and environmental abuse by the earliest inhabitants of Earth that had caused the alien-host to abandon it.

When the PNV was completely destroyed during Noah's flood, the regenerated tertiary space-time vault inflated by Earth's nuclear reserves became the atmosphere that we live in now. During such catastrophic inflation, some new and old damaged PNV fragmented remnants encrypted or re-encrypted as different types of good and harmful enclaves that remain hovering within our regenerated space-time

1

vault. Thus even up to the current date, there are still some well-preserved PNV enclaves on Earth, but their access points are barred from trespassers.

Just as oceans have high and low tides, PNV enclaves work in such a way that they interchange good and bad air with our environment. Well-preserved PNV enclaves that mainly concentrate and float over prime terrain within our space-time vault periodically release good living resources, healthy negative ions and oxygen to their immediate earthly borders but remove harmful air from their immediate earthly borders as necessary fuel.

In reverse, partially or incomplete encrypted harmful PNV ruins that hover in our atmosphere are likely accumulated in specific stagnant or catastrophe-prone regions. These ruins continuously exhaust their harmful waste to their immediate environments and also from their immediate environment they continuously extract their good living resources, negative ions and oxygen to use for repairing their respective damage.

Chinese *feng shui* masters have long discovered that the prime terrain on "dragon lines," also called "ley lines," generate higher concentration of good winds and water; in other words, many good PNV enclaves are concentrated on dragon lines. Thus during auspicious times their immediate habitats receive higher doses of good air and simultaneously these enclaves extract bad air from their immediate earthly habitats. In reverse, during inauspicious times, all malfunctioned PNV ruins directed by the nuclear resources from central earth are rectified by cosmic forces to exhaust bad air to their immediate earthly habitats and extract good air from their immediate earthly habitats.

Usually, meteorite impacts perforate the subsidiary atmosphere first before they reach outer earth's well-secured, thick, primordial atmosphere, as it can withstand or even deflect any regular extraterrestrial collisions. Thus a subsidiary vault was inflated upon Creation Day 4, as God began to create living things on Creation Day 5.

2

During the antediluvian eon, primordial amphisensus creatures in the ocean, on land and in the air traveled respectively in their daily navigations or seasonal migratory routes either inside the PNV atmosphere or outside its subsidiary atmosphere. These illuminated orientation signals were directed by nuclear reserves from hollow earth rectified by cosmic forces, unfortunately these signals are undetectable by our human eye pigmentation.

After Creation Day 7, as outer earth's PNV was abandoned and left to deteriorate by its creation host, the damaged PNV fragments either merged with its subsidiary vault's space-time or embedded as independent self-reliant enclaves, thus in the late antediluvian period, assimilation happened between both original and subsidiary vaults' inhabitants at such merged lands.

Would orientation signals be ruined or distorted when the PNV was abandoned?

No. Some proto-orientation signals had already been inflated and extended into the subsidiary vault during Creation Day 4. PNV orientation routes could not be easily ruined if the environment was not abused by man. Even after the PNV collapsed during the postdiluvian era, these orientation routes still inflated and extended along with the structural frame of the regenerated earthly atmosphere. The new earthly canopy was expanded under this situation, thus its new successions of living things gradually devolved to smaller sizes.

After the deluge, those very resilient old PNV remnants still re-encrypted and remained as enclaves by their respective auto self-recovery facilities. Thus some incredibly adaptive primitive giant creatures adapted and propagated through millions of years inside conservatories situated at the crossroads of suitable climate and abundant food chain zones, and their orientation routes were quickly repaired by the nuclear reserves from hollow earth through remote rendering.

3

The incipient regenerated earthly vault's regenerated orientation routes gradually contracted and become narrower as they radiated and extended toward higher altitudes with the expanded atmosphere. Such inflation finally stabilized a few generations postdiluvian. Eventually, most of the routes became impassable for creatures with large body mass to travel for their daily navigation and seasonal migration, and this was one of their extinction factors. These gigantic creatures could only survive if they happened to return or present on time at the safe zone of their old habitats during space-time regeneration and encryption.

The regenerated orientation routes remain today, but they only allow the smaller type of migratory birds and smaller creatures to migrate faithfully subject to seasonal changes and to navigate for their daily livelihood.

OTS – special sight senses by PNV residents and amphisensus creatures.

In addition, the speculation of a new color spectrum, which is suspected as the earth's most primitive ray spectrum called Original Tint Spectrum, is believed to exist abundantly in PNV enclaves and is still open for more discovery.

OTS can't be detected by our evolved eye pigmentation unless by some very limited rare recessive human eyes.

Some of these primordial rays from the OTS Spectrum were suspected as highly beneficial to human beings' physical health and could as well regenerate ones' mental and emotional well-being. Perhaps some rays from the OTS Spectrum have already been discovered but they are only applied currently in medical and scientific fields.

## 2. They Might be Giants

Let's talk about aliens.

When Galileo published his book suggesting the earth was not the center of the universe, he was placed under house arrest. His scientific facts presented in the 17th century would only become accepted and understood fully by modern clerics and theologians three centuries later. Any modern scholar will insist that Galileo was wrongly convicted by the Vatican.

Why do some of the world's most powerful religious authorities always want to oppress someone whose theories, ideas or discoveries are beyond what their era's human beings can comprehend? Even in this century, religious authorities oppress fiction writers who merely write stories to entertain their readers with imaginative adventure. Some days I feel like we're still living in the dark ages. You can imagine my theories have not been popular in some areas of the world.

I have said during the late antediluvian period, the subsidiary vault and open lands were an optimum habitat for different kinds of aliens from different planets to inhabit, invade and colonize. How did they get here and why?

I think they were more interested in our primordial earth's abundant natural resources, and also because our galactic disk was concave, curved like a bowl, intergalactic distance was shortened.

Now the galactic disk that we detect is flat, which denotes the inflation speed has slowed down, but if the space-time is continuously immersed by dark energies and transfer of dark matter from other universes, could this continuous expansion and acceleration cause the galactic disk to turn convex, a bowl-shape opposite to what it once had? Would a convex galactic disk indicate its doom? Such space-time distortion could shorten the galactic distance again.

I feel lucky to be born in this epoch when the galactic disk is flat and without alien influence. Aliens might not be entirely planetary beings from our physical universe. Have you ever read the book *Flatland?* We physical living things are limited by our own three-dimensional ordinance. Only those intelligent luminous energies originating from a higher

5

dimension would have abilities beyond our physical dimension.

That's why they could even change their features in different ways to adapt to different extreme temperatures, pressure and force changes in physical space-time.

And if there was any change exceeding the limits that physical flesh could bear, they would just transform back to other adaptable features or simply return to their original luminous energy state. They could remain dormant inside a rock, a piece of wood or subterranean vault to wait for a revival or a reactivation moment, or they could escape to another entity that they favored.

Or they could even possess a sick or weak physical body to let their hosts miraculously recover from sickness and gain incredible feats beyond our scientific explanation.

If the earliest antediluvian eon commenced when God began his creation, then I surmise the mid-antediluvian eon should have happened around Creation Day 5 when God began to create living things inside the PNV. Other luminous energies with variable transfiguration abilities began to emerge in a subsidiary vault into wilderness, and the late antediluvian eon should have occurred between post Rest Day and before Noah's flood when everything was experiencing change due to radiation caused by clear space and eroded subsidiary atmosphere—alien-inhabitants in the wilderness began to clone partially successful human-slaves and eventually they grew brave enough even to even steal God's created woman's flesh for cloning.

Genesis mentioned that angels' and human women's offspring were giants. They flourished during the late antediluvian. But many people think no such giant has ever existed on Earth before, all because it's not mentioned in their school textbooks. But our legends must come from somewhere.

Perhaps because they became obsolete beyond mention. Even the Book of Enoch had become obsolete for inclusion in the Bible. The Book of Jasher and Book of Enoch must have been used as the late antediluvian period's Bible.

The discovery of nodosaurus' footprints juxtaposed with humans really confused paleontologists and many people, because our knowledge and education taught us that there was no human existence during the mid-Cretaceous period.

I think unless our future students are taught that Earth initially evolved an intergalactic planetary ecology before known Earthly ecology took hold, the ancient mysteries will always stay hibernating or will be considered fake. Antediluvian civilizations, largely under celestial beings' and aliens' influence and occupation, would be easily taught unless the current evolutionary theories have been emphasized.

The mid-Cretaceous was about 127-89 million years ago. I surmise if those human footprints were not forgery, then they should belong to celestial beings somewhere around Creation Day 6.

Would Christians, scientists or atheists accept the hypothesis of extraterrestrials' existence during the antediluvian eon?

I think only a very low percentage of the population, regardless of what kind of background they have, could accept that aliens ever invaded the earth, although there is so much evidence from the ancient excavations showing extraterrestrial activity and whereabouts on Earth. Sometimes scholars and scientists are afraid even to mention extraterrestrials lest they be mocked and boycotted by their academic rivals or even religious establishments.

## 3. Adam and Eve and Snakes in the Garden

What do you theorize is the central goal of the PNV labyrinth?

In Alibaba Ma's writings, the PNV was presumably the land where Adam and Eve stayed after God kicked them out of the Garden of Eden. It was the place where Adam and Eve were originally created by God, and it was also the place where Cain and Abel were born. Before God banished Cain out of the PNV for murdering his brother, the PNV was almost a calamity-free canopy.

Those genetically modified forbidden fruit were actually formulated for amphisensus creatures to restore their general health from radiation after they returned from the wilderness. But it had adverse effects on humans. After humans ate it, they turned half-earthly and half-ethereal, thus God had to segregate them from him by expelling them to the PNV where he created them, as the PNV was also considered half-earthly and half-ethereal canopy. Since then God also commenced segregation between degenerated humans from purer animals and human babies by communication barriers.

Regarding those "whosever" or cannibals that Cain was afraid of, they could be alien-beings from other planets or genetically modified, cloned, earthly human-slaves or even hybrid giants. Initially, alien-beings were not able to clone female humans without knowing the DNA sequence of the human X chromosome. They knew that the God-created female was perfect, thus they plotted a subtle way to collect Eve's blood sample in order to produce a perfect female.

All primitive alien-inhabitants of human-hybrids, giant-hybrids and human-slaves were either exterminated later through Noah's flood or by natural selection due to abrupt environmental change of the regenerated earth.

If the catastrophic deluge had never happened to eradicate all those corrupted alien-inhabitants, the earth would have been continuously under the wicked celestial beings' counsel. Perhaps the earth and all its living things would end up demolished by antediluvian civilization's nuclear bombs, as scientists have discovered at least six ancient zones on Earth of depleted uranium with plutonium products. Perhaps over the course of the universe's history, these conscienceless celestial beings have destroyed one

8

planet after another; however, no inferior planetary beings could do anything to them. Only God could stop their malfeasance, that's one of the reasons God didn't annihilate those most cunning *albhly* living energy trailers—he knew that they could indirectly help to defeat and annihilate other evolved evil living-energy forms and wicked planetary beings.

Alien-inhabitants spread like wild-weeds after Eve's stolen cells were used by the fallen celestial beings to clone and improve their human slaves. Although dominant chromosomal abnormalities would occur on Eve's stolen homogametic XX sex chromosome, the eradication of any foreign alien genes was slow due to mutation induced by serious radiation. The deluge annihilated most of them virtually overnight. After the deluge, natural selection to eradicate incompatible alien genes still took ages to gradually subdue their occurrence to minimum, and even nowadays we still have cases of immune tolerance in pregnancy, stillborn cases with hidden hemolytic disease and other genetic defects.

Genesis mentioned that after Adam and Eve ate the forbidden fruit, their eyes opened and they could see that they were naked. My hypothesis is that this forbidden fruit contained rich growth hormones. Toddlers don't feel ashamed running around naked; as a matter of fact, they actually wouldn't be able to sense any difference if their parents didn't wear clothes.

Does such forbidden fruit still exist nowadays?

Yes, but my guess is only its subspecies evolved and remain to present day, perhaps as berries. I think the forbidden fruit was originally a genetically modified fruit that God planted for other purposes but not for human consumption. Alibaba Ma says it was the food for those giant spy birds, but since it looked so attractive to people, God cut down its size to benefit human beings later. The forbidden fruit may be nipple-tone reddish color, where older babies or young toddlers could hardly miss it. Logically it's the first

9

color they could instinctively detect. The forbidden fruit could be a giant red berry. Even so, the forbidden fruit was just a bait to hide the serpent's true motives.

Clearly the aliens' cloning was not successful. That prompted them to steal a sample of God-created human flesh and blood. Human chromosomes have been traced back through mitochondrial DNA across the globe, which comes only from the mother, and was found to have originated from the same female.

The secret to reproducing women was stolen by a thieving hominoid reptilian, the serpent. Genesis 3:15 only mentioned the enmity between woman and the serpent, so obviously only the female's flesh and blood sample was stolen, and it also hinted originally those fallen celestial beings didn't know how to clone a human female.

Nature only allowed one innate perfect creating host for the physical multiverse. I believe fallen celestial beings could clone human slaves, but as they were not innately perfect, their hidden flaws reflected on any of their creations. These transfigured fallen celestial beings became easily tainted by the physical world's insatiable lust, greed and ego, yet they wouldn't possess worldly emotion to feel love, longing and compassion. They were merely transformed as predatory, callous, thieving or parasitic galactic colonizers sojourning from one planet to another, or even from one universe to another. As the creator God was perfect, when he transformed into physical features to create Adam that He molded like Himself originally, he also reflected to Adam a hidden, perfect worldly emotional of love, tolerance, compassion and superior genes before the genetically-modified berry denatured such ethereal strength.

God obviously knew ahead of time that after the amalgamation of the PNV with wilderness, his superior humans would mate with those human-slaves and giant hybrids, resulting in inferiority and inconsistencies.

That could have happened eons ago on other, much older planets before. That's why God tightened his earthly vault's protection. Just before Noah's flood, the wilderness humans had fallen into extremes—promiscuity, murder and inhumane behaviors—because they were highly mixed by different aliens and hybrid human slaves with conscienceless aliens. God could only choose a family of his created human-descendants without blemishes and flush the rest.

I read some religious websites' commentaries of why, in less than three generations after the deluge, humans already became so corrupted again. They surmised it could be due to one of Noah's daughters-in-law not being pure. Perhaps this daughter-in-law was only mixed with those fallen celestial beings of God's own dimensional realm, thus God chose them as the second best selection.

That's why extreme behaviors diverged between human beings after that. One group would be god-fearing and humanely inclined but the other group would be against God and inhumanely inclined, callous and rebellious.

A godly-inclined man can't even bear to see blood, but in contrast, the earthly-inclined man enjoys seeing people being mistreated, abused and killed. A godly-inclined boss has compassion toward his employees, he pays them well, but an earthly-inclined boss has no compassion toward his employees; he treats them like slaves and refuses to pay them for their hard work.

Obviously, the slavery caste system on Earth was first implemented by those fallen celestial beings during the late antediluvian period to their cloned human slaves. But after the flood, mixed humans evolved to become more complicated than just two extreme inclinations; two extreme personalities in constant struggle were also developed among them.

That's why they say "there's a devil inside everyone."

# 4. PNV Affecting Modern Human Beliefs

In Genesis 1:16, the sun was known to be the greater light to govern the day set up by God in the expanse of the sky on Creation Day 4. Yet astronomical calculations tell us the sun had to coalesce before the planets could exist or orbit it.

Genesis clearly indicates that the sun did not exist on the first three creation days. Who would care of if there was a sun or not when no living thing yet existed?

Some astronomers presume that the earth was originally orbiting an immature, gaseous-state sun on the first creation day, but as the earth's atmosphere was hazy and opaque, the sun couldn't be detected.

Personally, I think if there really was an almighty creation God, he would be able to coexist over different space-time periods with the capability to transform different features. Nothing would be impossible for God—an alpha source of highest-level intelligent luminous energy that originated from hyperspace. He is said to be omniscient, after all—why assume time is linear for God? In order to cater to and work on any primeval planet, the most desirable feature He emanated should be a luminous energy source, hence if he was at work there would be light, and it would be a creation day. Whenever he left work, there would be no light, and it would be a creation night. That's why the world's earliest monotheistic Zoroastrians worshipped the Fire or the Sun God.

My belief is that monotheistic religions are actually worshiping the same God. Human beings are so unyielding it leads them to claim their own religion is the only true religion and their own God is the only true God. That's how religious diversifications, conflicts and wars begin. Religion is always the touchiest, most sensitive issue because it's subjective, and thus it's at the root of the most abusive practices throughout our human timeline. Although clearly all countries' history, past livelihood and cultures were tinted with strong religious overtones, with increased modernization of the world, we also see an increase in population of atheists and surrealists. Obviously, within the space-time expansion and acceleration epoch, human beings also could evolve to increasingly become self-reliant, self-centered and thus godless in order to survive those aliens' or God's long physical disappearance, and vice versa.

This leads us to creatures of human myth.

Was the legendary werewolf merely a myth or a real creature? If it was real, did it live in the PNV or the wilderness zone?

The creatures and human beings that were created by God supposedly should be aesthetically based on God's image, likeness and approval, thus the werewolf could be one of those prehistoric human-hybrids that were unsuccessfully cloned in the wilderness between genomes of fallen celestial beings and wolves. Due to the mix between ethereal luminous living energies and earthly wolf, the human features would be uncontrollably transformed into its original wolf features during a full moon night, as such ethereal living energies would be forced out by a co-existing true physical presence through strong cosmic and lunar forces. Maybe werewolves did exist once upon a time.

If ghosts really come to roam on Earth during "ghost month," a time in the Chinese Astrological calendar aligning with late summer, it would be a horrific month for those people born with recessive primitive eye pigmentation or senses. They would be able to see, sense or feel ghosts talking to each other or talking to them. A nephew of one of my Chinese friends could see deceased relatives when he was young, and this clairvoyance continued until he went to England for college. He had probably eaten an "Adam's apple" in England that he couldn't find in his equatorial country, and the fruit finally "damaged" his amphisensus eyes by turning them into earthly eyes.

Would having such a pair of extra functional eyes be a blessing or not for life in our earthly realm?

During lunar mid-July, many superstitious Chinese go to an extreme, not only refusing to go outdoors at night, but also avoiding travel, moving, getting married or delivering a baby. They believe this can avoid unlucky encounters or mishaps mediated by evil spirits. They also avoid hospitalization for elective surgery—including caesarean delivery—because they believe ghosts more likely to congregate in hospitals to bring those patients needless death or suffering.

This aligns with the timing of the PNV and hollow earth exhausting gasses and ions harmful to earthly life to replenish needed gasses and ions within hollow earth. Coincidence?

# 5. Cain into the Wilderness and What He Found There

Actually, the subsidiary vault's oxygen only abruptly increased when God began to abandon a segment of outer-Earth's PNV before preparing to banish Cain out of the PNV. When the abandoned PNV fitfully fused with its immediate wilderness zones, a series of catastrophic events was triggered to exterminate murderous alien inhabitants and carnivorous vegetation. It explains the repeated extinction events found in Earth's fossil record.

If all our fossil record happened at the same time, from the point of view of those in the PNV, only those less murderous human slaves that dwelled in hinterland subterranean caves could survive the extinction event. So if Cain was as good-looking as the fallen angels and was marked with a tattoo like one of their masters, of course nobody would dare kill him.

Initially, humans created by God never wanted to mix with any of those promiscuous "devil-cloned" gentiles. Also, those cannibals were practicing human sacrifice, thus whenever they saw humans created by God, they would sacrifice them, as they believed God-created humans possessed higher ethereal energies and powers, thus their life essence could enhance ethereal energies for their gods or kings.

14

That's why Cain knew he would be killed instantly in the wilderness zone if he encountered any human-slaves.


## 6. Deluge

When the oxygen level began to increase in the subsidiary vault, another secondary series of stronger alien and earthly mixed-strain inhabitants also began to adapt, evolve and burgeon like wild weeds; consequently, they turned out so corrupted that they even destroyed both subsidiary and original vaults. As a result, when a tertiary vault inflated, it spelled their doom too. The Noah's Ark flood and rain that drowned all living things could actually buffer the sudden inflation of a tertiary vault from the hollow earth's nuclear reserves.

That kind of powerful inflation could have ejected the earth from of its planetary orbit. But it didn't.


## 7. Animals and Telepathy and the Tower of Babel:

I read an old Reader Digest's article reporting that some animals can read their master's mind and intention even if kept in a separate room, and vets often receive cancellations of appointments from cat's owners, because those cats go into hiding right before their appointment time.

The higher strength of ethereal abilities with clairvoyant eyes and telepathic abilities was still retained among the purest animals and fragile human babies in order to preserve their survival fitness to prevent alien ethereal energies from occupying animals or human babies before their earthly consciousness could take hold.

Initially, living things and humans in the Garden of Eden possessed such strong ethereal abilities or subconscious will that they actually engaged in telepathic communications.

After Adam and Eve ate the modified forbidden fruit, some of their ethereal capabilities probably degenerated. In turn that was replaced by earthly consciousness. Thus their telepathic capability disintegrated.

That ethereal ability to understand other languages worked like an instant translator on every human. It might even work faster than an ff instant translator.

According to Genesis, what caused the confusion of tongues was the Towel of Babel. The construction of the Tower of Babel happened not too long after Noah's flood when an incipient regenerated atmosphere was found in lower altitudes.

Unfortunately, the Tower of Babel was like a pylon or giant antenna built under an uncompleted inflated atmosphere. It could actually induct radiation like radio frequencies and high-energy cosmic particles to cause degeneration and mutation to those people who stayed within its radial broadcast zone. This increased adult and newborn susceptibility to DNA alteration or breakdown to change their skin tones, which turned them into different races, lowered their intelligence, thus they wouldn't have the ability to learn other peoples' languages easily other than their own mother-tongue, and reduce their lifespan to half or even less of what their forefathers had lived before. According to the Bible, Eber lived up 464 years like his father and grandfather, but his son Peleg was merely 239 when he died.

Perhaps toward completion of the Tower of Babel, due to the massive weight asserted by its footprint, it collapsed, killed many people and destroyed their homes that surrounded it. Eventually, it forced the willful people to move away.

I prefer the version that God's intervention came like a lightning bolt—God just needed to extinguish their ethereal energies to minimum conceivability. They would be rendered to fully earthly conscious humans that could only understand their own mother tongue, and all other languages would instantly sound like gibberish. I think if the event was not catastrophic, willful human beings wouldn't have moved away from each other to faraway lands.

In either case, that's why the Chinese, with more than 5,000 years of history, won't build a house beside a tall tower, because they believe anything pointed and sharp could promote bad *feng shui* to their living environment. Who told them that? Obviously their direct ancestors could have suffered from living at the Tower of Babel's perimeter, that's why such a taboo was passed down to some of their descendants.

What about the intention of those postdiluvian people building Tower of Babel?

Many theories have been discussed regarding this issue, but I think this undertaking centralized King Nimrod's clan, power and authority and also reinstalled his family's dignity through his own abilities, strong will and capability. This included the course of provoking and mocking God deliberately, thus the Tower of Babel was also a grand temple to worship the Sun God intentionally against his patriarch's God.

This was the consequence of family conflicts and enmities between Noah's three sons and their descendants, exacerbated by Noah's prophecy. As Ham's clan's two eldest patriarchs were cursed by Noah, growing up within the closely-knitted feudal community he probably suffered constant insult and humiliation by his two elder brothers' clans' relatives.

Why blame King Nimrod from detouring from God when those supposedly God-loving relatives of Noah did no show their compassion and forgiving hearts?

Perhaps Ham's descendants were mostly perverts due to their deviant genes and bad parenting, thus their relatives chose to ostracize them instead.

But fairly speaking, God actually bestowed this lowest and least important of Ham's clan with a mighty leader of great strength in his generation, thus King Nimrod got a choice either to lead and strengthen his clan out of disgrace or disregard and abuse the endowment.

God commanded Noah and his descendants to spread out horizontally over the surface of the earth after the deluge, but Tyrant Nimrod built the Tower of Babel to go vertical instead. After Noah's deluge, God had a good reason to ask the fast-growing human populations to spread horizontally over the land, as the upper atmosphere of the regenerated vault had not stabilized yet; it was not wise to go vertically. Unfortunately, Tyrant Nimrod and his people wouldn't obey the command of their ancestor's God. They were unaware the incipient atmosphere could inflate and deflate extremely between the day and night at its upper expanse during that early postdiluvian period. The sky and the clouds probably also appeared a lot lower in those days. At one point they probably became frustrated, wondering why their tower could never reach the sky. The slaves and the workers were tormented by this colossal project.

Just about a century after the deluge, Tyrant Nimrod's arrogantly and perversely chose the Sun God to worship. He knew that his crafty profanation aggravated not just God and the other two elderly clans' patriarchs, it also promoted deliberate confusion between the sun as a god and the luminous-energy feature's creation god. He revived one of the most blasphemous antediluvian religions idolized by human slaves, probably under the direction of fallen angels who finally were eradicated during the deluge.

I suspect Tyrant Nimrod was actually an atheist. He became the mightiest of his generation, thus he probably only believed in himself. As he hated his two other immediate family clans, so he hated their God too. It didn't matter to him what his supporters idolized as long as it was not his ancestors' God.

Probably after the collapse of the PNV, God would not simply show up in our earthly space-time unnecessarily. When humans didn't see him physically, after a long while they would consider him powerless, unreliable and useless, and eventually the more earthly abilities human beings conceived, the lesser ethereal strength they would receive. They evolved and were inclined to godlessness.

The Book of Jasher says that three groups of people went against God when they built the Tower of Babel, with approval from King Nimrod. When God punished men's errors, he did it very intriguingly. If men attempted to kill God, God made their neighbors kill them. If men idolized apes and elephants, God detached them and their descendants from other human interaction; they were disposed to dwell among those animals in the savage uninhabited lands or forests. And if men thought arrogantly that an extremely tall tower could help them centralize power and make themselves famous to the whole world, God divided them and made them scatter all over the world; when they met each other again after many centuries, they considered their one-time relatives to be strangers.

Obviously the chaotic generation tortured by Tyrant Nimrod began at Perez's birth and that lasted about 300 years. Just like the predomination of his name, it forecast environmental, meteorological, ethereal, religious, demographic and geological uncertainty, confusion or separation to happen. Probably from that era onward, even fallen angels were separated from secular human beings by God through confusion of languages.

Alibaba Ma wrote that the colossal Tower of Babel was deliberately built on a specific location that could block God's communication access to the earth. In other words, when humans interfered or blocked God's communication networks, God in turn confounded their communication. If there was really such an almighty God who could breathe ethereal energies into his created beings, he should be able to erase such ethereal energies from them, and the communication confusion thus could happen instantly.

As God had promised he wouldn't annihilate humans by flood anymore, he extinguished their ethereal energies to the lowest strength, thus their language was confused. During this chaotic era, some fallen celestial beings or fallen angels could have returned to Earth through the eroded atmosphere to corrode God's pure human race. The confusion of languages happened stopped the mutual cooperation between humans and fallen celestial beings instantly, and the immediate calamities that followed forced these fallen celestial beings to leave the earth or become trapped in the earthly hyperspace we call hell. Cultures the world over have a name for this underworld, and many describe it as being subterranean. Perhaps from there onward God or angels only communicated with secular human beings during their dreamy subconscious state—a realm when human beings could resume and understand automatically the common tongue.

I read from an internet religious site's resources that the original human language is Hebrew. It was retained and named after Eber, who refused to help with the building of the Tower of Babel. Perhaps that's the reason angels could still converse with Abraham and Lot, and this happened right after the account of the Tower of Babel.

I offer a probable hypothesis that postdiluvian people still possessed formidable intelligence and the ethereal abilities to automatically enable inter-communication and understanding of different languages, thus all humans and their babies could communicate successfully with all others, and we could have commanded our cats to go to the vet's office in their own language.

But after the account of the Towel of Babel, human adults wouldn't be able to communicate with the babies and animals that possessed higher level ethereal energies, yet they could understand the human adults' speech to enable them learning their respective mother tongue quickly and to fulfill their respective master's requests.

Scientists have proven that babies' babbling contains every sound of every language—they narrow this down to the sounds of their native language through imitation of the adults around them. Bilingual children show great facility in learning more than one language at once with equal finesse. And they learn their dialects or languages quickest before five years old, as within this age range children still have the highest subconscious and their ethereal energies are retained at peak levels.

# GLOSSARY

## A

**ACAS:** Automatic Collision Avoidance System, it is one of MPPS pre-collision warning facilities, aiming to help pilot to avoid accidents.

*Albha:* the very first, unbeatable and almighty intelligent luminous living energy, host-of-all living energies of hyperspace.

*albhly* **luminous living energies:** originated from hyperspace. They could transform as angels, watchers, celestial beings or even as any other compatible features on earth. Some of them were ordered by *Albha* to protect specific earthly human or living things, but their defectors had low earthly conscience for any earthly living things and living beings

**aliens:** any foreign intelligent luminous living energies and living beings not originated from the Planet Earth. The luminous living energies from hyperspace could transform as different physical features under different circumstances since the earliest creation days on Planet Earth, and the living beings or extraterrestrials originated from different older galactic planets that particularly came to earth during the GEP epoch. All these aliens existed way before *Albha* created earthly beings, thus they were usually more advanced, more evolved and more intelligent than most earthly beings of the day. They carried along with them the advanced technologies and knowledge in astronomy, astrology and science to the ancient earthly beings.

**amphisensus creatures:** the earliest intelligent living things created by God during Creation Day 5, they were deployed by God to guard the Garden of Eden and also to spy upon outbound alien-criminals who tried to steal the earth's rich primordial resources. Their bi-senses could detect both living energies and living things, and their special physical prowess with resilience to extreme environments could enable them to navigate back and forth from wilderness earth and PNV during specific times monitored by the cosmic forces rectified by the earth's central core resources.

**Antediluvian:** all earthly time before the flood of Noah's Ark. Particular lengthy space-time phase where Earth was used by successive aliens to perform their different missions and activities on Earth. It was separated into three periods: the earliest period began at the beginning of Creation Day 1 to 4 when creator-God and his luminous energies pioneered the activities on Earth and settled inside the PNV heart. The mid period happened during Creation Day 5 to Rest Day 7; creator-God began to create living things inside the PNV and reprobate luminous energies first began to emerge on outer Earth to steal minerals and ship them back their own planets and other inferior luminous energies also began to invade outer Earth and possess Antediluvian wilderness creatures. The late period happened after Rest Day 7; some aliens would evade their planet's doom and calamities by sojourning on Earth and reprobate aliens started to clone unsuccessful hybrid-beings and creatures, but eventually human slaves were cloned with minimal success to work for their hosts. Their experimental human genes were progressively improved, especially after stealing *Homo albha* female's genes and deciphering her genetic codes, hence an assimilation period between aliens and human slaves commenced. Then PNV was partially abandoned by the

PNV host when he decided to kick out the first *Homo albha* murderer. The abandoned PNV amalgamated with its wilderness brought a series of major and minor calamities to the earth. When slave-beings, *Homo albha* and aliens assimilated and mated with each other, giant hybrids appeared on Earth. These offspring established a series of ancient civilizations ended by the Antediluvian Flood.

# B

**big bang 1:** also called the proto big bang; ruptured, fissured and inflated worm-vein webs, linked the hyperspace with the new entity and formed a void but mock universe.

**big bang 2:** an immediate auxiliary big bang that inflated a new mock universe itself, but the incidental inflation soon inflated a space-dimension within the previous mock universe. The inflating space-dimension would soon keep up with the inflating worm-vein webs and would intercalate them along its trajectory as formidable fundamental structural waves for the future universe, subsequently a much heavier and slower helical trajectory would levitate over the space-dimension trajectory to form incipient space-time dimension.

**big bang 10:** once the mega inferno of a wormhole called the white hole burst and ruptured to transform entities with duration, space and matter, a new auxiliary multiverse would commence once more.

# C

**celestial beings** transfigured features of *albhly* luminous energies that predominated on earth during

Antediluvian generations, some of them could be good *albhly*-watchers or angels but most of them were mutated and thus fallen as *albhly*-defectors with dissipated living energies, since eons ago these *albhly*-defectors either shirked their appointed duties by indulging their own secular activities, which they thought *Albha* wouldn't have known they were doing, or they were once hyperspace outlaws kicked out by *Albha* and thus hidden in different obscured planets from *Albha*.

**Commercial saucer Saucer BB1:** a smaller model commercial saucer usually used for short distance intercontinental domestic passages.

**Creation Space-time Belt:** incidental inflation from 4th auxiliary big bang would inflate the proto universe's Natal Space-time Belt into this new Creation Space-time Belt. Earthly Creation Day 2 and 3 fallen on this space-time belt.

**D**

**Doom Space-time Belt:** incidental inflation from 9th auxiliary big bang would inflate the proto universe's Stagnant Space-time Belt into this Doom Space-time Belt, the last or the doom universe of a multiverse.

**E**

**elixirantigen** a new age anti-inflammatory medication to replace the old age antibiotic.

*et*: a subjective personal pronoun for the host of hyperspace, *Albha*.

*etim*: an objective personal pronoun for the host of hyperspace, *Albha*.

***etis***: possessive pronoun for the host of hyperspace, *Albha*. *Albha* had compassion, patience and love toward earthly living things and living beings; *Homo albha* was basically created after *etis* image and characteristics.

# F

**ff**: mid-21st century evolved versatile smartphone, dubbed after Chinese traditional folded-fan, when folded it is a modern version of multitask tablet equipped with MPPS. When unfolded it turns into a computer screen or TV screen in different sizes' mode and it could also work as a projector. It is powered by a malleable auto-replenishing solar energy battery.

**fighter-saucers**: unpiloted experimental muted and repulsive propulsive energy hypersonic saucercraft.

**Flourishing Space-time Belt**: incidental inflation from 6th auxiliary big bang would inflate the proto universe's Living Space-time Belt into this new Flourishing Space-time Belt. It was the epoch after Creation Day 7, when Earth was colonized by aliens and they commenced Antediluvian civilizations but later they also destroyed their civilizations due to their sacrilege on *Albha* and his created *albhly* living things, as these aliens' moral and ethical practices were evil in *Albha's* eyes.

# G

**geopathic stress**: considered an empirical idea, but by mid-21st century scientifically it has proven its existence; enclosed mostly under the earth and trapped with all kinds of stagnant harmful energies.

**Grace Space-time Belt**: incidental inflation from 7th auxiliary big bang would inflate the proto universe's

Flourishing Space-time Belt into this new Grace Space-time Belt. The earth became a newly regenerated earth with an initially thin and low-altitude continuously inflating atmosphere gradually inflating to a stabilized thicker and higher altitude atmosphere. After catastrophic continental parting at the beginning phase of its distorted space-time, many aliens were exterminated. After that the space-time became very stable and thus could distance the galactic journeys and the dark energy and dark matters would act as absorbers and insulators. All these factors would protect living things and living beings living within this space-time belt from malicious alien-visitors. Additionally, dark energy, dark matter and thick earthly atmosphere also could protect the earth from frequent incidental big bang inflations' turbulences and harmful cosmic rays.

**Great Exposition Phase (GEP):** an epoch where its space-time belt was infused by harmful radiation to cause reprobation, diminishing ethereal energy or health hazards to any living energies, living beings and living things exposed to it.

# H

*Homo albha:* the man and woman created by creation God *Albha* during Creation Day 6.

**helix-time trajectory:** after big bang, as regular light and any other kind of plasmas were heavier, thus they would subsequently levitate along the preceded space-dimension trajectory.

**Hyperspace time:** very brief elapsed or lapsed of time when worm veins linked up both hyperspace and multiverse.

# I

**incipient time**: first unstable earthly time commenced at amalgamated open lands, when some segments of PNV that were abandoned by the creation God merged with the wilderness zones after Creation Day 7.

**J**

**K**

**L**

**Lau ban**: a Chinese word that means boss.

**leaking time**: very brief elapsed or lapsed of time during Creation Day 4 to resting Holy Day 7 when both boundaries of earthly space-time and PNV space-time merged during limited moment monitored by routine cosmic forces.

**living energy** or **ethereal energy**: Like human being's blood, it is the essence of life and prowess for living energies or luminous living energies. If any active living energy is retained in a human being, it would be permeated in the flesh and blood.

**living energies**: intelligent living energies or luminous living energies originated from hyperspace. There were some most intelligent and oldest living energies, secondary living energies and parasitic form of inferior living energies. When they emerged in physical universe at different speed according to their respective prowess and capacities, they could either possess a physical thing or living things, or transform to different features in accordance with different environments, or sometimes they could even co-exist as transitional physical and ethereal energy features.

**Living Space-time Belt**: incidental inflation from 5th auxiliary big bang would displace the proto universe's Creation Space-time Belt into this new Living Space-time Belt. Earthly Creation Day 4, 5, 6 and 7 fall on this space-time belt.

## M

*Morg*: *albhly* luminous living energy originated from hyperspace, due to *utis* innate deficiency of some living energies thus slowed down *utis* velocity, prowess and capability, *ut* illuminated right after *Albha's* existence.

**MPPS**: Multipurpose, Penetrating and Positioning System. A combo of user-friendly multiple function facilities and devices that could be used in aviation, seafaring and overland for searching, tracking and orientation. It also has odor and heat sensor orientation functions for different kinds of SAR operation. It is also known for its powerful ground penetrating and space-wise or solar system-wise outreaching advanced radar intelligence system to detect any strong or mega incidental inflation trajectory on its way to wreck a specific location on earth, thus it could forecast highly accurate pre-earthquakes' and pre-tsunamis' warning alarms.

**multiverse**: made up of a mock universe of void and eight consecutive inflating physical universes from nine consecutive big bangs.

## N

**Natal Space-time Belt**: incidental inflation from 3rd auxiliary big bang would displace the proto universe's first Space-time Belt into this new Natal Space-time Belt. Earthly

Creation Day 1 falls on the latest part of this space-time belt.

**Nodosaurs:** a group closely related to, and sometimes categorized under, the ankylosaurs. Flourished in the mid-Cretaceous period about 127—89 million years ago; these armored dinosaurs were characterized by their long, narrow heads, small brains, and lack of tail clubs. The most well-known nodosaurs included Nodosaurus, Sauropelta and Edmontonia, the last being especially common in North America.

**O**

**Open lands:** the amalgamated lands of abandoned PNV and earthly wilderness lands, where their space-time merged.

*Ornimegalonyx:* an extinct giant burrowing owl species that existed in the Pleistocene in the Caribbean and Mediterranean areas between 10,000 and 30,000 years ago; they terrorized the night sky of Cuba about 10, 000 years ago.

**OTS:** Original Tint Spectrum the most primitive color spectrum, it is unable to be detected by our evolved human eyes' pigmentation.

**P**

**PNV:** Primitive Navigational Vault, the earliest prehistoric enclosed canopy with its own independent atmosphere and space-time designed and built by a particular almighty alien-host (*Albha*) on Planet Earth. At the heart of these labyrinthine pathways scattered all over the incipient earth was *Albha's* earthly station, and PNV linked to *Albha's* outer space stations, too.

**primordial intelligent luminous living energies:** the most primitive forms of non-substantial living and creation powerhouse with varied intelligent levels originated from hyperspace. They had the prowess to transform any physical features subject to environmental changes; occasionally they could create living things or even living beings on some primordial planets. They traveled inter-dimensionally through periodically opened worm veins and wormholes.

**Q**

**R**

**reionization:** the process that reionized the matter in the universe after a big bang, and is the second of two major phases' transitions of gas in the universe. It cleared the dark opaque space and brought the first ray of light to the space. *Albha's* luminous living energy state at work during creation could automatically reionize a particular region of the opaque space.

**reserved electric cell:** most new age vehicles and aircraft in mid-21st century use solar energy, but it would convert to use its reserved electricity when its solar energy auto conversation system was running low or slow due to prolonged poor sunlight reception.

**S**

**SAR:** abbreviation for search and rescue

**saucer BB1:** mid 21st century's smaller kind of saucercraft flying domestically.

**saucer bridge:** mid 21st century's modern aerobridge.

**saucercraft**: mid 21st century's modern saucercraft that could fly a lot faster and safer than older jets.

**saucer-lag**: same meaning as jet-lag, except some passengers might experience an unknown symptom of temporary memory lapse right after flying.

**saucerport**: mid 21st century's modern airport for saucercrafts.

**serescopter**: mid 21st century's new age helicopter. CN999 Mini Dragonfly is a SAR serescopter; the latest serescopter model is CN888 Super Dragonfly.

**seres-drop**: heli-drop.

**slave-beings** or **human slaves**: earthly-beings partially successfully cloned by the *albhly* celestial beings outlaws that committed intergalactic minerals and gem stones theft during GEP; deployed as slaves to work in the mines to replace the living energies' hard toil on Earth.

**SEG Filling Station**: abbreviation for Solar, Electric and Gas filling station.

**space-dimension**: superluminal structural force trajectory could dilate faster than the light and any other kind of plasmas. This universe's fundamental structural frame would quickly pick up the worm-vein webs continuum and intercalate them while inflating along its trajectory.

**Space Lapse Rate (SLR)**: variable at space expansion, the rate at which inflation decreases with increase in space's expansion. The slowed down, distorted space-dimension that intercalated with worm-vein webs or gravitational waves that would flinch and turn into billions of swirling cauldron-like spirals.

**Stagnant Space-time Belt:** incidental inflation of 8th auxiliary big bang would inflate the proto universe's Grace Space-time Belt into this new Stagnant Space-time Belt.

**Space-time dimension:** a united pace-dimension intercalated with distribution worm-veins webs subsequently levitated by helix-time trajectory, the incipient space-time commenced during first SLR.

**T**

**U**

*ut*: a subjective personal pronoun for those mutated *albhly* living energies who went against their host, *Albha*.

*utim*: an objective personal pronoun for those mutated *albhly* living energies who went against their host, *Albha*.

*utis*: possessive pronoun for those mutated *albhly* living energies who went against their host.

**V**

**W**

**wormholes:** when auxiliary big bang triggered incidental inflation radiated on the older universes, two immediate space-time dimensions' distorted funnel throats meet and thus they inter-link temporarily. But if stars happen to fall into it and put pressure on the throats, they touch the worm-veins and tear its space-time beyond repair and then the wormholes turn into permanent wormholes.

**worm-vein webs**: links of hyperspace to the multiverse in the form of gravitational waves.

# X

**XZ-rays**: one of the routinely emitted primordial cosmic rays in space, when intercepted by dormant primitive communication signals on Earth, it might activate migration signals for certain migratory animals but they usually wrongly detour those animals from the deep sea to the beach, from the land to the river, etc. XZ-rays only worked properly before the great deluge.

**#XZ-ray**: this cosmic ray could neutralize OTS Ray Spectrum that infused the PNV protective atmospheric fence. If a legendary creature like a dragon or phoenix presented itself in a particular PNV remnant spot, it could become visible to any naked eyes or perhaps only to those extremely rare people born with primitive eye pigmentations.

# Y

# Z

**Zionizer**: the latest invention upgraded from the conventional ionizers, there were few kinds of newly discovered healthy ions top up with conventionally found negative ions to invigorate our vital energy and support general health.

**Z103**: the latest model laser gun.

# About the Author

E.F.Geller was educated in the USA, New Zealand and E. Europe, and currently lives in Auckland, New Zealand.


Contact the author

Twitter:

https://twitter.com/EFGELLER


Facebook:

https://www.facebook.com/pages/EF-Geller/899228726830867